What reade

M000223415

Epiphany
THE
GOLDING

Accolades

Epiphany
THE
GoLDING

SONYA DEANNA TERRY

Copyright © 2014 by Sonya D Terry

Print edition first published 2016

ISBN: 978-0994216793

Published by Sonya D Terry

Structural edit by Deonie Fiford
Copy edit (partial) by Abigail Nathan, Bothersome Words
Front cover image by Sergey Nivens
Front cover design by Jesh Snow of Jesh Designs
Back cover & spine design by Lorie DeWorken of Mind the Margins
Additional elements by Vecteezy

Here in the fairy wood between sea and sea
I have heard the song of a fairy bird in a tree
And the peace that is not in the world has flown to me
ARTHUR SYMONS

All that we see or seem
Is but a dream within a dream
EDGAR ALLAN POE

Not everything that can be counted counts
and not everything that counts can be counted
ALBERT EINSTEIN

Do not meddle in the affairs of dragons
For you are crunchy...and taste good with ketchup
UNKNOWN

Character List

18th-Century England

CORNWALL

Edward Lillibridge.......... Documenter of *Our True Ancient History*

Ned Lillibridge .... Edward Lillibridge's son

Lucetta: .... A Gypsy fortune teller

Prehistoric Norway
Portrayed as 'Norwegia' in Lillibridge's
Our True Ancient History

ELYSIUM GLADES

The elfin Brumlynd clan
Nature spirits of devic origin (sprites)

Maleika .... Clan Watcher

Pieter .... Maleika's firstborn son

Kloory .... Maleika's younger son

Croydee .... Maleika's nephew

Zhippe .... An adopted water sprite orphan

Carlonn .... Zhippe's twin

Forest creatures

Fripso...............................A young rabbit

Karee ....Fripso's mother

Sluken.............................Croydee's dragon

THE GRUDELLAN PALACE

Gold's Kin
Known to the sprites as 'body kings'

Eidred..............................Princess of Grudella

The Solen........................Gold's Kin Emperor/Eidred's father

Storlem............................Gold's Kin guard and crystal keeper

Zemelda ....Palace soothsayer/former bewitcher

Rahwor ....Grudellan sorcerer

The Dream Sphere
A celestial dimension featured in Lillibridge's
Our True Ancient History

Dream-Sphere dwellers
Passed-over beings of devic origin

Orahney...........................A passed-over autumn faerie

Alcor...............................The Brumlynd clan's Dream Master

Wallikin...........................Maleika's passed-over husband

Modern Australia

Rosetta Melki.................. Shop Assistant/Cleaner/Tarot Reader

Rosetta's Friday Fortnight book study group

Craig Delorey.................. Lawyer/entrepreneur

Edith Derby (Eadie)........ Beauty Therapy student

Royston Leckie .... Youth Counsellor

Lena Morris .... Health foods shop proprietor

Darren Eddings............... Former Hairdresser

Rosetta's employers

Caroline Trent................ Proprietor of Crystal Consciousness

Jack Barnaby................... Commercial cleaning proprietor

Izzie Redding.................. Rosetta's daughter

Glorion Osterhoudt .... Exchange student at Izzie's school

Charlotte Wallace............ Izzie's school friend

Diondra Wallace .... Charlotte's mother

Dominic Wallace .... Charlotte's father

Matthew P Weissler.........Investment Bank Trading Manager

Matthew's work colleagues

Charlie Sanders...............Director/Matthew's boss

Adam Harrow..................Trading Manager

Paul 'Davo' Davison........Trading Manager

Celia Owens.....................Matthew's assistant

Bernadette Weissler (Dette)...Matthew's wife

Sara Belfield...........................Dette's elder daughter

Laura Belfield..................Dette's younger daughter

Grant Belfield..................Dette's ex-husband/Sara and Laura's father/

ALICE SPRINGS

Conan Dalesford...Author of *Thoughts on Tomorrow's Tycoon War*

Jannali Dalesford......Conan's Wife

Prologue

An excerpt of a letter from
Edward Lillibridge
to his sister Meredith

— Written in the autumn of 1760 —

...*The boy has led me of late into an extraordinary situation.
Several days ago he traipsed to the wood on the morn, telling me
he would return to the cottage in time for dinner. Midday passed,
as did the afternoon. Ned was nowhere to be seen.*

*When orange and violet streaked the heavens, and smoke
whirled and curled from chimneys in the dale, I stood on my
doorstep, paced for a spell and watched the shadows beyond
the oak grove, anxious for Ned's return. Ned did not arrive
home, and so I donned my cloak and ventured into the darkly
mossy sanctum of the towering pines and elms.*

*At the edge of a clearing, I encountered a clue. Ned's wood-
cutting axe lay discarded upon a nest of pine needles. My heart
became chaotic then. All through my chest and head was the thud
of fear. I could not for the life of me see any sign of my dear son,
and I thought of my Mrs Lillibridge, peaceful now in her grave,
and my thoughts dwelt horribly on the morbid. In my fettered
imagination, I saw two gravestones side by side and felt the
familiar ache of woe that Iona's demise had so thoroughly instilled
in me.*

It is with great relief I report to you, Meredith, that this awful image I had conjured, of my son buried beside his mother at the mere age of one-and-ten years, was not to be a forbidding omen.

Presently, I heard the promising sound of rustling leaves. I dashed towards the leaves that alerted me and found my son by a thicket, prone upon the ground with eyes closed. I cried out his name in despair.

The thicket's leaves parted then, and there before me stood a woman of considerable beauty, her dark hair _not_ gathered upwards as is proper for that sex. In an accented voice, she said: 'He fell from the tree.' She gestured to the boughs of an oak above. 'He attempted to chop one of the higher branches.'

Ignoring her, I knelt by my son. Trembling and frantic, I listened for a heartbeat. Meredith, I speak the truth when I tell you I am certain his heart had stilled.

'Please...' The woman—a Gypsy—persisted with bothering me. Me in my ill-feared mourning! 'Allow me to return this boy to health,' she said. 'Allow me, sir, I beg of you!'

One who is immersed in the horror of a loved one's passing is loath to succumb to doubt when a ray of hope offers forth its glorious beams.

After consenting to her plea, I looked on dismally as the stranger waved her hands about in the air. She warbled a song—strung together with nonsense—and clutched at a pendant adorning her neck, presumably stolen, for it was an elegant gem of palest rose, one that would more than likely fetch a pretty penny at a London jeweller. She removed the pendant and placed the stone upon my Ned's left ankle.

Resigned to exclaiming, 'Cease mocking me, woman,' I was taken aback when I heard the word 'Father?' And there, in the

2

clearing of the woods, was my awakened son: recovered, sitting upright, a startled stare marking his ashen expression, blinking at the Gypsy, who bowed her head and retreated whence she had come.

Once I had established my lad was perfectly all right, I hastened after the mysterious Samaritan, intent on conveying my gratitude. Upon reaching her, I was overflowing with questions. 'Where are you from?' I asked. 'How did you learn to wield magic?'...

Chapter One

Autumn, 2008

A little after midnight, Rosetta threw down her tapestry and rescued the screaming kettle. Cluttered kitchens, she decided, were an unrivalled comfort. Earthenware, hanging copper pots...her latest home an echo of the last, complete with mottled assortments that brightened the emptiness between stove and sink.

Smoothing a strand of long hair aside—a lighter shade of brown now that the burgundy had washed out—she refilled the teapot and reached for the carton of soy.

Izzie dawdled in. Snatched up a slice of French loaf from the tray. Hacked away at it absent-mindedly.

'Teenagers,' Rosetta said with an affectionate smile. 'Always hungry.'

Izzie wandered out. What she did these days, Rosetta could only wonder. Giving the girl space, though, was a huge priority. The stern upbringing Rosetta had endured—in a Greek foster family who'd kept her away from friends—had, she supposed, compelled her as a mother to place freedom on a par with safety.

She returned to the couch with her mug, hopeful the tea leaves would cluster into hearts and flowers. The previous night's brew had only resulted in a bird with an impressive wingspan. A falcon in her future? Or had it been an eagle? Nothing romantic about that.

Maybe Izzie was doing homework. Maybe not. Talking to boys, perhaps, on the quirky phone Rosetta had saved up for months to buy her? Pencilling-in a new painting?

Rosetta's last boyfriend said it wasn't surprising the girl was artistic with Rosetta for a mother. One glance around the cosily crowded sitting room with its gallery-like walls, and guests assumed artists lived here. Or Gypsies. There was something almost Romani about the crimson rugs and vases of fake Spanish orchids. Lamps glowed ruby in the corners, illuminating a scattering of Victorian prints that spoke of dancing feet and caravans. Incense smoke rose in frenetic wisps to the sculpted ceiling as though eager to mock post-midnight stillness, clouding the crystal ball that glinted amber on the mantelpiece.

Yes, he'd been lovely, the one who thought the way she arranged things was arty, a refreshing antidote to cautious Benjamin, who considered her taste tawdry and dropped her with the explanation that drifters weren't his style. Poor precise Benjamin. If he'd understood the treasure status she'd given her belongings, he mightn't have been so dismissive, although 'treasure' was probably too mild a term. These were more than that. They were magicians, able to spin out renewed contentment to quell the strangeness of each new tenancy.

Izzie emerged from the hall and sorted through a pile of newspapers by the fireplace. The girl was not in an amiable mood. For this reason, Rosetta didn't rush to ask how her day was. Instead she sipped her tea and cuddled Sidelta, the silvery moggy they'd discovered in a thunderstorm and had struggled to soothe throughout every address-change trauma.

She scrolled through her mental checklist for the Lillibridge website. Blog page: now set up. Homepage: almost done. Background on the author: Lena had phoned earlier to say she'd get that written by tomorrow. Lena's research surrounding the eighteenth-century creator of fictional dimension-crossing people such as Pieter the elf had inspired speculation among Rosetta's book-group friends. 'Imagine if the events in *Our True Ancient History* were actually real,' Lena had said at the book group's last meeting. 'I mean, I know it sounds outlandish, but what if Lillibridge based his novel on intuitive visions? What if he'd somehow got a glimpse of a forgotten part of history?'

'Bunnies in bonnets. Sooo adorable.' Izzie held up a clipping of three live white rabbits decked out in beribboned hats, a news item promoting Sydney's Royal Easter Show.

'You haven't told me how your day was, Izzie.'

'Hm, well, it wasn't all that interesting.'

Sidelta curled herself into a spiral of softness. The faint oceanic rumble of her purr rose up amid the papery swish of tabloid-sorting. Warmth. Safety. She and Izzie were sure to feel more protected here.

The recurring images accosted her then, unexpected, as they always were.

The outdoor laundry in darkness.

An intruder's leer.

She calmed her breathing. 'Well, I had an interesting day.'

'Mm?'

'Did at least five tarot readings.'

'That's nice.'

Her daughter's tone was condescending. Ignoring this, Rosetta went on. 'Ooh, and that guy I like came into the shop again. You know who I mean...um...'

'The "gorgeous" GEG?'

'Yeah! The gorgeous Green-Eyed Guy. Looked like something out of a business-suit catalogue.' Rosetta smiled into her tea, enthused by the memory of her afternoon's work at Crystal Consciousness Books & Gifts in the city when the man whose name she could only dream of knowing had wandered into the shop. He'd thrown a packet of gift-wrap and some loose change on the counter, grinned at her and then sauntered out. On his way to the train he'd made another stop, to buy a finance paper at the news stand opposite. He visited the news stand every evening. Every evening, around the time she was due to shut shop, Rosetta looked out for him.

'Did you talk at all?'

'Say again? That rustling's drowning you out.'

'Did you find out anything about him?'

'Yes! That he's now the proud owner of polka-dotted gift-wrap and gives the exact amount in coins.' The cat blinked at her. She ruffled Sidelta's silken fur. 'It wouldn't have been appropriate if I'd launched into conversation. I had trouble enough managing: "That's three dollars eighty please", "Thank you", and "See you later".'

Izzie jumped to her feet. She fluttered the newspapers in each hand with the gusto of a fledgeling impatient to fly. 'Why is everyone so scared of rejection these days? I don't see why you can't just speak to him, Mum.'

'And die of embarrassment?'

Izzie, flapping her thin arms again, spun round to go and swung back.

Rosetta half-chuckled. 'Try the magazine rack in my room, hon. The Canadian travel brochures there might be good for the autumn part of your collage.'

'Geez, Mum! We're in another millennium, not the twelfth century. Girls *do* talk to guys they don't know.' Izzie gathered the papers in her arms together, tucking the corners into alignment. 'And it's not like you're someone who's low on confidence.'

'Nor timid normally.' Rosetta found it impossible to hide behind potted palms at parties or remain silent when someone endured an injustice. 'But I make life hard for myself with that silly big mouth of mine.'

Cheeky was how her Athenian mama had classified her. Rosetta's chatting freely to visiting tradesman, the postie, the proprietors of the corner shop, had rarely escaped the foster mother's hostile attention. 'Being lost for words every so often is kind of refreshing, but I do plan on speaking to him. Maybe after I lose a few kilos.' She circled the mug with her finger, scowling at the chipped nail polish. 'I'm just waiting for the right time.'

'Like when Venus contacts Jupiter. Or the cow jumps over the moon.' The cynical fifteen-year-old skittered off to her room.

'He's probably married. And he's too young for me, anyway.'

A slight delay. Then from Izzie's room, 'Anyone would think you were a great-great-granny the way you talk.'

'At the end of the year I'll be thirty-*nine.*' She said it rather than called it.

Izzie didn't answer. It wasn't Izzie's problem. Izzie was still a bright flower bursting with life, a pretty little beach gazania blooming in the sunshine.

What does that make me, Rosetta wondered as she eyed the 1983 Shiraz on the shelf.

A wilted flower. A withering rose. Exotic and full-bodied, but old, like the wine she was contemplating opening. What would a youthful executive want with a fading raggedy rose? Nothing, probably. She emptied the remainder of her tea into a potted fern and considered searching for the bottle opener.

Royston's copy of Lillibridge's novel lay open on the coffee table. She'd set it aside earlier when rushing to answer the phone.

She picked it up. Its yellow-edged pages held the familiar woodsy fragrance of antique books, although Royston's edition was nowhere near as old as those from original print runs.

She glided a hand across the first page.

Our True Ancient History

A tale from the People of the Sea

Retold by Reverend Edward Lillibridge
In the Year of Our Lord, Seventeen-Seventy-one

'The People of the Sea,' Rosetta whispered. 'Wish we could find out what Lillibridge meant by that.'

The cat opened a half-interested eye, then closed it again.

The book fell open where the narrative was musing on body kings, a rather disgruntled lot who made their presence felt in a number of antisocial ways.

...In the rubble of unjustified philosophies, they found comfort. In the ashes of a once flourishing faerie nation, they revelled in that race's diminishment. When the sun roamed their waking hours, searing its way through a screaming sky, body kings took to their temples to honour that sphere, which lent their gold its seductive sparkle, and when the moon floated placidly through twilight's hush, they spat words of hatred.

Within their solar shrines, they threw silver discs upon a central flame in a misguided effort to weaken lunar grace. And yet the moon continued to bathe their realm in her soothing beams.

Their only escape from that peaceful purgatory was sleep. And sleep they did, cancelling out an invitation to heal...imagine...dream of the future...reflect on the past...regard each other with an affection that held no lecherous intent.

> Hideous Luna
> Causes recline
> Silvers a world that is no longer mine
>
> Sleep I cajole for its cold clawing clasp
> A thrill to the body to die without gasp
> I 'waken to fire where Sol slathers Need
> And gold, solid Solar, indulges my Greed

Upon each of the body kings' sleeping-chamber walls was this tribute in reverse, a grudging ode to the luminary that presided over their death-like slumbers. Suffice to say, all in the empire enjoyed their terrors both real and imagined, thrived on the gift and receipt of punishment and cherished each nightmarish repose. While they could not fully cancel her out, they could at least kill off their conscious existence throughout Luna's silvering hours, and nightly rest allowed them the strength to welcome each dawn with fervour.

Those who woke to the day could only be pitied. At this stage in their evolution, they knew no better than to mock, uproariously, the silent glow of goodness.

Rosetta flicked through the novel's first few pages. She'd already read the beginning of *Our True Ancient History*–and more than once: firstly as a teenaged fantasy fiction fan and again at the initial book study meeting. Despite this, she turned back to Chapter One and settled into the cushions of her couch.

I

The modern world in which you and I now live, this flicker in time we call reality, was naught but an unimagined fancy in the Scandinavia of old.

In place of fields and villages, and within the heart of prehistoric Norway, lay Elysium, an ethereal forest whose dusk-wreathed silhouettes evoked spidery tendrils enmeshed in joy.

Here, colour would move in unison with mood. Crimson and magenta, the shades of passion, melded with violet sunshine over the wind-tickled surface of meandering streams. Beneath was a pristine silence, a mile long and heavy with the whispers of the water sprites.

Woven through Elysium's mood of serenity was the crystalline *whoosh* of a waterfall. Its music often masked the step of approaching predators. Maleika hoped this hadn't caused the faerie's delay. Truth be said, Maleika was unsettled over meeting Orahney so near to the body-king palace.

Maleika turned to the oak. Within its boughs were pixies immersed in their work. Tiny hands sculpted and smoothed the acorns. Minuscule asterisks of light, quiet effects of beauty-creation, filled the air at intervals in dancing, perfumed sparks.

Remembering scenes in contrast to the one before her, Maleika shuddered. Body kings–icy-eyed, golden-skinned, despising of devic heritage–had attacked and killed trees with their axes the day before, causing her fellow elves to flee or expire from shock. Sacred medicinal plants had been callously uprooted. Pastel-hued blooms, exquisite creations of the flower faeries, were now little more than severed ribbons of sadness.

Be at the oak tree by the caverns at dusk on the morrow, Orahney's sonic code had said, a code sent to Maleika in a Dream Sphere memory and deciphered with the consumption of Remembrance Essence upon waking. *There is an important task I must ask you to fulfil.*

Maleika had woken well before dusk mellowed the sky. As the evening clouds faded to apricot, her certainty dissolved into doubt. Had she deciphered the sonic code correctly?

A flutter of fiery colours emerged from around the trunk of the oak. Maleika asked Orahney if she'd journeyed far. 'It has occurred to me,' she added, 'that I know not where you live.'

'Earth is no longer my world,' Orahney said. 'I died of a broken heart one hundred season-cycles ago.'

'If only these body kings would move elsewhere. So very many of you are passing on before your plans are fulfilled.'

The ghostly faerie managed a courageous smile. 'My life was lived in the Pre-Destruction Century.'

Maleika voiced her envy for the faerie's uninterrupted stay in the Dream Sphere, and Orahney expressed her lament for the locks body kings had placed on Dream-Sphere memories.

'I pity you and your earthly clan,' Orahney said. 'Having access only in your slumber is limiting, to say the least. Remembrance Essence must be a comfort to you though. The power of crystal-infused Wondalobs water was still undiscovered when I lived here.'

Maleika lowered her tone to a whisper. 'Essence Bearers must be especially mindful now. Body-king courtiers have set up camp in the valley.' She gave thought to The Wondalobs, great rock surfaces deep within the Forest of Ivy: purple, jelly-like, and almost alive beneath their lichen covering. Once filled with spring water, each bore an astounding resemblance to the rounded back of a sleeping marsh monster.

'The Wondalobs appear no different to other rock surfaces,' Orahney assured. 'Take heart, Maleika. They are nondescript enough to go unnoticed.'

Maleika hoped Orahney was right. The faerie clans, whose task it was to plumb the essence, kept watch during the day in place of slumber. Fatigue had weakened their earthly life-force. Sacrifice indeed in their service to Elysium's sprites.

Orahney called forth the oak tree's dryad, a moss-coloured fellow with solemn eyes. She asked the dryad to uncover a wand deposited there a little under a century earlier, one that had been harboured within the oak's mighty trunk. The dryad waved about his gnarled hands, then vanished back into the tree. A rod crowned with a crystal of palest pink appeared. Part of the wand was swathed in dark fabric.

Orahney gestured to the manifestation. 'This, Maleika, was left for you by your future son.'

'I am to become a mother?' Overjoyed, Maleika flushed at the news.

'In three season-cycles, you and Wallikin will sing a boy into existence.'

'And so you are acquainted with him in the Dream Sphere!'

'Not quite.' Orahney retrieved the wand from the tree. 'I knew him in the Elysium of the past. After the twelfth anniversary of his birth, he will be trapped awhile in the Pre-Destruction Century.'

'A time-traveller in an earthly body? Is this possible, Orahney?'

'Not normally.'

'I would have thought the body kings' locks on our Dream Sphere access had prevented us from...'

'Unusual, I agree.'

'If you are referring to him travelling in slumber, I would understand.'

'He will not travel through any power of his own. The gold ones will force this upon him.'

Maleika took in a small, sharp breath.

'Do not let this vex you, Maleika. When he arrives in the Pre-Destruction Century, I will keep him safe. I can promise you this, for it has already occurred.'

'How I shall miss him!' Maleika contemplated the curling leaves at her feet. 'Tell me, though, he will return in good time, will he not?'

'I cannot tell you, Maleika. To reveal your fates might harm the natural scheme of events. Now listen closely, my friend. I must ask you to fulfil a task. If the task is not carried out correctly, many will suffer.' The fabric enclosing the wand unfurled into a hooded cloak. Orahney passed both cloak and wand to Maleika. The elf woman accepted them uncertainly. 'First of all,' said the faerie, 'you must adopt the disguise of a palace bewitcher, and then you must attend a crystalling.'

'A crystalling?'

'An infant-naming ceremony. It is a gathering in one of the palace temples where bewitchers bless newborns with crystal wands. I implore you to carry this out, Maleika. Infiltrating the Grudellan Palace will not be without risk, but it is crucial to the welfare of your son-to-be.'

II
FIFTEEN SEASON-CYCLES ON

By the fire, cloaked in silver, Pieter of the Brumlynds stared listlessly at the clouds. He'd not known how tired a boy of twelve season-cycles could become.

'Always sleep when the sky lightens,' Maleika told him. 'The nights here in Elysium Glades are sad imposters of the Dream Sphere.'

Pieter wriggled out of his silver cape to take another cup of berry cider. 'But I can never get all of it done,' he said. The boy, an impatient one, supposed he could return all of Elysium to its former tranquil safeness within the flap of a bluebird's wing. The body kings would be led elsewhere and then, he promised Maleika, he would sleep all the slumbers missed in one. In fact, he could wake to the Dream Sphere forever once this was achieved.

Maleika sighed. 'One day, my son, you will fully understand the importance of rest.'

When sun-up brought a glow to the hillside, Maleika sent off the fireflies and insisted Pieter accompany his clan in their journey to the Dream Sphere.

Pieter was less reluctant that morning. He stepped into the circle of candle canes where the sleeping wagons were stationed, as did his mother Maleika and the other four of their clan, then made a wish that courtiers clad in sprite-seeing cloaks would not happen across their otherwise invisible haven.

Once asleep, the Brumlynd clan floated in spirit-form up to the world that was theirs before birth and arrived at an ethereal twisting staircase and the sparkling gates of the Devic Great Hall.

The first in the Dream Sphere to greet them was Wallikin, Pieter's passed-over father, who had been taken by force to the Grudellan Palace when the youngest of the Brumlynds was an infant.

Body kings in sprite-seeing cloaks had stolen the elfin father from his clan many season-cycles earlier and had attempted to make him solid like themselves and unmagical. They were unable to drain him of heart-centred beauty-creation entirely, and so he had escaped being mesmerised by the illusion of lack and greed. The sand dunes of the Grudellan Palace, in which Wallikin was forced to mine gold, were rife with docile elves who believed themselves fortunate to be presented with tiny gold discs at the close of each season. In his frustration with the fellow prisoners' misguided loyalty, he expired of a broken heart.

Pieter had marvelled over the story many a time. 'The gold had to be offered back to the gifter,' Wallikin was wont to say with incredulous brow. 'Failing to give up our gift was considered worthy of malnutrition and death.'

'And so you had no choice other than to toil exhaustively and relinquish all rewards for your labours,' Pieter would say, as though puzzling over this would somehow deem it justifiable. 'You could not do your own work, you had to do theirs! And all so that you could momentarily hold gold droplets in your hand.'

A punishment indeed. Useless, flat pebbles traded for the life-needs that Wallikin already had in plenty before his imprisonment: nourishment and shelter! It was a currency born of the crudest ignorance.

Alcor, a silver-bearded Dream Master, floated swiftly towards Pieter. Those not fully aware of the Dream Sphere's hierarchies might have distinguished him as a father of the gods, and yet Alcor was but a guide.

Pieter observed the jewel in Alcor's crown, which emanated soothing light, and contemplated the anklets he wore, splendid cylinders of a metal unknown in the earthly world. Radiating the entire spectrum's colours, and then some, the anklets symbolised a humbleness to serve those of devic heritage: sprite clans of the Earth such as the elfin Brumlynds; and angels—passed-over sprites—of the celestial Dream Sphere such as Wallikin and the autumn faerie Orahney. The Dream Master was not fully rid of his recollections. He'd once had a life as a body-king trooper. Although his conversion was oftentimes harrowing, the more dark realities Alcor left behind, the further he progressed through the devic hierarchy.

Within the Corridor of the Dawntide, far-flung sunbeams lined the floors. Ceilings, although there were none, were made feasible by projected coverings: cobweb veils of aqua sea spray.

At the end of the Devic Great Hall were three doorways. Maleika chose the left this time. Pieter, undecided as to whether to step towards the one in the middle as he usually did, turned to a different door. Who was behind it and why? Who was he called upon to assist? 'The right-hand one, please, Master,' he said.

Alcor opened the door. 'You are to visit the future.'

Rosetta placed the book back on the coffee table. It fell shut with a muted thump.

On the next few pages were descriptions of a timeframe that could easily have been her own. How a reverend born in 1730 could have envisaged what appeared to be the digital age with such astounding accuracy was a topic of interest within the book club. Could Lena have been right about the author receiving psychic visions?

Considering Lillibridge wasn't the actual initiator of *Our True Ancient History*, this seemed unlikely. He'd been a scribe, a documenter. He'd attributed his ideas to those elusive People of the Sea.

She yawned. Time to turn in. She would open the Shiraz another night. Lillibridge's elf would have to step through the door without her.

Pieter stepped through the Dream Sphere's dimensional doorway. His spirit self was now embroiled in a state of affairs he had never thought possible, all while his physical self lay slumbering in the forest! Dream Sphere journeys were full of surprises.

Here he was, within a structure of sorts, pondering over numerals that flashed like glow-worms on upright black squares. The atmosphere was dank and angry and offended the elf boy's senses. Colour seemed not to exist, save for the odd splash in cloth strips that descended from each future man's collar. Did they fear colour's capacity for inspiration?

A haze, which Pieter supposed was tainted air, swirled densely around him. Heads popped out of this grimy mist and waggled stiffly, heads that roared nonsense, fists that punched the air.

Taut necks, hunched backs, cropped hair, foreheads that crumpled with a dull brand of concentration...Pieter mimicked this stance in an effort to align himself with the future men's hopes, strove to decode the symbols that triggered their militant cries, and felt the hunger behind their hope of foreseeing events, a desire for winning that gnawed at them.

The brightly lit symbols sharpened in significance. Understanding now, Pieter snapped his fingers. He seized up a coil-tailed apparatus beside one of the squares, held it to his ear, then shouted at the numerals. He had become one of these men, a willing participant in a fatally sombre game that hung upon decisions and held him in survival defence mode. Every heartbeat balanced on the flashing information; each breath another gasp of life-force for screaming down a price.

And at the end of his day in that sordid cavern, after having located the one Alcor expected him to assist: a man whose heart was muddied with anguish, Pieter followed the fellow, invisibly, into the cool night air and noticed him to be impervious to the moon and stars. He observed as the fellow switched off his mechanical side and donned a happy-chap expression so as not to glare at passers-by with the cold intensity of a servant of currency. The fellow marched to his chariot—an astonishing contraption of shining red that cocooned him roundly—and in this he returned to his dwelling through streets awash with artificial luminaries.

Alcor's sapphire eyes...The chime of sylvan bells...Spirals of aquamarine starlight...The Dream Sphere's Devic Great Hall had summoned Pieter back.

'That was utterly horrible,' Pieter told Alcor. 'Tell me, Master, that I never have to return to that place and those creatures'

'That place,' said Alcor, a wistful smile touching his eyes, 'is your world, the world you dwell in during your waking hours.'

'The earthly realm!'

'And those creatures aren't unlike you, less the devic wisdom of course.'

'Hampered joy! Limited peace! A wild, voracious race that feeds on itself? I have heard untruths in my time, but...a species like ours? From our forest in the world below? 'Tis almost an insult, Master.'

He thought awhile, however, remembering Elysium's gold-obsessed invaders, the species which chose to clash violently with nature, and wondered for once if his estimation of them remaining a minority or becoming extinct from sheer self-destruction might have been naive.

Could it be that these meddlers might flourish in a world grown older?

Before Pieter could wonder any longer, Alcor asked him if he wished to continue his assignment. Pieter admitted he couldn't be sure and mulled over what sort of insight he could offer a being such as the haze breather, insight that wouldn't be ignored. It was an ignorant one he would be dealing with after all. He would arrive at a decision before his next slumbering journey.

On waking, he joined his clan at the campfire, gazed at the dusk-streaked heavens, sipped Remembrance Essence and recalled only vaguely his visit to the Dream Sphere. He knew he'd visited the timeframe of someone discontented, but couldn't remember what he had witnessed while there. What he did remember was the sort of timeframe the person lived in. It had virtually gleamed with artificiality.

Many a time throughout the morning, squirrels had scampered over Pieter's sleeping wagon and nibbled at acorns in the still-warm ashes. Now that their day had drawn to a close, they nodded good evening to him and dashed back to their treetop homes.

Pieter spent his night rambling Elysium's forests and at the first hint of daylight returned to the campfire, now dissolved into a stream of smoke. When the robin trilled her herald to the dawn, he settled into his sleeping wagon once more and surrendered to the Dream Sphere's luminosity.

'And what is your decision?' Alcor asked upon ushering Pieter into the Devic Great Hall. 'Will you continue with this assignment?'

Able to glean the details of his last Dream Sphere visit now that he was free of his earthly mind, Pieter promised Alcor he would. 'I hope to do all I can to assist this fellow's evolution.' Although Pieter's thirst for growth and desire for kindness merits was strong in him, his motivation lay in the compassion he felt for the future creature. The assignment was his to make what betterment he could to another being's existence. Whether he could help, he wasn't at all certain. Through the Dream Sphere's wheel of transcendence he went.

Whirl of colour.

Clatter of shade.

Laughter of snowdrops.

Taste of stars.

And there again was that dutiful trooper...

...marching towards revolving glass doors. Matthew P Weissler, as the sign on his office and credit cards confirmed, with a presence that was neither striking nor displeasing; a lean, bordering on lanky, physique; hair the colour of perished leaves; a pallid complexion that went bronze in summer; and a passion for golf, mathematics, swimming, and any sort of music capable of giving him goosebumps. He was Matthew P Weissler, and he was in this building to get things straightened out.

Today he wanted to see those shares hiking. He'd be giving Gillings good news. Stable news. Perhaps not megaton lightning news, only because mega expectations weren't forecast on today's money scene.

He called a meeting, discussed the impacts of the Champion meltdown and told Plimpton on the trading floor to roll up the Gallilani deal. A nod from his assistant and he was in there with Charlie Sanders, straightening his tie while Charlie yelled into the phone. The tie was a particularly slippery form of silk, not his favourite shade of green. Were his eyes really that colour? Bernadette seemed to think so. She'd dolled-up the house and now her renovator's eye was trained on him. *We've got to get you less conservative.* Bernadette's current motto.

It was then, while he waited with toe-tapping impatience, that he discovered the art piece. It sat on one side of Charlie's desk, pushed up against a cluttered clump of papers and supported by a bottle opener and an autographed football. Comfortable, yet regal, even in Charlie's nest of mess.

Despite its mundane, even forgettable appearance, Matthew couldn't take his eyes off it. An eagle. Nothing unusual about that, but the thing somehow beckoned him as if it had a life of its own, inviting him to examine its texture.

Placing a hand on the eagle, he glanced at Charlie, who gestured, as he barked orders to his caller, for Matthew to pick it up. It was cool to the touch. Earthen. Iron and white gold studded its back and tail. Quite possibly a memento collected on a trip to the islands. He trailed his fingers over the smooth undulating wings and felt strangely comforted.

A memory came whirling back to him, something he couldn't be sure he'd ever replayed until now. It gripped him in a wild, fearful, free-falling state. Although Charlie was still booming into the phone, and the traffic and the yells of the guys on the bank's trading floor rumbled on, he remained undistracted, shutting his eyes and allowing himself to be engulfed by the rushing sensation that was drawing him backwards out of 2008 and plonking him into his childhood. Early childhood. Infancy more like it.

He was looking down at two fat little bare feet that were still unsteady at each step, and he could see a puffy plastic bubble surrounding his hips. In place of the familiar neck-tie on his chest was a bib with green and blue building blocks listing the alphabet.

Here he looked up, way up into the jacaranda tree, flowering light purple and sprinkling the grass with shadows, and noticed the faint circling of a bird. The bird flew closer and zoomed into the jacaranda.

Perching in the bough closest to him, the bird lifted its wings and began to...talk? No! A memory? But yes, the bird had spoken, although not by opening its beak to babble like a cartoon character. Communicating through thoughts. Words that came to him in another's voice. And although not yet two years of age, Matthew understood completely. What the bird said was where the memory went vague. Hadn't he been told something important? Something that might have even pertained to now?

Matthew didn't know why he'd supposed this.

Another hurling of colour. Another random memory. Winding wheels, fortress gates...velvet cloaks...pebbly roads. Way before his time though. Medieval almost, and yet he knew it well. How? What was going on?

'It's a great little artefact that one,' said Charlie, putting down the phone. 'Got it when I was in Oslo last month. Not cheap. Not too new either.'

Waking to present-day, Matthew nodded. As though stung, he returned the sculpture to Charlie's desk, letting the strange images leave along with it. 'How old do you think?'

'Dunno. Over a hundred-and-fifty I'd say. At least. Now, where are the reports you wanted me to see?'

Matthew looked one last time at the bird. He shook off a shudder. Snatched of his sense of the present a moment ago, he had almost forgotten his whereabouts. How could a crummy little carving have done that?

The reports were received good-naturedly. For all Charlie's compliments, Matthew should have been pleased with the outcome.

The emphasis was to be on the *should.* Irritated with his boss and not knowing why, Matthew stalked from the office.

His annoyance grew throughout the day. Judgements made about colleagues, which he'd normally ignore, today seemed to bite at him. Even the remark about blond-headed poser Adam Harrow, fuelled by Celia's disgust at the 'forgive me' roses Harrow ordered regularly for each woman he cheated on, became an aggravation to Matthew, a mite fanging at his throat. He found himself leaping out of his seat at intervals, grumbling to Celia about the gossip. It wasn't at all characteristic.

In the restroom mirror he noticed the colour rising in his face. Maybe he had a virus; the prickly temperature increase and dizzy lapse in Charlie's office were enough to indicate he wasn't his usual self.

But sickness prompted weakness and a need for sleep, and Matthew felt very much awake, readier than ever to shout down the hyenas that afternoon.

After a highly successful day, he headed home feeling empty. 'So I succeeded,' he said with a sigh. 'Succeeded at what?'

Before dinner he read Chapter Seven of a self-help book he'd untypically rescued from a garbage bin. When he got to the chapter that followed: 'The Ritual of Accumulation', he threw the book at the wall. 'What do you suggest we do then, Conan Dalesford?' he muttered. 'Ditch all our worldly possessions and live on buffalo grass?' He should have left it in the garbage where it belonged.

His narky behaviour continued throughout dinner. He got restless around the kids and snapped at his wife for being 'trivial' about Vanuatu. After apologising he went roaming the neighbourhood, numb to everything, very much alone in his people-rich world.

The moon was full and round. 'Explains the anger,' he told himself. His astrology-mad sister-in-law had told him the full moon triggered restlessness in those with a Cancerian Rising Sign. 'Maybe I should have been born there,' he said, nodding at the moon. A regular moon child. Homesick for the luminary that ruled his personality.

The silence broke. A flutter of wings ruffled the dreamy calm. Matthew searched the branches overhead. Gumleaves of blue, tipped with silver, parted to reveal...What was it? An eagle? His heart jumped. He scanned the leaves some more, only to see it wasn't a bird at all, but a bat. A silly little fruit bat, struggling to untangle itself from the branches. It hung upside down for a while, studying him with cherry-coloured eyes.

The bat's gaze was hypnotic. Immobilising. Matthew continued to stare, unable to free himself from the redness. Now everything had become red, a blur of scarlet blotting out the night, even the moon.

When this blanket of colour, which beckoned and caressed and embraced him, finally let go of his vision to vanish, he saw not the bat but a bird. The bird had a downward-curving beak. It blinked at him suspiciously in the way an eagle would, but there were no eagles in this part of the world.

It spoke to him! Without a voice, it said, 'Do you plan to waste the remainder of your life as well?'

Matthew looked away. Steadied his shaking body. No eagle met his sight when he turned again to the branches. Only the bat. The bat grunted, angry probably at its lack of privacy, then flip-flopped its wings and soared off, evidently in search of accommodation elsewhere.

'I'm delirious,' Matthew said in a gasp. 'And I'm talking to myself as well.'

He sat by the tree and stared at the sky. His eyes misted over. The stars looked better as wet silver blurs.

'I've gone mad,' he growled.

Sleep overcame him. The faint sound of a young voice whisked past. 'Master, I mean it this time. I will not visit the timeframe of that fellow ever again. Too much ire! He can visit me here in the Dream Sphere, though, if you wish...if you honestly think it would help.'

The tree trunk supported Matthew's head as he transcended one world for another...where everything made sense, at least until it was time to wake up.

Sleep had soothed Matthew. Leaning forward from the tree trunk, he stretched out his arms and blearily observed the playground. The square face of his German watch glowed an eerie green. Almost midnight. He mashed a hand against the leaf-strewn ground in readiness for jumping to his feet, but before he knew it his body froze, rendering him motionless.

He was plummeting backwards into a kind of well. He'd landed somewhere. Here there grew a magnificent forest, the type he'd hiked through in Bavaria—although these trees were decidedly older. Peace. A feeling of been-here-beforeness.

A flurry of movement caught Matthew's eye. He turned to see someone strikingly small in stature regarding him wordlessly, not unlike a gigantic-eyed child, with hair sticking out all over the place. Proud yet wholesome in appearance, like a Kalahari bushman.

A thin curling mouth twisted itself into an amiable grin. 'Hiyo!'

A child who still couldn't say 'hello'. Was he really a child this young though? The individual before Matthew was a bizarre blend of baby and teenager. Naivety in conflict with wisdom. Innocent trust at odds with a slightly mocking impishness. In no way was the little guy threatening.

So Matthew took a sharp stride towards him and said, 'Where the fu—' then gulped back his words. What was he thinking? He was speaking to a youngster. 'Where the *frack* am I, who the *frack* are you and what the *frack* is going on?'

The boy wasn't at all taken aback by this form of greeting. 'I'm Pieter of the Brumlynds,' he said, 'and I'm helping you with your destiny.'

'What destiny?'

'I don't know,' said Pieter with a shrug. 'Where exactly in your life are you?'

Matthew groaned. 'How am I supposed to know? Jeezus! I'm thirty-four, I've got a demanding career, an extravagant wife and two kids who I doubt even know I exist, and I'm in the throes of a nervous breakdown. Obvious, isn't it? I mean, you yourself, Peter of the Pumpkins or whoever you are, you illustrate this perfectly, the fact that I'm going mad.'

'I am not illustrating anything,' corrected Pieter.

'Christ! I'm hallucinating, and even my hallucinations answer me back.' Matthew rested his forehead in his hands. 'My boss, the guys at work, my family...everybody! Everybody answers me back. Why can't I just live?'

Pieter tilted his head to one side. 'Excuse me, sir, but I am not the avatar you mentioned twice. I'm an elf.'

'Did you just say you're an...No, this is getting too weird.'

'As well as that, I was not "answering" you "back".'

'See what I mean?' Matthew said, knowing deep down he was acting hopelessly sorry for himself.

'I was merely asking you where you were so I could more accurately direct you in your destiny. Secondly, I do not like to be referred to as a "hallucination" as I am no such thing. Had I been solid in form, as you are, I would probably have been insulted.'

Cautiously, Matthew lifted his head to study the hallucination. Who would have thought it might have an opinion? It felt things! 'Sorry,' he mumbled, unsure whether apologising to figments of his own imagination made him any crazier.

'Where do you live?' the strange boy asked cheerily. He was unfazed by Matthew's confusion.

'Cabarita Heights.'

'Where's Cabarita Heights? Somewhere high in the heavens?'

Matthew snorted. 'It's a suburb of Sydney. Aus-tra-li-a.'

'And the planet?' Pieter inquired.

'Are you out of your mind?' Matthew then realised the same question might apply to him, personally. 'I live in the world. The world! If you're inferring I'm off the planet—'

'What world?' chirped Pieter. 'There are many worlds other than yours, you know.'

Okay. Why fight it? He would play along and see where it led. 'Earth,' he said. 'Planet Earth.'

'Uh-huh.'

Could it be true the boy wasn't being impudent?

'And what timeframe? You'd be the kind to have a timeframe wouldn't you?'

'If you're talking about the year, it's 2008, and the month, since we're being fairly particular here, is March.'

'Where are you in your soul connection?'

'Huh?'

'Oh, I see. Never mind that question. All right, now that I have your details, I can finally give you an answer regarding your destiny.'

'And that is?'

'That is that—'

'Yes, yes, what?' Matthew was suddenly excited at the thought of the meaning of life, or, more importantly, that the meaning of *his* life would have some light shone on it, if only a glimmer, to inspire hope for the future.

'That is,' said Pieter, 'that I don't know what you're doing here either.'

'Great.' Matthew kicked the trunk of a tree. Its weirdly elastic texture gave him the sensation of having plunged his foot into jelly. 'And let me guess. You can't tell me how to get out of here.'

'Oh, I can.' Pieter was pleased to be of assistance. 'You're presumably a being with little soul connection, therefore I can safely guess that right now you are slumbering. I suspect your physical self wakes to the day. Do you remember falling asleep?'

It all flashed by. Storming out of the house, roaming the neighbourhood, a red-eyed bat, drifting into a misty sleep in the park. 'That's right,' Matthew said. 'I did fall asleep. I'm dreaming then!'

'You want to go now, I see,' Pieter said, turning.

'You bet.'

Pieter drew from his pocket a woodwind instrument fashioned from marsh grass. 'Perhaps we'll meet again. If so, I expect you'll be in a better humour. Then we can talk some more.' Wandering away from Matthew, he proceeded to play an odd little melody. Low and haunting. The soft, sweet whistle of a pipe made from reed.

'I *have* been a bit of a jerk,' Matthew admitted. He softened his tone. 'You'd better get home to your parents, kid.'

Pieter wound up his tune, then sprinted in the direction of a hazy crimson light. Matthew felt eerily alone in the twilit forest. 'Hey, Peter Piper,' he called. 'How do I get out of here?'

Pieter's voice pierced the silence. 'Wake up.' It sounded derogatory in the same way smart-arse Adam Harrow would address him: *Wake up, Weissler. There's no way Hong Kong's going to fix these deposits by Friday.*

Pieter's voice again. This time it sounded well-meaning. 'Just wake up, Matthew.'

How the creature guessed his name was a puzzle to Matthew. Logic gained upon waking alerted him to the obvious. The scenario had occurred within a dream.

Dreaming of saucer-eyed leprechauns who insisted they weren't part of his mind. Huh! Perhaps someone spiked his drink at the bar. If anyone were to do it, it'd have to be Harrow. That good-for-nothing loser. Yeah. Drugging drinks. Matthew wouldn't put it past him.

Shaking himself more awake, he became aware of the cold turning him goosebumpy and dampness settling into his skin. Rain. He was sitting in a playground while the clouds showered down.

He strolled back to his pseudo-Georgian eyesore and stood by the fishpond's waterfall in contemplation. The book he'd thrown at the wall: hadn't there been a chapter in it on supernatural sightings?

Intent on recovering Dalesford's *Thoughts on Tomorrow's Tycoon War* from the floor of his study, he marched down the garden path towards the chandelier's blaze, a swirl of crystal brilliance glinting in sharp, neat fragments behind the prim foyer windows.

Chapter Two

Rosetta set down a bowl of pretzels and took a seat between Craig and Eadie. 'What part are we up to?'

Royston tilted his head to the side, birdlike and alert. 'Chapter III. What's happened to Lena?'

'Working.'

'At 8 p.m.?'

'She's rearranging stock at her shop.'

Craig opened his book, then craned his neck round to Eadie on his left, deep-brown curls bobbing like a glassful of cola bubbles. 'Do you want to read next, Eadie?'

'But I read last time!'

'All right, I'll read,' Craig said. 'And then, Rosetta, could you read Chapters IV and V?'

'Sure. But before we start, I have some news that I've been absolutely aching to share. About our Friday Fortnight website.' She told Eadie, Royston and Craig that her Lillibridge-related site had rapidly gained international interest since its launch two weeks earlier. Her hope of connecting with other readers throughout the world was blossoming into reality.

Anyone who had managed to get access to an out-of-print copy of *Our True Ancient History*—available at only a smattering of antiquarian outlets—anyone wanting to explore its philosophies, was encouraged, on Rosetta's 'About Us' page to form a book-study group of their own. She'd had no idea the response would be so enthusiastic. 'So far we've had over 800 visits!'

Craig gave a low whistle, and Eadie shrieked.

'And five other Friday Fortnight groups are forming. Thirty-seven people in total!'

'Where are these groups situated?' Royston asked Rosetta. 'Are they mostly in Australia?'

'There's only one other here in Australia—it's in Melbourne. Every other group is overseas. I've got a list here with the exact numbers. Drum roll please, Craigo.' Craig pummelled the coffee table. 'England, Scotland, Canada, and two groups forming in the United States. A few readers in Ireland formed an *Our True Ancient History* group well before we did. They're going to stay connected with us through our website.' She scanned the list again. 'Ooh, and just one person in Sweden.'

'In Sweden?' said Royston. '*Where* in Sweden?'

'A little place called Perelda. It's an island just north of the mainland apparently. Just the one person in a group of his own. How amazing is that? Okay, Craig, Chapter III awaits.'

'At your service. Alrighty, people, listen up.'

III

Once Maleika woke, she was pleased to discover Pieter had readied the fire. When she asked where he'd journeyed in the Dream Sphere, he couldn't remember.

'Take another sip of Remembrance Essence, Pieter. You've probably travelled far.'

Pieter did so. 'All I recall is a forest similar to this one. And a fellow who got quite angry with me.' Pieter took another sip of the essence. Another small memory returned. The fellow had been dully clad, and he'd mistaken Pieter for one of the future's many great masters, having at one stage referred to him as 'Jesus' and then as 'Christ'. Pieter drained his cup. 'It's no use,' he said. 'I cannot recall it in detail.'

'Ah well,' said Maleika filling a cup for herself. 'Perhaps you aren't meant to.' Comforted by the familiar sights that now surrounded her, Elysium Glades bejewelled with moonlit dew, she turned to the campfire, sipped the Remembrance and allowed her memory of the day's slumber to return. 'Alcor asked me to observe a scenario. I expect what I saw was the distant future, and I expect it was our earthly world rather than another. I observed two people, a mother and daughter.'

'And...?' said Pieter.

'And they conversed inside a smallish dwelling which resembled *that* within.' She nodded towards the Grudellan Palace. 'Its walls weren't rounded but sharp and square.'

'What colours surrounded you, Maleika?'

'Sparkling colours of the Earth,' she said, recalling flashes of silver, copper, amber. 'Gold,' she added warily. 'Gold there was.'

'Were the people themselves golden?' This was asked by her nephew Croydee, another member of the Brumlynd clan who had crept out to join them. 'I hope they weren't body kings.'

'Not body kings, no. I assumed them to be sprites because the mother, obviously the Clan Watcher of the two, had skin and eyes of brown like us, dear, although her complexion was much lighter in shade, and no sign of superiority towards animals was indicated; a feline of grey sat loyally by her side. The younger one had a snow-pale face and tresses the colour of fire. The Watcher had wonderful lights streaming from her heart chakra.' Pieter and Croydee nodded appreciatively. 'Her aura was warm and of fire, which explained the inclusion of red in her environment. The youngster, her daughter, became exasperated at one stage and engaged in an odd little bird dance. The mother sprite's sense of hope is misted over. A sadness, a loss, has permeated her overall enthusiasm.'

'Why is she sad?' Croydee's long-lashed eyes crinkled in concern.

'She's missing a valuable part of herself. It's as though she's been tripped up by the gold-tainted illusion. Her mind has split into thousands of little facets—each yearning for the remembrance of other worlds—and yet there's little connection to the world in which she resides.'

'Then why, for goodness sake, does she stay?' said an incredulous Pieter. 'Why doesn't she get her Dream Master to mortally finish that silly useless life and go on to something better?'

'Patience, Cousin Pieter,' said Croydee. 'Not everyone understands how to pass over peacefully. I've heard that those of the future are rarely able to remain permanently in the Dream Sphere during one of their slumbers.'

Maleika agreed. 'And earthly life is the only existence they know. Dedication to the younger one is her motivation for living there. A huge commitment ribbon streams from one heart to the other. Whenever the Clan Watcher is tempted to float off, the heart ribbon returns her to the reality of the timeframe they undertook.'

'I wonder why you've been asked to help this one, Aunt Maleika,' said Croydee.

'I wonder too, Croydee. 'Tis all very exciting.'

An inky blueness was blotting out the twilight. The owl hooted. Crickets sang cheerily. The sprites' waking hours had sprung to life.

IV

When the golden hours descended upon Elysium Glades, Pieter called together several of his companions to share his Dream Sphere excursion: a foxling, an antlered deer and a mango eater, who each curled up outside his pumpkin-shaped sleeping wagon and settled promptly into slumber.

Once his physical self was immersed in sleep, he hastened to the Devic Great Hall. While in the Dream Sphere with his expanded memory of Dream Sphere occurrences, Pieter gave a great deal of thought to the body-king product who breathed grimy air, shouted at numerals and drove a chariot that roared. His ponderings over this fellow caused him to conclude that the future of the sprites would indeed be bleak, and so on this particular visit he asked Alcor whether his earthly home would plummet into this tragic, gold-grasping existence that resisted the quiet wisdom of the heart.

'For some amount of time it will,' Alcor said. 'And then grappling for power will retreat into history.'

'So it is, therefore, worth pursuing?' said Pieter doubtfully. 'A re-turn to our currency of kindness?'

'Very much worth pursuing, Pieter.' Alcor's smile hinted at sadness. 'Yet many will be whirled into the Cycle of Suffering before then. The outlook for the in-between time, I am afraid, is grim.' Alcor gestured to three doors at the end of the Devic Great Hall.

'Behind each of these is an individual requiring your help. Which door will you choose?'

'The middle one, please, master.'

Pieter was immediately transported to the other side and found himself atop a snow-caked mountain where a puffing breeze whipped clouds around his feet. An eagle was circling the rich violet sky.

Pieter had trouble getting the eagle's attention. Inhabiting an entire world with a faraway winged one wasn't the most comforting situation. The elf boy felt a coldness he'd seldom encountered. His mind became inflexible, as if of steel, and in his heart...Was it an ache? Although rarely dependent on his clan, he now longed to see the bright eyes of passed-over Wallikin...and where were his creature companions? There was no sign of them now, and Maleika was yet to fall asleep and travel there. She had mentioned her hope of revisiting the Clan Watcher sprite: a heartbroken mother of jovial temperament whose name suggested roses and whose futuristic dwelling displayed the shimmering metals body kings mined.

Alcor's instructions floated across to him from the other side of the Dream Sphere door. 'Bridge the gap between you and the ethereal eagle.'

How should he converse with one so conscious of its own magnificence? The emotion the bird expressed was remote, filmy, but a word penetrated the clouded pinnacle, and the word was 'vanity'.

Too strange to accept for Pieter, who had never known such a description. His higher mind narrowed it down to a word better known at that point in time where self-adoration was only in its infancy. Pride. A word used for body kings and not yet linked with arrogance.

For a moment Pieter took on the bird's thoughts and feelings.

'*Fearsome bird below, clad in a pointed cap. Does it not see this is my dwelling? Neither me nor mine. Inferior.*

Some try to encroach on me but are yet to win, for I ingeniously defend my territory. I leave them with little doubt as to who owns what. My plan is to skim the top of the sky. Look down, I shall, from there. And seen as God by all creation below, I shall smile and express gratitude for my marvellousness.'

The bird's chain of impressions grew hazy. Pieter gained only limited insight into what the eagle most wanted to achieve before his current life drew to a close. Was it simply to reach the top of a wind-wizened world and congratulate himself for having grasped perfection?

On these compulsory stay-awake Fridays, Izzie would shut herself away to finish art homework or her own little drawing projects. When she'd fallen asleep other times, she'd been woken by someone cackling energetically, like a bantam on amphetamines. She'd since trained herself to fight drowsiness and did her best to ignore the echo of undulating murmurs.

Her mother's voice rang out from the sitting room. 'Hey, I thought of something funny,' Rosetta was saying, having interrupted herself mid-chapter. 'That reference to the silver feline and fire-haired daughter...'

'I grinned to myself when I saw that.' Craig's voice. 'Who would have thought you'd feature in a book, Rosetta, disguised as a Clan Watcher?'

'Well, what can I say? Being associated with an Egyptian stone wasn't enough for me. I zoomed back to the 1770s and made Lillibridge give me a mention. And as you can see, he agreed to include Izzie and Sidelta.'

'Sounds like an obliging guy.'

'Oh, he is. Believe me, he is. Handsome too.'

'Jokes aside...' This was Royston's voice, but Izzie didn't hear what he said next. She was now fully absorbed in her latest art project.

Craig said something in a shout. Eadie giggled.

Rosetta was saying in lowered tones, 'Keep it down, you guys, Izzie's trying to sleep.' There it was. The usual token attempt of her mother to shush everyone. No-one ever took any notice, probably because soon after saying that, Rosetta would put her guests' volume to shame with raucous and passionate debates, roaring laughter and overly verbalised sympathy for anyone in her sitting room who happened to be facing any sort of 'challenge'.

The contrasting silence brought on by their 'World Peace Meditation' had last time caused Izzie to drop off at her desk, head resting on an unfinished charcoal sketch. She'd woken an hour later, but only long enough to tumble into bed. On the following morning, Izzie had glared into the bathroom mirror at smudges shadowing one side of her mouth. The smudges had melded together into a solid black circle, suggesting she was locked in a lopsided scream, the price she'd paid for dozing off and dreaming faeries dwelt in the backyard magnolia tree. The dream was so very real and so very tranquil it had made Izzie wonder whether she should use a sketchpad for a pillow every time she slept.

Rosetta's tone became upbeat again. She'd returned to the eagle chapter.

Oh dear, Pieter thought. The eagle has little desire to learn of his sad significance, and yet, in comparison to all populations of all cells—microscopic worlds of countless proportions—he is little more than half a grain of sand. Now to make his acquaintance.

Pieter resorted to sound. He conjured his marsh-grass pipe and whistled a lilting tune. His music ballooned upwards and invaded the eagle's dreams of conquering.

Although the bird thought himself to be a leader, he was, on the contrary, an excellent follower, for he allowed the melody to guide him down to Pieter, the 'strange bird'.

The eagle demanded to know why Pieter had trespassed.

'To learn of another's existence,' the elf told him.

'You do not wish to be another great one here?' the eagle asked in suspicion.

'Nay! Just exploring. Do you like to venture also?'

'Yes. I've made many journeys to various parts of the sky.'

'*This* sky and this sky only?'

'What other sky is there?'

'Are you saying you remain here and look not at worlds outside this one?' Pieter was intrigued.

'Don't be a fool. You're one of those strange travellers from that mountain over yonder who pop into my dwelling from time to time with dreams of discovering life in *other dimensions*. Such unfortunate optimism! Still, they trundle on their merry ways in search of a fantasy—as will you no doubt—only to remain here to the end of their days. They become content with the truth and blush at their former silliness.'

Was this how those of the future might feel, should they become oh-so-enclosed in their individual habitat? The Oracle had spoken of a scorn for nature and an obsession with contraptions. Pieter liked not to think of that time: when separation would take the place of unity; when Earth's non-faunal dwellers would create ever more things of a mindless capacity. Boxes on wheels, for instance, and segregated view cubes: unguided, contrived, spewing meaningless noise and imagery to a sadly deficient receivership.

Pieter reminded himself then that valuable thinking should not be spent on distant timeframes. Moulding murky thought-forms might cause even greater harm to the dreary future he had witnessed in the Dream Sphere. Instead, he had to focus on this world, the world his dream-self had entered. He had to extract the truth from the eagle's pride, to feel the pain if necessary. One of the elf's primary intentions for venturing through doors at the end of the Devic Great Hall was to learn how better to understand suffering, other creatures' suffering, so as to help remove it.

'I hail from another world,' Pieter began.

'Don't insult my intelligence.'

Unperturbed, Pieter went on. 'Whether you believe me or not is of your own free will, although I implore you not to call me a liar. I'm here with a gift of heartfelt enlightenment. Take it if you wish.'

The bird glared and blinked a golden eye.

'If so requested, I'll educate you wonderfully on worlds outside.' Pieter flung his arms out. 'From where I come, we care for your evolution.'

'Care!' mocked the bird.

'If it is not your concern, so be it. I shall depart to my own world and bother you no more.' Pieter knew he mustn't linger. If he got too empathetic with the eagle's singular-world consciousness, he could become mesmerised and trapped in that dimension. Then it would be a pretty shame, living in isolation and forgetting his traveller's identity.

'You have proven yourself to be deluded,' snapped the bird. 'Leave my sight at once, you nonsensical brat!'

The door of the Devic Great Hall opened. Alcor's wiry hand plucked the elf up by the collar and whisked him from the eagle's mountaintop world.

Alcor added Pieter's visit there to a record, which indicated the type of assignment the elf had set himself. Each act of compassion towards another individual via the Dream Sphere earned a certain amount of Kindness Merits. The merits enabled sprites to wield magic in their waking state on Earth, although magic was more commonly termed *beauty-creation*. All assignments eventually gained accolades, celebrated regularly at Alcor's Kindness Merits Ceremony, at which time the receiver was afforded a change. Some chose it to be bodily—many elves liked to be taller, thus becoming elfin adults—others chose aura expansion so that their capacities were better matched to more challenging assignments. It was all a matter of choice. Whether physical or ethereal was entirely up to the chooser.

Two cherubs guided the elf boy to the Dawntide corridor. A faint wave from Alcor. A tumble over an insipid pink cloud. Lighter and flightier, passing day-fleeing sprites who wished him luck. The closer Pieter got to his sleeping self the more that horrible stuff called logic infringed on his Dream Sphere adventure, causing the two worlds to become neatly separated. Otherworld longings had been renamed *dreams* or *non-reality* by the golden-skinned invaders. Celestial freedom frightened them.

The only memory Pieter carried back to the dying fire in the forest of his night-time dwelling was of a bleak sky and the whisper of feathers. The memory was as dim as his recollection of a dream the day before: the disgruntled fellow with hair the colour of perished leaves. The fellow's strange and cocooning chariot, one of those ridiculous wheeled boxes of the future, had amused Pieter greatly. He'd chuckled each time he'd recalled it, but apart from the odd man in an even odder vehicle, all else remained a mystery. Equally mysterious was whether he'd dreamt it at all. Perhaps the scenario was little more than a wondering, a fancy of his own invention.

Maleika's recollection of her slumbering travels was a piece of the puzzle surrounding something she referred to as The Silvering. She handed Pieter his mug of Remembrance Essence. 'Alcor says that in the distant future beauty-creation will be gone from the Earth.'

'Unimaginable,' said Pieter's younger brother Kloory, another member of the Brumlynd clan sitting beside the campfire.

Maleika took a sip of Remembrance Essence and gazed longingly at the star-speckled sky. 'There is hope, however. I now recall Alcor telling me that The Silvering will restore our currency of kindness.'

'And what *is* The Silvering?' asked Pieter.

'The Silvering is a time of repair in the extreme future. It is expected to occur when the gold-tainted illusion of *greed* equalling *lack* and *lack* equalling *greed* has multiplied to an unbearable point.'

'Hasn't it already done that?' grumbled Kloory.

'Apparently not,' said Maleika. 'According to Alcor, beauty-creation will one day return. It will heal hearts of body-king inflicted despair once it re-emerges.'

Pieter quietly wondered how the people of the future would rediscover the magic that he and his fellow sprites often took for granted.

Cousin Croydee responded to Pieter's musings and addressed his answer to Pieter's mother. 'I have heard this prophecy in the Dream Sphere also, Aunt Maleika. As I understand it, beauty-creation will be discovered by those with memory enough to recover devic wisdom, although for many aeons it will slumber unrecognised, deep beneath the soil of a faraway southern land.'

V

The next night, as campfire smoke rose and the planets above bounded into existence one by one—Jubilance in his golden ray and Venustus sparkling pink and silver, wielding their way around sleepy Luna—Maleika poured bottles of berry cider, tied them with leaf ribbon and combed Pieter's hair with a pinch of waking dust. The elf boy, she noticed, was not so much his alert little self. Worry perhaps? A dreadful body-king bred disease!

Danger perpetually lurked near the Brumlynd clan. Since the body kings had settled for themselves a suitable niche of control, a quiet brand of lament had marred each return from slumber. Maleika had received sorrowful news two evenings earlier. Grudellan Palace courtiers had invaded the Wondalobs. Genetically-tampered troopers, who took the form of eagles each twilight to surveil the Grudellan Palace's grounds, had stormed the sprites' secret location. They had drained many of the rocks for their own purposes. Faerie clans keeping vigil, clans who'd managed to protect the sacred spring water for fifteen season-cycles, had been forcibly taken to the mines.

'We have no choice other than to lessen our consumption of Remembrance Essence,' Maleika had told her clan. 'And so we shall only drink this again after the Clan Consolidation. Until all clans have gathered and agreed upon how often it can be drunk without depleting the Wondalobs, we shall not drink any.'

Pieter shook the starry dust from his hair and told Maleika he was off to the stream to see how two of his fellow clan members were faring. Maleika told him to say his five mantras before departing, reminded him to hum the auric protection song, then pointed to the owl in the tree who had succumbed to that 'worry' illness and couldn't stop hooting—a sobering reminder to keep emotions pure.

She then packed in her bracken-leaf bag a small bottle of Remembrance Essence and three large bottles of berry cider in preparation for a brief journey of delivery to a sprite family at the other side of the forest whose access to the Wondalobs had always been limited.

When setting off, she turned and looked back at her larger flagon of stored Remembrance. Why had she poured the family a small bottle this time? 'Because we are limited now,' she told herself. 'I am only being sensible.' And yet, remorse at her own meanness continued to gnaw. The amount she had allowed her friends, a clan of seven, was far less than the amount she had allowed her own little clan. She returned to the flagon and filled a second bottle. 'I have caught the contagion of lack,' she concluded, 'and now I'm resorting to greed.' An adherence to the belief of deprivation nearly always drew sprites into clumps of misfortune.

On the way back from her errand, Maleika rediscovered at the other side of the forest a path leading through a winding cavern, a place she remembered well. As a child she played hide-and-seek there with the daffodil faeries.

The cavern's atmosphere concerned her. No longer did it exude the scent of damp moss and mineral. Pervading the air was the faint odour of decay.

Maleika peered into the cavern doorway. Nothing there. And that was just it. Nothing! Nothingness did not feature much in the world these days and inevitably aroused suspicion if happened upon. Everything was gone from this cave.

Should she consider stepping in? Outer space to her people was far friendlier. Safer, too, than this bleak void. In the heavens, lightness and distance were obliquely understood. Planets and asteroids weren't a puzzle to be solved. They were old friends visited via the Dream Sphere, all with their own bustling devic population. Celestial bodies weren't perceived through a lens at the end of a cylinder and deemed globes of molten rock suspended in infinity. How the galaxies and their absence of floors and ceilings could be so baffling to those of the future was amusing indeed to the sprites.

'Limited is three-dimensional thought, sadly limited,' Maleika murmured. 'Truth insists that worlds are within worlds, merely as the cells are within each earthly creature.' Were not the cells of every life-form independent worlds of their own? And weren't Earth's peoples little more than a speck when viewed from a distance? 'All of us links in a greater chain,' she mused. 'All ignorant of the immensity within and without.'

A physical field emptied of everything! To determine if any life-force existed in the cave's etheric field, Maleika conjured a scattering of lemon and lilac lights, small and silver-edged, which she accessed from her supply of kindness merits.

Allowing the lights to guide her, she stepped in. Two goblin sprites crossed her path and sniggered at her, bony hands of grey cupping hollow mouths, hair like lava, eyes of black stone. Nodding pleasantly to them, Maleika shrugged and pressed on. Nothing as intangible as a goblin would deter her.

More eyes, a thousand eyes it seemed, blinked on like stars. Although unable to see these, Maleika could sense them. An emerald tinged blackness enveloped her. The lilac and lemon lights she'd called forth promptly vanished, the bothersome result of scanty kindness merits.

She became aware of foreboding sounds: whirring snarls and the scrape of scaled lids blinking. She peered over her shoulder. What sort of creatures lurked here? She had heard many chilling accounts of monstrous Grudellan carnivores. Sorcerers had created them from a dragon gene.

And then a tumbling rush of air like a wild spring gale whipped about Maleika's skirts and flung her to the far side of the cave.

Uneasily, she rose to her feet.

'Who is there?' she called.

If only they were dragons! But dragons had been ridded from Elysium several season-cycles ago.

Maleika moved warily onward.

VI

Dragons had been savaged throughout countless season-cycles. Memories of their demise caused pain to Maleika. The last dragon she had seen was much distanced from the earth. Only its shell had remained; its spirit having fled far away to the Dream Sphere, for its physical self had been cruelly left to shed golden blood by the thorn thicket.

Oh, how the body kings had gloated! Fine power they'd gleaned from the dragons they ingested. And then these predators would try to harm each other, since abruptly and voluntarily ending another's existence would only result in chaotic fates.

Dragon flesh, now imprinted on the body kings' genetic map, caused the skin of its consumer to glow golden. All of them, even the newer ones, had skin of this tone. Without their native grey-blue colouring they looked odder than odd, as though they weredusty-hued snails intent on sporting shells of flame-orange, a silly disguise worn with pride.

Maleika's thoughts, now muddied from these recollections, brought into the cave an army of bristly spiders the size of dinner plates. She whisked them back to their former homes with the blink-and-whistle technique and cautioned herself against creating negative fodder with her thinking, which poisonous creatures might be compelled to feed on.

An enormous bat soared to the cavern ceiling...yet was it a bat?

Doing her best to ignore the tremor of her shoulders, Maleika called, 'I wish to make your acquaintance. Please come forth and introduce yourself.'

The phantom animal fluttered down, and the telepathic question that reached the elf woman was: '*Do you mean to say you can truly see me?*'

'For certain,' said Maleika to the still-vague form. 'Why should I not? We all have our right to existence.'

'*Nay. Not I,*' the sad thing said. '*Nor them.*'

Turning, Maleika saw a number of filmy black wings. The sound of sobbing rose up and rippled through the cave. 'You cannot be a dragon,' she said. 'And yet...'

'*Well, that I was, once.*' Becoming more visible was a creature with long-lashed, faded turquoise eyes. The rest of him was a sooty grey. The tiniest hint of silver shone through all that darkness, hardly discernible as dragon scales, the most splendid feature of the animal.

He sent her another thought, too muffled to comprehend. The only word Maleika received was *nothing*, and then he eyed her carefully as though doubting her awareness of his presence.

'You'll have to think harder,' the elf woman said. 'I can no longer intuit your words.'

But at that, the poor fellow became grief-stricken. He folded his long neck in half, the very weight of him seeming to sag to the ground. Maleika could no longer see him, try as she might.

Certainly she wanted to help. Why had he said he was a dragon 'once'? Maleika resolved to revisit. Her dwindled kindness merits meant she could no longer access the invisible. She would gain more merits once she returned to the Dream Sphere at sun-up. Alcor was sure to have some owing to her for the work she was doing in guiding the heartbroken and rosy-named Clan Watcher sprite, the one with the silvery feline and fire-haired daughter.

Dawn was piercing the exit. Rocky walls glowed yellow and purple as though mirroring the colours of Maleika's magical stars. Birds and dryads basked in pools of light on rocks nearby. The atmosphere surrounding Maleika once again sprang to life. Leaving the gloom behind, she stepped out to breathe in the ferny air, the emerging daylight warm on her hair. Realising then that she was rather lost, she hastened towards another cave in the hope it would lead back to the Brumlynd wagons.

'Had you just gone into the cave over yonder?' a passing gnome with a wheelbarrow enquired.

Maleika nodded.

'It's filled with prisoners,' the gnome said. 'Passed-over dragons deprived of the Dream Sphere. Sorcerers have kept them grounded by clipping their celestial wings. So now the creatures live between worlds. They're too transparent for this one and too limited for the Dream Sphere. I've oft spied body kings release another poor victim into that emptiness.'

'At first I wasn't sure they were dragons,' said Maleika. 'Such meek, nondescript things! And to think they are simply dying giants, once magnificent and full of fire.'

'Dead,' corrected the gnome. 'With shackled spirits. And now as good as nothing, for they are emptied of their power. But heed my words, elf friend. The next cavern, the one you are about to venture into, has many dangers. Let the nothingness be. My brothers will transport you home via our own secret paths.'

The sun had climbed higher into the heavens when the gnomes led Maleika back to her clan. Much to her delight, Pieter and the other Brumlynds were already settled in their sleeping wagons.

'At last I may journey to the Dream Sphere,' Maleika said, after bidding the gnomes farewell and retiring to her wagon. She yawned, clamped her eyelids closed and removed her consciousness from the dazzle and jubilant bird sound of Elysium's golden hours.

When she and her clan woke from their slumbering journeys, they ambled out to the campfire and sat, unspeaking, for a while, swathed in the early evening's silence. A glimmer pierced the stillness.

'Not their electrical tricks again,' groaned Pieter, for lightning and thunder were the other ones' creation.

'Hush,' Maleika said with a smile.

There before them weaved and darted the faint impression of a butterfly, transparent like a dying dryad, wispy and white, a projected image, the equivalent of stumbling across a daydream in the dark. The vision took on colour—metallic gold—and stretched into proper form.

'Your presence feels familiar,' Pieter said to the apparition, an eagle image floating above his head.

'Elf boy, you know me from your dreams,' replied the creature. 'But now I dream. To be more specific, the aspect of me that dreams is the part of myself that is lost in limitation. And so I visit you in spirit form, and I ask for a little forgiving on your part.'

In response to the ghostly eagle's request, Pieter said, 'But you've not done anything to trouble me!' The boy leaned towards Maleika and whispered, 'How could I ever hold a grudge against a fine, harmless bird? One that I've apparently visited in the Dream Sphere?'

Maleika gave him a warning look.

'Perhaps I should not be so effusive,' he murmured.

'Perhaps not,' Maleika said, keenly aware that the eagle was more than likely a body king. Genetically-tampered troopers who changed into eagles were the very people responsible for robbing the sprites of their Wondalobs water. 'The appearance of innocence appeals to them,' Maleika added in a whisper. 'How often now have they attempted to embody devic or faunal grace?' Nature's harmonious beauty eluded the golden ones, and yet this was a quality they so strived to mimic.

The eagle continued to address young Pieter. 'You do not recall having spoken to me, and so I shall explain. You offered to enlighten my perception of space. You hoped to unveil for me the lands that lie beyond my mountainous dwelling. While my solid self slumbers, I am unchained from limited growth. From the standpoint of this wiser state, I ask that you return. My soul has been imprisoned by a sorcerer's spell and yearns to be free. In time I shall accept your offer of furthering my evolution.'

'I am not at all sure, sir, whether I can believe I visited you in the Dream Sphere,' said Pieter.

Maleika studied the eagle. The message was obviously nonsense intended to mislead. Even if Pieter were permitted to take a sip of the now rationed Remembrance Essence, Maleika doubted he would recall any visit to the fellow hovering before them. In contrast with these dubious claims, the eagle seemed not, in Maleika's opinion, to be the noblest of creatures. His aura of mustard yellow rang of self-inflation.

A constant game of pretence! Maleika marvelled at the body kings' endless attempts to confuse sprites. The female counterparts illustrated this perfectly. A great deal of their waking duration was spent painting their own lips and eyelids in a fierce attempt to resemble another species. Pieter had reported one evening upon returning from the Dream Sphere and sipping Remembrance Essence, that he'd discovered body kings knew nothing of those they tried so diligently to emulate. Those of the species from a world known as 'Have' on the other side of the looking glass, were seeing this and were going about their work with surprise in their eyes and smiling mouths. To be copied, of course, is the greatest form of flattery.

Devic sprite clans found it strange that the 'Have' creatures were so aware of the body kings and that—as Pieter had amazedly learnt—the body kings were blissfully unaware of any species but themselves, save for the 'wicked' plants, animals and sprites that they considered got in their way. And yet, the thought-forms from Planet Have were firmly imprinted upon all their operations. A body king was apt to say at any part of the day, 'I must *have...*' (this or that).

And so they continued to primp and preen, adoring each other with detachment for fear of egos withering, and continued to remain awfully sensuous creatures who reproduced at alarming rates.

'*Rahwor,*' said the eagle.

Maleika edged away. The word 'Rahwor' sounded foreboding. Was the eagle uttering the beginning of an incantation?

'Rahwor,' the eagle said again. 'That is the name of my spell caster. He has trapped my earthly self inside a shell of stony ignorance.'

Pieter proceeded to echo Maleika's concerns. 'This name you have given, sir. Its sonic signature confuses me...so I shall wish you goodnight and ask with the deepest respect that you continue on your way.'

'Your doubt in me disappoints,' said the eagle. 'I shall leave, then, and bother you no more.'

Charcoal glowed on the campfires. Lanterns high in the trees swung bright. A new darkness had encroached on the cricket-whistling wilderness.

The eagle bowed his head and vanished.

Rosetta snapped her book shut, reached for her document holder on the coffee table and turned to the others in her group. 'Karma do you think? Pieter rejected the eagle because he'd slighted him. Not intentionally though.'

'The eagle felt suspicious of Pieter when he met him,' Royston said, 'but I thought he had every right to be.'

Eadie, absorbed in examining the split ends of her dark hair, murmured, 'Really? I thought the eagle was unfair. He gave up on the elf before hearing him out.'

Royston tapped his knuckles against the back of Eadie's hand. 'But to give him credit, lovey, he would have felt intruded upon. Can you imagine someone walking up to you at your beauty school and saying "Hi there. I'm from Planet Quock. Do you want me to en-lighten you?" '

'It's a technical college, I'll have you know,' Eadie said pleasantly.

'Oops,' said Royston. 'TAFE then.'

'And I'm doing the make-up artistry unit of a Diploma in Beauty Therapy. But I get your point about the alien visitor, and the eagle was really sweet once his physical self slept. I wish Pieter had glugged some Remembrance Essence.'

'Speaking of glugging...' Craig said, 'will we start up the coffee now?'

'I'm interested in those gold pebbles we read about last fortnight,' Royston said. 'The ones Wallikin mentioned in Chapter II.'

'Aren't we all,' Rosetta drawled. 'Where can we get a few of those?'

Craig laughed a little and shook his head. 'The body kings' exchange of gold sounds like an alternate explanation for the beginning of money.'

'What did the sprites trade for survival?' said Eadie. 'The kindness merits they earned in the Dream Sphere?'

'Hm, don't think so, Eades,' Rosetta said. 'I think the kindness merits just acted as fuel for their magical powers. That's a good question. What would their currency have been? What do you reckon, Royston?'

'I think Eadie's on the right track,' Royston said. 'Kindness did happen to be their currency. I imagine they had some sort of bartering system.' He leaned back as Rosetta collected his empty wineglass. 'Off to bring out the supper already, Rosetta? I'm so pleased, my love, about the formation of those other book groups. And Perelda of all places!'

'It's brilliant,' Rosetta said. She swerved to collect the emptied pretzel bowl. Eadie, one step ahead, swooped on it instead. 'Better than we'd expected.'

'A lot of good things come out of Sweden.' Royston hummed an ABBA song, then leapt to his feet to do a celebratory little moonwalk. Eadie turned back and pounded the platter in time to Royston's reverse shuffles.

'Keep it down, you guys,' Rosetta said over her shoulder. 'Izzie's trying to sleep.'

Craig followed her into the kitchen and watched as she arranged Royston's European biscuits on a floral plate that used to belong to Mama. 'Looking good tonight,' Craig remarked.

'A good-looking supper,' Rosetta agreed.

'I was talking about you, Rosetta.' Craig chuckled softly. 'You always look good in purple.'

'Um...er...thanks! I do love dark colours. Would you mind popping these into the sitting room for me?'

Craig retreated. Rosetta settled the cups into their saucers and took the near-boiling kettle off the stove in time to stifle its heart-starting scream. All in the neighbourhood would remain asleep, forever unaware of her heroic attempt to protect their cardiovascular systems.

A shadow flitted past the kitchen window. Rosetta tensed.

Relax, she told herself. Nothing to worry about.

She sighed. Grasped the edge of the sink. They were safe here. He wouldn't be...

A crashing thump. Rattle of glass. Shadows.

She yelped. Stepped back from the sink.

His emotionless stare...a writhing lizard...smirking lips an unnatural red in the dull ray of moonlight...

Gaze still fixed on the window, she tried to call to the others. Couldn't.

A thud-thud.

Rosetta puffed out a sigh. The shadows continued to dance across the glass. She darted to the wall. Flicked on the outdoor light.

Yeeee-ow!

The culprit bounced away from the window, banging the pane once more.

'Thanks a lot, Sidelta,' Rosetta said in a groan. 'You scared me half to death.' Her cat had been skittering across the window ledge, clumsily pawing at a moth.

But the images...how did she stop the images? They were rolling in again in nightmarish flashes. '*Scram,*' she said under her breath, echoing the command Royston's American colleague suggested she use. 'Scram! Scram!'

He's not out there, Rosetta.' Royston had subtly arrived in the kitchen and was doing his best to calm her with butterfly-light back pats. 'He doesn't know where you are. You're safe.'

'You heard the yelp?'

'Nope. Only the *"Scram!"* All okay?'

'Absolutely fine. I freaked out for a sec, but it was only Sidelta on a moth quest.'

Royston plucked up the kettle from the stove. 'Now tell me. Who's having what?'

Safe, she reminded herself. Completely safe. Izzie secure in her bed, and me about to enjoy a chatty supper with a few of my closest friends.

When she returned to the sitting room with the tray of coffees, Eadie was saying, 'Shame Lena couldn't be here. Do you know if she's dug up any more background on the book's author?'

Rosetta passed a mug across to her. 'It's slim pickings so far. We're wishing we could access a diary of some sort, or letters even, but there's not much out there. Lena's found an article mentioning he fell in love with a Gypsy.'

'So I'm in good company then,' said Craig, 'if Lillibridge had a weakness for exotic women.' He raised an eyebrow at Rosetta.

Rosetta pretended not to notice. 'We don't know if it's just hearsay. Lena's attempting to contact the article's author, so we'll ask her about it next fortnight.'

'An eighteenth-century Gypsy,' said Eadie. 'I wonder if she had a caravan.'

'A painted one, probably.' Rosetta had already conjured, in her mind's eye, romantic images of a flamboyant horse-drawn wagon and a circular stream of tarot cards on a tiny round table, a page fluttering beside them, a secret letter, perhaps, from the People of the Sea.

But who were these sea people? Ragged beach dwellers? Yarn-spinning sailors? And why had Lillibridge chosen to document their story?

Chapter Three

The call of the whales had been in Rosetta's ears only seconds when the mobile meeped. It was a luxury, this rare morning of solitude. The past week had been a frenetic flit between processing purchases at Crystal Consciousness and emptying office bins for Jack Barnaby's firm. A day of freedom had finally arrived.

She wandered towards the phone, her thoughts drifting to the protein diet she continually pushed into the future. Why did listening to the whale song always remind her of the weight she wanted to lose? A few extra kilos didn't really equal whale status. She tore away the iPod and reached for her mobile.

The mature voice that greeted her was sweet and high, like a bell. The caller had picked up one of Rosetta's business cards at Crystal Consciousness Books & Gifts. Could she call in for a tarot reading?

This was perfect. Izzie was turning sixteen next week. Rosetta had wondered only yesterday how she could scrape up an extra fifty dollars. Whenever worry over her single-parent finances threatened to descend, she'd recall her Greek foster father reclining in the cane chair with the wobbly leg, a fedora pulled over his eyes, his caterpillar moustache undulating as he shrugged off concerns over their modest living standards. 'Ah well,' he would say, 'money can't buy happiness.'

Money spent on a teenager's special day to add a necessary dose of sparkle was equal to buying happiness, though, wasn't it? Or a portion of it, at least.

In answer to the appointment request, Rosetta said, '*Of course* you can call in for a tarot reading! What day were you thinking of?'

'Today.'

'Let's see...there's a cancellation here. How would three-pm suit?' There. That made her sound in demand.

'Three-pm won't suit at all. Can't it be this morning? Ten-thirty say?'

In half-an-hour! She'd never been *this* much in demand. Not ever. 'Ten-thirty it is then. I have a cancellation there too.'

'Eighty-nine Ashbury Avenue, Burwood? Marvellous! Cheerio, Odetta.'

'The name's actually—'

The call had already ended.

'Right!' Rosetta altered from drowsy to efficient. She flew to her wardrobe where a mish-mash of undersized garments lurked behind its doors. Half-an-hour! She snatched up two coat-hangers, one with a fitted blouse that tended to make her feel slimmer, the other with wide-leg pants that coordinated nicely colourwise. With clumsy determination, she flung them on in place of the pilled tracksuit she'd been pottering around in and reapplied her make-up before slipping on the dream weaver earrings she liked to wear for psychic work because of their cosmic design.

Izzie was on her mobile in the kitchen talking to Charlotte. 'Who's taking the oranges?'

Oranges? Ah. Netball. Rosetta collected the broom from the laundry. About to ask Izzie which parent's turn it was to take her to the courts, she drew to a sudden stop. It was her turn! She rushed to the hallway, seized up the home phone and dialled Charlotte Wallace's carefully groomed mother. Two Sundays free of having to ferry a bunch of gigglies. Hopefully this exchange would appeal to Diondra.

Diondra declined the apologetic proposal.

'That's fine, Diondra,' Rosetta said. 'If you're caught up we'll stick to the original plan.' She would need to stick a *Sorry – Back in 10 mins* note on the door for her new tarot client.

Silence. Had Diondra's phone cut out?

A symphony of tuneless voices and the roar of a hair dryer. Another burst of murmurs, then Diondra was back on the line. 'All right, just this once,' she snapped. 'But please don't make a habit of it.' The call ended in a savage click.

Rosetta delegated the dusting to Izzie, then rushed out to the verandah to shake out the hallway's crimson-edged rugs, their intricate swirls of olive and royal blue shimmering silkily in the morning light. She set up her tarot cards on the battered copper table and added an ornamental crystal ball to conjure a mystical mood, along with a nineteenth-century Turkish coffee pot, inherited upon Mama's passing.

Five minutes past the set appointment! Izzie was due to be collected in another twenty. Rosetta drifted back to the verandah and swept it, noticing the eaves could do with a clearing. 'Hope you've had your shower, darl,' she called, reminded of Diondra's propensity for turning up early. She reached again for the broom.

'Had it,' was the muffled reply from inside. 'Do you want those magazines near the fireplace? 'Cos if you don't I could use them for my four-seasons collage.'

'Fine with me.' Lost in concentration, Rosetta swished her broom through the wisps of cobwebs collecting in one of the eaves. She plucked them from the bristles and released the ghost-like fragments to the breeze. They floated in zigzags down to the lawn.

A motor purred into the driveway. A car door clicked shut. Her tarot client had arrived! At the clip-clop of fashionably elevated heels crossing the driveway, Rosetta turned to see not her client but a thunder-faced Diondra.

'Bummer.' Rosetta put the broom aside and dragged a cobweb-sticky hand through her hair. Diondra was nothing like a tarot client. So much for the psychic abilities.

Diondra marched up the verandah steps.

'Really sorry, Diondra, to have swapped shifts at such short notice,' Rosetta said. 'I'll do the next two of yours instead. It's just that I had a client call and—'

'You've already told me that!' Diondra's voice was angry and thin. Angry and thin could have also described Diondra.

Diondra glowered at a fallen cobweb on the verandah floor like a cat confronted with a rain puddle. She edged disgustedly away. 'Izzie ready?'

'I think so.' In an effort to buy Izzie more time, she moved to the screen door in a languorous amble. 'You ready, honey? The Wallaces are here.'

'I'll be there in two ticks,' called Izzie, which obviously meant she hadn't yet brushed her teeth.

Two ticks, in Rosetta's opinion, were two ticks too long to be spent small-talking with Diondra.

'A bit inconvenient, Rosetta.' An irate smile. 'You *phoned* me when I was getting my hair done.'

'And it looks great.'

'Thank-yooo.' The smile became more genuine. Diondra didn't need reassurance. Her smart swing-bob, bordering on artificiality with its several variations of beige, was ever immaculate. Eyes narrowed with feline slyness, she drawled, 'I see yours is natural.'

Rosetta tried not to laugh, although the appropriate action was probably to squirm. And who wouldn't be a teensy bit afraid, with a recruit from the Hair-Colour Police on their doorstep? 'Diondra, thanks! It takes a lot of work to get my hair looking natural.'

'You're due for a top-up, are you?'

'Not at all. I usually shorten the development time to avoid a fake-looking result.'

'Ah, so you dye it yourself. I didn't think anyone still did that.'

Sprung! Too early to congratulate herself on sidestepping the first innuendo. Not that it mattered. The conversation had nowhere to go.

Something scampered across Rosetta's scalp.

She screeched.

She threw her head forward. The ends of her hair brushed the knees of her wide-leg pants. With both hands she swiped at the crawliness.

This was all she needed: a client due any minute, a newly evicted spider about to wreak revenge, and a too-punctual fashion inspector smirking serenely down at her.

The screen door snapped open. 'You all right, Mum?'

The spider dropped to the verandah floor and scuttled towards the safety of the wall.

'I was cleaning cobwebs and...'

Slicing through the explanation, Diondra said, 'So *that's* what I saw in your hair.'

'Over here, Izzie,' Diondra's daughter, Charlotte, was leaning out of the car window.

Izzie waved goodbye to Rosetta and ran to greet her netball buddy.

Diondra turned and clunked her way importantly down the verandah steps. 'Poor you,' she said. 'I thought they were *greys*. I thought you were due for another semi.' Pausing on the path she added, 'Enjoy your day,' her frosty tone causing the goodwill gesture to sound eerily like a hex. She sailed across to her gold car, a gilded carriage wherein Izzie, Charlotte and another teen were chattering like starlings in the backseat, redonned her lipstick in the rear-view mirror and whirred out of the driveway.

'I do happen to have the odd grey hair,' Rosetta grumbled to no-one in particular. A couple of cobwebs were hardly a cause for pity. She was comfortable with those grey hairs, proud of what they signified. A departure from naivety. A journey towards the gaining of wisdom.

Sinking into a cane chair, she spotted a caterpillar on one of the steps. Its undulating dark brown bristles aptly resembled her foster father's moustache. Reflecting on Diondra's spiky remarks, she shrugged. 'As Baba always said, money can't buy happiness.' She groaned and glared at the sky. 'All I ask, though, is the chance to test that theory.'

Now where was that tarot client?

'What's the hold up?' Matthew glowered at the car in front. 'Come *on*.' All he wanted was a smooth run to the golf course, but a rugby game at the stadium up ahead had induced a thumb-drumming gridlock.

Dominic Wallace, his golfing partner for the day and husband of Bernadette's closest friend, would undoubtedly be using the extra time to brush up on his swing, one eyebrow raised for luck.

It wasn't just the time-wasting that made Matthew uncomfortable. Being alone in the Jag with his thoughts was not a favourite pastime, and yet whenever the surrounding vehicles puttered to a stop, he was forced into random mulling. Right now his conversation with a self-proclaimed elf insisted on overtaking. Throughout the week he'd had to continually remind himself that Peter 'Piper' wasn't real. The bat had been real though. Matthew had been fully conscious when the bat mutated into a bird.

'Do you plan to...?' He clamped his mouth closed. A waking dream. '...Plan to waste the remainder of your life?' A hallucination from lack of sleep. No significance whatsoever. And he of all people, Matthew P Weissler, contender for Charlie's glittering director's role, could not be accused of frittering away his future.

When he'd returned home after the bat/eagle/Peter Piper incident, he'd climbed the staircase of his neoclassical-style monstrosity and found Dalesford's book in the same place he'd thrown it, beneath the drapes of his study. A corner of one page had twisted from its laminated cover, and so he'd rescued it from the floor and pressed the cover flat with a paperweight. It wasn't the first time the book had preyed on his sympathies. He'd already saved it from a bin some weeks earlier.

The car behind him descended into a series of petulant beeps. He groaned and flicked on the radio.

Dalesford. Conan Dalesford, author of *Thoughts on Tomorrow's Tycoon War*, had loads of theories that were as challenging as they were intriguing.

The car in front had a twee sticker on its dusty rear window, weather-bleached to palest blue. Its faded words assured 'magic' did indeed 'happen'. What was the motorist like? No doubt a star-gazing fan of fairy tales, a bleary-eyed believer in seed diets and soul-travel, or 'OOBEs' as Dalesford referred to them.

To give Dalesford credit, the OOBE theory might well hold some clout. The suggestion that Out-Of-Body-Experiences actually occurred intrigued Matthew. Not enough to make him grow his hair long, chow down tofu, or pose lotus-style by the fountain in Hyde Park, but the idea that danced through Chapter Six was so logically explained it ultimately won his respect. According to Dalesford, an interdimensional soul-self was exactly like the physical self but separate and capable of travelling outside of it. Joined to the body by a silver cord, apparently, which detached in the event of death.

Pulsating from his speakers was a squeaky Top Ten single that contained about as much variation as a dentist's drill. On the next station, Doctor Cyanide was belting out a chaotic assortment of rabid chants.

The car in front rolled forward.

'Eureka!' Matthew pressed ahead.

'Gimme! Gimme! *Gimme!*' Doctor Cyanide's vicious demands were clawing tunelessly at his eardrums. 'More!' This had been uttered in a desperate snarl. 'More. More. *Moooo-wah! Moomoomoomoo-moomomomoomoo...*' Matthew flipped through the channels and landed within the tame harmonies of a Golden Oldies hour, a croony salvation from Cyanide's self-indulgent 1970s non-lyrics.

He knew Dalesford's chapter on OOBEs shouldn't really have appealed to him. Apart from mild interest in his sister-in-law's astrology obsession, mind-body-spirit topics had failed to impress. He did have to admit that her astro-predictions were rather apt. And a few months back he'd been amazed to learn that a couple of guys at work believed astrological trends affected the market. One had even hired an astrologer to advise on the best times to buy and sell. So if guys at work were into that stuff, his inquiry into OOBE theories hardly made him a New Age fruit-loop.

It was Dalesford's description of 'sprite visitations' that had captivated his interest most. Did that explain the Peter Piper puzzle? Or could it have been an Out-Of-Body Experience?

He veered through the gates of the Royal Sydney Golf Club and parked near the outdoor bar where Dominic Wallace was sipping a whiskey and goggling at the short-skirted attendants.

Once Matthew had signed in at the clubhouse, Dominic caught up with him on the conifer-shaded steps. 'I'm afraid I'll have to disappear for half-an-hour after the first round, Matt. Diondra wants me to collect Charlotte and her mates from netball.'

'Not a problem. And thanks for standing in for Davo.' Matthew would have preferred a stronger teammate today. Charlie Sanders was playing opposite them this morning, along with his eldest son, a trophy-magnet from way back, and Dominic Wallace's down-swing epitomised what that famous American golfing great, Lee Trevino, described as 'a caveman killing his lunch'. Everyone had to start somewhere, of course, but Dominic's evolution towards greatness seemed to have stalled indefinitely.

VII

Returning from the Dream Sphere was vexing for Maleika. She would not be recalling what she had done while in dream-self form. She had rationed her own consumption of the crystal-imbued Wondalobs water so that each member of her clan, comprising her two elfin sons Pieter and Kloory, her diminutive elfin nephew Croydee, and the two water-sprite orphans, were not deprived of it.

Sipping her berry cider, Maleika tried not to feel sorry for the state that had befallen them, of Pieter not yet returned to the Brumlynd campfire. She did not wish to dwell on the fact that the boy had recently celebrated the twelfth anniversary of his birth, nor did she seek a reminder of Orahney's unsettling prophecy fifteen season-cycles earlier, about gold-skins sending him to a previous century.

Pieter's younger brother was eager to make sense of his fragmented recollections. 'Ah!' Kloory said, having sipped Remembrance Essence. 'I now know where I went in my slumber. We were whirling through an azure sky in a hawkish vehicle. It was made of a similar substance to the gold those creatures pull from the earth, only it took on the colour of a thundercloud.'

'Silver?' suggested Maleika.

'Almost,' said Kloory, 'yet duller. The driver-sprite of this thundery chariot wore a solid head-bubble. He referred to it as his "helmet".'

'And so you took the form of one of these bubble fellows?'

'Indeed. I sat beside the driver.'

'Are you certain the both of you were sprites? Perhaps you were of gold heritage.'

'It's possible we *were* gold-skins.'

Maleika nodded approvingly at the term. The evening before, she insisted her clan refer to the Elysium invaders in a more honourable way than 'body kings'. The sprites' invented name, 'body king' emphasised an obsession with one's own physicality. The other term indicated appearance only and was discovered two evenings earlier by her nephew when he overheard two courtiers refer to themselves as 'We of Gold Skin'.

'We must use the name to which these people are accustomed,' Maleika had told her little clan. 'The leaders at the Clan Consolidation have deemed the other name offensive.'

Kloory continued with the description of his dream. 'Another hawkish vehicle hovered ahead of us. Spherical lightning bolts spewed from its base.'

Croydee trundled across to the berry cider flagon and poured himself a cup. Maleika observed her orphaned nephew with affection; marvelled at his dimples and dark curling hair; and noticed, not for the first time, how very much he resembled a fallen chestnut, for he outfitted his tiny plump body in furry seed husks. Having not been in solidity for long, Croydee was still linked to his most recent incarnation in the Dream Sphere. He was the least attached of all to this earthly world where fingers of darkness painted illusions of restriction. 'You've travelled far ahead to the future I think, Cousin Kloory. Would these fiery spheres have been miniature suns?'

'No, Croydee. These weren't golden. They met the ground in a blast of fury. Sprites were fleeing blazing cottages.' Kloory hid his face in his hands.

'Seems to be a continuation of body kings,' said Croydee.

'Of gold-skins,' corrected Maleika.

'Of gold-skins, I mean. For certain!'

'Who else would wear solid head bubbles and seek to harm other life-forms?' said Kloory.

'And so they will continue to live here on Earth,' said Maleika with a despondent shrug.

A grave stillness settled upon the clan.

'All we can do is keep working,' said Kloory. 'The more we can set an example of peaceable respect for them, the better chance this world has for the future. We might as well do it now while we're still permitted to exist here.'

They lifted their mugs in a quiet toast.

Reassuring herself that Pieter had been distracted on one of his rambles through forests beyond the Grudellan Palace and that he would more than likely reappear before dawn, Maleika pondered the life she was surveying in the Dream Sphere. She had come to learn the life was many aeons ahead of her own. She had taken an interest in this timeframe. The sonic signatures of the sprites she'd observed were resonating with those of the Brumlynds, and the sprite she'd been asked to assist, the one whose name suggested roses, had a genetic code that appeared to be tribal. Confusion enveloped this woman. The woman wanted to create beauty yet was limited by resources, and her hopes were eclipsed by the blandest brand of amusement, a swirl of dispiriting dealings and events.

The rose sprite was not engaged enough. Something had to happen to ground her in her material realm. It would not do to have her destroying her mission out of sheer forgetfulness, nor that of her fire-haired daughter. And what a mission it was!

Maleika leaned back and laughed at the irony of the situation. Putting up with deprivation and lovelessness and obscurity when...but all in good time. The plan would have to work. If the sprite were not reminded of the roles she and others like her were to play, all those of her timeframe would become known as 'the Insignificant Ones'. Maleika would do her best to allow this soul a right to her own significance. In doing so, the rays of elation would ripple through more than just the earthly world. All worlds would benefit from the freeing.

'Come along, then, Croydee,' she said, rising from the campfire. 'Tonight we're to visit those gnome friends of yours who dwell near the Grudellan Palace. They might have seen our Pieter.'

Rosetta stood on the footpath scanning Ashbury Avenue for signs of the latecomer. She returned to the verandah's cushioned cane chair with the local newspaper she'd collected from the letterbox and opened it to the employment section. A notice caught her eye. A bad speller in a neighbouring suburb was advertising for a nanny.

Will someone phone me urjently, i need someone to mind my kids ASAP in my home large inside moddern estate Cabarita Heights while im on holliday for 2 weeks.

Email Bernadette Weissler at the address below.

A flicker of lilac skimmed the verandah floorboards. Rosetta blinked, and flashes of pale yellow darted in all directions. She blinked again. Her vision was inundated with silver-edged star-shaped sparks. Not the first time this had happened. Time to book a check-up with the optometrist.

She opened the newspaper out again. The stars had gone now...hadn't they? No, still there, but bouncing above the job ad.

She read the advertisement again, this time minus any prejudice against its poorly worded presentation, and her vision cleared. Nannying wasn't the type of third job she sought. The last time she'd minded other people's children professionally was some twenty-five years ago, but maturity and being a mother might count for something.

Resolving to phone the advertiser on Monday, she settled back into the chair and slowed her breathing. Still optimistic that the tarot client who phoned earlier was late and not a no-show, she closed her eyes and cautioned herself against falling asleep.

The peace of the verandah soothed its way through her thoughts. Sleep beckoned. Surrender. Slumber. Drifting within a dream.

'Where am I?' she murmured and opened her eyes. Foliage in various shapes and forms splashed against her field of vision.

And then she saw it. Turrets of gold spiralled into a violet and crimson sky. A mint-scented mist floated about intricately patterned gates. Grand archways, which peaked at their apex in arabesque fashion, glittered darkly, as though beckoning from one angle and repelling from the other.

Whimsical. Mysterious. Displaying traces of modern and medi-eval design, although something about its impressiveness made Rosetta uneasy. The forest behind her emanated a blissful serenity, and yet this dazzling, golden enigma seemed to be wrapped in chills.

How did you describe a place so divorced from your own reality, so unlike anything you'd ever seen that it was a wonder you could see it at all? This would all be forgotten on her return to that other consciousness. Why couldn't her waking existence be as tranquil as the forest?

'Oh, there you are, Molly Carr,' a babyish voice from behind her said.

Rosetta spun round. 'The *name's not...not...*' She hesitated. 'What I mean to say,' she added without knowing why, 'Is, the *gnomes know naught* of Pieter's passing here. Let us go now, Croydee, to our sleeping wagons.'

Her senses numbed a little and she found herself wondering who she was.

She was Molly Carr, wasn't she? Who was she?

She was...

VIII

...*Maleika.* That was it. 'Thank goodness, I remembered my identity,' the elf woman whispered. For a moment she'd thought she had melded with another's existence. The sun had risen when they returned to their camp. Maleika looked forward to her journey to the Dream Sphere. Once there, she would choose to visit the tribal sprite who had lost her way. The poor woman had been spinning out a life-stream where the struggle for survival had clouded her mission. Even though the introduction of gold exchange was still in its infancy in Elysium, Maleika had immediately recognised its future effects.

Having fallen into slumber, Maleika, now in dream-self form, left her sleeping self behind and floated to the Dream Sphere. Upon her arrival she consulted Alcor. She asked whether she was to travel into the future.

'Yes, you must continue with this one's life-stream,' commanded Alcor. 'But in solid form. You need to remind her of who she is.' Alcor gestured to one of the Dream Sphere's doors.

Maleika stepped forward.

'Maleika...'

Maleika turned.

Alcor waved his hands in the air, and a scroll appeared, one that glowed of deep dark pink. 'You will need this.'

'And what is it, brother?'

'A personality,' he said. 'As well as a physical appearance. And an elementary knowledge of the ways of those in the future.'

A lingering feeling of returning from somewhere enchanted drifted around Rosetta when she woke. Twisting towers, dancing diamond foliage, a sublime sense of peace...all too elusive to grasp.

'No,' she decided with a yawn. 'Can't remember what the dream was about.'

So where was the woman who had made the urgent appointment? 'Might have something to eat,' she mumbled.

Rising to her feet, she stretched, then stumbled across the verandah to open the screen door. The cold steel handle of the door behind it did not give way. She groaned. Locked. Izzie had neglected to snib it when she left, leaving it to slam shut with the wind when Rosetta dozed.

What would she do for the remaining two hours while Izzie— who kept a key in her sports bag—darted blithely around the netball court? Rosetta had no phone handy, no money, just the clothes on her back and a mood that had switched from peaceful to peeved.

Wishing she could have left a note on the door for her tardy client, she made her way down the steps and crossed the front lawn. In under an hour she could track down Izzie's bag, retrieve the key and arrive back home. A compulsory walk instead of a calorie assault was a slimming consolation. 'Don't worry, Mum,' Izzie had said when Rosetta joked about her own weight. 'You're a meso-endomorph, so there's no point in aiming for the slenderness of a spindle-limbed ectomorph. It's all to do with frame and hereditary muscle mass. Just do more walking if you want to feel trimmer.'

Rosetta looked back at her home with its low-walled verandah, painted gables and stained-glass windows, and found herself smiling. The gracious California-style bungalow that enclosed its residents in nurturing warmth seemed almost to smile back. 'We've got two years of security ahead of us,' she whispered. She set out for the netball courts, a rapid march past autumn-tinged gardens and landscaped lawns. 'Two beautiful years!' The rental, a bargain for its size and location because it was marked for a 2010 demolition, felt far more like home than the ground floor flat they'd had prior: the inconvenient hub-jumble with mildew-infested walls. Here there was no barking blue heeler intent on shattering a good night's sleep; no neighbours dumping their rubbish in each other's bins to the point of overflow; no scraping up spilled debris from the road on garbage collection morning, courtesy of the sneaky neighbours and scavenging blue heeler.

More importantly, where they now lived was free of prowlers.

The images were starting. She tried to *scram* them away, but this time they persisted. The event that haunted her in nightmares played out in her memory like a Tropfest movie...

She was back in Punchbowl, collecting clothes from the communal outdoor laundry. Bringing them in after nightfall was never her favourite task. Not long after daylight-saving had ended, she'd underestimated how dark it would be once her wash-load had dried. Snatching up a torch, she rushed out into the chilly night air.

Grant, also known as Constable Belfield, was outside his garage with a carton of beer propped on one shoulder. He grinned, threw her a wink, then ascended the outdoor staircase to his second-floor flat. Thinking how pleasant it was to have a supportive friend for a neighbour who also happened to be attractive—in a sandy, freckly sort of way—and divorced, Rosetta smiled to herself and stepped into the laundry.

The sight within made her catch her breath.

Someone was crouched beside the washing machine.

Matted, serpentine hair flowed over a long dark coat that fell in folds across the concrete floor. Obscured by the coat's heavy sleeves were large pale hands. The fingernails—pointed, black, hideous—were curled into haggish claws.

Standing rigidly in the doorway, Rosetta struggled to recall any mention of a new tenant.

Which flat was this woman from?

The stranger turned to the right. Not a woman. The profile, half swallowed by shadow, was unarguably masculine. His thick red lips were twisted into a smirk. He was staring at the dryer, at the kaleidoscope of delicates swirling behind its door, nightwear belonging to Rosetta.

'They'll finish in a minute,' she told him. A warning from Grant flew back to her. 'In fact, I might as well...' Her voice stalled in her throat. The warning. Spotted the previous week: a long-haired prowler peering in bedroom windows.

Rosetta's breathing shrank into small gasps. She willed herself to remain focused.

The intruder continued to crouch. With mechanical slowness, he turned. He sniggered when he saw her. Was he relishing her fear?

He lurched into motion. A skink was scampering towards the washing machine. He grasped one of the skink's tiny legs and proceeded to dangle the creature languidly in the air, studying its terrified response with detached curiosity.

'No...' Rosetta whispered.

The creature wriggled back and forth, its brown scales glinting bronze in the shaft of moonlight descending from the window. Rosetta's fear gave way to fury. The intruder was watching her now; watching with unblinking eyes. His mouth widened into a mocking smile. He licked his lips.

Rosetta took an uneasy step forward.

He was now suspending the skink in front of his face, seeming to delight in the sensation of its frantic tail whipping the tip of his nose. He sneered ghoulishly. Then he lowered the skink onto his tongue.

Rosetta's voice escaped from her in a roar. 'Put that lizard down!'

The man's shoulders jumped. He stumbled to his feet. The skink fell to the floor and darted under the dryer.

Rosetta stepped out of the doorway. She pointed to the road. 'Go,' she commanded, power rising in her voice. 'Go now.'

Hunched and tense, the intruder slunk past her. He edged his way out of the laundry and then flitted away, a cowering wolf dissolving noiselessly into the darkness.

A clatter of footsteps rattled the metal stairs. 'Rosetta! You okay?' Grant was racing across the path.

He arrived at her side. Gripped her elbows to steady her. Rosetta folded forward, falling numbly against his shoulder. 'What's happening?' Grant said. 'What's going on?' He slipped the forgotten torch from her hand, flicked on its beam and shone it into the laundry.

She shook her head and signalled in the direction the man had run. 'It's him,' she said. 'The prowler.'

...Rosetta emerged from the memory and turned right into a street that led to Izzie's netball courts. The shouts of players were becoming audible now, squeaks and squawks of 'Here, here, here!' and 'Good one!' interspersed with the *froop-froop* of a referee's whistle.

A year had passed since that night. Grant had pursued the intruder without success. Not long after, she'd discovered the Ashbury Avenue home, and Grant's daughter had been super pleased that Izzie's new school was hers. 'You can hang out with Charlotte Wallace and me,' she'd said. And as an afterthought, 'Charlotte's dad sells houses. He does his own TV commercials.' Sara had then launched into impersonation mode, turning sideways, raising one eyebrow, and saying in Dominic's pompous mutter, "Call us at Wallace." '

Smiling at the recollection, Rosetta crossed the main road. Izzie's team was visible now through one of the high fences. Rosetta moved diagonally from the car park and hurried to Court C, where her little red-haired dynamo, all skinny legs and big feet, was bouncing about like Skippy on a caffeine high.

Clusters of sports bags were pressed into a corner of the mesh fence. Izzie's faded rucksack lay at the far end.

Hope no-one thinks I'm stealing the kids' stuff, she thought, rummaging through Izzie's bag.

'What are you looking for?' a voice demanded.

Rosetta jumped, swamped by unwarranted guilt. A smallish woman in her mid-to-late seventies stood over her.

Straightening, Rosetta said, 'Uh...hello! Where did you spring from? I didn't see you there.'

The woman failed to answer.

'I'm collecting something from my daughter.'

'Does she know you're here?'

'Well, no. But I'm not stealing from her.'

Another non-reply.

'I might be short of cash at the moment, but I'm not desperate.'

The woman didn't respond to that bad attempt at a joke, just continued to squint at her. 'Hurry along then.'

'Hurry along?'

'Yes. Hurry along and get that key, dear, and I'll give you a lift home. It's started to rain.'

Key! Rosetta couldn't remember mentioning the key.

The sky had been clear a moment earlier, and glary, an explanation perhaps for the woman's squint. Charcoal clouds now crowded out any trace of blue.

Feeling the odd *splish* tickle the crown of her head, Rosetta said, 'Thank you very much. That's really kind of you.'

'Don't mention it! Netball's not much of a spectator sport. You would know, being one of the mothers. I'm one of the grandmothers. We might as well get out of here or we'll either be deafened by that whistle or washed away by this rain.'

Rosetta followed the netball nanna to a faded pumpkin-coloured '70s hot rod Holden that made her own '96 model look positively modern.

The motor started up. Rosetta felt for a seat belt buckle, only to discover it glaringly absent.

Without warning, the car jumped forward and stalled.

'Sorry,' said the woman. The motor sputtered to a start again. She bumped the car over the grass, haphazardly dodging the dirt vehicle track.

Rosetta pressed back into the torn vinyl seat and seized hold of a strap swinging from the ceiling. She became aware of a calming aroma, a smoky, woodsy blend that suggested pine trees, campfires...roasted hazelnuts?

The rain had stilled once they reached the road. The woman pulled an enormous pair of sunglasses from her handbag and pushed them onto her nose. Rosetta embarked on a lively summary of the no-show, the lock-out and the walk to the courts. After *tsk-tsk*-ing in all the right places, the woman said, 'Some people are just plain unreliable. I don't think your tarot client will call again.' She looked rather blank behind her beetle-eyed sunnies. The sun glinted on her unlined skin, a rich deep-brown like Craig's.

'I'm Rosetta, by the way. Rosetta Melki.'

'Molly Carr.'

'Pleased to meet you, Molly.' Laughing, Rosetta shook her head. 'I thought at first you were going to accuse me of going through those bags.'

'Goodness. Poor Rosetta!' Molly gestured to the seat behind her. 'And that, in the back, is Curry.'

Expecting to see a casserole, Rosetta turned to the back seat and was surprised to find a rabbit, a live one, white with a grey splodge on its back. It was standing on its hind legs, its face half out of the open window. Intrigued, she watched the small creature wallowing in the air that rushed by, its ears flapping backwards in the breeze. Why Curry though? Unusual name for a rabbit. 'Hello little Curry,' she cooed. 'Aw, how gorgeous, a car-friendly bunny! Amazing.'

She told Molly about Izzie's obsession with rabbits as the scenery whizzed past. 'Oops!' she said finally. 'It's this street here, the one coming up on the right. I've been too busy blabbing.'

The car skidded to a maniacal stop. Rosetta felt a nasty twinge in her neck as her head flew forward and her hair swung across like curtains. Peeling away the strands that had settled across her face, Rosetta glanced again at Molly. The unlikely speed-demon looked as tranquil as a lamb.

The rabbit leapt into the reckless lift-giver's lap, then scrambled onto the dashboard. Molly lurched the car around to the right and stepped hard on the accelerator. Fearing for the rabbit's safety, Rosetta snatched Curry up. The rabbit's fur was luxuriant. It brushed the side of its face against her fingertips the way Sidelta the cat did and nudged the back of her hand with its snout.

'So you're a tarot reader, lovey?'

'Certainly am.'

'I've never had my future read.'

'Then here's a way I can say thank you for giving me a lift home. That's if you're not busy of course.'

'Nope, not too busy! If I hadn't been at a loose end this morning, I wouldn't have been mooching around those netball courts.'

Rosetta indicated her house was on the other side of the avenue, and Molly slowed the car. 'Okay, Rosetta, which of these lovely little homes is yours?'

Relieved to have access to indoors once again and refuge from the erratic driving, Rosetta ushered her new friend inside, heated the kettle and checked the phone messages. Nothing so far from the tarot client.

Once she'd prepared Molly a cup of raspberry tea and generous slab of semolina cake set out on a silver-edged Athenian plate, Rosetta voiced her concern about Curry remaining in the car. Molly assured her the windows were ajar and that the visit wouldn't be long.

At the copper table, Rosetta asked Molly to shuffle the tarots. 'Then I'll set it out into the Celtic Cross, and we'll see what's on the cards!'

Before Rosetta could hand them to her, Molly scooped up the cards, bending them in the process, and threw them into a violent shuffle that threatened to dog-ear the corners.

Rosetta tried not to let this get to her, although she couldn't help feeling that Molly was treating one of her treasures—a birthday present from a boyfriend some twenty-something years ago—like a two-dollar shop dispensable.

The shuffling drew to a stop. Rosetta held out her hand for the pack, but Molly seemed not to have noticed. Instead, she snatched up a card on the top of the pile, a card Rosetta couldn't see, studied it, nodded, then tucked it back into the pack.

Rosetta half-laughed with surprise.

The mysterious pumpkin-driver leaned forward, her face solemn and owlish. 'Green-eyed,' she said. 'You need to make contact with him.'

'Um...Wow! Um...'

'And you need to make contact soon. The two of you sail past each other like there's infinite time to spare.'

'Really? Ha! That's just amazing. Did you actually say *green-eyed*? I think I might have misheard.'

'No, you didn't mishear, I did indeed say that. The man in your future, Rosetta, is the man with green eyes.'

Chapter Four

Rosetta watched Molly Carr seize up the tarot pack once more. The cards flew in a blur, animated by the sprightly hands that shuffled them.

Molly was yet to provide further insight into her optimistic GEG comment, and there was no explanation for snaffling Rosetta's role of reader. Was it so surprising, considering the craziness of all that had happened so far? An otherwise peaceful morning had been whipped out of control with the no-show, the lock-out and the walk to the courts. And Mercury wasn't even in retrograde!

Molly set the cards face-down into a Celtic Cross formation, pressing each one against the tarot silk's azure and magenta loops. 'Rosetta...Melki,' she said ponderously. 'You have another name.'

'My married name was Redding, but I changed it back. And my surname at birth was changed by my adoptive parents to Melki.'

'What was your original surname?'

'Don't know. My foster parents didn't know either. I was adopted in New Zealand. Lived there till I was three.'

'Do you remember anything about New Zealand?'

'I remember...Hmm. What do I remember? I think the only thing I really remember is a shaded yard. There's a bird in the yard with a curved beak. And flowers in a tree that I've never happened upon since.'

Molly turned over one of the cards, the Queen of Cups, a Celtic version of the Queen of Hearts. 'Your foster parents. These were the people who gave you your surname?'

'Well, yeah. And my first name. My baba named me after the Rosetta Stone. He was an Egypt-loving Greek.'

Molly's face conveyed displeasure.

Strange reaction. A handle was just a handle. *A rose by any other name...*

'I'm not criticising your actual title, dear. That would be most impertinent.'

And hijacking a tarot reading wasn't?

'I'm concerned about your sonic signature. It's changed since you were first named. I'll have to check back with the Oracle.'

What did Molly mean by the Oracle? And what was wrong with her surname? Keen to see what the first card was, Rosetta flipped it to reveal its colourful underside. The King of Cups.

Molly gave a flourish of her hand. 'As you would know, The King of Cups—Hearts in the ordinary card pack—is nearly always representative of a suitor.'

Green eyes and a dazzling smile flashed past Rosetta. She recalled their last encounter.

'Just came in to tell you your A-frame got knocked over, but I put it back,' he'd said.

Stunned to see the star of her imagination materialised, she'd looked, and kept looking—to the detriment of listening—then doubted she'd heard him correctly.

'Your A-frame shop sign. I've put it back where it belongs.' Exactly what she'd thought he'd said. 'I think one of the school kids might have toppled it.'

Returning to reality and Molly's unanticipated fortune telling, Rosetta deemed the prediction a lucky guess. She wouldn't stand a chance with the gorgeous GEG.

'Have you heard of sprite visitations, Rosetta?'

'I have. It's mentioned in a chapter of a book we're to launch at Crystal Consciousness.' Perhaps she should start on it. Conan Dalesford's 300-pager on money, OOBEs and the future could always be brought forward on her To Be Read list.

'I believe you're being helped, Rosetta, by one or two of these otherworldly beings.'

But sprites were meant to only belong in novels, fairy stories like Lillibridge's, although to those considered gullible enough, herself and Lena included, a question mark hung over *Our True Ancient History*'s fiction claim.

'What the Otherworldly beings want you to know,' Molly said, 'is that you mustn't let anyone talk you out of your dreams.'

Before Rosetta could react with friendly scepticism, a scrap of the past rushed back, a glimpse of those teenage years when her foster father repeatedly despaired of her airy notions. 'Rosetta-Rosetta,' he'd said. 'What are we gonna do with you, huh?'

She'd been guilty of thinking aloud about ending world poverty.

'You don't have to be Mother Teresa, okay? Just be a good person. Be good to your mama and baba and sister and brothers, and when you marry, be good to your husband and kids. That's it.'

'But I want to be more than that. I want to be part of a team that addresses global suffering.'

Her baba shook his head. 'That takes a lotta money, Rosetta, to build up something like that.'

'Then I'll make sure I have money. I want to initiate community programs.'

'Better find a rich husband then.'

Her mama eyed her critically. 'She's not skinny enough to marry a rich man. A rich man wants a woman with a good figure.'

Rosetta's baba chuckled and said, 'Better lose weight, then, Rosetta,' before murmuring something in defence of her *child-bearin'* hips.

'But her voice isn't soft or sweet enough,' Mama shrilled.

Baba winked. 'So that's why your mama married a poor man like me!'

Rosetta had assured them she would never rely on a man for money. 'I'll be wealthy in my own right,' she'd said, and marched to her bedroom, head held high.

...In readiness to confide in Molly about her life's mission, Rosetta drew in a breath. Could her goal ever be realised? Would she one day have earned enough to fulfil her hope of becoming a philanthropist? 'There is *one* dream I haven't given up on, Molly.'

'Don't abandon eggs.'

'Sorry?'

Molly thumped her fist on the copper table. Again she said, 'Don't abandon eggs.'

'That won't happen. Meat's definitely out, but I'd be hopeless at sticking to a vegan diet.'

Molly scanned the ceiling. 'The work in which you're involved. The green-eyed fellow is connected with your work.'

'The work I do at the shop?' Meeting anyone through her cleaning job wasn't an option. Apart from Jack Barnaby's chirpy delegations when she scoured various offices in Martin Place, and the disgruntled notes from finance traders like 'MW' whose pens were marked *Royal Sydney Golf Club*, human interaction remained rare.

'Perhaps it *is* the shop,' Molly said.

The possibility of the GEG calling in again to Crystal Consciousness was practically a certainty!

'But there's often more than one way to meet your fate. It could happen any day. Any day or night. You might be hurrying down the street...and there he'll be.' She waved a hand in the direction of Ashbury Avenue beyond the sitting-room window.

'Haven't we all heard that before.' Rosetta smoothed out a small crease in the tarot silk.

Molly collapsed the Celtic Cross formation. She crunched the cards into a pile again. Sixteen cards left in the reading and yet the self-assigned reader was closing it off, wrapping the tarots into their silk and rising from her chair. And now she was scurrying into the hallway.

Rosetta leapt from her seat. 'Molly, I hope you didn't think I was being sarcastic just then.' She followed the hasty lady towards the door.

'Not in the slightest, dear. And what you said is true. We've all heard it before: that we're soon to invite a handsome stranger into our lives. The difference is my insights are quite sound, but I must get back to the netball courts. My granddaughter might well be on an orange-eating break by now, and I don't want her concluding I've been beamed up by aliens.'

Perplexed by unpredictable Molly's predictions, Rosetta snibbed the door to avoid being locked out a second time, then followed her onto the verandah. Molly bustled across to the driveway where the Holden, with its black-scraped orangeness and tilted headlights, conjured up the image of a grimacing Jack-O-Lantern.

Molly reversed from the driveway, calling, 'Your life is going to take on a brand new purpose. It's all about commitment.'

'Sure!' Rosetta gulped.

Molly's car revved.

Commitment was not a good word. She'd paid the price of commitment ever since Angus had stomped out of her life, leaving her with the sole care of a child he'd refused to support and a mortgaged house the bank repossessed.

Molly's car lurched forward, then zoomed recklessly backwards.

Rosetta checked that the garbage and recycling bins were pushed far enough away from the driveway. An echoing *bumpity-bang* resounded, followed by a rumble.

Curry's startled head popped up at the window, swivelling left and right.

Had Molly really hit the bins? All three of them? Rosetta swung round to inspect the damage. The wheelie bins, now skittled, lay drunkenly across the driveway.

'Oops! Sorry!' Molly's voice had become faint and far away.

A feeling of listlessness overcame her.

Darkness fell swiftly, like someone had turned off the sun.

'What's happening?' Rosetta asked herself. '*What's happening?*' Her arms might as well have been made of stone. Her legs, too, had become immobilised, as though the soles of her feet were suctioned to the lawn.

'Mum!'

Rosetta's eyes snapped open.

'You were snoring!'

She was back in the verandah chair! How did Izzie get there so suddenly?

Dominic Wallace, young Charlotte Wallace and Izzie were standing at the bottom of the steps. Staring at her.

'Where's Molly...the bunny...' Rosetta stopped. She'd been asleep. Curry and the enigmatic tarot reader weren't even real.

Unsteadily, she rose to her feet.

Dominic Wallace, tall and cardboard-cut-out handsome, was thumping up the steps. With the self-aware strut of a man inspired by his own potential, he crossed the verandah. To Rosetta's chest, he said, 'And how is Rosetta?'

A blatant opportunist. She hadn't forgotten the time he'd asked if she'd consider meeting him for a drink at a plush hotel. Was it any wonder Diondra suffered from perpetual anger? Who wouldn't, with a husband who never missed an opportunity to advertise his contempt for monogamy?

'What was that about a bunny called Molly?' said Charlotte blinking.

It was all very quiet on the verandah.

Dominic lifted his eyes to Rosetta's face and smirked.

'Just sleep-talk I guess.' Rosetta attempted a laugh. 'Must have been dreaming.'

Dominic's voice took on a suggestive tone, starting with a stage-whisper and ending in a growl. 'The bunnies in my dreams have names like Sindi or Candee.' He gestured to the tuxedoed rabbit-head logo on his polo shirt. 'Oh, what I'd give to be buddies with Hefner.'

IX

Body kings, so named by the devas, goaded and strove and desired. Plundered treasure tokens. Smashed apart sacred caves intent on shattering their mysteries.

Within the centre of a treeless plain, and at the edge of Elysium Glades, lay a glimmering palace guarded by eagle-winged men. In one of its chambers, a body-king daughter sat by a loom. As daybreak lit the motley patterns formed, the young maiden's face took on radiance, a glow that died at the shadowing of a cloud. Filtering from the rafters was the stomp of the Grudellans who guarded her family's much-coveted gold. By the well were three hundred sprite slaves chanting numbers that made no sense to them, in an effort, enforced by the Solen, to segregate little from lot.

Buckets mounted and filled and overflowed. The elves' secret Wondalobs water, plumbed and consumed excessively, was rendering those of the royal court overly powerful. Power, only beneficial in small doses, would turn against itself like a two-headed asp when utilised to extremes, and yet those of Gold's Kin, unperturbed by suggestions of danger, continued to gluttonise their pilfered prize.

Shaking her head at the wail of another sprite sent away to the mines, frowning at the squabble of guards in the tower above her chamber, the golden girl heard her minders' voices and resisted the temptation to run and to hide.

'Eidred,' they snapped. Sharp voices, crisp as autumn leaves and twice as icy, filled the gilded chamber. 'Eee-dred! Where are your tables?'

'They are away, good minders, away.'

'Enough of your tiresome impertinence! We command you to work two dozen hours in the laundries.'

'Yet I addressed you in the manner you ask.' Eidred's heart became heavy at the thought of an entire day and night without nourishment, scrubbing flaxen cloth.

''Tis rude not to have multiplications tables ready at this sun's degree.'

'Lessons, I thought, are, and always were, at the 31st sun degree. If I see correctly from my sill, we are still in the 30th.'

'Then the 30th it is to be. From yesterday onwards. Since you avoided waiting with times-tables ready, in the possibility of us changing our minds, you now have greater work to contend with as punishment. Start immediately.'

Swallowing back her sobs, the Princess of Grudella tucked her woven craft carefully into a jewelled treasure chest and sat down to work on numeral perfecting. She glanced sideways at her minders, but they continued to stand over her. Terrifying shadows they were, with cruel beaks and eyes that were barely there.

If their excuse for her punishment was based on logic, the prime component of her lessons, then she wanted no part of logic. This daughter of the Solen dreamed of freeing herself from the cold, skeletal creatures forever.

She despised the content of the lessons as much as she despised her Grudellan teachers.

They were ghastly, those pterodactyls.

X

'There,' the princess said as she folded the last of the linen. 'Finally done.'

No more had she thought of her loom or attended to dreams of future happiness. They were ripped from her heart when she'd clicked into counting mode. At last her thoughts were her own again.

If only she had a faerie godmother; someone who would listen comfortingly to all her woes, who would understand her inability to feel safe in the family she was born into and who had the power to manifest Eidred's heart's desire. A magical gift. A wish materialising into a truth.

With one magic spell all to herself, Eidred could revel in freedom. No longer would she be confined to a medium-sized chamber in a sprawling prison of a castle, she'd have a larger chamber, and she'd make the imposing castle smaller. The Grudellans—pterodactyls that haunted her day and night and never let her be—would, upon her wish, only be able to annoy her once a day. Once a day and no more than that.

Oh, to have freedom! She'd wish for an extra colour to add to her tapestry. She'd lower the voices of the slaves so that their screams wouldn't startle her as much. She'd make her skin a shade golder than it already was, and all the linen they made her scrub would scrub clean in half the time.

What fun to feel what free people felt! Life would no longer be mundane. It would be challenging. She'd even go so far as to change her name. No longer would she be known as Eidred. She'd be *Eidredelda*. What a splendid name! It made her feel important.

And her father would be made, upon her wish, to lessen his grumbles about the faeries. Secretly, Eidred didn't think it fair that the fey should be so resented. This she confided to no-one. If her sympathy towards them became known, the Solen would end her worldly existence there and then for such insanity. Eidred wasn't meant to be aware of the sprites. No-one else of the royal court could discern them without the aid of their fey-detection cloaks, and yet Eidred saw them perfectly—no doubt a breach of palace law—and was constantly in awe of the faeries, elves, gnomes, dryads and pixies who dwelt within Elysium's glorious forests and glades.

She'd stumbled across these elusive people twice in her life. The meetings had been quite by accident, during punishments when she'd been ordered to transport two parcels of gold to a shipful of Ehyptians on Grudella's shore. The gold had been such a strain on the princess's tiny frame, her arms had still ached and trembled three daybreaks later.

It had been night, just as it was now. That was when these people awoke. Came to life, rather. During the sun's hours they retreated to their invisible sleeping wagons.

When Eidred's people went to sleep, the world was no longer theirs. It became a silvery land of shadows and belonged to the fey. So different were they to those of her realm. The fey were quick, gracious, colourful. Their words rang with kindness, and they rarely expressed anger or loathing. Twice they had helped her carry the gold through their forest by making the weight of it vanish. This they did by sprinkling stars over Eidred. The stars had made Eidred dizzy in a pleasant sort of way, giving her the impression of treading through silken clouds.

Eidred was still unsure as to whether she admired or despised the fey. She was supposed to despise them. And she did. She despised them. She despised them with affection. Torn by creed and all of its laws, Eidred—from the time of her arrival in the world five-and-ten season-cycles ago—had spun out her existence cocooned in guilt and armed with fear. Who was she, anyway, to entertain the thought of faeries being in any way adequate? Those mites were *inferior*. Why else would they sleep through the gods' finest hours and wake to the depths of nocturnal gloom? To wish for a faerie godmother was a wicked thought. Away with it at once!

The thought was almost gone when Eidred settled down to sleep. Almost gone...and it would have been forgotten had the girl not halted it for a further moment.

Supposing I was wicked and trusted the inferior fey folk, she thought. Suppose a faerie godmother appeared and promised to present me with the magic seed of freedom. I know more than any-one that they wield mischievous powers and are best avoided. But suppose the fey are such people who happen to be superior. Wiser than even *us*. People who know more, can do more and can call in the energies of change far quicker than any of our sorcerers.

How would a being like this appear? Eidred fancied she could see a creature, dark-eyed and of fey origin, hair like her own but skin that differed in tone to hers: as luminous as an oyster gem, and eyes too big for the face. It wore a gown the colour of fire. It had butterfly wings in all shades. Its voice was opposite to the voices Eidred most often heard; free of screeches. Simply a whispery breeze of a voice that didn't assault the ears. A faerie godmother! What would she be known as? Eidred closed her eyes to allow sleep to engulf her.

What would this faerie godmother be called?

The answer came back from somewhere unknown.

Your godmother is Orahney.

And it sounded like a blessing, carried in the arms of the soft night air.

XI

Eidred woke to find her chamber different. The walls were half dissolved and veiled in a radiant mist. Her ears were filled with a shrill whirring, not unlike the buzzing of bees.

There came a flash of light, so bright it filled the darkened room with the essence of daybreak.

Eidred blinked rapidly, surprised at her lack of alarm. The most she felt was a calm awareness of things going according to plan.

Appearing at the end of her bed was a satiny light. It might have been a firefly, for it was surrounded by a halo. The light grew larger. Eidred discerned a person within the glow—a moving, breathing person.

'A faerie!' Eidred said. Her dreams were coming true.

'Orahney,' a voice murmured. 'Can you hear me?' There before Eidred stood a little, plump lady with eyes as bright as suns and a dimpled smile that spoke of pure kindness.

'Who are you?' Eidred asked.

'Maleika,' the being said. 'Orahney, is that you?'

The princess was puzzled, aware she had heard the name Orahney somewhere before. Why had it repeated? 'I am not the person you seek,' she said with apology. 'You have evidently lost your way.'

Before responding, the fey woman studied her. 'Well I never! Tell me, then, child, who you suppose yourself to be.'

Eidred shrugged. 'I don't suppose anything. It just *is*, that's all. I am Eidred, Princess of Grudella. My father rules this particular realm.'

'Your father is a *king*?' Maleika shuddered. 'How is this so?'

'His father was a solen also,' said Eidred, at once feeling a sense of pride regarding her heritage. 'He has hundreds of men who are slaves to him, and he is in constant contact with the gods.'

'Who are....?'

'I will not state all their names, but Grudas, the pterodactyl god, oversees the Grudellan realm.'

'Oh dear. I'd never thought my search would become so complicated, Orahney...er...Eidred, I mean to say. Tell me, Eidred, have you befriended any sprites of the devic realm?'

'Apart from you, none! To do so would be the death of me, you do understand. How strange. Here you are, appeared in my room, and 'tis almost exactly what I had wished for, only I'd somehow supposed you'd have hair like mine and would be clothed in orange. Never mind, you're here now. Let me state my wishes.'

'Wishes, child? You want me to grant you a wish with my magic?'

'I asked for these before slumbering. Please hurry. We cannot have the guards finding a member of the fey here. It would be the end of us both! I shall tell you my wishes now.'

'You don't remember a thing, do you?'

'I beg your pardon?'

Maleika sat down by the tower window, a moonbeam silvering her downcast eyelids. To Eidred she appeared as tranquil as a lamb, despite the danger that lurked in every corner of the palace.

XII

Maleika was in turmoil, filled with concern for the golden-haired creature before her. Surely this being was Orahney reincarnated. But Orahney choosing to be royal? How could this be? While she had not enjoyed any luck in her search for Pieter, Maleika had at least accessed a clue to finding him. She'd travelled to the other universe and consulted the Oracle there. The Oracle had told her of an eagle statue.

> Three flights of stairs
> The lost one's room
> Is sanctioned off in lofty gloom
> Revisit where the eagle's flown
> Its earthly shell
> Is set in stone

The only information the Oracle dared to give. The stone eagle was perched on a towering post in the Grudellan Palace grounds, just beyond the golden gates and thicket of poisonous thorns, which flanked the glittering monstrosity gold-skins called home. The hill the palace had impolitely risen from, once ferny and vital when part of Elysium's forest, was a sandy, treeless plain that faerie and dryad clans had been forced to desert.

The Oracle's mention of revisiting this site was a puzzle to Maleika. Her only other journey to the Grudellan Palace had taken place many season-cycles earlier. She had disguised herself as a bewitcher back then with the cloak Orahney had asked the oak dryad to conjure. Armed with Orahney's crystal-crowned wand, she'd infiltrated a temple where a crystalling was in progress, an infant-naming ceremony for one of the Solen's newborns. The temple had been nowhere near the eagle statue, and so she could not agree with the Oracle that she was in any way revisiting it.

Maleika heard crashing stomps on the staircase. Marching, echoing, marching on upwards while a menacing screech violated the tower room's moon-bathed stillness.

'You must go, Faerie Godmother,' urged the girl. 'It's *them*–the sons of the gods!'

Maleika immediately called forth her beauty-creation powers—magic earned from the gleaning of kindness merits—arriving, after an interval, back at the forest of her dwelling. Kloory, Croydee and the water sprites had already journeyed to the river, leaving a nest of embers that threw out dying warmth.

Prodding the embers with a twig, Maleika mused over the gold-skinned girl's aura. Wracked with fear. A heart frozen by examples of cruelty. A body-king daughter, not especially dark, but victimised by darkness, thus identifying with this more than with light.

'Why this concerns Pieter's whereabouts, I do not know,' muttered Maleika, gazing at the yellow sparks flying upwards amongst fluttering ash. 'The likeness...something in the features—or perhaps it was only the length of hair or facial expression—had me confused initially. I thought the princess to be Orahney with an altered persona, returned from the Dream Sphere in a new earthly life.' She resolved to consult the Oracle again about Pieter's disappearance. 'I am obviously not regaining my Dream-Sphere memories correctly. To err like this is proof itself.'

On the way to his car, Matthew paused in the Martin Place Station arcade, contemplating the sign in a shop window: *Book Launch 5.30pm Friday. Purchase* Thoughts on Tomorrow's Tycoon War *and have it signed by visionary Alice Springs author Conan Dalesford!*

Matthew already knew about the launch. Dalesford's book, second-hand because he'd retrieved it, fully wrapped, from an arcade bin, had come with a bookmark advertising the event. His chunky wristwatch and the lifelessness of the store told him he'd missed out, but he couldn't have left work any earlier.

A clunk rang out from the darkened shop. The door swung open and a warm female voice said, 'So that's your Sydney launch complete, Conan. What next?'

He could see the source of the voice now. A smallish woman with neat brown hair and spectacles was efficiently locking the double doors alongside a wiry tanned bloke with a close-cut snowy beard.

'A Scandinavian holiday,' he said, 'which we're very much looking forward to. Caroline, I truly appreciate all you've done. And please thank charming Rosetta for all her help.'

The two said their goodbyes and the man, Conan Dalesford himself, turned, gave Matthew a nod and veered a trolley bag towards the escalators.

Encouraged by the kindness in the author's eyes, Matthew stepped forward, his hand outstretched. 'Matthew Weissler. I enjoyed your book.' Conan Dalesford shook the hand Matthew offered. 'I was sorry to miss the launch. I'd hoped to ask what inspired you to write *Thoughts on Tomorrow's Tycoon War.*'

'There's a short answer to that,' Dalesford said, 'and a long one. Which would you prefer?'

'Take your time. I'm in no hurry.'

'And I need a Sydneysider to direct me to a good place to eat, so if you're in no rush to get home, Matthew, we can discuss the book over dinner.'

Matthew hadn't been relishing the evening ahead with Bernadette. She hadn't spoken to him now for three days. Why, exactly, he wasn't sure, but having a pub meal with someone affable whose work he'd grown to admire sure beat the prospect of those icy stares.

Once at the George Street brasserie that adjoined the bar with the fancy lampshades and boasted an eclectic bill of fare, Dalesford said, 'So tell me. How did you happen upon the book I wrote?'

'By accident,' Matthew said. 'I hate to have to tell you this, but I found it in the rubbish.'

'The rubbish!' Dalesford shook his head. Grinned slightly. 'Interesting way to find it.' His blue eyes glimmered a little. 'Do you know who threw it out?'

'I do, as a matter of fact. It was a colleague of mine.' Matthew thought back to the day of the incident. He'd been heading to his underground car park via the Martin Place Station arcade. A conversation with Adam Harrow about the Greenknowe takeover had bled into the domain of after-hours, but only because they'd caught the same Mezzanine Level lift.

Matthew had unwittingly followed the guy on a detour into an eccentric little shop, the same place Conan Dalesford exited earlier, a mystic's paradise that sold cards and wrapping and reeked of burning myrrh. An autumn-toned poster at the far end had caught Matthew's eye. Harrow had hung around to make a purchase, and Matthew had continued on to the news stand, noting in his BlackBerry to get Mothers' Day gift wrap there the following day. Laura's request was for 'something pink and dotty'.

Harrow had caught up with him, the package he'd bought now shoved under one arm. 'Don't waste your breath on the Greenknowe bastards,' he'd said. 'If we're lucky, they'll hang in their own noose.' He'd then powered towards the escalators and flipped his unopened purchase into a bin.

Matthew had glared at the back of his colleague's blond head. A sense of injustice at the wasting of something new had compelled him to cross to the bin and peer inside. Before long, he'd found himself reaching into the chaotic assortment of sticky drink cans and poly-styrene burger boxes.

...'Literally bought and binned,' Matthew told Dalesford. 'I was right behind the guy, so I nabbed it. Opened it when I got home and from then on out I was hooked.'

'Well, well,' said Dalesford. 'What sort of fellow would throw away an unread book?'

Contemplating Harrow and the slippery dishonesty that defined him, Matthew tried not to grit his teeth. 'A very unlikeable fellow.'

He left the table to get drinks. On the way to the bar, he collided with a hefty geezer carrying a full tray of steins. The tray crashed down. One of the steins smacked painfully against his left knee. His knee locked, a flare-up from a previous sprain. Intent on delaying lurching into the embarrassing half-limp these flare-ups generally caused, Matthew spent more time than necessary collecting each of the spilled glasses from the floor, alongside the apologetic tray carrier, then walked as steadily as he could to the bar.

When he returned to the table, Dalesford said, 'Running injury?'

Matthew handed Dalesford his schooner. 'I used to compete in marathons.'

Dalesford dug out a small black box from his trolley bag, took something from it and held his fist out to Matthew. 'Here,' he said. 'Hold this for a sec. It might just settle the pain.'

Something jagged and cold fell into Matthew's palm. A crystal. Clear quartz probably. He closed his fingers around it.

A shot of heat ran up his arm. He jumped. He opened his hand again. Could the stone have changed colour? He mustn't have observed it closely enough at the start. Its white flecked facets had lively veins of electric blue running through them.

He blinked, and a flash of silver engulfed the room. 'Whoa!' he said. 'Did you see that?'

'See what?'

'That storm must be close!' Matthew turned to one of the bar windows, perplexed by the absence of accompanying thunder.

'You sure about that? The sky looked pretty clear on our walk here. We Territorians keep attuned to impending storms.'

'The lightning. It lit up the room.'

'I think,' Dalesford leaned forward, 'that it came from the crystal. It was only you who saw that, Matthew.'

'You're kidding.' Matthew held the gem up to the light. Examined it in disbelief. He didn't have much knowledge of crystals. Hippies and the like tended to attribute mysterious powers to them, a claim that was, in Matthew's opinion, the product of misguided idealism. Perhaps he'd been too sceptical. Perhaps the New Age fruit-loops had something on him. Always prudent, he supposed, to keep an open mind. 'Where do you get one of these?'

'You don't.'

'Huh?'

'I ran that one up in my workshop back in Alice Springs.' A smudge of a smile played on Dalesford's lips. 'It's a poor imitation though.'

Matthew tried to dilute his surprise. 'A poor imitation?'

A poor imitation of what?

Friday night, a non-book-group-meeting night, and two more sleeps until her day off for the week. Rosetta would have stayed longer at the launch she'd organised, but Izzie needed to be driven to Charlotte's birthday bash.

Once she'd stumbled inside with full bags of groceries, Izzie flew into the hallway and told her a lift had already been arranged.

Rosetta groaned. 'If only you'd texted me about that, Izzie. I could have stayed and talked more with Conan Dalesford!'

'Sorry. My phone's been charging.'

'Ah well. It's done now.' In truth, she was pleased to be home. When she'd leapt onto the Burwood-bound train and flopped into a seat, her legs had protested heavily against all the overtime.

She went to work preparing an old Greek favourite, rosemary and lentil soup. When the kitchen all but pulsated with the sharply comforting aromas of homegrown herbs and butter-fried onion, she left the medley to simmer and updated her Lillibridge site.

Izzie scooted into the study and asked for suggestions on what to pair with her slimline jeans. They settled on the sweet little top with medieval sleeves that Izzie had bought with her bowling alley earnings. Although simple and blue-grey, the top was an uncanny match for Izzie's eyes and complemented the trimness of her sportsy figure.

Once a car rolled into the driveway, Rosetta gave Izzie a quick hug and handed her the little rose quartz pendant from Crystal Consciousness, which she'd managed to wrap before introducing Conan Dalesford to a gathering of launch attendees.

'Charlotte will love this,' Izzie said, waving the package above her head. 'Just about everything she owns is pink!' Then she was off for an evening of girlish babble, punctuated probably, with the drumbeats of Boyd Levanzi songs. And boys? Rosetta knew boys were invited. When she'd asked if any 'hotties' were going, Izzie had become untypically evasive.

Later that evening after drying the dishes, Rosetta staved off dieter's guilt and indulged in another slice of jam-on-toast. Wishing the breadbox had originally come with a dieter-proof lock, she turned away from it and fixed herself a cup of cocoa. Keen to breathe in the cool night air, she scanned Ashbury Avenue through the sitting room window. No-one lurking near the front garden. She relaxed her shoulders and wandered out to the verandah.

I'm getting paranoid, she told herself. We're safe at this new address. Completely safe. The lizard eater can't creep up on us here.

Inside, the antique clock relayed the half-hour in a single dramatic chime. Izzie would be home soon. The Wallaces had promised to drop everyone back by eleven. Sleepy chirrups of baby birds filtered through the stillness. Amid a clump of lacy ferns by the letterbox, the Japanese maple stood sentry over the footpath, deep maroon against a darkened sky. In the daytime breeze its leaves were a vivid conglomeration of shivering scarlet stars. Izzie was planning on immortalising these with her pastels.

The pastels, a Christmas gift two years earlier, were now little more than a spectrum of squashy stubs. Laughing slightly at the recollection of her daughter's dogged perseverance with them, Rosetta made a mental note to keep an eye out for discounted art supplies. At this stage, affording Izzie's birthday presents was still looming large. Caroline had mentioned there might be an extra shift at the shop. She'd snap that up on Monday if it became available. While one more shift would mean working fifteen days straight without a break, lately she didn't mind how often she worked there. Now that the Green Eyed Guy had potentially become a regular customer, the notion of serving at the Crystal Consciousness counter had taken on a peppy new radiance.

Deep in thought, Rosetta sat down on the verandah steps, re-calling last Sunday's bizarre events. Oddly, the unnamed tarot requester on the phone and Molly Carr, the woman in the dream, seemed as though they were one and the same. Both had lilting inflexions and bell-like laughter. And in true Alice in Wonderland style, Rosetta's subconscious had conjured a white rabbit. She could still feel its soft fur on her hands. It had been a startlingly affectionate creature, more puppy than bunny.

She reached for her mug of cocoa. With a clunk, the mug skit-tled over the side of the step. 'Saves a few calories,' she reasoned, reaching for the cup at the foot of a chrysanthemum.

A flash of white leapt from the garden bed. She jolted forward.

A rabbit with a grey splodge on its back.

Molly's rabbit?

'But that was a dream,' Rosetta reminded herself.

Curry was only a dream.

The curving line of ruby taillights had drawn to a stop.

Matthew settled his foot on the accelerator, eager to get home and online to check next Friday's flights to the Northern Territory. When he'd mentioned remaining in contact, Dalesford's suggestion of visiting him and his wife at their Alice Springs property appeared to be little more than a nicety, but Dalesford had repeated the invitation by adding, 'We'll only be there for another fortnight, then we're off to explore Denmark, Iceland, Norway and Sweden. Why don't you fly up and stay with us next weekend?'

Time seemed to have passed quickly in the bar. Dalesford's stance on the global monetary system mostly opposed Matthew's own views. They'd discussed where they believed the world was heading, and Matthew had seized upon the challenge of defending an imperfect but workable survival framework. 'The world will always run on money,' he'd told Dalesford.

The author had countered this with, 'Don't be so sure. Time is a cycle. Returning to the values of aeons ago, before money or bartering came into being, might well become a necessity.'

The traffic lurched forward. Matthew jiggled his foot in time to the '50s swing rhythms on the car radio. His knee had recovered remarkably well, considering the force of the tray's jolt. He'd been expecting to ice-pack it, but the usual damage control of numbing the pain and arranging a physio appointment didn't appear to apply. He'd been surprised at the ease in his step when he'd descended a concrete stairwell to the parking station, probably one of the reasons he hadn't succumbed to impatience at tonight's dawdling traffic. A sense of collectedness was kerbing his usual white-knuckled reactions. He felt focused and unhassled, and surprisingly upbeat.

He was pressing ahead now, aware of a tune, an overriding whistling sound that conflicted sharply with Sedaka's carefree take on relationship bust-ups. He tinkered with the radio. The melodious whirr had invaded every other channel! It was even backdropping news bulletins and accompanying the late-night rants of a shock-jock, a semi-lullaby softening every livid exclamation. He leaned forward to switch it off just as a P-plater swung out in front of him.

'What the...!' Matthew's reflexes snapped into action.

His car tyres screeched. The steering wheel escaped from his grip as though controlled by invisible hands and spun him into a side street.

A collision with the median strip. A diagonal skid towards the kerb.

He steadied the Jag and pulled up to regain his cool. The median strip prevented any immediate chance of returning to the highway.

He breathed out forcefully. The shock, seeming to have settled in shards at the base of his lungs, had begun to ease. He leaned forward to read a badly lit street sign. A couple of right-hand turns would lead him back.

After a few seconds' reflection on the catastrophe that might have transpired, Matthew became aware once more of the faint melody. Low and haunting. The soft, sweet whistle of a pipe made from reed. Again he attempted to deaden the radio, only to realise he'd succeeded the first time. The radio's lights were off, and yet the tune was still playing.

Perhaps the sound was coming from within. Perhaps there was something amiss with his ears. Whistling from Tinnitus? A possibility, but he'd never heard Tinnutis described as tuneful.

Trying to ignore the mellow tones that were disconcertingly similar to music Peter Piper had played, Matthew started up the motor and continued along a street peppered with double-gabled homes: interwar cottages exuding mustard-gold light from their square and circular windows.

He made a swift turn into Ashbury Avenue.

The tune quavered and rippled, then dissolved into silence.

Rosetta watched in fascination. The rabbit, possibly one of the neighbours' pets, was now bouncing across the moonlit lawn. At the letterbox it paused to smooth a paw across its whiskers, dandelion tail twitching feverishly.

Grooming complete, it zipped between the rockery and driveway, then lolloped right onto the road.

A glimmer of car lights flickered at the end of Ashbury Avenue. The hum of a motor drew near. The rabbit turned to stare.

Rosetta rocketed to the kerb. In a frantic attempt to wave down the motorist, she flung her arms above her head. Her vision had blurred. Both the rabbit and approaching car were almost entirely blotted out with a random burst of those lilac and lemon silver-edged splodges. She shook her head and blinked twice. The car slowed and eased to a halt.

She flew to the centre of the road and stooped to gather up the bundle of fur. The bundle of fur sprang sideways. Rosetta sprang after it. It hesitated, then hopped forward. Rosetta hopped forward. Missed.

'Everything okay?' a self-assured voice called from the car.

The voice seemed to have a clearing effect on the stars in Rosetta's eyes. They twirled upwards, then disappeared in a mysterious puff of light. Still doubled over, she raised her hand in silent response. Calling out at this stage might cause the rabbit to shelter under the vehicle in fright.

Becoming aware of a rumbling whirr that sounded frustratingly like the approach of another car from the opposite direction, Rosetta tiptoed towards her target.

The rabbit bounded up to her. Rosetta dived on it. 'Gotcha!' Her hands encompassed the trembling fluff-ball, but when she curled her fingers into a clasp, her knuckles smacked against the asphalt. The rabbit had somehow slipped across to the other side of the car; was now blinking at her with dewy eyes. 'Who do you think you are?' she grumbled. 'The Energizer Bunny?'

Her hands had gone right through the rabbit! She grasped at it again. The animal eyed her and then seemed to fade. Melted gradually into the darkness.

How could this be? She knew she wasn't dreaming this time.

And then it vanished altogether.

Utterly confused now, Rosetta rose unsteadily, palms thrust out. Her mouth had dropped open. She could barely manage to speak. Finally addressing the open window of a car she'd stopped unnecessarily, a Jaguar the colour of cherries, she called faintly, 'Wasn't a rabbit...'

She'd been pursuing a hallucination! Imagining how this must have looked, her confusion turned to embarrassment. She rose to her full height, tossed her head and marched smartly back to the house.

A hallucination! What could have caused her to hallucinate? People were known to start seeing things when they'd missed out on a severe amount of sleep, and yet she'd never suffered from fatigue. And those weirdly disrupting purple and yellow silver-lined stars...were they a hallucination too? She still hadn't sourced the reason for their randomness.

Once at the verandah steps, she heard, 'Mum! What were you doing?'

She turned to see Dominic Wallace, his daughter Charlotte, and Izzie, standing next to Dominic's four-wheel-drive. Staring at her. Again. This must have been the true meaning of déjà vu!

Adopting her best in-control manner, she said, 'You must have crept up on me. I didn't realise you were here.'

'You did look fairly busy,' said Dominic, smirking.

'Had you lost something on the road?' said a polite Charlotte.

'Ah yes,' Rosetta said. 'I had. But I've found it now.' Changing the subject, she added, 'And you enjoyed your birthday, sweetie?'

While Charlotte answered in the affirmative and voiced her appreciation for the rose quartz pendant, Rosetta became aware of Izzie glaring at her.

'Thanks so much, Dominic, for bringing Izzie home.'

'You're very welcome, Rosetta,' he drawled, analysing her cleavage. 'Always welcome.'

Izzie stomped up the steps ahead of Rosetta.

Once inside, Izzie turned to her, face red with what looked to be a mixture of anger and humiliation. 'Mum, can I ask what you told the person in the car after you stopped leaping about?'

'Um...nothing of importance. We weren't having any sort of conversation.'

'But I was sure I heard you speak to him. Something to do with a rabbit. That's the second time you've muttered about bunnies in front of Charlotte and her dad. Any reason for that?'

'I don't like your tone, Isobel.'

Izzie's voice mellowed. 'I didn't mean to sound bossy. Is everything okay though?'

How could she explain this away? Shaking her head at the likelihood of an animal vanishing into thin air, Rosetta drew in a deep breath to answer. She hesitated. Where would she start?

'Er...Mum,' Izzie had taken on an expression of concern. 'Can people go senile at thirty-eight?'

Nervously, Rosetta glanced away. 'Not normally, honey.' She darted to the side-table, and with forced enthusiasm, rearranged the autumn flowers she'd placed in a vase the day before. 'Why do you ask?'

Chapter Five

Izzie found the leaves of paper she wanted in the corner of her local newsagency. Edged with silver, bronze and gold, each had a luminous watermark with hints of peacock and plum and watermelon.

A chill slid over her arms. She lifted her head and glanced around the shop. No-one there except Marla's dad Louey behind the counter, smiling calmly at the sunlight streaming in after a day of clouds. Izzie had got a lot of that lately, the feeling of being watched. She shrugged and returned to the paper shelves.

A man's shadow fell across the linoleum. Outside the shop a darkly dressed figure turned from the headline-cluttered window and disappeared up the footpath.

Trying not to feel unnerved by this, Izzie concentrated on the papers and counted out twelve. Ideal for the invitations she planned to design. She would pay for them with the money she earned cashiering at the bowling alley on Saturday nights.

Would he be impressed if he received a leaf of this paper in his locker? Or would he think her kooky and desperate if she, barely more than a stranger, asked him to her sixteenth birthday picnic?

His accent was freaky, and yet hearing it was just as exhilarating as listening to Boyd Levanzi's 'Ain't Been Nothing No More'. Izzie would have much preferred screen-saver images of the boy she was inviting to her birthday than images of Boyd Levanzi. The African American hip-hop phenomenon who teens referred to as 'boydiful', beautiful and all as he was with his puppy dog eyes and sensuous smile, was nothing in comparison to a certain person in tenth grade at Burwood High. A certain person who pronounced hello 'halo' and wore weird snow boots in a place where winters weren't especially cold. Izzie knew nothing of the Dutch culture, except, perhaps, that if one of them asked you out to lunch, they'd probably split the bill.

She would never have believed that she'd one day be interested in a Netherlands boy whose name suggested a distant galaxy. Glorion. Six feet tall and coolness personified. Eyes Izzie felt she could swim in. Lips that were a hundred per cent worthy of winning Best in the Solar System.

The recurring dreams she'd had from the time she was seven were always about a tall boy appearing in her teenage future. She'd wake up marvelling at the memory of kind brown eyes and a husky voice. He'd told her she'd have some years to wait, of course, before they met. 'And then,' the Dream Boy had said, 'the world is ours to share.' Totally mushy these days and unchanged from the first dream all those years ago: the fairy-floss output of a seven-year-old's subconscious.

The fact that Glorion Osterhoudt looked exactly like the boy from the dream was too freaky to explain. She'd met him thirty-eight days ago when he'd bopped her on the head with his maths book in the canteen queue. Someone in her group had called a 'first-to-the-canteen-queue' challenge, but Izzie's undone shoelace hampered her start. When the others rushed into the crowded canteen, she'd scrambled to the front of the queue, pushed in and stifled her giggles just long enough to holler, 'I won!' Her friends at the other end of the line had laughed along with her. She'd turned to the tall boy behind her, the new boy, and he'd playfully brushed that maths book over the top of her head. She'd said to him, 'I'll go. Just did that to surprise them,' and stepped out.

He'd grinned and said she was welcome to remain where she was, and when she'd protested, he'd murmured, 'Please stay.' Those eyes and that smile had felt bizarrely—and dreamishly—familiar.

She'd never thought cardboard could be a precursor for such good feelings; the very thing in fact, five-and-a-half weeks later, that reminded her of Glorion while wandering through Louey's shop. Her gaze settled on a tray of half-price stationery. A book just like the one Glorion used, to pretend-reprimand her, lay atop a pile of A4 notebooks. It looked the same as his. Dark-green in colour with those large E's zipping diagonally across the midline. Resisting the temptation to glide it across her head to check if it felt the same, Izzie turned her attention to the I-Candy chewing-gum. Ha! *Eye candy.* Why did everything remind her of the future boy?

She paid Louey for the invitation papers. 'You very quiet today, Izzie,' he commented. 'You freakin' out or something?' Chinese-born Louey never missed an opportunity to practice Aussie slang.

Izzie assured him she was fine and stepped out onto the foot-path. Honey-locust leaves, transparently yellow with the afternoon light, quivered like butterfly wings in a barely-there breeze.

Her birthday picnic. Brighton le Sands was the perfect setting for fun and/or romance. If anyone mentioned that this happened to be the same area Glorion lived in, she would have to act surprised. Advice from her mother rang in her memory. 'Never make it too easy for a guy you fancy, Izzie. Boys love doing the chasing.' Was holding her party in Glorion's home suburb considered chasing? She threw off the idea with a shake of her head. Rosetta's advice was just a Greek matriarch's outdated notion that teenagers of today could ignore.

She scampered towards the corner of Burwood Road and thought for the third time that day how unfair it was that the guy she liked wasn't in any way mediocre. Glorion Osterhoudt's every move literally *screamed* popularity. For admirers, this equalled the prickly prospect of competition. And could the others be blamed? Any suspicion Izzie might have had about shallowness lurking beneath an awesome façade was cancelled out when Glorion, in his role as captain of the Silver Tongues school debating team, stepped up to the podium on the library's second floor. The topic had been *The world is in need of an alternate exchange system,* and Glorion's team were arguing that money, and credit in general, had become a mouldy paradigm. He'd begun with, 'Imagine a world that rejects the wheel of suffering, a world that refuses to perpetuate war.'

Izzie approached the corner. Ahead of her was the same faceless stranger she'd glimpsed outside the newsagency window. Dark clothing. Head down. Wending around one of the trees lining the pavement. He made an abrupt turn back, leaf shadows veiling his downturned face, and hurtled towards the corner.

Izzie started. Stepped sideways.

Ker-thud!

He'd smacked against her right shoulder. Izzie teetered. The stranger flung round to glare at her. Izzie stumbled backwards.

Long black hair. Long black nails. Snarling red lips. The goth guy from the Punchbowl flats.

'Sorry,' Izzie said. But was she at fault?

The goth said nothing, just slouched forward, staring wildly with pale eyes. Izzie turned the other way and quickened her step. She could still sense his presence.

He was creeping alongside her!

She wheeled round and hurried back to the newsagency. Once at a safe distance, she peered over the magazine rack to observe him.

Louey's voice filtered across from the counter. 'I swear you freakin' out, Izzie.'

The stranger passed Louey's shop and then turned into the next street. Izzie breathed in deeply, trying to calm the fear in her chest.

Probably harmless. His clothes were normal enough: Coat, black jeans, black boots—no different to the garb of any other man wandering along the street. The neighbours had said he'd been spying on them. Could easily have been a rumour. Maybe the guy was just quirky and misunderstood. But the cruel stare and curling talons...Izzie winced and darted back onto the footpath.

At their old place, her mother had crossed paths with him in the communal laundry. She ran into the flat looking like she'd spotted the abominable snowman in the detergent cupboard and said in an overly cheerful voice, 'Next time you need to go to the laundry, honey, make sure you let me know, and I'll go there with you.'

Izzie had asked why. Her mother had murmured that the 'weird window peeper' had been in there and added that as long as they were sensible about where they went, he probably wouldn't be a bother.

'But did the guy *act* weird?' Izzie wanted to know.

'Sure did. Ah! There's my ginger cake recipe. Yeah, I got out of the laundry pretty fast. Grant was there, and he chased him away.'

Izzie asked her mother then whether anyone had any proof he looked in windows. Radical hair and nails, she felt, shouldn't automatically brand someone a burglar or a pervert. Her mother's evasive answer concerning a neighbour telling a neighbour that they thought they saw him loitering one night was no proof of guilt. 'He *might* just happen to *live* here,' Izzie said. 'He goes and washes his socks, and everyone gets their knickers in a knot.'

'Believe me, Izzie, he was acting really weird, and he shouldn't have been there. Be careful when you're outside, okay?' Rosetta was now emptying cupfuls of flour, sugar and soy milk into a mixing bowl with the zeal of someone competing in a baking race. She whirred a wooden spoon through the batter while humming a non-existent tune. The shuddery tone of her voice told Izzie that a few darker details might have gone unmentioned. From then on, Izzie made a habit of looking over her shoulder whenever she left the flat. She'd seen him skulking about twice after that.

Today, after her flit from Louey's newsagency, Izzie couldn't help feeling some of the edginess she'd felt at Punchbowl. What was the matter with the *Walk* sign? The red pedestrian light seemed intent on holding it hostage. By the time it turned green, Izzie's pace, along with her pulse, had quickened. Checking behind her every so often, she veered across to the more populated side of the street. She'd be home in another ten minutes.

She wouldn't tell her mother. Rosetta would only worry. Back when they were living in Punchbowl, Rosetta had gone all out to protect her from the suspected 'peeper': dropping her off and picking her up from school and delivering her door-to-door to friends' places. Highly embarrassing. Izzie couldn't bear a repeat of that. Moving to Burwood had meant moving to freedom.

The goth guy was nowhere to be seen. Maybe just picking up dinner at the local Thai.

Once the double-gables of the vintage home she'd grown to love came into view, Izzie raced down the footpath, hurried through her mother's garden and leapt up the three verandah steps. Sidleta sprang from the hydrangeas and followed her. She let Sidelta in, locked the door behind her and called out, 'Hi Mum.' No answer. After-work grocery shopping most likely.

She took a last look out of the sitting room window, shook off a shiver at remembering the coldness of the stranger's eyes, then sat down at the dining table to write out her new party invitations with the metallic gold texta her mother kept by the phone. Her cat looked lovingly up at her with a small soft *brrr.*

'Nice to see you too, Sidelta,' Izzie said. She'd never been so glad to get home.

XIII

Pieter tried to remember how long he'd been away from his clan. He'd been distracted by a terrible event. An elf from a neighbouring forest had been taken away to the mines. Pieter had secretly followed the gold-skins responsible and had spent a number of evenings camped outside the Grudellan Palace trying to devise a way of freeing him. Alas, when the opportunity for escape arrived, the wretch was too influenced by their powers to leave.

Which night, exactly, had this occurred? The last night he'd spent with his clan felt faded and far away. Maleika had been immersed in one of her Remembrance recollections, which she'd spoken of drowsily to Pieter's younger brother, Kloory, a being of the sky. Unlike Pieter, who spent his days trundling through thickets and paddling through streams, Kloory was quite often found hovering above trees with the birds and butterflies.

'Should have been a sylph,' Maleika would say of him when he was found once again in his preferred element.

'But my work belongs here,' he would reply. 'Although I cannot, for the life of me, let go of my other existence.' His previous incarnation had been that of a cosmic cherub.

Pieter had overheard, as he'd poured himself a cup of berry cider, some of Maleika's gabble, and he'd understood only a quarter of it, for it was spoken in star language and needed to be interpreted by one from the galaxies. This was where Kloory's help proved useful. Having lived more than one life in the Pleiades star system, Kloory understood much of their language and had managed to retain a smidgen of knowledge, despite body-king sorcerers having almost entirely cancelled out past-life remembrance.

'Ah well,' Pieter said, smiling at the recollection. 'I shall see my clan again soon I expect, but not until I find a way to lead those captives to freedom.' He found a clearing in the forest and settled down to sleep. When he arrived in the Dream Sphere's Great Hall, Alcor wasted no time in ushering him through one of three doors.

XIV

Back at Eidred's place of dwelling, where the pterodactyls had burst forth into her tower room and caused her visiting faerie godmother to flee, Eidred was consumed with terror. Her hands were shaking the way grass shivers in a gale. Concealing them under the gold satin bed cover, she willed herself to sound puzzled at being the object of suspicion at an hour such as this. 'Talking? You heard talking?'

'Don't be impertinent,' they snapped. Eidred's four minders all spoke in unison since pterodactyls shared the same mind. Their voices rang high. They rasped in a way that sent her blood cold; spat and hissed their words, forked tongues flashing from glinting beaks.

'I could not sleep, and so I recited.'

'Recited what?'

'My times-tables in readiness for the morrow.' Eidred held her breath.

'Stupid girl,' they sniped. Remarkably, they were satisfied with this answer. Without further questioning, they crackled and crunched their way through the chamber's exit and down the stone steps, their horrid squeaks and squeals lingering long after their presence.

Never failing to leave things as they weren't, the minders had scraped a jagged hole in the door, and one of the chairs they'd thrown now had a loosened leg. As neatly as she could, Eidred straightened up the furniture, if only to destroy the memory of their invasion. She folded one of her tapestries into a cushioned wad and pushed it into the door's splintered gap. The thought of awaking to witness cold, black, prying eyes peering through it was all too horrible.

Although a feeble attempt at self-protection, the tapestry filler was in some way comforting to Eidred. Knowing it was there might allow her to succumb to the vulnerability of slumber. Despite this attempt at safeguarding her sanctuary, sleep was not forthcoming.

The princess ran to her dressing-quarter at the other side of her chamber. She opened the quarter's doors, although they were more like gates than doors, with jewel-studded vertical bars. Beneath an ornate seat that one could recline in while deciding what to wear, and hidden within the lining of a small silk cushion, was the crystal that her nursery maid had given her many season-cycles earlier. The nursery maid had told Eidred, with quiet caution, of her royal naming ceremony in infancy when this crystal had been secretly placed beneath the pillow of her crib.

The stone was imbued with calming properties that comforted Eidred whenever she felt distress. Now, as she tucked the crystal beneath her pillow, a feeling of floaty peace swam through her heart.

Eidred had no sooner drifted off than she awoke to find she was clad in a gown and not the plain calico nightdress she'd donned earlier. Peculiar, certainly, yet in its own way fathomable to Eidred whose body felt lighter than ever before. She looked down at her hands. They were filmy, ghostlike. It was as though she had died and become spirit.

Eidred knew she should be afraid, and yet she felt nothing but a sense of peace. She felt in some way whole again, like a jigsaw puzzle having received the final piece.

Below and far away was a round window edged with snow. Through the window was an image of herself, and this self of Eidred's slept, golden hair fanned across the cushions of her chamber's canopied bed.

It had to be a dream. And her dream self was not within her mind, it was a separate entity, able to observe her denser body in slumber!

The gown she now wore displayed colours she had never before seen nor imagined could be real. Colours Eidred *could* recognise were those similar to the sun's fiery rays, the others watery yet metallically alive, swirling within a velveteen glow.

Here she stood by a misty lake pondering over a name, a familiar sound that had whispered to her before she'd fallen asleep earlier in the evening: the name her fleeing faerie godmother had used.

No longer was she acting out her role as daughter of the Solen, eyes closed in soft repose, wrapped in a room of moonlit hush. Now she was a being of greater significance possessing a depth of knowing. She even knew a boy was approaching and sensed the boy to be an elf.

Filling the air was a lilting tune. Low and haunting. The soft, sweet whistle of a pipe made from reed. The boy emerged from a misty wood. He paused within a sweep of speckled shadows and concluded his spellbinding melody, then greeted Eidred with a gallant bow. He meandered towards her through dawn's misty haze. Once at the lake's shore, he drew to a stop.

To Eidred, the boy was the most perfect creature she had ever seen. Lustrous brown skin, eyes as deep as the ocean, a sunburst of a smile so warm it could melt glaciers.

How old was he? His height suggested he might be perhaps five-and-ten season-cycles as Eidred was, or younger, perhaps, there being too much innocence in those eyes for the boy to have lived through fifteen world-weary years.

XV

If time were measured in elf terms, Pieter's normal appearance was that of a twelve-year-old. Alcor had made him step into his 'later self', a more mature vehicle that would create greater resonance with the person he was assigned to visit.

He observed a young lady by the lake. 'My godmother Orahney,' Pieter whispered to himself. 'The Dream Sphere dweller who prophesied my arrival upon the Earth.' Was it truly Orahney though? Pieter took in the flame-toned hues that swirled about her. These certainly were the autumn faerie's auric-field signature, the reason he recognised her in the first place. Orahney in a younger form, no more than five-and-ten season-cycles. Orahney wingless, and with fair skin and hair. Why would she take on the form of a gold-skin?

Although he wanted to greet her heartily, the elf proceeded with care. According to Alcor, the individual behind the Dream Sphere door would be disoriented. Just how far removed from reality the faerie would be was not yet known. It was Pieter's assignment, he supposed, to determine this.

'Hiyo,' he said cheerily but without any amount of familiarity.

'Oh! And who are you?' said Orahney with a sigh.

Pieter's heart sank. He hadn't realised how much he'd hoped Orahney would still remember him, a rather proud expectation for someone as insignificant as he. Pieter had only ever met his faerie godmother twice before, and only in the Dream Sphere. Orahney had been disanchored from her former life on Earth well before Pieter's time.

'I am Pieter.' The elf smiled and took Orahney's hand in his.

'I am Eidred,' said the faerie shyly. 'Princess of Grudella. My father is Solen of the Grudellan Palace.'

'Oh.' Pieter blinked and released the maiden's hand. More than appearing as such, Orahney *believed* she was a body-king daughter. Orahney coy and lacking her usual stateliness! Stranger things had happened.

Her presence reminded Pieter of waking to the whirling intonations of star language the night before his journey to the Grudellan Palace. Maleika's utterances had been thin and wavering, like the clinking of sylvan bells. Kloory's interpretation of the words had been an announcement Orahney made to Maleika and other sprites during their slumbering visit to her Dream Sphere home. Sprites were concerned body kings would make the devic race extinct. Orahney had assured them that all those of devic heritage would continue on in the future but in another genetic form. 'And Maleika,' she'd said. 'Tell my godson he must never fear any creature bearing bovine horns.' Why he should be afraid of the bulls and cows on the hillside, Pieter could not fathom. Those whose souls had originated in the Taurus constellation were dependably mild-mannered.

The faerie who now called herself Eidred turned to gaze at the lake mirroring stars amid a sparkle of moons and suns, and she appeared to marvel at the glassy reflections that smoothed its dark blue glimmer. 'The name Orahney,' she said. 'I have heard it before.' Her eyelids fluttered drowsily. 'Goodness! I'm beginning to tire. I must return to the Grudellan Palace. Can you help me, please, sir? My legs are weakening.'

Shocked, Pieter stared at the faerie, whose small frame was folding unsteadily, fluttering downward like a withering leaf.

'Orahney,' he cried. 'We are in our Dream Sphere bodies! Spirit-selves *never* grow weak! And you mustn't believe yourself to be a gold-skin. If you enter that palace you're sure to lose your heart.'

Unbelieving as the boy was of Orahney's collapse, he rushed to her aid, steadying her with his arm while she grasped at his elbow, just as a more solid being would do.

'You mustn't believe it, Orahney!'

The colour of the faerie's gown and the fiery lights around her head were dimming, dying like the twilight dies when darkness creeps into the sky.

'I see the image of a golden chamber shimmering beneath me,' Orahney said quietly. 'Ah, the chamber is mine! I am soon to wake.'

'Please stay,' said Pieter. 'Stay in the Dream Sphere a little while longer. It appears you are bewildered. If you remain here some more, I can enlighten you on who you truly are.'

Orahney nodded. 'If you so wish.'

Pieter clasped Orahney's hands, calling to Alcor to usher them from this dawn-gilded lakeside world of Orahney's choosing and into the safety of the Devic Great Hall. The power in the spell had neither enough energy nor compliance to work. The faerie was masked in something dark, a force not representative of good, and she was unwillingly deserting the Dream Sphere, much to her dismay.

It was too late to free Orahney. She was now enveloped in a cold grey bubble. A bright sickly light beamed upon her and lit up the sphere of grey in a flash of lightning. All Pieter could see was Orahney's gentle eyes clouded with fright.

Only when Orahney vanished did the door to the Devic Great Hall appear.

Pieter glared at it in frustration and shed a rueful tear.

Cruising through the outskirts of Alice Springs in his rented sports car, Matthew turned up the volume—a liberty Bernadette rarely allowed him—and punched the air with his fist. 'I'm free,' he said with a laugh.

An elderly man clutching a brown-papered bottle stepped onto the road. Matthew pulled up to let him pass. The man fell into a lethargic shuffle, then rose on tiptoe and waltzed to an inaudible rhythm, his aim of reaching the other side lost in a sea of forgetfulness.

A couple of weeks ago I would have been fuming at that, Matthew thought as the guy halted on a third-beat and wobbled to the kerb.

But something had changed since that talk in the bar with Dalesford. For some bizarre reason, aggression no longer motivated him.

The wonky pedestrian farewelled him from the roadside with a ceremonious salute. Any pangs of sympathy he might have felt for the poor pathetic stranger were promptly superseded by sparks of anticipation. Waving in return, Matthew hit the accelerator and flew towards the Stuart Highway.

Travelling to the Northern Territory might put an end to the sleepless nights he'd endured over the past month. Ever since the bat/eagle had asked him whether he planned to waste the remainder of his life, he'd been assailed by insecurities. Nothing felt right anymore: Bernadette's monotonous fashion babble, his spirit-sapping career. Days and nights had been blanched of colour. All that seemed to matter was the eagle's unanswered question.

He was looking forward to speaking with the Alice Springs author again. Not that Dalesford could solve this relentless uneasiness about the expected changes at work. Charlie had been hinting at retirement since the beginning of the year. He'd be recommending Matthew to the board of course. Providing Adam Harrow hadn't found a way to weasel his way in, Matthew could be smoothly settled in the role of trading director before the end of 2008.

He'd already promised Davo and others that he'd never let Harrow reign smugly over their team. What bugged him was his passion for the promotion had waned. Discussing the author's insights in Chapter Nine—'Success in the Modern World'—might reignite that compulsion to go for gold.

Bernadette had been angered by the notion of a weekend without him. He wished he could have told her the truth. Rather than gritting his teeth through a tumult of accusations, he'd resorted to renaming his trip 'a golf weekend'.

You're cheating on me! Bernadette's famous catch-cry. *I know you are!* The words wouldn't have been so infuriating if they'd held a skerrick of truth.

Bernadette. Dette. Mostly Matthew avoided the shortened version her friends used. Its pronunciation, no different to that of a word he despised, conjured up a superstition he'd never been able to shake. Debt must be avoided. Regardless of his robust financial situation, Matthew feared debt more than he feared death.

Since selling up all but two of his properties—and sinking much of the profit into blue-chip shares that proved excellent in their returns—the dread of being in the red had thankfully stayed under its rock. The only ownership left was the over-indulged pseudo-Georgian he lived in, probably the most frequently redecorated home in Sydney, and a Lower North Shore penthouse that made him extremely popular at the close of each calendar.

New Year's Eve: when fireworks spectators crammed sardine-style around the Harbour Bridge. His seventeenth-floor balcony with its rooftop garden was the envy of many, including his guests, most of whom had been invited by Bernadette's acquaintances. They'd gush over how 'gorgeous' the penthouse's gilded Egyptian bathroom was while raiding Matthew's bar.

To avoid all that, he'd take the family to Manhattan next time. A Crosby-esque Christmas would be novel for the kids—they'd never experienced a wintry festive season—and nothing beat the glamour of an N.Y.C. N.Y.E.

Quebec in the autumn. Paris in the spring. Dette was never happier than when they were touring Paris. More partial to the City of Light than she would ever be to the City of Angels. In Los Angeles she'd been too busy with beautification to venture from their hotel. The spa's slim-wrap had taken precedence on the day of their Disneyland trip. 'Don't forget that *I'm* on holiday too,' she'd said in a gentle voice when the girls had protested. She'd then smiled winningly and patted Matthew's back. 'You've still got Matthew going with you. Matthew isn't bored by that sort of thing.'

Venice, though, had been spectacular; quite nearly one hundred per cent. Bernadette had loved holidaying in such a romantic location for her birthday, right up until their final night. She'd refused to speak to Matthew at the ritzy restaurant they'd decided on for their final meal, owing to the fact that the famous Italian boot maker she'd arranged to see had cancelled his appointment with her.

Once dessert was over, and they were onto the espresso and mints, her gas-flame-blue eyes had snapped up to his. 'Why would a Venetian shoe designer get a cold?' She'd then hurled a teaspoon of sugar into her cup. The brown granules that hadn't made it into Bernadette's coffee were scattered across the white linen of the tablecloth, sparkling in the glow of candlelight like specks of forgotten stardust. 'Doesn't garlic cure colds? There's enough bloody garlic in this city to sink a gondolier.'

'I think you might mean gondola.'

'Gondola, gondolier. Same diff. I wish I'd known you before you swallowed that encyclopaedia.'

Harmony. At this stage of the marriage it felt like a faraway fantasy world that insisted on eluding him, but he'd sort things out eventually. No partner was perfect. Relationships had to be worked at, after all.

The wind flickered warmly through his hair. He was rocketing along an open road now, yelling along to an '80s song and soaking up the transient freedom.

A Saturday afternoon spent zooming through The Red Centre's azure and burnt-umber vibrancy minus all complicated trimmings. He was his own man today, free to do as he pleased and answerable to no-one.

'Lucetta, don't do that, sweetheart, Matthew's married,' Dalesford said.

Ignoring the white-haired man before her, Lucetta fluttered her eyelashes. She took a tentative step forward, then rested her head on Matthew's shoulder.

Not knowing what else to do, Matthew laughed. The gorgeous creature had been at his side from the time he'd arrived, her large dark eyes following his every move. Although chuffed at being the recipient of such blatant adoration, he couldn't help feeling that chewing someone's hair was a little over the top.

'Do your alpacas yield much wool?' Matthew asked as they trudged towards a weatherboard house beside a grove of palm trees.

'I just have them as pets,' Dalesford said. 'But their wool is prized. They're much better adapted to the Aussie environment than sheep are. And they don't pull the grass from the roots. Living, breathing lawn-mowers.'

'Not to mention affectionate.'

'Cuddliest grass-cutters you'll ever find.' Dalesford gestured towards his house at the other side of the paddock where a lanky red-haired kid stood. 'Here's another one of the tween-agers.'

'Granddad!' the boy called from the porch steps, 'Jannali phoned just then.'

'Is she on her way home?'

Matthew felt something ticklish on the back of his neck. Lucetta again! He turned around and shooed the docile animal back towards her herd. She skittered across to another alpaca with dark brown fleece.

The grandson called back, 'Said she's leaving now.'

'Good one!' Dalesford punched the air. 'Get everyone together then, and set up the guitar for Matt.'

Matthew blinked and turned to Conan Dalesford.

'You'd be musical wouldn't you, Matthew?' The eyes that briefly met Matthew's were direct and honest.

Matthew nodded. 'How'd you know that?'

'Just a lucky guess.' Dalesford adjusted the brim of his Akubra. 'You'd be auditory dominant, wouldn't you?'

'Auditory dominant?'

'A reliance on the hearing sense, when taking in the environment, slightly more than on the tactile or visual senses. People whose auditory sense dominates are generally smooth in speech. And very aware of the sounds around them. You speak in the modulated tones of a singer. There's no flatness in your voice. I'm willing to bet you pestered your parents for a guitar when you were young.'

Matthew grinned, shaking his head. 'Much loved fifteenth birthday present.'

'And I'll bet it didn't take you long to get a backyard band together.'

'We were convinced we'd be famous by the time we were twenty-one.'

'Weren't we all,' said Dalesford. 'Ah well, better luck next time.' Dalesford led Matthew up the porch steps. 'At being famous, that is. Well, you'll certainly be in front of crowds in the future, but not as a rock star.'

The man was respected by many for his uncannily accurate psychic predictions. A number of questions regarding when, in future years, Matthew might trade in his current career and return to law, and whether that whim of entering politics when he reached his forties would grow into a blazing ambition, were waiting patiently in his BlackBerry. Could Dalesford's casual mention of renown be a nod in the direction of political leadership?

He thought over Dalesford's theory about the senses. 'So you're saying anyone who enjoys singing is auditory dominant.'

'Not at all.' Dalesford opened the front door, and they stepped into a foyer with ceilings of pale turquoise. Out on the porch, wind chimes jangled. 'Some singers take in their environment more through their visual senses. And then there are the tactile ones, singers who tend to have a rich texture to their tone. Tactile singers' speaking voices are generally low or husky. And they look down a lot when they converse, rather than upwards or side-to-side. When we look down we become more aware of emotions. Tactile people need to *feel* what's being said.'

'Interesting theory,' Matthew said. 'Don't know whether I go along with it though.'

'And I don't know whether I *suggested* you go along with it. Anyway, it's not my own theory. It's been around for years. I'm surprised you've never heard of it. But that's only a fraction of the story. Our senses are compartmentalised these days. Becoming enlightened has a lot to do with returning to full use of them. But then, you already know my take on that. I discussed the fuller senses in my "Epiphany" chapter.'

'Chapter Twelve I think it was. Page 197.'

'Ha! Now, someone who deals with words rather than numbers finds info like that hard to remember. Probably the reason I don't work in finance.' Dalesford went to close the door, looked out of it and said, 'Where's Lucetta now? Ah, back at Edward's side. Soulmates for sure. On the subject of books...' He strolled to a cabinet at one side of the foyer, opened one of its glass doors and produced something antiquated. The book he held had a faded cover, red and plain. 'I named Edward after the author of this tale. Do you know of it?'

The gilded title, typical of novels published a hundred years ago, read: *Our True Ancient History.* The author's name sounded terribly British: Reverend Edward Lillibridge. 'Nope,' said Matthew. 'Never heard of it.'

'Funny that.' Dalesford squinted at Matthew as though he didn't quite believe him. 'Ah well. It's been pretty obscure throughout the twentieth century. And now that we're nearly a decade into the new millennium...but never mind, you'll connect with it when you need to.'

Why would he need to connect with a novel published before the advent of racy spy thrillers? Matthew was rarely interested in fiction. Least of all old fiction.

Dalesford did not expand on this. 'Anyway, come through to the living room and we'll get this party started. I actually forgot to tell Jannali you're staying.' He'd pronounced the name Jan-*nal*-ee.

'Forgot?'

'I've always been a bit vague, I'm afraid.'

'Not a problem. I'll book into a hotel. Don't want to just land on the two of you.'

'You'll do nothing of the sort. Jannali loves having guests, especially surprise guests.'

Within minutes Matthew found himself hooked to an amplifier and strumming a Gibson Slash—the Rolls Royce of electric guitars—along with four of his host's grandkids, and rehearsing a Torres Strait Islander birthday song while Dalesford went ballistic on bongos.

Dalesford's wife, Jannali, whose birthday it was, would be home any second. The windowed doors at the side of Dalesford's makeshift studio opened out to a courtyard shaded by mango trees. Beyond rolled a rambling panorama in varied tones of green, a refreshing contrast to the slick, greyed-out orderliness of Martin Place. Getting nudged and nuzzled by an undersized llama, and belting out the words to the homeland ceremonial song of someone he'd never met, hadn't been on Matthew's agenda. Additional questions about *Thoughts on Tomorrow's Tycoon War* were listed in his BlackBerry alongside those personal queries about where his life was heading. Their conversation, however, had only surrounded the farm and the grandkids, and the only mention of any book had been that casual reference to the unexceptional relic on Dalesford's shelf. Not that Matthew was complaining. There were few things he loved more than jamming.

'She's here,' shrilled one of Dalesford's granddaughters, a golden-haired munchkin no older than five.

'Okay, guys,' Dalesford shouted. 'Hit it!'

Embarrassed by Dalesford's old-school attempts at coolness, Matthew kept up in 'G' as young Brantley had recommended, and hummed along in harmony with the kids' unfamiliar lyrics.

Through the door whirled a portly woman with glowing eyes and a face that emanated joy. She danced, stamped and clapped her way up to the inexpert band, her dress in its ice-cream shades of pineapple and vanilla swishing in accordance with the *boom-ker-boom* of Dalesford's bongos.

When the song ended, she placed her hands on her hips and said, beaming, 'I thought I told you guys I've finished with birthdays.'

'We weren't listening, babe,' said Dalesford.

'And who's this good looker over here?'

Matthew turned. No-one behind him.

'You, darlin',' said Jannali. 'I'm talking about *you.*'

'He's Matthew,' called one of the smaller grandsons. 'Granddad invited him over.'

'The hotshot merchant banker from Sydney, sweetheart,' said Dalesford.

Matthew stepped forward. 'I'm really sorry to intrude like this on your birthday.' He reached out to shake Jannali's hand. 'If I'd known,

I would have...' The guitar swung with him and clunked against the nearby table.

'Don't apologise,' Jannali boomed. She stepped forward and looped her arm through Matthew's. 'You happen to be the best present I could wish for. It's not often my husband gives me a *handsome man* for my birthday!'

To mask his awkwardness, Matthew laughed.

'You're mistaken, love,' Dalesford said. 'He's only on loan.'

Still clutching Matthew's arm possessively, Jannali sidestepped closer. She frowned up at Matthew before bursting into chuckles that proved to be contagious. 'I certainly hope you're staying for lunch,' she said. 'Auntie's donated a super-sized Pavlova, and we won't get through it all ourselves.'

'Um...'

'Brantley!' she commanded. 'Set an extra place at the table, then come back and do some more jamming.' She took a seat beside her husband at the drums. 'Okay, guys,' she said. 'What are we playing now?'

XVI

Pieter's previous Dream Sphere memory was unclear. It came to him every so often in glimpses of the autumn faerie calling to him for help and referring to herself as a princess.

He was on the hill tonight with his water-sprite siblings, Zhippe and Carlonn, two orphans under his mother's care. The three were somersaulting high above the tree-tops, then zooming to the ground in bundles of chortles.

The sweet smell of night breeze on clover permeated the air. For these children, evenings were spent revelling in movement and laughter. Even guardian devas such as Maleika, although able to harness greater calm, never lost that sense of play as they matured.

The water sprites, or undines as they were known, were both adoring and adorable little people. Zhippe and Carlonn's sea-sprite parents had passed on to the Dream Sphere many season-cycles earlier after having been stolen away and robbed of their heart radiance by body king troopers. The twin orphans frequently reminisced about their coral-garden playground beneath the ocean, and often told the other Brumlynds detailed and lively stories about sprites who had shared their environment: a beach east of the Grudellan Palace with powdery lilac sand. A storm had swept them into one of Elysium's rivers but they'd since been embraced by the Brumlynd clan and thereafter enjoyed residing in Elysium Glades alongside Maleika, Pieter, Kloory and Croydee.

Zhippe, the one at Pieter's left who was scaling the elm tree, had a large head and long autumn-toned hair, which stuck out in fluffy spears. Bony features, softened by a permanent dimply smile, made up Zhippe's jovial face.

Carlonn was greener and daintier. Lichen grew from Carlonn's wrists, and hair like moss floated around the creature's shoulders. The eyes, like Zhippe's, were a curious black with golden glints. Carlonn would bound like a playful tiger cub when on land, but once submerged in water, resembled a gliding fish.

The gender of these creatures was not important since they lived not for reproduction but for keeping strong the river's life-force. Their nurturing senses of the female and protective senses of the male were not expressed from within them, instead, transferred directly into the water so that the river would not evaporate. Evaporation meant the undines' home would be gobbled up by air sprites: sylphs, who were converted to the body kings' vengeful ways. This had begun the creation of drought, a terrible ailment to inflict on such an essentially moist planet.

The three were chatting with the rabbits who had emerged from their burrows. Shy ones were Elysium rabbits, impeccably polite too. Getting them to say anything louder than a whisper took quite a lot of coaxing.

A fledgeling mother was anxious about the plight of her firstborn. Carlonn offered to search the entire river bank, and the mother rabbit agreed that this might be best, for she hadn't seen Fripso all day.

Pieter searched the high road above the dell with Zhippe. He had an awful inkling that Fripso may not be returning, but refused to give the thought entry to his emotions. Vexations such as fear and heartache, all newcomers to this world, having been introduced by the chaos-hungry body kings, were not entertained if it could be helped. Weeping, cowering and lamenting was frowned upon by Clan

Watchers. It only perpetuated the gold-skin notion that all should suffer.

Zhippe supposed the young bunny had explored the higher hills, having been born under the pioneering sign of the mountain goat, and Pieter agreed that this was a sound suggestion. They headed for the foothills where the sheep grazed. Fleeces like scallop-edged clouds studded a mountaintop blackened by night. The ewes, rams and lambs were similarly concerned. The bleats they sent out to relatives on neighbouring hills were answered with, 'Naught discovered, we are sorry to say.'

The rabbits searched their hill again, careful to avoid the burrows on the western side, which now belonged mostly to weasels. Since their contact with sorcerers, weasels were no longer amiable

Though they weren't entirely converted to the rogue doctrine, their clan leaders were considering such. To do so would turn them very nasty indeed, a great change from their gentle, almost cow-like natures. Earlier on they had been friends to everyone, most of all to the rabbits, yet now suspicion corrupted their eyes and their heart chakras were miserably clouded over.

The three found nothing and returned to Karee wishing they had. Fripso's mother sighed and bade them farewell. She would send Fripso around, she said, to show his appreciation when he was found. She'd then added bravely that she would insist he explain to them where he had gone. And then they would all laugh together over berry cider and sing a gratitude song or two.

The undines were looking forward to the refreshment of the river. Pieter was intent on searching some more. Waving goodbye, Zhippe and Carlonn somersaulted over the bank and did a crazed little jig in the shallows.

Pieter smiled at their silliness. He knew he should return to his dwelling. He had not been back for many a night, and on this partic-ular evening, he'd been seized by a sense of urgency, fearing Fripso had been taken by a gold-skin. Hadn't he, himself, been visited by a gold-skin disguised as an eagle? Could the eagle apparition have gone to Fripso after Pieter had sent it on its way? He must trek to the Grudellan Palace in search of the poor creature.

Dawn was soon to arrive. Pieter's search through Elysium Glades for Karee's son had been in vain. He found a clearing under a filigree tree and laid himself down, his concerns for both a missing rabbit and deceptive eagle apparition soon to be dissolved in slumber. 'I am no doubt attempting to visit my clan in the Dream Sphere,' he told himself. 'But without the aid of Remembrance Essence I will never know, and the undines won't see Maleika till after their ocean sojourn.'

The radial spokes of cobwebs in each tree branch, snowflake-intricate symbols, gleamed sedately while altering from silver to gold.

The forest's night world was growing lighter. Inhabitants, all, were lost to a better existence.

XVII

Certain Fripso was imprisoned by the gold-skins, Pieter trekked to the edge of the forest to observe their gilded residence.

He passed through a cavern, drab in contrast to the rest of Elysium due to a dark emptiness that reeked of decay, and emerged at the edge of a thicket of poisonous thorns, which enclosed and concealed the body king palace.

Pieter had almost reached the spires of gold when he heard a crackle of twigs. Expecting to see a squirrel or a goblin even, he turned, only to witness a fleeting shadow; graceful, like the shadow of a deer, although not of faunal origin. The girl, whose shadow it was, stepped further into the thicket.

'Oi!' yelled Pieter. 'Who are you, if I might ask?'

The slight figure turned. Because of the darkness, Pieter could not discern her colours, seeing only flowing tresses and rather large, startled eyes. 'Like a deer, but not a deer,' he whispered to himself.

'Who spoke?' said the girl. She stepped through a moonbeam, and Pieter saw then that her colours were golden. A cascade of yellow-gold hair, bright as the sun, and skin that gleamed golden as well. A body-king maiden. One of the others.

Take caution, Pieter, the elf warned himself.

'I apologise for startling you,' he said impatiently. The apology, he knew, was a useless thing. Gold-skins could not communicate with sprites without the aid of sprite-seeing garments and court witches, terrifying sorceresses who dwelt in black pyramids in the palace grounds.

Naturally hearing nothing, the girl continued on her way. Pieter followed her noisily—twigs snapping beneath his feet, leaves crumpling angrily—yet not once did the golden girl turn. Instead, she waltzed onwards, a basket of berries swinging in one hand, stooping to look at toadstools or to peer in rabbit burrows, then continuing on while Pieter scuttled behind.

It was then that Pieter glimpsed the gold-skin fully. She had seated herself on a mossy fallen tree trunk to rest and drink from the stream. Subtly as ever he could, Pieter observed her through the bracken, only to encounter a pang of familiarity.

Yesterday's visit to the Dream Sphere had been unclear to him, yet now he remembered losing Orahney, seeing her sabotaged by greyness. She had visited him in a different form; had looked exactly like the girl by the stream. If it hadn't been for her aura's colours, Pieter would not have recognised the faerie. Now, as he looked upon this child of perpetrators, he couldn't help feeling sorry for her, if only for her birthright and ugly colouring, for in these times fair hair and lightly tanned complexions were considered frightening to those of greater souls.

To Pieter, however, it was more than a sense of sympathy that crossed him—it was a feeling of attachment. Of knowing, although he didn't quite understand what it was that he knew. Despite Orahney and the girl being entirely different in physical appearance, Pieter now noticed a similarity. Was it the hair?

Orahney's hair was far from golden of course. Mostly it shone mulberry, but at sunrise, it grew almost like that of the body kings. The Brumlynds had often laughed and told the Dream Sphere dweller she frightened them when the sun lightened her tresses. She'd made a turban of sorts, from lunarised birch leaves, so as not to scare them, and they all teasingly referred to this headdress as 'camouflage' for her other 'more sinister' side.

Why then had Pieter, in his last visit to the Dream Sphere, heard Orahney refer to herself as a princess? How could she ever assume herself to be such a horrific creature? To see a deva whose numerous kindness merits had elevated her to Watcher of an autumn sprite clan descend into that sort of confusion was disheartening indeed. She may as well have been a leopard determined to dwell in an ant nest.

'I know she does not see me,' Pieter said of the gold-skin, with a satisfied grin, then said even louder to prove his point, 'Those eyes rarely witness the goings on of sprites.'

A look of astonishment crossed the girl's face. 'Who said that?' she said.

Pieter started and stepped back.

'Who is talking? Please do not mock me. I am afeared. Please step forward and introduce yourself. I mean you no harm.'

Just as wary as the girl who had spoken to him, Pieter crept out from the bracken. The girl blinked her wide blue eyes. Surely she couldn't see him!

'I am sorry to frighten you, lady,' said Pieter, 'for it was not my intention. Is it true you can not only hear me but see me as well?'

The girl gasped. 'Of course! You're a faerie! Oh my goodness.'

'An elf,' Pieter corrected.

'I beg your pardon. An elf. This seems to me to be no coincidence. I had a faerie godmother visit me only two nights ago, but she vanished before I got my wish. Have you come to grant my wish instead?'

So typical of these creatures, Pieter thought. Full of self-serving values. Still, I shall try to remain understanding.

Aloud, he said, 'In actuality, no. It is not to my knowledge that any sprite grants wishes. Are you certain you heard correctly on this matter?'

'I read it in *The Book of Rightitude*,' said the girl, now obviously impatient with Pieter for not arriving in the guise of a faerie godmother. 'It says if someone like me, who has proper lineage, happens to capture a creature such as yourself, I may use its power to make real my wishes. It is the law. It is fact. Even so, I am not permitted to associate with the likes of you, elf, so I had better be on my way. Good evening.'

'Sorry to be of no use to you,' Pieter said, and there was more than a hint of sarcasm in his tone. How could she hope to capture him when he was taller than her? Younger perhaps—he was probably her junior by two or three season-cycles. Far less juvenile though.

He covered himself with a cloud of temporary invisibility—even the palace's eagles circling the thorn thicket did not see him—and ran on after the hoity-toity maiden. He was determined to find out who she was and why she could access a sprite with her vision. Very few of that type had any awareness of devic peoples. They could not even sense sprites, yet would dream up wrongful stories about them. Sprites never knew these days when they were being spied upon, or tricked into confiding in a body-king magician.

What an unusual creature, thought Pieter as he stole after the body-king daughter through gilded gates held open by winged guards.

Something here was not as it seemed.

The hush of darkness enveloped Pieter. The golden girl sprang up lamp lit steps where stone gargoyles threatened the entrance.

Guided by gleaming hair that shone like a beacon in the artificial light, Pieter followed the girl inside, into the cold, dark, fear-ridden palace; saw the hideous pterodactyls clawing at their food, and crept like a lamb behind her. A lamb in the shadow of lions.

Chapter Six

Matthew stepped out to his car amid a cacophony of hoots and excited farewell squeals from the kids and Jannali on the porch.

'Call me, son, if you need to,' Conan Dalesford said.

Matthew assured him he would. Jannali Dalesford had insisted he stay over. He still had those questions on the BlackBerry to ask. He hadn't got round to them, but who cared? Encountering the hospitable Dalesfords, their eclectic collection of musical instruments and their smoochy alpacas had exceeded his expectations and yet hadn't involved alcohol. A good time in Sydney usually meant celebrating a win with his colleagues at the bar with the fancy lampshades, congregating at the arched windows to laugh and guzzle liquid-stupidity before trundling across to the taxi rank.

'Your loving wife'll be happy to have her man back,' Jannali said when she hugged him goodbye.

'Let's not forget the children. They'll be pleased to see their dad again,' Dalesford said. 'There are two, aren't there?'

'Stepchildren,' Matthew corrected. About to say they wouldn't have missed him, he hesitated. No point in attempting to make others understand his home situation.

He shook hands with the author, climbed into his rental car and sailed towards the property gate, Jannali's well-meaning words circling in his mind.

'Gimme!' Doctor Cyanide shrieked from the radio. 'More! More. More. *Moooo-wah*!'

'Aargh.' Matthew thumped his fist on the steering wheel. 'Not you again.' An additional reason for hating Cyanide's music was the image it threw up of Adam Harrow at a microphone stand. Work's annual social club concerts were embarrassingly bad. Never intended to be good, of course, but comedy could so easily descend into blather.

The task of impersonating a famous musician had become a steadfast tradition among many of Sydney's investment bankers. If it hadn't been for the proceeds going to a good cause, Matthew would never have taken part, but he believed The Royal Children's Hospital to be more than deserving. Bringing along his guitar each year, and a pair of fake sideburns, was a hassle. Burdened by the knowledge that his act would do Don McLean a terrible injustice, he'd sing about the Chevy and the levee, and Jack being nimble and all that. Harrow was invariably first on stage, giving voice to his grasping conceit, stabbing an accusing finger at the admin team and screeching the lyrics to 'Gimme'.

Matthew reached the airport at sunset when the sky was vacillating between rose and gold. Hunger gnawed at him. He strolled around the restaurant section, searching for something more appetising than plane food: hardly a challenging task.

He checked his Rolex. Not enough time for an a-la-carte dinner at a local restaurant. He'd have to grab a simple main from the airport bistro.

Chicken Kiev beckoned, but he couldn't go past a burger. The one served to Table Four overflowed with fillings and was huddled against fat golden chips.

Did he really want beef though? Or even chicken or pork or lamb? The meal Conan Dalesford prepared at lunch had been a meat-free barbecue of all things: organically grown herb-dusted veggies, char-grilled and basted with garlic. The thought of it tickled his tastebuds. A dinner of stuffed mushrooms, spicy pumpkin patties, zucchini fritters...

When he'd asked Dalesford the reason he'd given up meat he'd said cryptically, 'Something to do with a guy comparing a lamb to a puppy.' Later he'd elaborated, and the story he related had been a thought-provoking one, both tragic and inspiring, the moral of which Matthew would never forget.

In the queue, he found himself eye-to-eye with the back of an autograph-plastered baseball cap. Its wearer had a restless head. Each time Matthew attempted to read any of the signatures, the cap swivelled frustratingly.

'Ahem!'

A freckled hand held a plate of food out to him. 'You want this?' A big bloke in an Akubra was offering him the meal he'd been eyeing.

Keen to accept, Matthew thought it prudent to check why anyone would give their meal away.

'Asked for a beef burger and they gave me a veggie one by mistake. Not into eating green stuff.'

No suspicion of Windex, fly spray, spittle or staleness, just a gift, an actualised desire of a meatless meal, minus the wait-time. 'Thanks for that. How much do I owe you?'

'Nothing,' barked the benefactor but Matthew was already scanning the overhead menu and reaching for twenty-two-fifty in his wallet.

'Nothing I said!' The bloke bristled. 'Take it or leave it, mate.' He shook his head in disdain and strolled away.

A small reunion was going on outside the bistro, a guy greeting his wife and young sons. The mother and boys were obviously freshly alighted from a U.S. vacation—each had donned Mickey Mouse ears for a snapshot. This image of jet-lagged domestic bliss, a mum acknowledging a trip to that famous fun park with an affectionate arm around each child, prompted for the second time that weekend a recollection of the Disneyland day trip. The memory of how he'd felt about Bernadette returned to him.

She was descending the hotel stairs to the hotel's spa while her youngest held Matthew's hand and howled. 'Bernadette...' he'd said in exasperation.

'Don't cry, Laura sweetie,' she'd called over her shoulder, voice marshmallow soft. 'You have to understand that Mummy needs some "me" time. If Mummy doesn't have that fluid-reduction slim-wrap, her clothes will look silly on her.'

Matthew had told Bernadette they'd wait. Went to call the travel agent to arrange a later tour, but she'd been looking forward to the detoxifying properties of Tahitian clays ever since she'd read about them in the brochure. So Matthew and the girls had visited the magical kingdom without her...and without her getting to hear her daughters' giggles when they'd been whirled around in the Mad Hatter's stop-start teacups.

Resisting the urge to wallow in resentment, Matthew shook away his residual bugbears and reminded himself that a conflict-free life had to be earned. Dalesford had earned himself a tranquil existence by living off the land. Escaped 'corporate tyranny' as he called it, long ago. Worked for himself, and from then on out, money had miraculously flowed.

From the airport lounge, Matthew observed the stars beyond the tarmac. Roddie at work was right. They did resemble icicles this far inland. Translucent like crystal. Spiky white purity. Sharply edged and brimming with sparkle.

Shortly before his plane touched down in Sydney, after viewing his problems from a perspective he hadn't ever adopted before–from a place of peaceful insight–a realisation struck him. He sat forward with a jolt. The guy next to him spun round. Matthew sank back into his seat. The guy went back to his airport novel.

'They're all answered,' he said under his breath.

Without knowing anything about the BlackBerry list, Conan Dalesford had illustrated, by example, each of the answers Matthew had sought.

Within the arabesque splendour of a palatial walk-in wardrobe her husband called 'Aladdin's Cave', Dette riffled through her autumn frocks. *An actress,* he'd said when he'd taken her to Chavelle's. *You'd make a brilliant actress.*

'It's exhausting,' she'd told him. 'I get so tired of playing all these different roles.' Wife. Lover. Mother. Friend. Guarding everyone's secrets, including her own. Being married to Matthew should have been cosier than this, but those initial feelings of safeness had slipped from her grasp. And Diondra was always heaping guilt on her, telling her she should think herself lucky. She'd said, when Dette had called in last Saturday, 'You found yourself the best kind of man,' while gazing out at her lavish garden in glum resignation where Dominic, red and flustered, was inexpertly wielding the pool net. Diondra was right. Matthew certainly had some endearing qualities. Even-tempered...nice-looking, and Dette was most of the time able to overlook his mid-brown mildness, even though it excluded him from dark and mysterious or golden Apollo definitions.

The fuchsia dress. She'd wear her fuchsia dress into the city this afternoon. Having always favoured feminine colours, she was forever grateful for pinks, but whether to accessorise today with gold or with silver had become the next dilemma.

Clutching the dress, she briskly exited the haven that housed her clothes and reviewed her diary on the dresser. Today was important. She was to book herself tickets and accommodation for that Vanuatu trip. The nanny she planned to hire would have to be older than Matthew and plain. The trip was to be early May. The childcare agency would need to organise interviews with Dette by the end of March. So much for that notice she'd placed in the *Inner-West Times*. Only one response!

Today she'd lunch at Raffaello's in Phillip Street and then she'd embark on a search for swimsuits, new pairs of sunnies, lingerie sets, flirty accessories and half-a-dozen paler lipsticks to see her through Vanuatu's dazzling golden days and sultry nights.

Pilates at ten. Mani and pedi, a quarter past four. If she were lucky, she'd get to purchase everything she wanted in those few precious hours in between.

XVIII

Pieter was now standing opposite a door within the palace. Flickers of gold and red—garish hues of hair and gown—disappeared behind it. The maiden had gone to her retreat and Pieter was foolishly sheltering in the dark nook of a cold, forbidding castle.

She was speaking to someone in silvery tones, but Pieter could not discern her words.

'Wait!' Pieter whispered to himself. 'This part of the door has been damaged.' Although achingly aware of the scurrilousness of eavesdropping, he was compelled to glean all he could from the conversation she had begun. Mentions of his rabbit friend's whereabouts might suddenly emerge.

'I suspect I met an elf this evening,' she was saying in a quavering voice. 'He didn't seem to want to grant me my wish. For all I know he might have been rather dangerous, perhaps not of fey origin after all.' With whom might she be speaking? The maiden gabbled on with hardly a pause and there came no response from her listener. For Fripso's sake, he must observe. Just one glimpse, to see who it was.

A piece of cloth, a tapestry in fact, had been stuffed into the door's damage, but over and above a corner of this, the elf could see the golden girl kneeling and facing a shelf by the window. Beside the shelf was a closed-in basket, which, against the room's gilded starkness, appeared comparatively decorative in its lattice patterning. Painted upon this basket was a scowling circular face framed in radiating beams, which Pieter mistook for a personified daisy, but recognised it soon after to be a grumpy depiction of Sol. Was this what body kings practised when locked away in their palace during Pieter's slumbering hours? The worship of sun faces on baskets? He knew they were reputed to adore a number of inanimate objects that represented the searing circle in the sky: stone sculptures, totem poles, flat pebbles of gold from the mines, referred to as *coins*, stamped with a likeness of the god they worshipped in profile and circulated obsessively to nurture inflated importance.

'Ah well, shining friend,' the girl whispered. 'I bid you a wonderful slumber. I too must sleep.'

The face continued to regard her with mute disapproval.

Drawing away from the door, Pieter smiled, touched at the simple kindness that had sweetened the girls' speech. He was sure he could never talk to a painted construction of cane this pleasantly.

Diagonal light was permeating the luminous French windows of Dette's bathroom. She hung her fuchsia dress and fresh undergarments on the door's brass hook and navigated her way through steaming clouds toward her Jacuzzi, a frothy cauldron laced with the heady scents of Shady Lady Supremely Sensuous Bathing Emollient.

She turned off the tall golden taps and sighed. She would probably feel better if she wept, but tears didn't come easily these days.
She'd grown tougher out of necessity. Easier to be angry than sad
anyway, although when it came to him, despite his infuriating ways
that spun her into rages she could never control, a cold and watery
desperation hid behind her got-it-all-together façade. Four days! He
hadn't spoken to her in four whole days.

'I can't give you a hundred per cent,' he'd told her last Tuesday.
'But I'm here for you. Remember that.' Those words spoke volumes.
They told Dette she couldn't quite reach a corner of his heart that
should only have been reserved for her. Failed ownership of
something she valued. If it were something tangible, she would have
given every cent she had, but the lack of admiration in those green
eyes of his continually mocked her passionate declarations.

Perching on the edge of the heart-shaped Jacuzzi, Dette waved
her fingers beneath the bubbles, rainbow-winking splodges exuding
the florally citrus notes of ylang-ylang, lime and hyacinth. The water
was still a bit hot. If she cut out and pinned Sara's needlework
assignment, the temperature would be perfect when she returned.

In her sewing room, she flicked on the rhythms of Boyd Levanzi,
the hot hip-hopper everyone—including her ladies' tennis group—was
listening to, fastened the tissue-paper pattern in several swift moves,
and steered the scissors through the length of pale pink chiffon that
Sara had chosen for her summer blouse.

'No-one will know you ran out of time,' she'd told her eldest with
a secret smile. Helping with this kind of homework was easy. Dette
had been an ace at sewing throughout school—she'd had no other
choice! How else could she have dressed as prettily as she had when
the people who raised her were such awful misers? And even though
Sara was much better off materially, the style-conscious teen had been
previously unkempt; had only in the past year learnt to appreciate the
art of garment creation.

Dette's youngest, on the other hand, was already a fashionista,
and she hadn't even started first grade. When they'd shopped at the
haberdashery on Thursday evening, little Laura had marvelled at the
many and varied textiles in a series of overjoyed shrieks. 'This one,

Sara,' she'd squeaked, after running across to point out a luxuriantly textured but highly inappropriate synthetic.

Sara had rolled her eyes. 'Are you on drugs?' she said to the six-year-old. 'Why would I want a summer top made of grey faux fur?'

'You'd look like Izzie's cat,' Laura had explained.

'Exactly.'

'And Izzie's cat is bee-yoo-tiful! Why don't you buy it, Sarie?'

'Now, who's Izzie, again?' Dette had asked. 'Remind me, girls,' and Sara had told her she was the friend whose mother had encountered that weirdo in Grant's outdoor laundry.

'But they've moved,' Laura said. 'So we don't see them at Dad's flats anymore.'

Dette rounded the pattern's corner with a single fierce snip. Always burdened. Always worrying about *him*. Why was he so enamoured with 'funny' females? Why was pointless banter so attractive to men?

She shook her head in annoyance, huffed out a sigh and rolled her eyes to the amber ceiling, a shade she found pleasing when she'd first had it painted. 'You *still* haven't booked Dan to re-do it,' she chided herself. This was the third time she'd resolved to phone the interior designer. Metallic sheens were a sharper look this year. Petulant Peach on the sample card looked promising, but then so did Turnabout Teal.

Dette placed the sleeves on one side of her sewing table and slipped the scissors through the chiffon once more.

She'd ask Dan, while he was there, about the ceilings in the bedroom and robes. It wouldn't take much to talk her into something more upbeat—easily earned cash for Dan. Given a nudge, she'd embrace the challenge of livening up its appeal.

Two pins dropped from the table. Disgruntled by this, she knelt and patted the floor. Here was one of them, but where was the other? Where had it *fracking* gone?

Mulling over her ceilings again, and the overall colour scheme, Dette groaned. The choices she'd made six months back were now too dull for her liking. Too uninspiring. Too yesterday. Michelle was already getting into the creams and sparklies on offer in furnishings. So was Diondra.

Dette knew Matthew enjoyed the luxurious haven she provided for him. After the bright lights of a sterile trading floor, their three-storey, square-topped, beige-clad home, elegant and the epitome of class with its subdued lamp lit ambience and enterprising décor, was quite obviously somewhere he was able to relax in style. The problem with Matthew was he wanted everything to stay the same. She was better off sticking to accessorising for now. He'd agree to the new lounge suite idea soon enough. She'd bloody-well make sure of that.

The renegade pin would be lost forever once Rhoda vacuumed. Well then! It could stay where it liked. 'I don't have time for this,' Dette muttered. She rose to her feet. She'd have to finish up after the yoke was done. Her bath was getting cold, and she wanted to get moving.

Dette slid her scissors noisily through the fabric, her thoughts liquefying into anguish. Why hadn't she worked on her sense of humour from the time she was young? *Snip! Snip!* That recent admission of his, about admiring comediennes and upbeat women in general, *Snip! Snip! Snip!* had irked Dette, *Snip!* largely because she'd spent year after year attempting to follow her great-uncle's adamant advice, and now, through sheer necessity, she was forced to emulate a behaviour she loathed. 'You must be pretty and amusing, but never a jokester,' her great-uncle had insisted. 'Leave jokey-pokey to women of the lower classes.' No-one ever argued with the magnanimous Colonel Doulton. He was arrogant of course, but he had a right to be: he'd been born of good stock! His fondest childhood memories had been playing hide-and-seek in Langton Castle, his uncle's sprawlingly impressive Welsh estate, and playing Gin Rummy in a supposedly haunted garden grotto with the children of European royalty.

Dette packed the cut-out pattern pieces away and descended the stairs to the bathroom, planning her necessary transformation into slapstick femme fatale. She would need to make herself thoroughly irresistible with an alluring new winter wardrobe, and she'd visit the salon for eyelash extensions that were a teensy bit thicker, to give her an air of exotic mystery. Blue-black perhaps, rather than the tentative brown-black she'd had with her first lot. Tina at Luscious had mentioned two appointments ago that the blue-black was significantly more glamorous.

And she'd force herself to be extra attentive to his needs. No more arguing. He would get to see the better side of her nature. The sweeter, more pliable Dette. The Dette who was going to spoil him like crazy in her determination to become one of his obsessions.

In the bathroom, she paused a second to consult the mirror. A wisp had managed to escape from her showercap. She pushed it under the elastic, pondering over the possibility of going copper for winter. The new season's light reds were gaining steadily in popularity. While Ronaldo told her the combination he mixed up—of Butterscotch, Straw and Platinum Pearl—was still in keeping with the latest 1960s look, especially if worn teased and teamed with hoop earrings, she was fearful the sun-kissed image would wane without warning, that she would risk looking outdated if she didn't act fast.

Once submerged in her bubble bath, Dette snatched up her bathroom mobile and phoned her ex, greeting him with a no-nonsense: 'How could you let your daughters down like that? I have to find a babysitter now.'

'And that superhero of a husband of yours can't look after them while you're away?'

'Matthew's refusing. Insists I pay someone to supervise them. I can't believe you. How could you just—'

'I'll call you back.'

Dette's voice grew to a roar. 'You will not! Explain why—'

But Grant had meant business. The phone call dissolved in Dette's ear.

Diondra Wallace called a few minutes later to gloat about Dominic's entry into the Real Estate Business of the Year Awards.

Pleased to have the phone free again once Diondra's smug monologue had ended, Dette called her cousin, a single parent living in one of the seedier parts of Sydney. 'How would you like to make an easy five hundred during the school hols?'

'Are you serious?'

Of course Dette was serious. She needed someone to cover. An alibi to make her look more virtuous than she really was.

'It's Bernadette, is it?' droned the voice on the other line. The voice became animated. 'Gawd! What are *you* doing ringing *me?* Can't imagine it'd be for a social chat.'

'You're kind of right about that. Not that I wouldn't love to catch up, but I'm in a little bit of a hurry at the moment.' Dette reclined against the Jacuzzi's waterproof pillow. 'Just wanted to ask you a quick five-hundred-dollar question.'

'Wait a minute...don't tell me, you're doing market research. Matt's lost his millions, and you've turned to telemarketing.'

'I won't tell you that, because it's not the case. Sorry to disappoint.'

'Bernie Weissler! Well, well! When was the last time the two of us caught up?'

Angry the conversation was going nowhere fast, Dette employed a decisive tone. 'Probably at Nan and Pop's diamond anniversary three or four months ago.'

'Didn't go to that. Jackson was sick with an ear infection.'

'Should've got a babysitter. You missed a great get-together.'

'Jackson was *sick*. And strangely, Bernadette, even if he hadn't been, my pay cheque wouldn't have stretched that far! Babysitters to me might as well be pixies living on Mars.'

'Not anymore.' Dette scooped up a handful of foam and blew on the compacted bubbles. They puffed outwards and drifted back into the water in irregular gleaming fragments. 'I've got a feeling you'll soon find they do exist. Five hundred might get you a few evenings out minus the kids don't you think?'

A sigh and sniff on the other line hinted at late nights, early mornings, a severe case of survival stress and a run-down constitution. 'Bernie, Bernie, Bernie,' she scolded. 'What are you up to *now?*

XIX

In the depths of the royal residence was a silence so eerie that Pieter almost felt fearful. At eventide the forest became lively. Inside the Grudellan Palace, a heavy gloom tainted nightfall.

Where the golden girl's chamber lay was a chill that evoked Arctic fog.

It was little wonder these people vacated their solid selves, in this uninspiring patch of time, to visit a realm more radiant. And yet, did they go anywhere other than the Nightmare Realms in their slumber? Pieter was vexed by this question as he watched, from behind the scowling sun basket, the sleeping body-king daughter.

Also unsettling him was the notion of having trespassed, of having followed a maiden into her home and of now observing her living quarters without permission during her private hours of sleep. When he'd stood outside the chamber door earlier he'd heard rabbitish snuffles and wondered whether this might be the sound of Fripso snoring. He'd discontinued weighing up whether tiptoeing into the maiden's chamber was wrong once his beauty-creation powers allowed him to walk, invisibly, through a wall. If his intentions for doing so had been anything but noble, his kindness-fuelled magic would have refused to manifest. He would be careful not to disturb the slumberer. He would promptly retreat once he found the source of his search.

While doing his best to adjust to the suffocating darkness, the elf thought about his clan and found himself missing the other Brumlynds. True, Maleika had said to feel blue, grey or black must be resisted at every opportunity, and although pain was rarely welcome in a sprite's emotional sphere, Pieter could not deny he felt it in a fluttering, greater than insignificant amount.

It was then that he heard the screams, crystal-sharp shrieks that made the room he was cringing in even colder. 'Nay! Nay,' the voice cried. 'Dream Sphere ancestors, I pray that you help me!'

Unable to resist rushing to the window and yet dreading what might be perceived, Pieter found himself at the arched stone vista—as if ushered there by invisible wings—staring out to an empty square courtyard where the shadows stretched menacingly across tiles of bronze and copper. Who had been calling out? Who was in peril? He looked up, not knowing what he was expecting to see. All that greeted him was a charcoal wash of sky and one lone meteorite, for its brothers were misted over by a cloud that hung above the Grudellan Palace.

The sky in this part of Elysium, masked and muted by the palace's artificial luminaries, was alien to the forest's sky. There, after waking from the Dream Sphere, Pieter had only to look upwards to feel refreshed by the heavenward magic. Above the deliciously ethereal treetops was the dance of the cosmos where asteroids and planets made their brilliant entrances in an effervescent blaze. Pearly, incandescent, and blossoming into mirthful sparks, the skies of Elysium Glades never ceased to delight those below, those who were not too taken up with their own goings-on to witness them. In a timeframe further along, Pieter supposed, this spectacle might be compared with those bursts of fire future peoples used for celebratory purposes.

Now, as Pieter scanned the lonely stretch of copper-bronze yard and thicket of poisonous thorns beyond, he became privy to a faint scuffle and glanced at the fountain where the gold-skins got their nourishment. Bubbling over with ferocity, hissing steam, glowing golden, a sorry reminder of dragon's blood, of harmless animals' lives habitually stolen.

Beyond this, a pair of shadows smothered sparkles on the tiles. Pieter peered further out of the paneless window, then ducked himself back in again—mindful of being noticed—and took in two figures crossing the square, both cloaked in dark fabrics that melted into their even darker reflections. Gold-skins on their way to their sleeping quarters. Nothing unusual about that. No sign of anyone crying out to angel ancestors for help. A picture of simplicity, albeit bleak.

One of the hooded heads turned, noticing a poktador slither towards a tunnelled-out burrow in the fountain. Pieter shuddered. Poktadors were nasty creatures indeed, a cross between a snake and a spider. They slithered and scampered, and sniped at anything living that got in their way. Two heads, four eyes, two deadly sets of fangs and the ability to spy, stalk and devour at a speed that was horrifyingly quick. The poktador that Pieter and one of the gold-skins now watched was monstrous in size. This one was larger than the whole of Pieter and dwarfed the two 'midnight marauders', who were giants of sorts themselves. It lashed its razor-edged tongue against the fountain's cascade as though striving to slice from the liquid each suspended bauble of gold.

Unlike his preceding moments spent in the palace, at this point Pieter felt gratitude for the shelter of that icy chamber. To share the courtyard with the gold-skins and poktador would be far from desirable. Able now to tear his eyes from the fountain-guzzling display, he espied the cloaked one watch the poktador, wondering in vague amusement whether he himself was also being spied on from some undetected corner. He noticed a flicker of movement. The cloak's hood fell away, revealing a shock of curling hair, grotesque skin tone and glacier eyes. A ringed finger pointed. Sandalled feet with bejewelled toes, which the cloak only partially covered, changed direction and stepped lightly towards the fountain. The gold-skin bared jagged teeth that dazzled in the fountain's glow.

But then—and Pieter's astonishment was absolute—the gold-skin's face reduced in size. Smaller, smaller, shrunken, withered, purple, creased. The nose branched rapidly outwards like a tree growing in a faster timeframe. The eyes sank back in the head to become little more than black dots. With twisting talons the altered being grasped at the snake-spider. A beak came down upon the hapless creature. A scream of hideous proportions pierced the stillness.

The bulk of the poktador had been swallowed, but the poktador's tail was thrashing from the edges of its predator's beak. The bird-monster threw its head back, gulped, and then voiced its satisfaction in a squeal that vibrated harshly in Pieter's ears. Flinging its hood back over its head, it glared up at the princess's tower window. Pieter slipped out of sight.

From his new vantage point, Pieter could see that this body king, the poktador's killer, had returned to his former identity. He was gazing up at the tower window with a sickening gleam in his pale, glassy eyes. He turned to his counterpart, at which point both bowed to each other and moved onwards, footsteps seemingly joined, necks folded at the same angle, marching with united finesse away from the elf boy's line of vision.

Pieter sat down, cross-legged, on a frozen floor. He concentrated on conjuring a small healing to rebalance his emotions after the unexpected violence. As he did so, he felt the prickle of a warning that he was being watched. Someone was observing him... staring tensely.

He jumped to his feet. The previously sleeping body-king daughter had risen. She stood not on the floor by the bed, but upon the bed itself.

In her hand was a glinting slab of metal. An axe! The body-king daughter was holding an axe made of gold.

She proceeded to stomp towards him, the golden axe held high.

XX

his Clan Watcher had told him many a time that when elves encountered the threat of mortality, they froze for a second or two to calculate whether survival remained an option.

This is exactly what Pieter did when he saw the glinting axe.

Is this, Pieter wondered, the way I am to finish my assignment on Earth?

And still, within this moment of crystallised mobility, he pondered the irony of expiring this way—under a slab of gold. He'd hoped his lifetime would see the cessation of body kings reigning over the sprites, that he'd succeed in persuading these war adorers to quit Elysium and take their tawdry residence with them. Alas, the elf's dreams were doomed, fit to crumble under a single strike of extravagant body-king weaponry.

'Ah, our Pieter,' he envisioned one of the Brumlynds saying in a tone that would primarily creak of affection. 'He dissolved in the influence of body kings. Was taken to the palace against his will, or so the rumour goes, and it is confirmed by our Dream Master that he passed on to the Dream Sphere's pearl-encrusted gates and will not be available to tell of his earthly demise until he has left the recuperation state.'

Would their magical abilities be enough to see *how* he'd been dissolved in the earthly realm, or would they only be permitted to rely on hearsay? An unsavoury thought: that up until the complete healing of his more ethereal and passed-over Dream-Sphere self, an embarrassing misapprehension might prevail.

What a useless way to pass to the next world, he told himself, still within this fragmented moment in time where an axe was meaning to conquer him cruelly. No pride, no heroes' celebration, no certainty. Was this how he wanted to leave his sprite allies? Did he honestly wish to spend the entire duration of his Wake explaining to everyone what had truly occurred—the way Crookwell was obliged to do after he overdosed on Wondalobs water?

Nay, not my fate he decided, and he slipped beneath the cane basket.

There came a *crash* and a *clack-clacking* of wood.

Pieter looked up to see the basket—the funny, idolised basket. It had split into two remarkably even halves.

The body-king daughter, quite forgetting her previous moment of rage, had shed all signs of brutality. She threw down her axe. Whimpering now, she clutched at scattered basket pieces and held them to her heart. She was on her knees, rocking and clutching and squealing out pleas for forgiveness. Pieter now noticed her headdress, which would have been donned prior to her predatory shuffle: dull metal, a knight's helmet almost. Protruding from either side were horns. Mournful for the creature body kings would have slain for these, Pieter took a step back. Remembering Orahney's coded warning to not be upset by anyone bearing bovine horns, he pushed the tragic thought away.

A snuffling noise caught his attention. Knowing he was no longer in the hysterical maiden's sights as a suitable chopping target, he darted across to the mysterious sun-faced basket with its odd capacity to make a gold-skin talk kindly to it—not to mention grieve over its demise—and found beneath it and before him, two sparkling, heavy-lidded eyes. Pieter recognised these eyes at once. 'Ye Gods. Fripso! It is *you.*' He shook his head in disbelief and sighed. 'Thank the heavens no harm was done.'

'Am I safe now, Pieter?' said the long-eared captive.

'You are safe, my friend. Thank the heavens and rejoice. You are safe, and, to my knowledge so far, so am I.'

The darkness faded. Had it really been an entire evening since he'd infiltrated the palace?

Within the orange veil of dawn, the Solen's daughter was altered into a menacing array of golds, her skin grotesquely luminous. Strands of garish hair fell forward over eyes that resembled a frozen lake as she stared at the elf, agog. She removed Pieter's friend from the damage and said, 'You *know* my rabbit!'

'By the way, Matt, Melissa's posting the wedding invitations on the weekend,' said Davo, idly drumming his fingers on the table. 'I said I could hand you one on Monday, but she wants to mail them. She's got a wax seal for envelopes that she's determined to show off.' He shook his head , amused. 'Women and their weddings! Always want to do things the "proper" way! She needs to know the address for you and Dette.'

Matthew didn't want to answer that. He took another sip of black espresso. It was late afternoon. He and Paul 'Davo' Davison were taking a rare break to discuss the café meeting they'd just had with a representative from Gallilani's. He could see the guy returning to his office on the other side of Martin Place, shackled to his briefcase, marching the worker-ant march along with every other eight-to-sixer. Matthew leaned back in his seat. For the first time since he could remember, he was not in a rush to get back to the twenty-third floor.

Davo was watching him seriously, mobile poised for the address. He'd never noticed it before, the amount of tension in his workmate's face. Of the two of them, he'd always considered Davo to be the more relaxed. Somehow things had changed since meeting Conan Dalesford. The trip to Alice Springs must have refreshed his outlook, but then ever since Dalesford had handed him that crystal, his perceptions seemed to have heightened.

Conan and Jannali had made him feel understood, and Conan Dalesford had described with Sherlockian accuracy events in Matthew's past. At one stage Dalesford had referred to Jannali's umbrella as a 'brolly', adding, 'For your sake, Matthew, seeing you spent a certain amount of your formative years in England during primary school, and probably most of high school too.'

'How'd you know I went to school in England?'

'From the way you round your vowels. You wouldn't have been born there, that's a different accent again, but you've sure as hell got most of their mannerisms.'

Dalesford's guess was right. In 1978 Matthew's parents bought a place in Wimbledon. He'd attended British schools from ages six to seventeen.

'Your address, Matt.'

Should he let Davo in on his secret? He'd have to tell him. He'd tell him now. 'I don't know whether that's such a good idea,' Matthew said, 'inviting the two of us.'

'Why? You've got plans?'

Exactly what he didn't have. There were no plans in place for Matthew and Bernadette.

The traffic up on Castlereagh Street had fallen into its own kind of rhythm, a metropolitan throb that he'd never previously noticed. Everything seemed to have its own song. Even the sounds that used to grate on Matthew, had, in the past week, become more bearable...interesting even.

'Davo, this is in confidence, right? Dette and I aren't doing a lot together these days.'

Davo did well in hiding his surprise, although Matthew could hear the *whoosh* of his breath as he exhaled. 'Bad as that, huh?'

'Yup.' Matthew handed over the address. 'Hasn't been good for a long time. But we'll make sure one of us attends your big day.'

Davo waited for further facts. Whose fault had it been? Was one cheating on the other? 'So you're splitting up.'

'Just working through it.' Discussing the futility of the marriage wouldn't be fair to Bernadette.

Since his weekend away, the absence of a pre-nuptial contract had dramatically lost its importance. Financial damage loomed ahead of course. He'd accepted that. He'd also come to terms with the realisation that if he didn't act fast in the divorce department, he could well be left with a lot less. Dette's out-of-control spending might turn debt into a reality.

Her shopping addiction had compounded with each year. And despite his ongoing reassurance that she was still young and would always be beautiful, she continued to visit surgeons who agreed to remove the invisible wrinkles that the reputable ones denied were there. He wasn't going to tell Davo that. Nor was he going to tell him that his other-half's temper tantrums—typically winding up with screamed name-calling—humiliated him no end.

'I need a holiday! I have to do something about my stress levels,' she'd screech, but how would a second trip to Vanuatu in four months make her yell at him any less? Matthew suspected that if their relationship had been one Bernadette was happy in, her stress levels might never have got so chaotic. He was doing her no favours by staying.

Matthew and his colleague finished their coffees in relative silence. Nearly six pm. Home-time for many. They'd remain at the office for another two hours, at least, while they finalised the logistics for the Gallilani deal.

Rays of a lowering sun had gilded the crowds of after-workers trooping towards the street. Their faces showed signs of impatience when the red pedestrian light blinked on.

'Incongruous,' Matthew said, mostly to himself.

Davo took another gulp of coffee and flicked through the Gallilani file his assistant had prepared. 'When relationships fall apart?' he said. 'Yeah, I guess it is.'

'I was talking about us worker-ants.'

'Us?'

Matthew nodded towards the stampede outside the floor-to-ceiling windows. 'We're all trapped in the rat race and don't know how to get out of it.'

'That's not incongruous. That's just life.'

Matthew gazed at the luminance enveloping each pedestrian paused at the lights. For a second he wished he were an artist able to capture the glory of that image, of the sun turning each of them golden. No longer were they worried, rushing little life-forms. To someone apart from them, who they would never know—someone observing them quietly from a café—they'd become magnificent. Solemn angels sporting afternoon halos.

Incongruous, he thought. We're all so unaware of our own empowerment.

When he'd held that crystal at the bar, something quite inexplicable had happened. It was as though he'd turned into Dr Suess's newly reformed Grinch, complete with ballooning heart and benign Grinchy grin.

Driving home after his meal with the author, he'd sensed a lightness in his chest, and he couldn't help smiling at things that would have previously gone unnoticed. The crazy woman in the middle of the road, whose outline was barely visible in the darkness, hadn't annoyed him at all. When he'd searched for the next right-turn, he'd been startled to find the woman waving him to a stop before frog-hopping in front of his car and diving at the asphalt. She'd called out cryptically, 'Wasn't a rabbit,' then wandered off with her head held high. Instead of zooming onward in impatience, he'd sat back and laughed.

He was back in the office now. The chair he'd borrowed from the tea room—to replace his swivel until Maintenance re-gassed it—was starting to bug him. Taking a break from charts on the screen, Matthew leaned back. He tilted his chair—so that he was balancing on its back legs only—placed his palms behind his head, and linked his fingers.

'And whaddaya think *you're* doing, Weissler?' Charlie was thundering towards him with an unpleasant look on his face.

Matthew scrambled to unlace his fingers, which now felt awkwardly stuck. In so doing, he lost his balance.

His weight shifted, tipping his chair forward, then back, and then forward again, and his knee banged against the underside of the desk. Bullseye. Right on the old injury, and not a single pain-clearing crystal in sight.

Just when he thought the worst was over, the chair tilted further forward. Despite his rodeo rider's determination to stay on, Matthew slid off.

From under his desk he called to Charlie, 'Sure is dark under here.' And untidy. Dozens of screwed up papers that had missed the waste-paper basket taunted him now, as did the expectation of Charlie's next few words.

Within his cubbyhole landing spot, he could feel the responding tremor of floorboards with Charlie's retreating footsteps. The trading director's voice filtered back to him in a deadpan roar. 'My office, Matthew Weissler. Pronto.'

XXI

'My rabbit is the most wonderful creature in the world.' The girl hugged small Fripso to her neck and choked back a sob. 'Elf,' she said, after whispering to Fripso. 'I hadn't intended to kill you. For the attack I apologise.'

'Only meant to remove some of me then?' Pieter was incredulous. 'Why, that's crueller than killing. Still, you are a body-king daughter after all.'

'Body king? Whatever that is, I am no such thing. I am of Gold's Kin.'

'I beg your pardon. Of gold skin.'

'Again you are incorrect. I am of Gold's...' The girl shook her head. She smiled ever so slightly. 'Ah well. If you insist. What is a body king though? Is it an insult to my family? I expect it's no term of endearment.'

'Neither,' said Pieter throwing the rabbit a wink.

The animal gazed across at Pieter with half-closed lids, appreciative of the attention after his prison had collapsed around him. Pieter's kindness merits enabled him to listen to some of the rabbit's thinking.

'My wish has come true. One of the Brumlynds has freed me! Now to shake off my captor, who I must admit has endeared me to her in the way she worships my very existence.

'What a brave thing Pieter has done, smashing my jail open without prior thought to his own security! My only memory of the ordeal is a dream about my hillside blanketed in buttercups. I awoke to the faraway echo of crackling wood. The tapestry roof-cover of my prison was whisked away and there, behind a mere skeletal reminder of my too-small enclosure, and surrounded by the dazzling light of morning, stood Maleika's heroic son.

'*I shall pay special attention to Pieter's conversation. I must observe any signals concerning our escape. In the meantime I shall savour the last of my coddler's affection.*'

Turning to the maiden, Pieter attempted an interpretation of the term he'd used. 'A body king idolises his body. His physical vehicle alone is all that he believes he is.'

'What nonsense,' snapped the girl. 'We are far more than that! We have a magnificent palace, we have hundreds of slaves, and we have a dragon font and regular banquets where we eat more than we need. As for myself, I have tapestries and gold spun linen and...and my rabbit.' Momentarily she lifted the little creature nestled at her neck as a dramatic way of demonstrating to Pieter that this was who she meant.

Pieter's heart wept for her. He knew that among all she considered she owned, Fripso was the dearest to her. And sadly, she was yet to learn he was the one thing mentioned that couldn't be possessed. The elf would delay this sorry news until he found exactly the right words.

'Friend,' he began good-naturedly—it was best not to make an enemy of an axe-wielding materialist—'you state things outside of yourself. Outside of your body. All these are physical still, just as the body is.'

'Are they really?' she said in surprise.

'Indeed,' said Pieter prolonging his 'friendly' face. 'Your riches, you see, are not *you*, nor is your body. Your body—'

'I know all that.' She cast a guilty glance to the side. 'Elf, I have no desire to end your existence, and I have already offered you my apologies. I was dreaming. A nightmare had me in its grips. I could have sworn there was a monster in the corner.' As an afterthought, she added, 'I expect you are not at all monstrous.' She set Fripso down, ran to her window, took note of a sundial in the courtyard and gasped. 'Goodness! Dear Sol is almost at two degrees. I must ready myself for the Four Seasons Ball.' She hastened to the end of her chamber where a smaller room was partitioned off with gilded bars and opened one of its gates. 'I wonder now, elf, whether I could ask for your assistance. One of my minders has placed my dancing slippers on that shelf at the far wall of my clothing quarter, and I can no longer reach them. You are greater in height than me. Would you be so kind as to...'

'Say no more,' said a gallant Pieter. He stepped into the alcove, the rabbit at his heels, and strode towards the shelf.

He halted when hearing a *clang* and a *click*.

'Oh dear,' Fripso said. 'Ah, no! Oh dear.'

The maiden was now by her canopied bed, placing the key to her clothing-quarters in a box that shone of tawdry gems.

'She has trapped us here,' said Fripso, eyeing the indoor gates that had closed behind them. 'The cunning creature is imprisoning us both!'

Chapter Seven

Standing beside Charlie's desk—he'd not been invited to sit—Matthew recalled the stomach-churning apprehension, which, since contact with the crystal, had remarkably grown wings and left him.

Charlie threw down Matthew's spiral-bound reports, one after another, chanting in robot tones when each one hit the desk, 'Not good enough, not good enough, not good enough...' as though they were worm-infested apples failing a quality test. Charlie raised his eyes to Matthew. In a voice that rang of sarcasm he said, 'What's up? You in love or something?'

It was quite the opposite. What he'd always believed had given him emotional security was nothing more than an illusion.

Charlie's account of these fruitless efforts was jaw-dropping. Matthew drew in a breath to explain, but words escaped him. What had happened?

He went back to his desk, checked the reports, found Charlie's complaint to be abysmally justified and shook his head in despair. 'I need a holiday,' he said with a groan. And to top it all off, he was resorting to one of Bernadette's insipid whines. How had he managed to mangle a task he'd been competent at for years? Checking his staff's updates was something he did meticulously. Nothing escaped his eagle eye, and that was the easy part of the job! How could he have got it so wrong this time?

He returned to Charlie's office and said, 'I can't believe I approved those. I'm as disappointed at this as you are.'

Charlie frowned at him, a reaction that usually inspired a certain amount of ire. Today it felt comical.

Did Charlie ever realise how crazy this all was? The threatening act towards subordinates...the mandatory flexing of seniority muscles.

Matthew had done it all before with his own team. It was a role. Just a role the corporation insisted they play.

The eagle sculpture on Charlie's desk seemed to be frowning too.

Could Dalesford have messed with his mind when he'd handed him the crystal? Knowing no-one else had seen that flash of light was more than a little unsettling. Matthew remembered back to an event when he was fourteen and living in the UK. His parents had taken him and his brother to a hypnotist show in Leeds. For weeks afterwards he'd puzzled over how the showman had manipulated semi-sleeping volunteers into doing the strangest of things before commanding them to forget it all upon waking. Bernadette frequently acted as though he'd done something awful to her, and yet he had no recollection of having done anything. This, of course, had been going on well before meeting Dalesford.

He had to acknowledge he wasn't his usual self. The recent disjointed yet freakishly connected experiences had disturbed his equilibrium. What about the night he'd slept under a tree in the park and stumbled across a bat that turned into a bird? And a small boy with a big attitude in a forest he'd never seen before? He'd put it down to someone spiking his drink. He'd secretly blamed Harrow, probably because Celia inferred Harrow was 'on something'. If the guy were indeed guilty of substance abuse, he wouldn't be wasting anything on Matthew. If Harrow were known for anything, it wasn't for his generosity.

A knock on the open door, and Charlie's assistant stepped in to deliver another stack of reports.

Dalesford a hypnotist and Harrow a drink spiker! Matthew staved off a chuckle. Looking for someone else to blame was hardly helpful.

The assistant left, and Charlie opened his office door, saying to Matthew, 'Anyway, we'll discuss this later. I've got a meeting at six.'

Matthew headed back to his desk. 'I'll get these patched up.'

And then the dreaded words arrived. 'No. Get on with other things. I'll give them to Adam Harrow.'

Of all other trading managers Charlie could have issued the work to, he'd had to settle on that good-for-nothing slime. Just like Adam

Harrow to get in the Board Director's ear about inheriting Charlie's role. Two seats would have been set out for Harrow no doubt. One for him, the other for his overblown sense of entitlement.

Harrow with the Nordic good looks and selective charm that women fell for time after time. Harrow who believed the starving throughout the world were meant to starve. Said with conviction they'd dug their own graves.

Matthew recalled the last time he had to endure the bloke's unstoppable arrogance when he'd witnessed him chatting up the girl with the seductive eyes. The poor girl had fallen for it of course, as they all did. Matthew had wanted to shout out to her about Harrow slinking into the tea room a week or so earlier to announce in a barely audible mumble that he'd got engaged. Five minutes before asking this girl if she were single he'd been phoning his fiancée to advise he'd be home in the next half hour.

Despite the annoyances of his own relationship, Matthew could never do that to Bernadette. Having once been on the receiving end of infidelity, he knew being cheated on was the worst kind of hurt. He also knew Bernadette would never do that to him. Loyalty at least was something they had going for them. But Matthew couldn't see a future there anymore. The only honourable thing to do was to tell his wife he was no longer happy.

Outside Charlie's office, Matthew caught himself pacing and stopped.

I could always leave, he thought.

Surprised by the impulsiveness of this idea, he promptly dispelled it. His loyalty had taken on an urgent voice, was telling him he had to shield his team from the inevitable havoc that Harrow would cause if armed with extra power. It told him in a growl that he was expected to do the right thing by an employer who had only ever rewarded him with advancement, and yet something else, something like an elusive wisp of muted silver sunshine, was insisting he break free of the game.

He turned and strode back to his desk. Conan Dalesford's mention of escaping 'corporate tyranny' had been lurking in the back of his mind since the plane trip home. It had since increased in decibels, a jingle blaring at him like a feel-good commercial for jogging shoes.

In his imagination he revisited Conan and Jannali's ocean-green foyer. A recollection of the crystal's blast of silver light spun seamlessly into the haunting echo of a pipe made from reed.

The eagle's sombre words were dancing about him now in starlit streaks. *Do you plan to waste the remainder of your life as well?*

Freedom.

Emerging from a treadmill of a dream.

Waking up. *Wake up, Weissler.* A sound-bite of Harrow's voice, cold and imperious.

Wake up! The forest kid's voice cancelled Harrow's out, fortified with the same self-certainty yet infinitely kinder. *Just wake up, Matthew.*

It struck him then, a resolution to his endless obsessing. A dawning of possibility. A sudden insight into how he'd been tripped up by his narrow definition of security. A flash of realisation. An epiphany.

He returned to his workstation. 'What's stopping me?' he said.

While Charlie met with the human resources manager, Matthew emailed admin with a request. Remembering the mess he'd discovered under his desk, he reached for a post-it note and scribbled down the words: *Cleaner, Please don't miss the floor* and initialled it.

An hour later, Matthew was back in Charlie's office.

'I'm sorry this had to happen.' Charlie's tone was grim. 'You've been a great asset to the bank, Matthew, but with your background in finance and law you'll have no trouble finding another financial management role.'

'Or a legal one,' said Matthew.

'Or a legal one, yes.' Charlie strode across to where Matthew stood, clamping a hand on his back as they went to exit the office door. 'Eleven years, Matt! Tell you what. Don't decide yet. Think it over tonight and we'll have a chat about it in the morning.'

'I'm not doing this lightly,' Matthew told him. 'The decision won't be any different tomorrow.'

'Concerning those reports. Your staff members let you down badly.'

'Absolutely not, Charlie. If I were going to go blaming, I'd blame it on stress.' Matthew stopped short of the door and turned to his boss. 'But I take full responsibility for having stuffed up.'

'I can't persuade you to stay?'

'Resigning has been on my mind for some time now, to be honest.' The truth was his restlessness had crept up on him only recently, having begun the day he'd discovered the eagle sculpture on Charlie's desk. Associating eagles with that sudden urge for freedom had been strengthened further—courtesy of the shape-shifting bat— although fatigue-related sleepless dreaming signalled the need for swift action. It had to be treated seriously.

He reached for the office door and opened it. The door, as though ripped from his hands, crashed shut. He stepped back to see Charlie, red-faced and fuming, leaning against the handle.

'For *Chrissake,*' Charlie exploded. 'Whaddya think you're doing?'

'What did you think? I was opening the door!'

'You're throwing your bloody future away, that's what you're bloody-well doing!' Disgusted snort. 'For five years I've been grooming you for my role! *Five* f***ing *years!*'

Matthew looked down at the puffed-up trading director and realised with a shock that it wasn't rage twisting Charlie's features. It was anguish. He planted a hand on his boss's shoulder. 'It's okay, mate. It's okay.'

'What's getting to me, Matthew, if you must know, is this.' Charlie's voice lowered. His words were hurried and urgent. 'I'm retiring in six months. Six months and all this is yours. Maybe, as a mentor, I haven't encouraged you enough, but when it comes to leading GM teams, you're one in a thousand. The sky's the limit for you here.'

A fire engine siren in George Street screamed through the silence.

Sweat beads had settled across Charlie's forehead. 'And you *know* who's lined up behind you.'

A lot had happened in the past hour. Matthew had conquered a grimy fear. The threat that once taunted him, of Adam Harrow snatching the promotion he'd continually striven for, had vaporised like steam from the tea-room urn.

He'd feared loss of control. What he'd failed to realise until now was that he'd lost control long ago in succumbing to that fear.

Weirdly enough, now that Charlie's trading director role was almost imminent, the thought of rising higher felt strangely unexciting, like having neared the crest of Everest only to decide he'd rather be in the tropics.

It was clear to Matthew, but Charlie would never understand. How could he, from that vantage point? 'There's more to life than the corporation,' Matthew said.

Charlie sank into a rapid slouch and hissed out a sigh, reminding Matthew of a deflating bicycle tyre. 'Fair enough.' Charlie glanced away. Smiled down at the carpet. He swung open the door. 'I'd rather not say you're right, Weissler, but maybe you are, in some other reality out there.'

XXII

'First Fripso and now Pieter,' said Maleika. 'Dear, dear! Both of them missing and no sign of their whereabouts. They're nowhere in sight in the Dream Sphere. When am I to make any progress?'

Kloory stared solemnly at the ground. 'It is a mission of importance for them,' he told his mother. 'Perhaps they don't want to be found just yet,' but Maleika thought otherwise.

They sat awhile by the campfire in silence. Fireflies, intent on the blaze beneath them, zipped about the rising smoke.

'I know we will see our Pieter again,' Maleika said. 'He's a loyal member of the clan. He would not abandon us without warning.'

Kloory detected a hint of uncertainty in this last statement. Deep in thought, he surveyed the glades where streams of iridescent light draped from shadowed branches. 'Two others are connected with Pieter,' he said. 'And each of the three shares the same soul-path. No-one knows how far from us it will lead or how long it will last. Perhaps eternity. Or perhaps Pieter will return tomorrow and Fripso in a day or two.'

Finding little comfort in this revelation, Maleika gathered up her bottles of Remembrance Essence and in readiness for dawn retired to her sleeping wagon, quite forgetting to bid Kloory a happy wakening.

The glades lost their mystical shimmer and turned a brazen gold at the emergence of daybreak. Maleika was lost in a dream where three silhouettes—one of a boy wearing a crown, another of a flowing-haired girl and the third of a timid animal baby—were crossing a stream that separated now from then.

XXIII

Each evening, Maleika and her clan went bravely about their work as though they were not in the least concerned about the disappearance of two vital members of their forest.

Instead of wasting time pitying herself for the emptiness she knew was there, Maleika became busier than ever seeking their whereabouts and spent much time pondering. Even if Pieter and Fripso were taken by gold-skins, somewhere, in some reality, was a decision to allow it, and so Alcor offered as much assistance as a Dream Master could by encouraging her to open the door that held the most answers. Frustration at her inability to unpuzzle these riddles plagued Maleika, yet she refused to weaken and warded off temptations towards dark emotion with the rays of hope that the moon offered on each silent waking. Was her son with the rabbit? Was the gold-skin maiden aware that she had taken on some of Orahney's characteristics? Kloory's suggestion that somehow all three were connected might not have been as silly as it first seemed.

It was the far-distant future that weighed most on Maleika's mind. If Pieter were deterred too much from his life path, the evolution of the world he had volunteered to rejuvenate might become lost in the Cycle of Suffering that gold-skins were known to have inflicted upon Earth's future.

They did not suppose he would vanish without a trace. Whenever he ventured outside his home-forest the clan located him promptly, or he returned with the aid of his beauty-creation powers.

It was as though she must cross a chasm to reach him, a looming black hole that echoed the one in the Bastion galaxy, where those whose souls had not yet developed hearts would escape to extinguish the evidence of their creation. Somewhere and somehow, the frameworks of these souls had been noted. Somewhere and somehow their re-creation occurred, at which time the maker was indeed careful to include the potential for love in future evolvements.

Nothing in existence was a mistake. Nor was anything that escaped existence. Whether a thing existed or not was supremely important in at least someone's dimension. And in thinking of this, Maleika was reminded of the dragon cave, where life had been ended and not renewed. She thought, as she sipped cider by the just-built fire, of the thorn thicket, of the eagle statue that loomed over it and of the Oracle in the Dream Sphere who she hoped would tell her more about Pieter in words free of poetic ambivalence.

She went to a ferny ledge, lay herself down and asked again, 'What do you have to tell me?' and although it was not yet dawn, almost too early to exit her earthly world, Maleika became immersed in sleep, curled up in bracken like a fledgeling deer, gliding towards that city wherein the Oracle was held, peering into the Oracle's silver-gold ocean. It glimmered with texture and colour and light and shade, and all things profound and powerful. It chose a rhyme in which to speak to the elf woman. It said:

And now
Those few
Will choose
Anew
To delve the caves
Of darkness through
A gilded vortex
Fringed with blood
Those linked in memory
Maimed by mud
The shadowed prowl
To herewith prey
On star-spun souls
Their heart-warmed *fey*

146

But trace all progress
Through the maze
Of solar stealth and toxic haze
To one point where
Those lives are freed
Thus vanquishing the glut of need

Then crumbled is the horned ones' wall
Where grizzly beasts are prone to fall

And once a winged man acts with grace
By gifting magic framed in lace
The Silvering will fast descend
To mark the greed-lack ailment's end

For now Maleika put to rest
Your search
It is a fruitless quest

Unperturbed by the nonsensical references, Maleika bowed deeply her thanks and intentioned herself to the Dream Sphere's Devic Great Hall where Alcor stilled her shaking shoulders. As he wove from his wand a pastel-hued calmative to her shuddering collarbones, she told him of the Oracle, reciting the prediction so as to remember it on her waking. 'Can you offer me any direction on this, brother?' she asked.

'Maleika, I offer only opinion on what I have heard. My Clan Watcher has given no advice, but it seems to me that those you seek are under a dark influence at present. If I were you I would next be searching for the horned ones' wall.'

'This I agree to during the next slumbering.'

'Then so be it. I shall prepare a triplicate of dimensional doorways, all holding knowledge pertaining to such. I shall advise my master in readiness for the morrow.'

'Thank you, Alcor.' Maleika felt her voice vanish as she spiralled towards Earth and her temporary bracken bed in Elysium Glades. Awaking to crickets' comforting chirrups, she rose, journeyed back to her clan and settled into a place by the fire where her small nephew Croydee was already preparing heated Remembrance Essence.

'You, Aunt Maleika, are more important than you think,' said the other Brumlynd, and he said it nobly, as though he'd been given authority to do so.

'Ha! This is what I say of Pieter, but I am merely his Watcher, so I suppose in a way I am drawn into his important missions.'

'Nay, Aunt Maleika,' said Croydee, pouring the essence into a star-shaped mug. 'Cousin Pieter is part of a devic crew, but you are the captain. You are the one who will alter the future eternally.'

Glorion was sure to have received his invitation by now. Izzie hadn't told anyone she'd invited him, figuring that his acceptance could be dropped into the conversation during lunch break.

His refusal would be extra devastating if she had to convey it to six boy-crazy teens. Izzie knew that while her pals might always appear to be cheering each other on as far as lassoing a guy went, the truth was they kind of hoped for failure, unless, of course, they'd won the heart of someone just as good.

'Pity we don't have boys coming along,' Sara said in a whine.

'Well why don't you invite some?' suggested Izzie. 'It's everyone's party as far as I'm concerned.'

'But if I invite Alexander or Glorion or Tyson it'll look like I'm asking them out. If *you* invite them it's just you including them with a whole lot of others. You've got the advantage being the birthday girl.'

Izzie smiled to herself at that. Alexander and Tyson could in fact be excellent decoys, allowing her to get together with Glorion unnoticed. The last thing she wanted was to find her party being had by someone else. 'Okay.' Izzie shrugged. 'I'll invite Alexander and Tyson.'

'And Glorion?' Sara, daughter of Izzie's former policeman neighbour, watched Izzie closely, eyes bright with hope.

This called for some bluffing. Sara, the ninth-grader with the neatly braided single plait, the kid who'd been delighted to have tenth-grader Izzie move to her area and start at Burwood High, and who'd prior to that knocked on Izzie's door every second weekend when staying at her dad's Punchbowl flat, was surprisingly easy to coerce. 'Don't know about Glorion,' Izzie said in reply, adopting her best 'bored' expression. 'Glorion's the one with the weird boots, isn't he?'

Sara coloured. 'Yeah. Weirder than weird.'

'Then Alexander and Tyson—even though there's a humungous chance they're busy—are okay to invite anyway don't you reckon?'

'Yeah! I reckon.' Sara, about to clap her hands in excitement, caught the juvenile gesture before it had a chance to manifest and forced her arms to drop to her sides.

Getting a 'no' from Alexander and Tyson would not be a stress. Although cute, Tyson was a bit of a big mouth. Alexander Whitford was absurdly formal, like he thought he was his own great-great grandfather. The other girls said he was sophisticated. Izzie just saw him as old.

Glorion, on the other hand, was quiet and loud in all the right ways and so effortlessly up-to-date he was actually ahead of his time.

In the afternoon, Izzie bumped into Tyson on her way to French class, Tyson who was trying to get to French class too, darting between kids with backpacks like a boxer dodging strikes. The tee he wore had sliced off sleeves that showed off his bumpy biceps to advantage. Hot, in a stocky sort of way. That was Tyson. Not that he was anywhere near as nice as a certain Dutch boy. She handed him a party invitation. And then everything went wrong. She walked away from their conversation feeling angry with herself.

The day rolled on. Once the bell rang, Izzie dawdled home, wishing she could think of a way to put things right. It wasn't until she reached her front door that a realisation dawned. She'd forgotten to look over her shoulder every so often, like her mother suggested she do after that fingernail dude turned up at Punchbowl. Since that day outside Louey's newsagency, when the same guy collided with her and glared, Izzie had taken the backward glance thing a whole lot more seriously.

Her mother's voice, low in tone and loud in volume, was reverberating in the hallway of their 1920s bungalow, Rosetta absorbed in a phone conversation with one of 'the girls'. She beamed when she saw Izzie and waved energetically.

Izzie marched down the hallway, the Persian rug softening her step, and made a right-turn into her room, wishing she could activate some sort of mute switch on all that blah-blah-ing.

'But meet me for a coffee on Wednesday, darl, and I'll tell you all about it....Yeah. Happened two Sundays ago. Well it started off with a potential client phoning for a tarot reading...Oops, sorry! Just checked my diary. Would Thursday be okay with you? I'm rostered on for serving lunch at the refuge on Wednesday. Then I'm cleaning offices for Jack Barnaby Wednesday night...'

Izzie plunked her bag down next to her bed and moodily re-called her chat with Tyson.

'What's your number, Busy Izzie?' Tyson had asked.

'My phone's stuffed at the moment. I'll give you Sara's number.'

'Cool!'

'Anyone else you wanna bring?'

'Aargh! I'll check with the guys. Glorion could be in on it.'

'Gl...Glori... you *know* Glorion Osterhoudt?' At Tyson's mention of that name, Izzie's totally-in-control persona had morphed into that of someone who felt young, unsure and disproportionately lost for words.

'Yup. Dutch guy. You like him, do you?'

Izzie's face burned. 'Glorion? N-no!'

Tyson, who'd at first been fazed by Izzie's instigating of the conversation, nervous even, had gone on to chat calmly like he'd known her for years. 'Yeah, I'll tell him about it 'cos he's pretty much new here and he might want to go. Thanks Iz, I'll let you know.'

'Yeah...um...do that...um...'

'Do you know if Mr Fisher's back teaching Maths?' Tyson had taken a step backwards then, his spiky-lashed eyes seeming to treble in size. 'You're going red, Izzie! I reckon you do like Glorion.'

Re-living those final moments of the conversation made her uncomfortably warm again. She slapped a sketchbook onto her work desk and thumped down her tin of pastels.

Rosetta's blah-blah-ing had got even louder. 'Yeah the evening shift's going well. Apart from rude notes from people like "MW" it's not bad at all...Wonder who MW actually is. I imagine him as grey and bristly. High, pessimistic-sounding voice, bossy with his wife, a bit mean, a bit miserly. One of Lillibridge's *body kings*. Ha-ha-ha!'

'Blah, blah, blah,' moaned Izzie, head waggling from side to side as she hung up her schoolbag. It was always when she wanted to sulk in silence that her mother's exuberance got especially annoying.

She shook the pastels from their tin. She'd overheard the story twice already, something to do with the tarot cards and an uncanny experience. Wasn't Rosetta going to tell this friend all about it on Thursday when they met for coffee? Apparently not. Izzie had now been gifted the good fortune of hearing the story a third time.

She took out a purple pastel and ran a hand over the cream coloured page of her sketchbook. Rosetta's anecdote – told from the sitting room and made louder by the house's absence of carpet as a sound block—wound up now after some stunned and amazed superlatives. 'Don't abandon eggs! Ha-ha! Yeah, that's what "Molly" in my dream said!...More real than any dream I've had in the past!'

The conversation moved predictably to Rosetta's 'Gorgeous GEG': the Green-Eyed Guy. He'd gone into the shop where she worked, and he'd talked about something other than his purchase. Izzie already knew this.

'I already *know*,' Izzie grumbled. 'I know, I know, I know.'

'...I know,' Rosetta's voice chimed elatedly. 'I know, I know! I can't believe it either!' Laughter. 'And it was all because of that bloody shop-sign—*you* know the one I'm talking about, Lena, that A-frame pavement board I had so much trouble painting. Had it in the back seat before the paint had dried and Izzie accidentally sat on it when I collected her and a friend of hers from school one day. Dalia had the front seat, luckily...It *did* happen!...I'm serious, Lena, it did! Izzie has the paint marks on the back of her uniform to prove it. *Had* I should say. I mean, it's not like I'd get the poor kid to keep wearing it...Use it as a floor rag...Compulsive recycler...'

Izzie whispered, 'Please don't mention that I needed a roomier uniform.'

'No I got her another one...A bit roomier for her boobs and hips...Great little second-hand uniform kiosk next to her school canteen...These kids grow so fast!'

Izzie drew a circular chain that spiralled and spiralled and spiralled outwards. Kind of like how life was supposed to be, ever expanding into new possibilities, although Tyson referring to Glorion as a buddy had sprung her own spiral into reverse. She turned the page of her sketchbook, picked up a pastel of palest pink and concentrated on creating a luminous oval, flecked with white highlights to give a dimensional illusion, then drew a grey and gold frame around it, loops of lacy metal, which lent her oval the look of a brooch or pendant encased in lunar-gilt, a rare silver-gold metal she'd learnt about yesterday in science.

'...You're kidding!...The last time I saw Ben he was, say, up to my shoulder, and when you and I ran into each other at the markets, I was like, "Who *is* this? Oh, it's Lena's son!"...Not too tall I hope! Although it'd save you getting the ladder out when he does the roof gutters. Ha ha!'

Izzie eyed her picture of the jewellery piece in satisfaction and pinned it up on her corkboard, then began on an abstract of the sun and moon locked in a kiss. She added caramel splodges and black stars, and thought of Glorion's eyes. Glorion's weren't just intelligent eyes, they were far beyond that. Those eyes held some kind of genius. That had been proven at the debate. The memory of his words seemed to float about Izzie in heart-shaped speech-bubbles:

Picture a world that has forgotten what it is to feel ailments such as fear, worry, grief.

Picture a world whose many varied peoples have learnt, after having weathered the storms of deception, to trust each other once more.

He was so...so world-minded! So interested in society and the human race as a whole!

Worldly Glorion would already have had countless romances. The question hung like a raincloud over Izzie's mostly unswayable optimism. Was he already in love with someone? Could he be pining for someone in Holland? She cringed at the thought of Glorion, light-brown hair and silver snow boots glinting red in the morning light, solemnly waving goodbye to a weeping girl with plaits and staggering away with his hand on his heart through a windmill field blooming with tulips.

'Why did I make such an idiot of myself in front of Tyson,' Izzie whispered to the fluffy, curled-up heap on the bed: Sidelta resembling a silver-grey pom-pom. 'What if Tyson tells Glorion I like him?' If Glorion didn't turn up to her party, she'd know he had laughed along with Tyson about her crush on him. And even if he didn't have a girlfriend back in Holland, he was probably far more interested in getting to know some other tenth-grader, someone three-hundred per cent prettier than Izzie, with shampoo-commercial hair.

Now that Tyson was set to speak to Glorion, Izzie felt sure his failure to turn up to her party would feel like a double-rejection, the first being his non-response following the invitation she'd left in his locker.

Low-pitched laughter exploded in the hallway. Rosetta was still yabbering to Lena. 'And I'm glad I'll never know what the guy in the Jaguar was thinking...Ha ha ha! Tried to walk away intelligently... Ha- ha!...could hear this sniggering sound coming from the car. I was *mortified.*'

Mortified!

'That's the word,' Izzie said to the cat. Prickly with inadequacy, Izzie again recalled her downward spiralling talk with Tyson that morning. Why this compulsion to revisit an incident she'd prefer to forget? She spoke once more to her pointy-eared pet. 'I thought mothers and timid people were the only ones who got mortified, but that's exactly how I felt today!' Prior to that she'd only ever referred to the feeling as 'being weak'. 'I was mortified, kitty-cat.' She pressed the side of her face against the purring bundle's silvery back. 'And it's a stupid, *stupid* emotion, Sidelta. Cats don't get embarrassed, do they? Why wasn't I born a cat?'

XXIV

All that they saw was the cobweb lace of moon-illuminated ferns and the mossy dells that loomed ahead. 'Are you sure it's safe to go to the Grudellan Palace at this hour?' the rabbit mother asked Maleika.

Maleika nodded. 'We would be better off in the Dream Sphere at this point, Karee, but 'tis only a glimpse of the palace that I want. I wish to make certain our sons aren't trapped in the grounds.'

The rays of Sol were not far away, and the moon was a sad fragment of its former self. Karee, lolloping beside her, strove to conceal her distress. She would rather have stayed away, and yet here she was, bound for the foreboding Grudellan gates.

What would they want with a rabbit baby? Perhaps Fripso would be overlooked. Apart from dragons, and the unfortunates the dark-hearted had mesmerised, Elysium Glades was almost, although not altogether, a sanctuary of protection.

'Ah!' cried Maleika. 'Do you see those luminaries—the artificial ones I mean to say.'

'I do indeed.' Karee twitched her whiskers and blinked at the overly bright array of citrus yellow that swirled around an ominous silhouette of geometric lines.

'That is the gold-skins' royal residence, which includes this monstrosity of a construction and the sand dunes over yonder where the mines are. I expect all are sleeping. We'll try to alert our loved ones to our presence should they happen to be there.'

'Fripso and Pieter might not be in the palace at all,' Karee remarked, although she said it more to reassure herself.

'Dear Karee, you are right. 'Tis hardly likely they've ventured this far, but let us eliminate suspicion no matter how small it might be, by searching from a distance.'

'Perhaps we should look closer, go inside the palace gates?' whispered a cautious Karee.

'We won't concern ourselves with anything so perilous this night. If we see anything unusual, we will discuss our next steps on the morrow.'

Sighing gently, Karee relaxed at the mention of vigilance from a distance. She could never forgive herself if she were captured. What help would she be to her baby then?

The statue in the grounds appeared to be a raven stationed upon a bough, but as Karee neared, she discerned it to be a stone eagle upon a tall pedestal that competed for height with the palace's towers. 'Maleika, do you see anything?' When it came to spying upon the Grudellans, stature was hardly to Karee's advantage.

'Ooh! I see troopers: eagle-men guarding the gates.'

'And?'

'And there's a pond-ish pool of water in a container that sparkles of gold. It has spouts and cascades. It is, I think, what they refer to as a "fountain", the essence they drink to keep their skins that dreadful colour. And I see...oh yes, it is she.'

'Who, Maleika?'

'The maiden. One of the daughters. I vaguely see her outline in the paneless window. I see artificial light brightening half of her face. She is reading...she is reading aloud. Karee this is very strange. Shouldn't a gold-skin be afraid of the moon? The people of that species are ever intolerant of the fresh night air.'

'Yet the guards are out here, all the same.'

'Guards are hybrids. Not full-blooded.'

'They do have dances, I understand, and those are held in the evening.'

'Yes, Karee, this is true, but their dances are enclosed within the walls of their fortress. Artificial luminaries containing a portion of captured sun shine upon them. The moon, to gold-skins, is a loathsome scallywag.'

'You mentioned this maiden had similarities to Orahney.'

'I did think this at one stage, although why Orahney would journey away from her peaceful life in the Dream Sphere to play the earthly role of a princess, I cannot fathom. In fact, I swear by the light of Luna that she's unlikely to do such a thing. No, I believe this girl at the open window delights in imitating passed-on sprites, simply to taunt us. They are cruel, the gold-skins. Never be swayed by their charms, Karee, for they have many. I almost felt sympathy for the wretch when I visited her residence. Demure, she was, and terribly polite, but as Orahney says, they are never who they seem. Their natures are forever remoulding. They match their mood to whatever surrounds them, camouflaging the bad to lure in the good.'

'Too-hoo,' wailed an owl. 'Hoo-oo! Hoo-oo!'

'Ah, he who hoots reminds us of how worry can weaken the will. Our sage friend was taken in by them. Where he once uttered words of wisdom, he now moans in a language none of us understand, and his eyes have turned sorrowful.'

'Do you think he might be warning us, Maleika, about venturing any further?'

'I think he might. We shall go.'

'Race you home!'

'Only if you promise not to run as fast as you did when I sent you into the future.'

'Promise. I hear the poor lady sprite got a terrible fright when I returned to the Dream Sphere. It would have appeared as though I'd vanished.'

'In that part of time, magic is scarce,' said Maleika. 'And disappearing is considered to be impossible! Having you lead her to that fellow's red chariot, Karee, did not serve its purpose, but I'm sure I'll succeed in ushering her fate to her sooner or later. All right, then, dear. Race you home.'

The two forest-dwellers then hopped and ran respectively, back to their haven of harmony, a dew-glistening festival of foliage, to greet the peach-toned mists of morning.

XXV

Pieter could not recall how long he had been in the Grudellan Palace. Certainly it was a matter of several evenings.

He and Fripso lived meagrely. The rabbit was at least grateful that 'home' had become a larger prison. For Pieter, Eidred's dressing-quarter was just a prison and gratitude was in fact the opposite of his regard for body kings.

'Only if you use your magic in the way I advise,' the Solen's daughter had said to their request for freedom. Pieter had consistently refused each self-indulgent suggestion. To corrupt beauty-creation was unthinkable. The girl's entrapment in a dynasty she did not care for was hardly Pieter's concern. While he wanted to further her enlightenment he could not do so by enabling her access to more of the things she already had.

The commands for wishes remained unaltered. She wanted the linen to clean more easily, the voices of men-at-arms made quieter. A small amendment to her given name was also on the list. And much to Pieter's disdain, she'd asked him to vanish into thin air.

Although he'd refused to partake in such petty showmanship, he knew that even if he'd wanted to, he was incapable of doing this. The kindness merits that powered his magic were all used. Being unable to access Remembrance Essence meant he had no way of recalling whether his Dream Sphere self had gained more merits through actively guiding those in the future.

The wishes granted might free Pieter from his jailing but would only serve to entangle the girl further in hers. Besides all that, he knew that sprite magic, the beauty-creation residing within his heart, differed greatly to the magic of Grudellan sorcerers. It could not work on selfish demands.

All that Pieter had at his disposal was a fragile bond of friendship. He hoped to cultivate this as a means of steering the poor wretch towards better knowledge. For the moment he must endure the suffocating listlessness of a residence devoid of all signs of flora. He must make the most of these restrictions. He and Fripso told stories much of the time, tales of their slumbering sojourns, to keep their spirits lively.

Their captor at least was kind enough to feed them well. She would talk to them with an odd brand of stilted affection and, mindful of their nocturnal constitutions, respected the sleep they required during the day. When they woke at night, however, they would witness through the gate-like golden bars of the chamber's clothing quarter, in itself the size of a small room, two opal-blue eyes scanning them keenly. 'Oh goodness, the two of you have woken! How lovely to see you again,' Eidred was wont to say.

'Eidred, friend, these hours are yours now to sleep,' Pieter would scold after the girl had conversed with them almost to sun-up. 'You must treasure the night as your time for renewal. Do not let us weary you with conversation.'

The girl would yawn and nod, then tiptoe to her bed. She would call 'Good night', and when her breathing became regular and slow, her reluctant companions spoke of escape and longed for the beauty of their starlit stream.

'Might someone find us do you suppose, Pieter?' Fripso asked one such evening.

'Possibly so, but in the end it is up to us to free ourselves. It is not just you and me who are the victims.'

'We must free *her* as well,' agreed Fripso, his eyes aglow with admiration for the girl with the gentle heart. She had treated him as his own mother had.

'All three...must be free.' The elf paused. The words struck him as familiar. Echoes, perhaps, from the Dream Sphere.

'Free all three
Then safe are we.'

Not long after they had gone to sleep, Pieter and his fellow inmate were awoken by a sound. It echoed the memory of Pieter's first evening in the palace when a poktador had been slaughtered by gold-skins so fiendish the very knowledge of their presence was enough to induce violent chills. Remembering this, he smiled at the next recalled occurrence. The Princess of Grudella back then had stood above him terrifyingly, looking to all intents and purposes like a creature driven to kill. Thankfully, the axe had not been seen since, and the carrier of it had immediately been sheepish, thereafter accosting him only with apologies. ''Twas strange,' mused the elf in a whisper 'that she was unaware what possessed her to believe a monster dwelt in the corner.' What to gold-skins could ever be considered monstrous when they themselves had capabilities of devouring ill-fortuned fountain drinkers? Their disregard for life was as alarming as it was perverse.

In fairness to his captor, he did not believe she had the same capacity for cruelty. It puzzled him that one from such a hideous race should exhibit personality aspects that were so decidedly faerie-like. Her love for the forest was all-encompassing. Had it not been for her demands to magically alter small parts of future history, Pieter felt sure she would have returned him much sooner to his home. Often when he spoke of the Brumlynd clan a flutter of guilt would mar her expression. She would then begin on a persuasive speech about being freed at the cost of a mere three wishes. Pieter would change the subject and talk to the princess about sprites gaining kindness merits, to which she would listen with fascination. He told her how they earned these through their work in the Dream Sphere, abilities that assisted them in their creation of beauty—or, *magic* as it was commonly known among those of the empire—much of which had been robbed from sprites many season-cycles earlier.

Back then, body-king sorcerers had placed a lock on the devic realm's internal gateway to the Dream Sphere. Devic access to this dimension now was through slumber only. Locked off along with it had been the exquisite bodily senses that they all possessed, made possible through their unlimited connection to the slumbering world.

They were far more like mortals now. When sprites woke at the close of each day, they could only appreciate its beauty through *seeing* the fiery colours of sunset with only their eyes and *hearing* the call of night birds with only their ears. The feel of coolness that pervaded the air along with the fragrance of moonflowers and taste of berry cider were experienced separately also, through the other three senses. Enjoyment of their surroundings was now compartmentalised, causing them to be less intuitive.

Pieter continually nudged at Eidred's conscience. He thanked the gods that she did indeed have a conscience to nudge. He and his rabbit friend could just as easily have been captured by one of her monster relatives. Then they would never again see the silhouettes of trees around the Brumlynd camp, nor revel in the aroma of dancing wood fires.

This gold-skin was benevolent. Her sympathy for other life-forms appeared to be aptly developed. Her eagerness, also, to please those she'd trapped, had Pieter pondering over her parentage. It was as though amongst the rubble of hatred, which tainted the much afeared Grudellan Palace, a small spark of goodness had been buried, a tiny gem that thought itself to be nothing more than greyness, as a pearl might regard the oyster-shell that cocoons it.

Heredity and cocoons soon became a subject of discussion between Pieter and Fripso. 'Caterpillars do become butterflies after all,' noted the rabbit upon one waking. He'd been referring of course to the creature that was only half darkened by body kings. It retained its goodly mind and thus was able to evolve out of its cumbersome, genetically-tampered vehicle by weaving together the rays of both moon and sun: an enveloping fabric made solid by the creature's capacity to transform the density of frequencies. Lo and behold, for all the sprites to marvel at, emerged a magnificent specimen of light, colour, freedom and hope.

Prior to its degradation, the butterfly had been a flower faerie who was, to the sprites' dismay, seduced by an Atlantean solen's radiance at the end of the Pre-Destruction Century. Such a delicately exquisite being was this faerie, so empathetic was the faerie's regard for all living things, that through busying itself in understanding others, it forgot to identify with the self. Becoming susceptible to powers of possession: a faerie's demise and a lesson to all sprites. Self-respect was precious armour. Behaviour of an all-trusting nature was detrimental to the continuation of what body kings called 'the fey'. Was it possible this fair-haired maiden might be a hybrid like the butterfly? Could Eidred be partly devic origin or had she only recently been bestowed sprite qualities when unknowingly taking on Orahney's auric-field colours? Had a partial exchange of minds occurred?

Another shriek scattered the stillness. It made Pieter especially uncomfortable knowing his trapped and mesmerised elfin friends were identifying with the dark ones just as a dark one had befriended and identified with him.

Remembering the hundreds of bony, soil-crusted figures moving about the dunes like mechanical twigs, he turned to Fripso. 'Many elves have been taken by gold-skins,' he told the rabbit. 'Twelve of my friends are slaves in the mines.'

'Pieter, I am sorry for you.'

'And I am sorry for them. They were made to work during their time of slumber.'

'Toiling under the sun!' Fripso was aghast.

'I sacrificed sleep once so that I could rescue them. I hid within the thorn thicket and stole across to the sand dunes.'

Fripso's eyes were made large with concern.

Pieter slumped forward. He shook his head. 'It was awful, Fripso. Their auras were knotted into hideous yellow coils, heavy with thoughts of lack and fear. I stayed by them through the day. Once night arrived and the guards slept, I made myself known. Sadly, few elves could see me. In their solidity they'd lost the ability to perceive anyone who hadn't been robbed of heart power.

'Those who did see me were vacant-eyed. I told them I was there to assist their escape.' He recalled how the elves had refused; how each had insisted they were to labour for their birthright to appease their 'protectors'.

'You are sprites,' Pieter had cried. 'You do not live by the currency of gold!'

Protesting, they had said, 'We need our food and shelter.'

Pieter had persisted. 'The guards are sleeping,' he had said. 'Now is your chance to return to your forest.'

Pieter buried his face in his hands. 'I couldn't persuade them, Fripso,' he said. 'They insisted the forest would soon be built upon with the empire's expansion and praised their captors for remaining true to the "Century of Progress". I couldn't convince them that body kings were only dwelling in Elysium due to the compliant nature of their captives. "You're keeping them here," I said, "by working for them! There are many of you and few of them. Discard your dangerous obedience, and you will be free!"

' "But that would be dishonest," they'd said. "Our protectors provide us with all we need." '

Fripso snorted. 'How silly of them not to escape when they were able.'

'Yet I cannot blame my poor sprite brothers,' Pieter said. 'Any empowering decision would have been erased by the tangle of beliefs whittling away at their life-force.'

'They have lost heart,' said Fripso.

'Heart and higher mind,' Pieter said. 'No longer are they able to create beauty.'

Later that evening, when the two sat in silence within a moon-beam filtering through Eidred's window, Pieter was alerted to the sound of hiccupping whimpers.

'I weep for your fellow elves,' Fripso said.

'I am sorry, my friend,' said Pieter. 'I should never have told you of this tragedy. When the maiden sends me to the mines, I shall do my best to escape.'

'I do not believe Eidred would do such a thing.'

Relenting to a torrent of pessimism that clawed at his throat and constricted his chest, Pieter gazed woefully at the glittering chamber beyond the wardrobe's bejewelled bars. 'She is a body-king daughter, Fripso.'

XXVI

Dawn arrived glaringly. Pieter settled down to sleep and thought back to the last conversation he'd held with his dear Clan Watcher.

After having woken to the night, he'd sat by the fire. She had been at his side, passing him a cup of Remembrance Essence.

'I vaguely remember,' he said to her, 'a crystal dome and a leader in the future who is to address a large number of people. Their congregating as such is known as the Sonic Unity Gathering.'

Maleika, eager to learn of his last Dream Sphere visit said, 'And what does the leader say to these people at the gathering, Pieter?'

'There is something to celebrate,' Pieter told her. 'A return to the currency of kindness. The leader then announces the name of an individual who has been greatly responsible for this.'

'And who should this creature be?'

'The name is...er...it is difficult to recall.'

'Take another sip of Remembrance Essence, Pieter.'

Pieter did so. 'Oh!' he said. 'Det.'

'Det,' repeated Maleika.

'Ah...'

'Take another sip, Pieter.'

Pieter did so. 'Wise...'

Maleika nodded encouragingly. 'Wise.'

'La!' said Pieter finally.

'Well done, Pieter.' Maleika clasped her hands together. 'You have been shown someone who will one day restore this world to its former beauty. And we now know the sonic signature of this wonderful sprite. Det-ah-Wise-la!'

At that moment, they heard a rustling in the leaves.

Maleika and Pieter turned. Behind the oak tree, which arched across the Brumlynds' camp, silver-tipped and calm, hovered the silhouette of a tall, thin figure in a hooded cloak: a body king sorcerer eavesdropping on their Dream Sphere recollections!

Maleika rose to her feet. 'Away with you,' she cried. 'Away with you now, or I shall cast a spell so that you are no longer handsome!'

The silhouette fluttered off into the darkness. Pieter and Maleika chuckled at the idea of sprite magic used with nasty intent: a thoroughly amusing presumption. All that they wielded was for the benefit of nature, and nature was inherently kind. That sprites were meddlesome spell-casters was only a rumour amongst those of the royal court.

'I do not think, Maleika,' said Pieter, 'that this golden-skinned pryer will bother us further.'

'His pride will keep us safe,' said Maleika with a satisfied nod. 'And what is handsome or ugly anyway when it is little more than opinion?'

'And yet body kings believe their opinions to be truth.'

'Indeed they do, Pieter, indeed they do. I implore you, though, *do* remember to refer to them by their proper name. They like to be known as gold-skins.'

Wistful now, Pieter smiled at the memory of his conversation with his mother, the Clan Watcher. He would find a way soon to return to her.

Somehow he would return.

Chapter Eight

The Friday Fortnight evenings were always a bore for Izzie because the house then belonged to her mother.

Izzie and her friends wouldn't usually catch up until Sunday. While other kids whooped around the streets to celebrate the weekend's approach, Izzie's group conserved their energy so that Saturday mornings meant feeling fresh enough to get up before noon.

And so the lamps were traditionally Friday-Fortnight low, and the glass doors of the cabinets sparkled after Izzie had Windexed them. A platter of pretzels was placed on the coffee table, six wine goblets were set out on the kitchen counter, and the verandah light was flicked on so that it blazed like a persistent star through the gap in the sitting-room curtains.

Taking in the cosy scene, Izzie imagined capturing it in pastels and decided she'd have to use reds, golds and ambers to recreate that glimmery, forties-movie effect. 'This is what peace is,' she told herself, feeling proud of the house her mother had secured for them. The home's interior no longer seemed fuddy-duddy formal. Izzie had grown to regard it as gently elegant, with its patches of stained glass and whirly-curly ceiling cornices.

The doorbell chimed. 'See ya round, Peace,' Izzie groaned to herself. 'Hello, screech-fest.'

Her mother, reeking of patchouli aromatic essence, sprinted past her to the door looking embarrassingly like a teenager eager to go on a date. While Rosetta's hair looked shiny that evening, like a flat sheet of polished rosewood, normally it was dull, dark and boring. She opened the door and screamed, 'Royston!'

'Rosetta!' Royston screamed back. 'Your hair looks *fabulous*. Blow-drying it with that chia-seed serum makes it sooo much glossier! And I really dig the reddish highlights.'

'Well, I had to make an effort for you guys.'

From where she stood in the hallway Izzie could see a finger wagging. The finger belonged to Royston. 'But you don't always make that sort of effort for us, do you now? Still, I appreciate the fact that you've turned over a new leaf. Now all I have left to do is persuade you to get it slashed off and styled into an elfin bob.' He scissored his fingers.

Rosetta bunched the lengths of her hair protectively and gave Royston's shoulder an affectionate shove. She steered him inside, then turned to the man who had trailed in behind him. 'And I think I know who this is!'

'Rosetta, meet Darren. Darren, this is my dear, dear friend Rosetta. How many years has it been, sweets?'

'Ooh 'bout fifteen?'

'No, it'd be longer than that...wait a minnie...' Royston, having balded considerably in the past year, had grown a layer of facial hair to compensate for the loss of his Liberace curls. He rested his fingertips on the stubble and stroked his lower lip in an effort to recall. Hovering tentatively by Royston's side was a man of fine-boned proportions with a habit of smiling and nodding in a series of quivery bursts. The man was clutching a cake laden with strawberries, which Izzie knew would obliterate Rosetta's dieters' willpower. 'Yeah, has to be fifteen. I thought it could have been more.'

'It just seems like more,' said Rosetta laughing, 'because of all I've put you through! I've put him through a lot, Darren. It's a wonder he's still speaking to me, but then that's the person he is. He's a really, *really* beautiful man.'

Just great, thought Izzie. The screech-fest turns into a love-fest.

In theme with Izzie's supposings, Royston, who had spotted her doing the last of the dusting at the telephone foyer table, ran towards her with arms outstretched. 'And how's my little Izzie-Whizzy?' he said in a tone so filled with fondness it made Izzie chuckle.

'Not so bad, Roystie,' she said, allowing herself to sink into his hug. 'That aftershave: it's legendary.'

'This girlie's got excellent taste, Rosetta,' Royston hollered with a bulging-eyed nod, but Rosetta and Darren had already disappeared into the kitchen to prepare drinks.

In his left hand was a faded edition of *Our True Ancient History*. 'Except it's cologne, darlin'. Cologne for men. Simmering Pine it's called.'

'Cool!'

'So has this pretty little gal got herself a boyfriend yet?'

'I'm too young for a boyfriend,' Izzie protested, not adding that if that boyfriend happened to be Glorion Osterhoudt, she was way, *way* old enough.

'That's what you say,' said Royston, giving her ponytail an indulgent ruffle. 'But I can't see our Izzie staying solo for long. Mark my words. Some fella's going to sweep you off your feet in the next six months or so, and you'll be like: "Hey I'm not so young after all!" '

'That a prediction Royst?'

Royston, sensitively intuitive and known for his accuracy in foretelling occurrences, tilted his head to the side, adopted a more sober expression and said, 'It wasn't at the time, but now I think it is. It really is.'

Intrigued to know whether this might mean getting to go out with the boy she idolised, Izzie's voice became an excited whisper. 'Do you think he's Australian though...or would he be from overseas?'

'Got your eye on someone already, Iz?'

'No, no, no!' Dammit, the man was psychic. Or maybe she'd just been too obvious. Why did she have to bring up Glorion's nationality? Royston would detect her denial was a lie.

Luckily for Izzie, Royston did not look sceptical. Instead, he seemed to be locked in a contemplative state, judging by the liquidity of his faraway gaze. 'He's certainly not from here.'

Izzie wanted to clap her hands and leap about the hallway.

'But then again, I don't even feel he's from...anywhere. It's like there's this emptiness...this void.'

'Yes?' Izzie was desperate to hear more. 'What do you mean by that? What else do you see? What—'

'Royston bay-bee,' her mother trilled from the kitchen in a witchy squawk. 'Are you going to help us get these snacks prepared, or will I have to do something threatening?'

As though he really were a smidgen scared, Royston gave Izzie an apologetic smile and hurried to the kitchen.

Muffled, now that the walls acted as barriers, Royston said: 'I was giving Izzie a reading.'

And just as muffled from Rosetta: 'Oh, you were giving Izzie a reading! That's okay, keep going, I'll bring you out your drink. Do you want claret or...?'

Listening intently in the hope that she'd soon see a wineglass-in-hand Royston returning to the hallway, Izzie grimaced once she heard: 'Nah, that's fine, love. I'm sure Izzie would rather be phoning friends than getting a psychic reading from an old fogey like moi.'

Izzie trudged up the hallway towards her room.

'She's really blossoming, that girl,' Royston's voice echoed. 'Turning into quite the fatale.'

'Well she takes after her mother...' Mumble, mumble, mumble.

'Rosetta, we *know* you're a femme fatale, no need to brag about it. Sheesh! Can't tell you, Darren, how many budding romances and make-ups and break-ups I've endured hearing about with this fly-about woman...' Mumble, mumble, mumble.

'...Am not a...' Mumble.

'Yes you...' Mumble.

'Fake arguments beginning and the others aren't even here yet,' Izzie said to herself. She straightened the vase of homegrown Easter daisies on the foyer table facing the bathroom and dawdled to her bedroom.

The door was answered twice more. Curly haired, lanky Craig, a chilled kind of guy with a law firm in Surry Hills, was next to follow Royston and boyfriend. Craig at this stage was encouraging her mum to finish the law degree she'd resumed when Izzie began high school. Way back in the mid-nineties when he was a Legal Aid solicitor, Rosetta had been his client. She'd gone to him about child maintenance when trying to locate Izzie's father, a man who had left Australia with a new wife and seemed to have never existed.

When Izzie was little, she often heard her mother telling people that her father had 'done a disappearing act'. In Izzie's child's mind, he was a fascinating mystery. By the time she lined up for show-and-tell in her first year of primary school, she'd concluded he was a magician who had 'just vanished' and considered it newsworthy enough to share with her fellow finger-painters.

Mrs Priestley hadn't been so entertained by the revelation. Years later, Rosetta related the parent-teacher interview when she'd been asked if she knew that Izzie 'sometimes made up stories' and 'might have been compensating for the absence of her father by purporting he was "magical" and able to "disappear".'

Rosetta had confided she wasn't the least bit concerned. 'You were being *creative*, Izzie,' she'd said emphatically. 'And logical too. In a literal way. I went home from that interview full of pride for my imaginative little five-year-old.'

Craig's floorboard-creaking strides made a rhythmic accompaniment to Rosetta's ribbings about his 'secret project', some kind of cash cow that Craig wasn't prepared to talk about until its official launch. 'I don't think he's going to reveal anything tonight,' Rosetta said in a mock whine to Royston and Darren.

Next to shout greetings in the hallway was Lena the fair-haired health food shop owner, a friend of Rosetta's from first-year mature-age uni. The two always reminisced about that year as though everything in it had been nothing short of hilarious. The year after the hilarious one hadn't been as much fun. Whenever Rosetta mentioned it, she would gaze out at the backyard and shrug. Probably the year had been less full of laughs because the vanishing man she'd married demanded she drop uni to help out in his accounting firm. He'd left her soon after, for another woman. Left her holding the baby, and the baby had been Izzie. Rosetta's hopes of gaining a degree had then 'gone out the window' as she'd put it. Izzie supposed this was the reason her mother always stared out of windows when recalling those years. To subconsciously search for lost opportunities.

'Okay, Lena lovey,' Royston's voice echoed from the sitting room. 'You were busy with your shop last fortnight, so you can be first to read. Next two chapters please.'

'Two chapters? Oh, good!' Lena's voice lifted in volume. 'I like getting to be reader.'

XXVII

When Pieter became used to the home of a prisoner, he almost began to enjoy the role cast upon him. He and Fripso had become confidantes, just like soldiers of a later time united by unjust conditions.

He'd resolved to view this restriction as a learning opportunity. While dwelling within a royal residence, he would find out all he could about gold-skins and their mysterious rituals. At every meeting with Eidred, he asked about her family and her early life, at the same time noticing her auric field shrink and darken as storm clouds do. Gold-skin auras were rarely pretty. They exuded basic hues, nothing of the gentler, illuminated ones that graced those of devic heritage, although Eidred's colours softened whenever she spoke to her captives.

Fripso was eager to hear Pieter's findings. Explaining them allowed Pieter to better remember the accounts Eidred had given him, of the Norwegian invasion not so many season-cycles ago that had robbed so many of the chance to complete their soul-fulfilling assignments.

From whence they had come, no-one could fathom. That they were from a universe which opposed the one they had infiltrated was understood. Where exactly this topsy-turvy location marked its existence had little bearing on the work devas had set out to complete: the advancement of all things goodly so that *beauty-creation*—the only honourable brand of magic—could flourish.

Still, some hint as to where they were from might help his fellow sprites better comprehend the powers they were doing their best to deflect. And so the question evolved one starless night when clouds crowded an inky sky.

'Here I am, lovelies,' sang Eidred. Her dish, which still held bones of marsh birds, disgusted Pieter and Fripso. 'Oh I am sorry. Let me rid my platter of these. I know how much it vexes the two of you to see the animal carcasses we ingest, yet you must understand we need this.'

'But you don't,' grumbled Fripso. The rabbit was newly accustomed to conversing with a gold-skin. Faunal parents warned their young against trusting gold-skins enough to speak to them, and Fripso doggedly observed this rule, but Pieter's arrival had changed all that. The elf encouraged him to communicate with the girl as the pretence of being mute would mean he might only speak to Pieter, and then that he might only speak to Pieter outside of the girl's presence. 'Rabbits graze on the grass the land offers,' Fripso continued. 'And Pieter and his family only ingest liquids. You would never see them eat at all, Eidred. They are mostly spirit.'

'How you maintain your weight, elf, is beyond me,' said Eidred with a sigh. 'And you have grown so much taller! You were little over my height when you first arrived here. Still, your species is made of more transparent stuff than ours. Your atoms are lighter, as you said. You are non-dependent on nourishment.'

'Not non-dependent,' Pieter said. 'We still require nourishment as you know. The only reason I've survived here as long as I have is the water that you conscientiously bring for me. That is my sustenance. But preying on something living...Hurting it! Ending it! Ingesting it! This is something our species cannot imagine.'

Eidred pushed through the bars of her clothing quarter a plateful of Wakkel-Weed for Fripso and a cup filled with stream water from the dell for Pieter. 'I wish I could be noble like you, and kinder to animals.'

Pieter watched her pityingly. 'What stops you, Eidred?'

The girl bowed her head, and Pieter thought he heard a sob from behind her veil of hair.

'Baff-Daaaahmly,' she said.

'What did you say?' said Pieter and Fripso in unison.

'My family,' said Eidred. 'I said "my family",' and with that she broke into a cascade of sobs.

'Poor Eidred,' said Fripso. ''Tis not your fault you were born into such a grotesque genetic code.'

'Perhaps there was a mistake,' murmured Eidred. She gazed up at the grizzly clouds that filled the stone vista. 'Perhaps under the rubble...Nay, forget I made mention of it.'

The rubble! Hadn't this been a thought of Pieter's? Surely not. Of all things they were, gold-skins were certainly not intuitive. And yet a princess from the Grudellan Palace had echoed his sentiments about a gem lost in rubble. Coincidence, he supposed; little more than that. He had been encaged for too long, was making somethings out of little nothings that were best left alone.

He became aware of the girl regarding him. A small crinkle had formed on her forehead. 'Uncanny,' she said, mostly to herself.

'What is uncanny, Eidred?' asked Fripso.

'The resemblance,' she said. 'Pieter looks very much like a boy in a painting of ours.'

'No-one would ever paint *him*,' said the rabbit. With a chuckle he added. 'He's far from remarkable, this elf.'

At the thought of vainly posing for an artist who might think him worthy of replication, Pieter laughed too.

Eidred placed her hands on her hips. In a flurry of passion, she said, 'The boy in the painting I tell you of is in no way unremarkable!'

'He is not?' said Fripso pretending surprise.

'No. In fact he is very fine to look at.'

In an effort to explain this, Fripso said, 'Ah well. I suppose by gold-skin standards our friend Pieter might be considered fine. I imagine his features and proportions would agree with the golden mean.'

'Indeed they do,' said Eidred nodding importantly.

'What is the golden mean?' Pieter wanted to know. Whatever it was, it sounded intriguing.

'You must have been dozing through one of our conversations Pieter,' said Fripso. 'The golden mean is a measurement of architecture and, among other things, facial features and bodily proportions that these people's gods insist is the formula for beauty. As you know, Eidred's relatives are obsessed with measuring. Measuring, measuring! Always measuring.'

'I wish you could see this portrait,' Eidred said to them. 'It is displayed in my father's gallery. I'm sure you'd both agree upon the likeness.'

Unsure as to whether resembling a body king, who by body-king standards possessed an agreed-upon level of handsomeness, was either a compliment or an insult, Pieter dismissed these thoughts as useless and approached the subject that was weighing on his mind. 'Do you know, Eidred, where your family hails from?' he asked. 'Originally, I mean.'

'They hail from the South East,' said Eidred decidedly. 'Remember how I told you they built their triangles then travelled to the North West?'

'Save your geometry and mathematics and directions for someone who understands them,' grumbled Fripso, unaware of his gracelessness towards someone who had delighted him with a generous amount of Wakkel-Weed.

'I fear I cannot translate into fey or fauna language,' apologised Eidred.

'Yes, yes, I understand this.' Enthusiastic now, Pieter nodded. 'I remember it clearly from the last time you told me. But what about before that, Eidred? What of your true origins?'

'Do you mean interplanetary?'

'Interplanetary, yes!'

'I...to be honest...I have been afraid to ask. My schooling is for telling, not asking. My minders educate me on the triangles of the east and the gems of the south, but they do not care to reveal anything further back than that.'

'Pity,' said Pieter.

'Mm. Pity it is. But Pieter, if you wish, I could obtain the answer you desire. I could intrude into the library when all are asleep. I have grown quite fond of remaining awake in the silvering hours. It will be no trouble not sleeping one night in order to search for the script that speaks of the world we are from.'

'Eidred, friend, we want not to put you in danger. 'Twas just a small wondering. Don't trouble yourself any longer over it.'

'But I want to know, Pieter!' The girl threw her arms out to her sides with a kind of drama Fripso and Pieter weren't used to. 'Since I stumbled across you and Fripso, I have learnt much. This, I realise, is the faerie wish I was hoping to have granted, not the other things. I wanted *wisdom,* my friends, and wisdom is what you are giving me. I do not need magic. Like you told me, Pieter, expecting this is both disrespectful to your species and manipulative, and I don't fancy myself to be either of these things. In truth I believe magic, if allowed to be used, would have prompted your successful escape, but you blatantly refused to wield it.' She sighed. 'I feel we have been thrown together.'

Pieter turned and addressed Fripso. 'Well you and I have, cer- tainly,' he said to the rabbit. 'Dwelling together in an alcove reserved for frocks, coronets and dance slippers has not been an ideal of liberty.'

'Do you forget,' said Fripso, growing again in impertinence, 'that you have in fact thrown *us* into a prison, Eidred, and haven't enabled our release?'

'Oh no!' The girl's eyes widened. For a moment she looked genuinely stupefied. 'No, you do not think this is what I do?'

'Eidred,' Pieter said, leaning against the bars, 'we are tired of living in your wardrobe. We pose no threat. Why won't you set us free?'

'Oh my goodness,' squealed Eidred. 'We misunderstand each other! You think I am trapping you here against your will!'

'Well aren't you?' said Fripso, now thoroughly confused.

'Indeed not! You do *not* understand! I am responsible for your freedom! I am here to ensure your survival! Why else would I have pleaded with Pieter to use his magic? I wanted nothing more than for the two of you to return to Elysium Glades. Protected by magic, however, to enable a safe escape. Pieter would hear nothing of it though. And now, should the two of you attempt to leave the palace, you would end your existence immediately. Already, Pieter, the power of our surroundings is solidifying you more. It's made you less magical.'

Pieter knew he had become heavier in heart and body since having been locked away in Eidred's chamber. Healing was more difficult to access now. His daily dreams were fainter than ever. Although his prime concern was visiting Maleika and the other Brumlynds in his slumber, without the aid of their Remembrance Essence, he had no recollection of what would have occurred. Providing they had enough Remembrance Essence to go around, his clan would recall having spoken to him. They would know by now that he was inside the palace.

When Pieter had tested invisibility on himself, he was unable to make it work. His physical vehicle had matured. No longer was he younger than the Princess of Grudella by three season-cycles as he'd been when his earthly self held a finer vibration. To anyone who might have observed, he was now her peer.

'Yet if you hadn't stolen me in the first place,' Fripso said to Eidred, 'we wouldn't be indulging in such a dismal discussion. I think you have put me into a terrible situation. I think—'

'Wait, Fripso.' Pieter held a finger to his lips. 'Listen to what the maiden means to say.'

'Fripso, my pet. Do you not remember a weasel in the glades? The weasel intended to pounce. I felt it would traumatise you to recall, but it appears you are unaware this ever happened. The day I concealed you in my basket and made a home for you here was the day you evaded death.'

'All I knew,' said Fripso with startled eyes, 'was that someone had stolen me.'

'Rescued you,' said Eidred. 'Sadly you saw this in reverse. And as for you, Pieter, had you not realised the danger of infiltrating a realm such as this? A species such as yourself? Did you not know that they can end your time here in the blink of an eye?'

'But I could have fled earlier if not caged in your dressing-quarter and—'

'No, Pieter, let me continue. You trespassed! You hid in my room. I concede you did this out of concern for Fripso, and fortunately for you, I gave up my dressing-quarter to provide a hiding place. This division of my chamber is one of the few areas of the palace unlit by fey-and-fauna-depicting luminaries. You are thankfully not visible to our guards.'

'And I made myself completely invisible to all when I followed you in here.'

'Which is just as well. Do you see those bright circles up there in the eaves? The guards survey just about every inch of this residence. There is a room beneath the palace containing a magical mirror broken into many squares. Each of the squares contains a view of the areas that the luminaries send to them.'

'And so they spy on you through these fey-and-fauna-depicting luminaries?'

'Not on me. Not on Gold's Kin. They are watching out for intruders. 'Tis for our protection, you must understand. The guards cannot be everywhere at once. What would we do if an evil gnome trundled in and attempted to slay us all?'

'Gnomes do not kill,' said an indignant Pieter.

'And they certainly aren't evil,' said Fripso. 'None of the sprites are.'

'A mango eater then. What if a mango eater tried to devour one of our courtiers?'

'Eidred! Friend!' To hide his amusement, Pieter turned away from the ill-advised maiden. 'The only things mango eaters devour are mangoes!'

'Still, there are many dangers that lurk in Elysium. You should be pleased that I am respectful of the fey. I am grateful I do not need such contraptions. My gift of faerie sight means you are *not* invisible to me as you are to everyone else of the court. But the matter-depicting luminaries display you in their fragmented mirrors. That is how they *can* perceive you!'

'That and the donning of those sprite-seeing garments.'

'Fey-detection cloaks which are worn in the forest. Oh dear!' Eidred covered her eyes with her hand. 'I worry, constantly, about the two of you plotting an escape in my absence.' Eidred anxiously searched their faces. 'Please do not try this, I beg of you! If either of you ventured outside my clothing quarter, our troopers would find you. Those spying luminaries are trained on each and every exit. You took a terrible risk, Pieter,' Eidred scolded. 'You've locked yourself inside and...'

'And?'

'And I care enough to conceal you. From *them,* but if ever you tried to flee, you would be swiftly discovered. Neither you nor Fripso would return to the forest alive.'

XXVIII

At the murmur of voices outside Eidred's chamber door, Pieter opened his eyes and rose to his feet. Two Grudellans were speaking in hushed tones.

'And so,' said one of these voices, 'we await with interest this journey to the previous century. Are we to expect much in the way of disturbance?'

A cold laugh echoed throughout the hall. 'None at all, save for a moment or two of thunderous rumbling. You must understand that our palace is to be preserved in its transportation to the Norwegia of old. Nothing we have or need will be changed. Apart from the forests and glades of Elysium with all its beastly fey, and the land that surrounds it, everything will remain true to the century in which we currently reside.'

'And I hear that Rahwor is later to travel in time by himself!'

'Rahwor,' Pieter whispered. 'I have heard this name before.' The image of an eagle returned to him then, in flashes, a glowing-eyed creature making its plea above the merry orange sparks of the Brumlynd campfire.

The other voice in the hall was replying. 'Yes, but Rahwor is to travel *forward* in time. Once prepared, he will travel aeons into the future.'

'And Rahwor is to seek out the enemy who plans to disrupt gold-skin law?'

'A traitor by the name of Det-ah-Wise-la.'

Det-ah-Wise-la! Was this not the name Pieter had pondered over when he'd remembered, prior to sleep, his last words with Maleika? He thought of the Sonic Unity Gathering announcement that Alcor had shown him; of a leader, whose name was Nikolaus, introducing Det-ah-Wise-la as someone respected, and wise too, perhaps, as her name suggested.

The voices—moments before quiet, although clear—were faint with distance. Pieter thought of Det-ah-Wise-la, who appeared to now be in danger, and looked back with regret on his and Maleika's carelessness. Had they been more vigilant, Pieter and Maleika would have discovered the eavesdropper earlier. Had they spoken in careful whispers, the woman yet to incarnate in the faraway future would still be unknown to body kings. Inadvertently, they had beckoned adversity; had invited attention of the cruellest kind.

The sun was now risen. Its fiery beams splashed the chamber floor with bold sparkles. Pieter settled himself down to sleep. Rarely did he recall his visits to the Dream Sphere. With no Remembrance Essence to sip, he was at a loss. He could at least resolve what to do there. And so he vowed to ask Alcor how the currency of kindness might be preserved; would request the task of keeping safe this noble aspiration of future people.

Contemplating that place, thousands of seasons-cycles separate from him and yet still very much real in its future place on the earthly timeline, Pieter floated off to his slumber.

Not long after, a faint rumble outside shook Pieter awake.

Hearing a wail from Eidred in her bed, he sat up.

'Ah no! Ah no!'

'It is only a storm, friend,' he called. 'Or you are under the influence of a nightmare.'

'No, Pieter,' Eidred called. 'This is no nightmare. Nor thunder of any kind. 'Tis what I feared! Ah no! Ah no!'

And then the floor of the dressing-quarter dipped suddenly sideways. It had shifted of its own accord!

'Fripso,' Pieter yelled. 'Brother, are you all right?'

A small voice called back, 'Goodness me, whatever happened?'

The rumbling increased to a deafening roar. The floor shook violently. Pieter was flung onto his back. The rabbit whimpered. The gold-skin girl sobbed.

Dazed by the unfamiliar light of the early sun, Pieter tried in vain to see Eidred. The palace's jolts and starts, lesser now, yet disconcerting, were disrupting his view.

Another bout of quaking hurled Pieter to the wall. There was nothing he could hang onto; nowhere he could anchor. The quakes were mercilessly throwing him from corner to corner.

At last he saw her. She was leaning against the chamber window, clutching her head in her hands and shouting. 'The Backwards-Winding! No, no! The Backwards-Winding has begun and it is all my fault.'

All before Pieter dissolved into a blur. The image before him, of Eidred and Fripso, and of the dressing-quarter's barred doors, and of the very chamber that surrounded them, was now whirling into a peculiar combination of stripes, undulations of colour that rippled and radiated alarmingly.

'Pieter, are you still there?' called Fripso. 'All that I see is fragments of nothing!'

'I am here, Fripso,' called Pieter. 'Eidred, what is happening to your palace?'

'The empire is winding backward,' Eidred called. 'The Backwards-Winding is taking place!'

Pieter slid across on his belly to take hold of the dressing-quarter bars, which shuddered beneath his grip. Fripso's small body tumbled to his side. The soft pressure of Fripso's front paws kneaded against Pieter's elbow. Letting go of one of the bars, Pieter held the vulnerable animal to his chest.

Silence at last arrived. The quake subsided.

Fripso, evidently the first to recover and remarkably unaffected by all the surprising somersaults he had endured, said, 'Eidred, what in heaven's name was that?'

'It is something too, too awful to explain,' said Eidred. She hurried to the dressing-quarter and asked Pieter to pass her a gown of ivory silk. 'It is over now, though, so you must go to your slumber. And I must prepare for my schooling.'

Pieter folded his arms. 'You care not to tell us why this chaos has occurred?' Like Fripso, he was mystified, although after having overheard the talk between two body kings earlier, he already suspected he knew. He could not understand, however, why Eidred had woefully uttered that it was all her fault.

Eidred was replying to him now. 'I care not to even think of it,' she said. 'So I shan't, and nor must you. Sleep well now, my dears. And rest assured that all will be calm again from this day on.'

Fripso fell swiftly to his slumber, but Pieter did not. His mind was taken up with the memory of the Grudellans' icy voices and their references to the hooded eavesdropper, Rahwor.

Rahwor, the eagle had said. *That is the name of my spell caster. He has trapped my earthly self inside a shell of stony ignorance.*

'And I failed to help,' Pieter said, astounded at his own callousness. 'He asked me to free him, and I inferred he might be a sorcerer himself.'

It was then that Pieter recalled a dream, otherwise known as the spontaneous retrieval of a Dream Sphere visit without the aid of Remembrance Essence. He could now remember the events that took place directly after his conversation with the mountain-circling eagle. Prior to exiting that rocky world, when he'd called to Alcor to open the Devic Great Hall door, he'd intuitively projected himself into a future life of the eagle's.

A spinning wheel was all Pieter had seen, then a sad girl at it, shredding wool and shedding tears. But the eagle was not the living one. He was the spindle, solid as rock, with only etheric ears to listen as the girl spoke lamenting words to herself, of a love now lost. But Pieter's eagle friend had grown. For in his unmoving consciousness he was *absorbing* and he wanted to know what it was to feel love and pain.

As he delved further into the eagle's future lives, Pieter was projected into a little hut where a crone sat nursing a crying child while stirring an iron cauldron. The eagle was still in a natural element like the rock—a product plumbed from the earth—as he was when a sculptor's craft, but warmer, heated by fire and basking in the tenderness the old woman provided for her grandchild, absorbing the care that was unconsciously spilled into the stew.

Yes, learning more about serving, about other worlds, yet still unmoving. If the eagle had taken a step towards learning of spheres other than his own, he would not have needed to revert to such non-progressive embodiments. Next, if warmth were mastered, he would become a moth; if light learnt, a blossom on a tree; growth understood, a tree himself, and then...but Pieter told himself he mustn't steal glimpses of another's future. He changed his mind and glimpsed two more. Warm-blooded once again, and again a bird, a sparrow though, in search of humility. Humility gained, a kingfisher.

Sleep claimed him once the owl in Elysium embarked on a slow, sad lament. Wearied by a quake that Eidred had called 'the Backwards-Winding', and sobered by the memory of having turned away an eagle's earnest request, the elf boy drifted up to the Dream Sphere, his heart leaden with sorrow.

Izzie, confined to her bedroom while the sitting room was taken up by Rosetta's Friday Fortnight group, concentrated on pasting onto her four-seasons collage photos of the front garden's red Japanese maple, courtesy of the camera Sara had lent her.

She'd been in the hallway when Royston and the quivery-nodder had arrived, and had soon after heard Craig's amused reluctance to discuss his 'secret project'. Someone else was buzzing the bell now. Had to be Eadie.

New Zealand Maori Eadie had left a cryptic voice message earlier in the evening, saying in her lovely NZ accent: 'Have to give tonight's Friday Fortnight a miss, unfortunately. I've been involved in a small disaster. Not serious though. No need to phone me back, I'll tell you all about it tomorrow.' But now she was here.

'Caught a cab,' Eadie was telling Rosetta. 'Had a last-minute change of heart.'

According to the hallway explanation that Izzie would rather have not been overhearing, Eadie, on her way home from late-night shopping the evening before, had crashed into her garage door. She'd forgone wearing her contact lenses and forgot she'd closed it on her way out.

'Duh,' was all Izzie could say to that.

Eadie's hospitalised car was at present getting an eighteen-hundred-dollar patch-up, and Eadie had reached a place in her life where she was hating short-sightedness, garage doors and smirking teenaged mechanics who she suspected regarded her as some kind of 'airhead' when hearing the gory details.

'Duh!' Izzie said again. Why hadn't Eadie at least popped on some specs before getting into the car? Feeling bad about eaves-dropping on, and scoffing at, someone's account of their own bad luck, Izzie resolved to focus on the winter corner of her collage.

Poor Eadie was always getting into scrapes, similar to Izzie's mother in that way, only flightier. Funnily, this was not where their similarities ended. Both had flowing hair and olive skin tone. Both had in common the characteristics of generous features within a broadish oval face, although from Izzie's portrait-painter perspective, the differences would show up on a sketch-pad if each likeness were broken into grids. Rosetta's mouth was wider and fuller than Eadie's, as were her eyes, which although dark, were known to display golden glints that Royston considered to be 'tigerish'.

'You've gotta have a bit of Maori in your background,' Eadie would tell Rosetta, but Rosetta wasn't so sure. She had her heart set on one day finding out that she had some indigenous Australian in her blood—like Craig, whose grandparents were Aboriginal—because the idea of ancestors who'd lived through the Dreamtime appeared rather glamorous to her. People had usually assumed Rosetta to be

Greek because of her mama and baba's ethnicity but even now, twenty years after she'd left home, remarks that she looked Mediterranean weren't uncommon. Rosetta had put it down to being brought up amid warmly demonstrative mannerisms often seen to be typical of her foster family's culture. 'But I doubt that I *am* Greek,' she'd say.

With the silent ten minutes of their 'World Peace' prayer complete, the voices had risen over the *charp-de-woop-choo* of the reggae that Craig would have brought.

'Amazing what happened to Rosetta last Sunday, Craig.' This was Lena. 'Did you hear about it?'

'Nope. What happened?'

And so the hostess embarked on the story that Izzie now endured a fourth time, about the tinkly voiced lady on the phone, and the nap she'd had when she dreamt she got locked out and encountered a tarot reader of indigenous Australian origin. She'd gone to the netball courts in this dream and had been given a lift home.

Previously, Izzie hadn't seen significance in the anecdote. Its continual playback meant she could just about mouth everything from memory. Tonight, though, while she listened more attentively to the events, she realised that what happened two Sundays ago did in fact have a spooky quality.

Craig and Eadie, new to the story, said things like 'Wow,' and '*No way*' over and over, which, Izzie supposed might have swayed her to empathise with her mother's amazement.

'And that's not all,' Rosetta said. 'But the last thing we want is burnt vol-au-vents, so we'll break for a commercial while I go and rescue them.'

'Wait,' Lena ordered. 'Let *me* get them out of the oven. And keep talking!'

The kitchen clattered with the oven door opening and the retrieval of a baking tray.

The story rolled onwards from where its narrator had chased after someone's rabbit.

Best part: the part I'm starring in, Izzie thought with a smile as her mother related in minuscule detail how 'thoughtful little Izzie' had offered to make her a cup of cocoa.

Izzie had never bothered to hang around and overhear this bit of the story. It embarrassed her too much recalling how her friend and friend's father had reacted when they'd driven up Ashbury Avenue only to see Rosetta prancing about the road and stooping forward, grasping stupidly at the air. Charlotte's dad had said 'What the...?' in the same way he had when they'd found her asleep on the verandah muttering about a rabbit. And then she'd rambled on, again, about a rabbit, this time to the driver of a stationary car, telling the man she'd been mistaken, that there hadn't been a rabbit at all.

To hear the story's conclusion now was freaky. 'Speak louder,' Lena called above her own cling-clanging, obviously trawling the cupboards for a savouries platter.

'It disappeared! The rabbit had actually vaporised!' In quieter tones, Rosetta told them she'd been terrified she was losing her marbles. 'Poor Izzie,' she said between laughs. 'She's convinced I'm going senile. And whenever I try to explain the real reason for waving my arms about on the road, she escapes to her room with the excuse of having to do homework.'

Lena, Craig, Royston and Eadie reassuringly insisted that she'd witnessed an apparition. Spirits, they said, were capable of crossing dimensions. The rabbit must have not only visited her in the sleep dimension—when she'd dreamt about the Molly woman—but also during her waking hours.

'If I'd been there, I would have told the rabbit to go to the light,' Royston said.

'I think it did anyway,' Rosetta said, 'without any prompting from me because it vanished with record speed.'

'I feel sure Molly and her rabbit are ghosts trapped between worlds,' said Eadie. 'I mean, it's not hard to imagine they're no longer alive if Molly drove as recklessly as you say. And I realise this is a really sad thought, but you did say her car lacked seat belts.'

'I'd happily argue that there's no way Molly could be a ghost. Dreams are supposed to be the result of our imaginations shedding their garbage, but I can't be so sure anymore because there was another weird thing in all of this.'

'And what was that?' said Darren.

'Something that happened when I got changed for bed.'

Craig's voice chimed in again, this time huskily. 'Just forming a mental picture of that,' he said. 'Right, gotcha. Go on.'

'I plumped up one of my pillows, and...you won't believe this! Underneath it was one of my tarot cards.'

'Which one?' said Eadie. 'Not the King of Cups!'

'That's exactly what it was. I rushed out to the sitting room and went systematically through each of the tarots. The card was definitely one from my pack, but how could it have got under my pillow?'

Rosetta gazed around the room with a pride that bordered on motherly. The Friday Fortnight group. Friends who shared her passion for Lillibridge's book. Five faces aglow with dancing orange light. Craig had made the hearth's flicker of flames possible with the firewood he'd brought.

She was pleased her guests had backed her up on the conclusion that Molly and her rabbit might have been real, in some dimension at least. They continued discussing the dream-woman and Curry the way others might discuss celebrities, analysing, re-analysing and singling out parts of the dream, some of which Rosetta argued weren't relevant at all.

'Like my old man might say, it's not a Bob Dylan song,' Craig pointed out. 'I think the major message concerns Rosetta not allowing herself to lose hope in finding a soulmate. Forget all the other stuff.' He then asked Rosetta, as he often did, how her love life was faring.

'Not good at all,' she said, 'but then, since I hit my late thirties it's been slim pickings. Men prefer slim women.'

Craig was quick to disagree. 'Not every guy wants someone stick-insect thin, Rosetta. Plenty of us go for brunette bombshells.'

Rosetta couldn't help laughing at Craig's exaggerated view of her. 'I'm not sure "brunette" could ever precede "bombshell".' To Lena, she said, 'Isn't the term only ever used for blondes?'

'Generally speaking.' In an effort to look the part, Lena adopted a hand-on-hip pose and fluttered her eyelids at the ceiling. 'Although, foils aside, I think I'd have to be buxom to comply.'

They returned to discussing the princess feeling alien to her family, and the friendship she'd formed with the elf and rabbit. Royston and Lena speculated on what royal Eidred must have meant in Chapter XXVIII when she referred to a random quake as 'the Backwards-Winding'.

Rosetta and Craig threw in ideas as to who the mysterious Det-ah-Wise-la might have been and which timeframe in the sprites' future she might have lived in if credence were ever given to the crazy rumour that Lillibridge's book was an authentic account of ancient events and not just a quaintly fanciful fairy tale.

Rosetta thought Det-ah-Wise-la might have been a code name for Joan of Arc. 'She freed her homeland of domination. Maybe that's what Maleika meant by restoring the world's former beauty.'

'Nah,' said Craig. 'Too warlike. I reckon Det-ah-Wise-la was someone whose actions never reached the history books. Will we start up the coffee now?'

'Sure,' said Rosetta. 'But I just want to let you guys know about the launch of yet another overseas Friday Fortnight group. It's in the United Kingdom, and it's going to be run by Glynis and Dudley Hampton of Tintagel in Cornwall.'

'Haven't been to England in years.' Craig flicked his iPod onto French Classics. 'One of these days I'll plan another trip.'

'Visit that new group, then, if you do,' said Lena. 'And ask them where in Cornwall Reverend Edward Lillibridge was supposed to have lived. And died...although I doubt there's any record of his death.'

'Absolutely I will!' Craig fine-tuned the volume, and the sounds of a lone accordion bounced into life.

Eadie had already put the kettle on. Rosetta buttered scones, sliced the cake Darren had brought and readied the cups and saucers while the guttural strains of Edith Piaf rolled in from the sitting room. She sang along, uttering gobbledy-gook in place of lyrics she didn't know, and whipped up a brew on Royston's borrowed espresso machine. A comforting aroma of roasted coffee beans wended its way through the kitchen. Royston and Darren wandered in from the sitting room. She poured them each a cup.

'Smoky tones with a unique brand of melancholy ardour,' said Royston after taking a sip, and Rosetta was surprised to learn that it wasn't the coffee he was talking about but her singing. 'Sounds like a velvet-voiced blues singer, doesn't she, Darren?'

Looking impressed, Darren nodded a series of nods.

'Even with my pseudo French?' Rosetta pretended to look injured. 'You're not having a go at my language skills are you, Roystie? I did happen to learn French. At school.'

'It was your voice I was talking about, not your crazed attempt at masking the words.' Addressing Darren, Royston added, 'She was definitely one of those cabaret artists from the golden age of jazz.'

'We should talk Rosetta into entering that comp my brother hosts at the Bondi Diggers,' Darren said to Royston. Turning to Rosetta he said, 'So you were a sultry songstress in another life!'

'If reincarnation happens to be real, then apparently I was. I crooned my way through the art-deco era, but only according to Royston.'

When the evening came to an end, Rosetta told Darren how happy she was to meet him finally and agreed to be his guest at a poetry club get-together. 'I'll try to dig up some verses I wrote, back when I was my daughter's age,' she said when they walked through to the hallway.

'Please do,' said Darren. 'Look at that! How beautiful.' He gestured to the hallway's floorboards turned into a pool of reflected colour from the front door's stained-glass. 'Hm! Must be the placement of your verandah light globe. Yes, definitely come along to Poets Garret, Rosetta. We love having guests who recite their work.'

After the door had thumped shut behind them, Rosetta rinsed out the cups and wineglasses. The phone rang when she was settling them into the dish rack.

'Just checking what you're having for breakfast tomorrow.' Craig on his mobile.

Aware he was referring to the command in her dream to not 'abandon eggs', she said, 'An omelette of course.'

'Just as well. You don't want Molly haunting your dreams again. Hey, I reckon I've worked out the symbolism in that statement.' He asked what she and Lena had settled on for the name of the charity they hoped to form.

'We were thinking of calling it Promoting Peace on Earth.'

'PPE?'

'Yeah, but we've since decided on Ending Global Suffering.'

'Aha! I was pretty sure that was the name you chose. Well, there you have it.'

'Have what?'

'Where Molly Carr's reference to a non-vegan diet came from, although as it turns out, it's nothing to do with food. It's a message to persist with Ending Global Suffering. EGS.' Craig laughed at her expression of surprise, said goodnight in a whisper and ended the call. Encouragement to do with Ending Global Suffering? If her friends were right, if the dream was in fact an encounter with someone from another dimension, then perhaps a gift had been presented, an insight into her future.

She moved to the sitting room, peeked through the curtains as she was in the habit of doing nowadays before bed, humming a power anthem and whispering '*Scram*' when the intruder images threatened to encroach on her tranquil state of mind, then ambled to the bathroom.

While brushing her teeth and dissolving, with her cheap-and-cheerful cleanser, the gunk resembling boot-polish that caked her lashes, she mulled over Izzie's birthday picnic. The dining room clock had chimed midnight ten minutes ago. Her daughter's birthday had just moved from eight days away to seven. In a week little Izzie would be sweet sixteen! Rosetta scowled into the mirror. Her

cleanser-foamed face scowled back. 'You should be in a position to afford more for her,' she said. 'Why couldn't you have found an extra job?'

The sooner she managed to get back to her uni course, the closer she would be to a nicely paid law career. Being on Jack Barnaby's roster was fine for now, but it got degrading when staff at the offices she cleaned scribbled down tense little complaints. MW's gripe the week before was a prime example of this. A Post-it note stuck to an empty desk had read: *Cleaner, Please don't miss the floor. MW.* Jack had given her strict instructions to clear the bins of the office only. Nothing more. Jack's workers were not required to tidy under desks, disappointing news to anyone too squeamish to do a quick check of their misses at the end of the day. Inflamed at receiving the anonymous command, Rosetta had seized up a pen and written underneath: *Banker, Please don't miss the bin. RM.*

The idea of an additional job as a nanny had gained traction since she'd spotted the newspaper ad two Sundays back. On Tuesday she was off to Cabarita Heights for a meeting with Bernadette Weissler, who explained in a businesslike return call that an unavoidable trip to Vanuatu over the school holidays had necessitated the search for a 'firm but amiable stand-in mother'.

A job like this for up to a fortnight wasn't so bad. Small amounts of temporary work might eventually lead to something permanent.

It was the silver-edged stars of lemon and pale-purple that had done it. The optometrist had since peered at her over his tortoiseshell half-specs and declared her vision perfect. A day later, she'd remembered two previous instances when she'd seen those ethereal blobs and wondered whether they might be a lucky omen, courtesy of her guardian angels. They'd appeared years ago when she'd read Jack Barnaby's ad. She hadn't thought of cleaning at the time, but despite an abysmal lack of experience, Jack had told her the job was hers. Four years on and she was yet to thank those lucky stars for the stream of regular work that followed.

Those same stars had hovered jubilantly around a rental notice until she'd taken a second look. Her landlord had decided to sell, and she'd had to find somewhere fast. Admittedly, living in the Punchbowl block of flats had been anything but cosy. The creepy guy in the laundry had seen to that, as had the barking blue heeler and rubbish-dumping neighbours, but a friendship had sprouted—Grant Belfield phoned her fairly regularly these days—and Izzie had done beautifully at Punchbowl High. Getting to be Year Nine Captain didn't happen to everyone. So if Rosetta's guardian angels were responsible, the focus had been more on neighbourly spirit and scholarly accolades than on boring old security.

After those stars made their most recent appearance, a wholly unwelcome one when ghostly 'Curry' lolloped with staccato speed onto the unlit road, their reason for showing up had remained a puzzle. Something significant might still happen. Perhaps the incident was just training, a quantum kind of rehearsal for saving the life of a real animal someday.

Would going to Bernadette Weissler's interview for the child-carer's position also lead to a happy result?

She splashed off the cleanser's glinting bubbles and drifted off to bed.

Chapter Nine

XXIX
The Devic Pre-Destruction Century
Or 'The Pre-Glory Century' to those
of the Empire
THE TIMEFRAME IN WHICH
THEIR PALACE NOW RESIDES

The precious gems the body kings had moved so very long ago were a source of fascination for Pieter.

Because he was familiar with the rocks and minerals of his native surroundings, Pieter felt sure that if he garnered more awareness about the gems Eidred mentioned, he would understand their importance to gold-skins. He wondered what the body kings were like in that prism of time when they first invaded Norwegia. He knew little of their origins. He knew, for instance, that their skin tone was the result of the dragon blood they consumed and that their original countenances were grey, but their lineage remained a mystery.

He had heard that the troopers who *weren't* gold-skin hybrids, like the eagle-winged guards and the Solen's family, were in fact a type of vulture, 'pterodactyls' according to Eidred; guards of a higher order, referred to by those at court as 'the Grudellans', some of whom were Eidred's minders. This mass of hideously snatching, squealing, power-squandering one-mind was divided into many angrily inhabited bodies. The chilling unison in which they spoke was a terrifying sound to poor Fripso.

Eidred continually reassured Pieter. 'Never mind,' she would say, before emphasising that no-one in the palace, other than her, had faerie sight. 'They have to rely on the luminaries to see anyone of your heritage. None of them will see you when they stomp into my room, but they *will* see Fripso. You must always ensure he stays hushed beneath his blanket.'

Pieter suggested she use the same blanket to smuggle Fripso out of the Grudellan Palace and back to the forest. Eidred had hidden him beneath a cloth in her berry basket, hadn't she, when believing him to need her protection after the weasel incident? Couldn't she do this in reverse?

Eidred threw her hands up in frustration. 'He insists he won't leave without *you*, Pieter. If you could change his mind, I'd be eternally grateful. Even better would be seeing you restored of your magic. Invisibility is far less dangerous than donning a disguising cloak and stepping out of my dressing quarter in full view of the spy lights. And that is only the beginning. The guards on the staircase would seize you within the blink of an eye.'

Whenever Eidred's minders invaded her room, most often the three were given a smidgen of warning, heralded by footsteps on stairs, and Eidred would close the doors of the quarter. On the odd occasion that they'd been taken by surprise, Pieter would rush to cover Fripso, who risked becoming frozen with fear and incapable of hiding. The cover, as well as concealing Eidred's small, long-eared charge, thankfully shielded him from the upsetting sight of those creatures.

'One day, my friend,' Pieter would soothe every so often. 'One day I will find our way to freedom.'

'We must trust Eidred,' Fripso would say, 'and not abandon her without a goodbye if we find our chance to leave.'

The elf agreed. 'Leaving in secret would be horribly impolite. And unless I am wrong about the pterodactyls, we are her only friends.'

It certainly was a sorry sight each dawn, the pterodactyls screaming at Eidred to begin on her education. Counting, counting, always counting. And weighing. Gold was to be measured, and measured again. One must repeat...and repeat...and repeat...number upon number until one lost all sensitivity to nature, creation, the cosmos and the heart. The minds of palace students became heavy with a concrete-laden and contrary logic that tore at their higher ideals and left them in shreds by the time dusk arrived.

'And now I must sleep,' she would say in a toneless, passion-robbed voice when returned from her schooling. Her eyes would be dull with a greyed out drowsiness. Of course she never could sleep after running across to 'her rabbit'. 'How is my rabbit this evening?' she would say, and some of the beige-greyness would leave her, prompting more of a blueness and a sparkle.

After spending time talking, feeding and nurturing her involuntarily immobilised guests, her thirst for stories of the other realms would revive. She loved to hear of Pieter's journeys to the Dream Sphere where Alcor would send him on a mission, often to help another being's enlightenment. She knew that at present Pieter had been commanded to observe the life of someone *not* from their time. Pieter explained that this individual was from the future and, if able to unite with a certain woman, would have a significant influence upon the world.

'He wasn't very accommodating with you, though, was he, Pieter, when you met him in his dream-state?'

'Quite arrogant,' agreed Pieter shaking his head. 'Just as you were, maiden, when first we met.'

Eidred's eyes widened. She appeared much taken aback, which made Pieter laugh. 'Was I indeed? Well, well, Pieter of the Brumlynds, I suppose you expect you are beyond reprieve in the way you spoke to me? I am royal remember!'

Pieter put further comment aside. Let her think her people superior to his own. It didn't matter. Over time Eidred had grown. Her increased understanding of devic lore might take others of her family a good several lifetimes to grasp. Considering the meaningless chatter she tolerated daily: prejudiced trivia designed to twist her thinking processes into something steel and mechanical, she still maintained enough resonance with sprites to allow their presence into her consciousness.

So many more would never, *never* see. But the time when sprites were to become invisible to all but their good selves and the animals was much further along, and at least their existence was an acknowledgeable one in the time that Pieter lived.

Grown also, although not so much intellectually, there being no stimulus for new thought in the gold-adorned chamber, was Pieter. He was a tall elf now, having grown older overnight, appearing to be seven-and-ten, one season-cycle older than the princess who was now six-and-ten.

Fripso was determined to value his time as a palace stowaway. Pieter and Eidred had become his fondest friends. 'If ever I die,' he said dreamily one evening when they'd talked about life and the afterlife, 'I shall return to this world as one of your children.'

Eidred glanced at Pieter shyly.

'Our children?' Pieter demanded.

'I mean, as a child of one of you, depending of course on who weds first.'

Pieter breathed a thankful sigh. He might be growing up, but he hardly thought it right to entertain the idea of having children with a body-king daughter. He would marry someday of course. Someday, long after he and his companions had devised an escape, he would marry a forest faerie probably, or an elf maiden from a faraway clan.

An escape seemed further away than ever now. Eidred confirmed to him eventually that the Backwards-Winding was indeed the palace travelling to the Elysium of one hundred season-cycles ago.

'And so,' said Pieter, 'this construction has been lifted out of our current time, The Century of Ruin and—'

'Incorrect. Our current time is known as The Century of Progress.'

'Only according to gold-skins.'

'Then let us choose to disagree on this, Pieter, but yes, as you say, the Grudellan Palace has relocated to the Elysium of yore.'

'And now we reside in the Pre-Destruction Century.'

'It is actually known as The Pre-*Glory* Century. Despite your odd terms, elf, you perceive the general concept. It is not just our Norwegian realm affected. Every other empirical palace has joined us here in the past.' She regarded Pieter with a comforting smile. 'Try not to concern yourself over this,' she said. 'After my eighteenth birthday something will happen to restore us to our proper timeframe.'

When Pieter asked further, Eidred grew secretive. 'Only six of us here in Norwegia know of this,' she said. 'Although had it not been for my nursery maid confiding in me when I was young, I would be entirely ignorant of the Backwards-Winding.' She nervously eyed the door of her chamber. 'I invite danger when speaking of palace confidences.'

Until the day he was returned to his clan in The Century of Ruin, and until he left his boyhood behind, Pieter would treasure the remainder of his youth. It felt unfair that the Grudellan Palace frequencies had already robbed him of four or five of his season-cycles. A great deal of his magic too. The healings he carried out to clear his mind of the palace's chaotic thought-forms were now slower to access and milder in their effect.

Reflecting on Fripso's comment concerning children, Pieter thought for a moment about the kind of offspring Eidred would have. Her future marriage might have already been arranged. He hoped with all his heart that her firstborn would be a son. As Eidred had said two nights earlier, if a lady of court bore three daughters in succession, the Solen commanded her execution. Eidred was a third daughter, the reason she had never known her mother.

By Grudellan Palace standards, an absence of sons meant a decline in power. A certain amount of daughters was deemed acceptable. As future incubators, they would ultimately further the genetic line. If they managed to marry into realms more affluent, they were considered to be useful. Other than this, royal women were seen as tiresome inferiors, kept separate from their siblings, goaded by pterodactyl minders and subjected to servitude. Eidred was a launderer. She did not believe the title equated to slave. 'This is the sort of work royal ladies are expected to do,' she said indignantly.

'Have you never questioned the way you are treated?' Pieter asked.

'Whatever do you mean? I am royal. Part of the privilege of being born a princess is to work for the good of the empire.'

Pieter told Eidred that childbirth was his other reason for pitying the women of her heritage. As with the faunal realm, gold-skins' young grew in their mothers' bellies before birth and echoed both parents' family lines with genetics that restricted creative capacities.

Eidred was shocked to hear sprites relied not on incubation. 'Although I agree that *singing* a child into existence rather than birthing it would be far less vexing for mothers.'

'Children of sprites arrive in this world directly from the Dream Sphere,' Pieter told her. 'Clans sing the sacred song of life in music and dance ceremonies with the intention of inviting a soul to manifest in infant form.'

'And so, if gestation is unnecessary then there must be an absence of marital ...' Eidred lowered her lids. 'Forgive me, Pieter. 'Tis an inappropriate subject. I should never have mentioned it.'

Amused at the maiden's coyness, Pieter told Eidred that sprites were *not* non-sensual. 'The physical delights of marriage aren't exclusive to gold-skins,' he said, 'even though they like to think all things pleasurable are of their own invention.'

Eidred murmured the words, 'I see,' then blushed and turned away.

XXX

One evening, when Eidred had recovered from her day of re- lentless sums, she stepped inside the dressing-quarter, sat herself down on the rose-coloured chaise and said, 'Pieter, I might as well reveal the secret I have kept from you.'

'And what secret is that?'

'The secret that surrounds the Backwards-Winding. You have been whisked away from your timeframe. I fear you are bewildered.'

'It is a strange thing, for sure,' Pieter said, 'that this entire palace has been swept up and then moved to a previous century. Although I trust that you are right in what you tell me, about us returning again after your birthday.' He told Eidred how pleased he was for the sprites of Elysium Glades. 'With the Grudellan Palace gone from their timeframe, my clan and others will be free to live as they have before. No more enslavement! No more offensive gold coins!'

Eidred turned away. 'As I understand it, the sorcerers have replaced our vanished residence with a hologram. The forest-dwellers won't be terrorised but will continue to fear my family, I'm afraid, because they'll see the Grudellan Palace's replica above the thorn thicket.'

'I see. So the forbidden, treeless part of Elysium will remain unchanged.'

Eidred nodded solemnly. 'All due to this holographic replica. And not just its exterior. The goings-on within will be a projection of our own lives here.' Her face brightened. 'I shall tell you how we are to return to the future, Pieter. As I've said earlier, few in the palace are aware of this. I am not supposed to know, but I shall tell you what I learned when young.'

And so, Eidred related to him a story explaining why the Solen decreed they move the royal residence from one century to another.

At royal infant naming ceremonies, or 'crystallings' as they were known, twelve former faeries, all in hooded cloaks, would be called upon to issue blessings. To enable the blessings, a crystal-crowned wand was given, temporarily, to each of the twelve.

Eidred's crystalling was a private affair, since daughters were not to be celebrated, and was attended only by the Solen, four Grudellan minders, Eidred's nursery maid and an eagle-winged guard whose task it was to allocate a wand to each bewitcher.

After the bewitchers bestowed small Eidred with proper husband-attracting qualities such as gracefulness and the ability to sing like a nightingale, there came a terrible commotion.

A wicked faerie magically appeared. She snatched up the twelfth faerie's wand. Ugly lightning flew from her taloned fingertips and into the wand. She announced that Eidred would pierce her finger on her eighteenth birthday, and that shortly after she would die. The bitter creature then threw the wand to the floor before vanishing in a flash of flame.

The crystal on the wand she had flung was smashed into two.

The twelfth former faerie, of course, was yet to give her blessing. To help soothe the sting of this ominous spell, she held her wand aloft—now damaged, yet still crystal-tipped—and decreed that the princess would not die, she would only slumber. 'All will sleep,' she had said, 'for a hundred years, and all will wake refreshed and unchanged by the hands of time.'

...'Thank goodness, Eidred,' Pieter said gravely. 'I would hate to think you were doomed. How do you know all this if it is meant to be secret?'

'My nursery maid told me in whispers one day when I asked how she came by the jagged fragment of crystal. She told me it was part of the wand the wicked one broke. She said no-one else of our court was to know of the Backwards-Winding because the wicked one might be an infiltrator, someone in disguise who resides here. If this cruel intender were to hear her spell was partially undone, she might wreak further havoc upon us. I don't believe she's an enemy within the palace. My feeling is she would have been a faerie once—drained of her heart powers and thus made into a bewitcher—perhaps one of the fortunate ones who found a way to escape.'

'How does this explain the Solen ordering a removal of your palace, indeed all other palaces across the globe, from their current century?'

'Eee-dred!'

Eidred jumped. 'My minders! I fear they have heard me.' She hurried to the door of her chamber.

Pieter waited anxiously for Eidred's return. At last she burst into the room again, flushed but smiling. 'It was only tables reciting that they wanted,' she said. 'They had not heard, Pieter, although their being so near to my room has acted as a warning. I should never have spoken of this. I shall say no more.'

Pieter's question, therefore, was not to be answered. He soon concluded that now they were residing in the Pre-Destruction Century, the sleep everyone in the empire was to fall into on Eidred's birthday would return them to the timeframe in which they began. After one hundred season-cycles, they would wake to the Century of Ruin. This would have been why Eidred had said all would be restored once she was eight-and-ten. He now looked forward to this day.

The next evening, Pieter woke to see Eidred watching him bashfully through the bars of the dressing-quarter doors. 'Pieter, regarding those gems you asked me about,' she began. 'I've thought much of this, and I do believe I have a way of gleaning our family's history.'

'How?' said Pieter and Fripso in intrigued unison.

'I shall visit my father's soothsayer.'

'His soothsayer? It is a type of magician is it not?'

'Yes. An alchemist who is privy to the astrology you talk of, Pieter. I have heard plenty about this soothsayer at court. There is always much gossip amongst the noblewomen, as you know. I have learnt I am entitled to an audience with the soothsayer.'

'Be careful, then, dear Eidred,' warned Fripso. 'I daresay someone like that is dark like the rest of them.'

'Oh, I have no doubt of that,' Eidred assured the rabbit. 'But 'tis one way I can ask as many questions as I wish without being shouted at, or threatened, or interrupted.'

'As you are during school,' said Pieter. He gazed at the floor, feeling great compassion for the poor waif having to endure treatment she did not deserve.

'Yes. I may ask the soothsayer as many as three-and-twenty questions. Is that not wonderful?'

'Useful certainly,' agreed Pieter. 'But inevitably dangerous as Fripso warns.'

'Still, it is worth the danger. I shall be careful, I promise you, my dears. It is conditional of course, my visit to the soothsayer.'

'Isn't everything in this godforsaken place?' grumbled Fripso.

'What condition is it based on, Eidred?' Pieter asked.

'Oh, the condition it is based on is not unachievable.'

'Whatever is it then?'

'That I marry.' Eidred's face had taken on a dreamy expression.

'Marry the soothsayer?' Fripso was horrified.

Pieter was equally horrified. Surely she would not go so far as to wed an aged—and quite possibly toothless—magician of darkness!

'You're quite the jester,' Eidred said to the rabbit with a sigh. In a manner far more pensive than usual, she sashayed to her bed, blew out the candle and neglected to bid either of them goodnight.

'She must be in love,' Fripso commented.

'I don't think so,' Pieter scorned. He thought a moment before adding, 'With whom?'

'How should I know?' Fripso said yawning. 'Probably with a prince from one of those banquets she tells us about. She doesn't seem too concerned about fulfilling that condition, if you ask me.'

Very soon, the soft, sleep-induced breathing of the elf's dwelling mates permeated the silence. It was then that a wide-awake Pieter, in an impulse quite foreign to his normally placid nature, took aim at the nearest wall and gave it a kick.

⚜

After an exhausting workday, Matthew pulled into the garage and leaned against the steering wheel, contemplating staying at home that evening, getting an early night.

He had to remind himself he wasn't exactly looking forward to sleep. In going out again, he'd be buying himself a temporary escape, ensuring the slumber he had after a late night was shorter and therefore less dream-filled.

The Peter Piper kid had bugged Matthew again, hijacking a dream that had teetered on the border of wakefulness. An elf and an eagle standing by a dawn-drenched autumn tree. The soft, sweet whistle of a pipe made from reed. That was all he remembered. That was all he ever remembered. The dream had recurred twice.

This most recent dream was much the same as the first in the series. The second of the series also had the golden-leafed background and bird but differed. The kid, taller now, having a similar appearance to music's current man-of-the-moment, an American teenage idol whose name Matthew couldn't recall—had held up a floor mop and a pair of overalls. Was this an indication to Matthew that he should have worked harder? That he should not have written a letter of resignation, which would come into effect in two weeks' time? That someone was going to dupe him of an investment by 'taking him to the cleaners'?

But there he was again, doing what Dalesford suggested he do but doing it badly: interpreting symbols. It might have been a symbol, the dream, a coded instruction as to how to make his future life better, or it might have just been the result of that mustard and pickled onion sandwich he'd fixed before bed, a sure-fire way to induce psychedelic nightmares.

Now inside, Matthew rested his briefcase in the hall, then scooted up the marble staircase. The Audi was not in the garage. He didn't need psychic powers to know Bernadette wouldn't be visiting at the hospital. That was something Matthew would be expected to do on the weekend, with Laura and Sara. How was he going to say to the poor lady coughing her lungs out from pneumonia that her granddaughter was still 'a bit busy' a second time?

'Tell her I'm ill if you have to,' Bernadette had roared. 'She hates me you know. She doesn't deserve my attention.'

Any mention of Grandma Carmody or her frail condition infuriated her, and yet Matthew was sure the senior woman—a sunny and motherly sort—did not hold grudges in the way Bernadette did.

From what Matthew could gather, it had been two upsetting incidents that Bernadette could never forgive. The first had been the grandmother telling her at seventeen that a red dress she'd worn to a disco made her look 'a tad too provocative'. The second had been undiluted criticism of the buttons on a jacket she'd made in high school needlework. Grandma Carmody said they were too big. Matthew had seen the 1987 yearbook. Grandma Carmody was right. Venturing all the way up to Bernadette's chin had been a line of flat circular objects the size of mini-compact disks. Bernadette, normally stunning in anything she wore, had quite possibly channelled Pierrot in that pic, the teary French clown who'd snatched at the moon.

As far as Matthew knew, these comments alone were the basis of Bernadette's wounded indifference, despite Grandma Carmody's unswerving loyalty. Birthday and Christmas gifts sent by the war-widow pensioner, whose financial situation was far from healthy, were ever extravagant, quite beyond her affordability and smartly presented with ribbons and bows, along with letters in elegant copperplate requesting photographs of the kids.

He galloped up a second flight of stairs and strode down the hallway to his study, intent on checking for emails from Gallilani to ensure no nasties lurked around what seemed so far to be a clear deal. Ten minutes before he had to go out again. He'd grab a drink, spruce up a bit and look in on the girls to make sure they weren't killing each other over some minor dispute.

The computer was taken. Sara had beaten him to it.

'Hey, sweetie,' he said.

No answer.

'Why here? Everything okay with your notebook?'

'It's not working. I want another one.'

'Not working? It's not that long since I got it for you.' All Matthew could see of his stepdaughter was the back of her head and a single straw-coloured plait. He watched for signs of nodding. 'Why not go and get the notebook and I'll try and figure it out.'

'Nah, too much trouble. I'm busy.'

'Sara, I'm sorry, but I'm about to go out, and I'll need to look at my emails before I do. You can have that back once I jump in and check them.'

The young teen turned, making a face. 'Matthew, I'm online with my two favourite buddies. I can't leave them hanging.'

Getting impatient now, Matthew consulted his watch and said, 'Okay, five minutes longer then, in order to tell Tyson and Lizzy—'

'Tyson and *Izzie.*'

'...In order to tell Tyson and *Izzie* that you'll be leaving them hanging for two.'

'Whatever.'

He wandered across to Laura's room, knocked on the opened door and smiled down at the little girl chatting on her mobile. 'Hi Laura Lou. Everything all right?'

'Fine,' she snapped in a six-year-old's squeak, then whispered something into the phone. 'You can go now, Matthew!'

'Huh?'

'Matthew!' The little girl rolled her eyes in exasperation. 'Can't you see I'm having a private conversation?'

Not bothering to answer that, Matthew wandered to the bathroom and wrenched the shaving cream out of the chrome cabinet, looking forward to the time Bernadette's daughters would learn to value manners. He'd now come to accept that they didn't like words such as 'hello', 'goodbye' and 'thank you'.

He'd looked forward to being a father, even though it was only the role of stepdad. Next to making exorbitant amounts of money, marrying a glamour and buzzing about in a sports car, having a couple of kids to care about had been one of his major goals.

He lathered his jaw and proceeded to shave. He'd always fancied he'd have children he could make a fuss over, perhaps even spoil occasionally, but spoiling Laura and Sara had already been efficiently seen to, long before Matthew's time. The most coveted technology had been handed over to Bernadette's girls within nanoseconds of their asking. Every movie they'd viewed or wished to view bought outright, although never revisited, and archived in a towering DVD spine that looked as though it were trying to nudge the fifteen-foot ceiling.

Eyeing the imposing cornices, he undid his tie and strode to his room. It hadn't been his first choice, the pseudo-Georgian, but its location was closer to the girls' schools than his Milsons Point penthouse, and joint decisions were to be expected now that he was responsible for a family.

Since Bernadette had her heart set on hiring the flamboyant furnishings consultant known to be an Einstein when it came to colour schemes, Matthew put mention of the cost aside. Quibbling over the cost of gold-plated faucets or baroque-era chandeliers was hardly productive. Decorator Dan had turned Sara and Laura's bedrooms into the sort of living spaces princesses would envy, each with a walk-in robe to rival the coat-hanger-clanger of their mother's. 'Aladdin's Cave,' he called it. She'd had it done out to resemble a Turkish circus.

He crossed back through the elaborate indoor balcony hallway. A quick long-black, a squiz at the inbox and then he'd be on his way.

It was possible she *wouldn't* be upset with him for going out. She'd surprised him the night he returned from Alice Springs. Instead of ranting or freezing him out, she'd been gentle, demure even, the woman he'd originally married. If she'd always been like that, he'd have no cause to question the partnership's longevity, but he also had to caution himself against judging her too severely. Whenever he recalled the disturbed Burwood woman hopping about in the dark, he felt a surge of gratitude at being married to someone sober. Before getting trapped in substance abuse, she might have been as dignified as Bernadette. Assuming she had a husband, how would the poor sod be dealing with all that? Would he have contemplated breaking up, as Matthew was doing, or was he resigned to enduring the strangeness?

'Where are you going, anyway?' Sara yelled as he passed the study in a brisk march.

Matthew grinned at that. The one time one of Bernadette's girls wanted to know where he was going, it was somewhere embarrassing. 'Poetry reading,' he called back. 'On a friend's recommendation.'

The younger daughter poked her head out of the bedroom and chanted in a sing-song voice, 'Little Miss Muffet sat on a tuffet eating her curds and whey.'

'That's a good one, Laura,' Matthew commented. 'I might use that.' Laura collapsed into a fit of squealing giggles, ran to her bed and began jumping on it, aiming her hands towards the ceiling. 'When are we getting a trampoline?' she shouted. 'I'm sick of jumping on this.'

It was the ingratitude that got to him: the girls' dissatisfaction with all that they had and bottomless pit nagging for all that they hadn't. He didn't blame them of course. Kids were primarily a product of their upbringing. 'I don't know whether Mum wants you jumping on your new bed,' he said finally.

'You can't tell me what to do. You're not the boss of me. Mum is. And so is Dad. And Mum's here all the time, and she doesn't care what I do.'

'Where's Mum tonight, do you know?'

'Nope.'

'Shopping, I bet,' Sara shouted from Matthew's study.

'You're probably right about that.' He headed towards the kitchen. 'Anyone want a drink?'

'Nah.'

An equation concerning the role of stepfather often nagged at him, especially on the nights he woke from unpleasant dreams. Numerals would rollick through his thoughts to a rhythm as insistent as a military drumbeat. Company totals, his own personal budget. He'd calculate and re-calculate them until his eyelids grew heavy or the alarm clock went off. The equation that assailed him in the early hours, though, was a formulation of conundrums rather than digits and caused him to ask how his stepdaughters could grow into considerate, disciplined adults with the ability to live within their means when raised by an indulgent mother and obliging stepfather.

Bernadette's housekeeper was in the kitchen, chopping vegetables for a roast.

'Hello there, Rhoda. I didn't expect to see you here this late.'

Rhoda beamed. 'Mr Weissler! 'How are you?'

'Matthew. Please.'

'I mean Matthew. Sorry.'

Matthew filled a mug from the espresso machine and took a few gulps, then filled two glasses with spring water.

'Your Mrs Weissler had a late appointment and asked me to cook dinner tonight and supervise the kids. Normally it's my day off.'

'That's good of you. Loved the celery and watercress soup you made the other day.'

'You liked it? I'll cook it again on Thursday then.'

'Rhoda, you're a star.'

The girls would at least have someone looking after them until Bernadette got home, although it niggled at him that she might not be there to say goodnight to them when they padded off to their beds. 'Sara's old enough and responsible enough not only to babysit her sister but to look after kids professionally,' she'd say when he'd offer to bring in a minder on their nights out. 'I babysat my cousins from the time I was twelve. And you couldn't get a more secure home than ours, Mattie.' She was right of course, and Laura and Sara were never far from her mind. She would discuss them on dinners out, her face aglow with tender pride, and once home, would smile down at their sleeping faces before filling their slippers with after-dinner mints, careful to ensure the wrappings protruded conspicuously enough to prevent crunch damage from warmth-seeking feet.

Nights out, nowadays, of course, were blemished with disagreement. Vanuatu had been brought up again, and again he'd opposed her plans. Bernadette wanted to go during the school holidays. Matthew felt she was being unfair to her children. 'They need to be with their mother. Take them with you. Give them a chance to see the islands.'

'But don't you get it?' she'd wailed. 'I need time to myself for once.'

'What fun are the girls going to have at home on their own while I'm at work? Most nights I can't get back any earlier than eight-thirty. What sort of school holiday is that?'

Bernadette had frozen him out; had eaten opposite him in a fork-stabbing sulk.

On the way home, they'd arrived at a compromise. He'd agreed that a nanny for the entire two weeks wasn't such a bad idea, a firm but amiable stand-in-mother whose duties would include keeping them company during Matthew's work hours and taking them to the movies or friends' parties, or Luna Park. They'd given Rhoda first option, but Rhoda could only maintain her evening cooking shift—on the days of the holidays she'd be minding her school-age grandchildren—so Bernadette had conducted interviews with candidates. He'd coached her in interviewing, and she'd quite enjoyed the responsibility of chatting to potential employees.

Returning to the study, Matthew found Sara tapping on the keyboard while talking on his office phone. 'Charlotte, *wait*,' she was saying. 'Is Tyson getting online? Cool. Speak to you soon.'

He placed a glass beside her as she smacked the phone down, and said, 'All wrapped up now?'

'Hardly,' Sara said. 'I've got heaps to speak to and I have to speak to them now. What's that? Water? You *know* I hate water.'

'It's good for you,' Matthew murmured, retrieving his laptop from the stationery cupboard. 'Soft-drink dissolves teeth. Okay Sara. I need my computer please. Now.'

Reluctantly, Sara stepped aside. Matthew settled into his seat and clicked onto his emails. Nothing in his inbox from Gallilani's. He'd check again on his laptop once he found a parking spot at the venue.

He knocked on Laura's door and placed her glass on the bed-side table. Her back was turned. Matthew smiled to himself at the sight of the silent munchkin busily arranging new outfits for one of her dolls. 'Water for Laura Lou,' he announced.

'Okay,' she said softly.

'Now if Rhoda asks you to go to bed, you have to do as she says, okay?'

'Okay.'

'Not like last time, okay?'

'Okay, Matthew. I'll go to bed nicely.'

'Good girl, Laura. See you tomorrow morning.'

He called goodnight to Sara as he thundered down the stairs.

'Night, Matt,' she called. 'Have a good time.'

Matthew halted on the landing. Have a good time? Was that Sara Belfield speaking? Touched by this, he called back, 'Thanks, sweets. Try to have some of that water if you can.'

He was two minutes late arriving at the community hall, a stubby building strangled by the sort of gigantic ivy leaves that protruded from stone walls and overlapped compactly like the scales of a mythical fire-breather.

Matthew reached for the laptop on the backseat. He'd risk another couple of minutes for peace of mind over the Gallilani deal.

Within a matter of days this relentless grapple for deals would be history. Just a fortnight more and he'd be finishing up as a mere manager in his mid-thirties, immediately following a task that had floundered pathetically. Not that this had been the final decider. The stifling level of discontent and the feeling of not making any tangible difference in an occupation that threatened to beckon mundanity had pushed him to think the unthinkable.

Comforted by the good news of no news in his inbox, he snapped the laptop closed, switched off his phone, grabbed the folder of loose-leafed poems he'd packed in the glove-box that morning—a leftover from his youth, which he believed still held merit—and sauntered down a ferny path to the doorway, wondering why the hall's committee didn't get a gardener in to smarten things up.

In the foyer on his way to Room Five, Matthew could hear the meeting had started on time. Someone was introducing a poet's recital.

Great, he thought, angry at himself for not leaving work earlier. The other thought he had was: *You bastard, Dalesford.*

Poetry reading? Was the man the product of a first-cousin marriage? What was the alpaca farmer-turned-author thinking when he suggested Matthew attend something as wimpish as this? 'I predict you'll be addressing great amounts of people in the future,' Dalesford had told him. 'Get into practice by speaking to groups. This mustn't involve heading meetings at your work, mind you. Try a local type of gathering. A writers' club would be good. Somewhere people go to read out their work.'

'I've toyed with the idea of getting into politics,' Matthew had said. 'So getting up in front of people makes sense. I want to make a difference to society.'

'You'll be making a difference to society all right,' Dalesford had said. 'But I don't think it'll be through politics.'

Aware that he was just as crazy as Dalesford to go along with those pie-in-the-sky presumptions, Matthew wondered whether he'd be wise to quit now and return home. At the exact instant of that thought, something seemed to buzz, or trill, in his ear. He drew to a stop. Waggled his head.

'Okay, first up tonight, we have a lovely new guest, courtesy of our fellow member, Darren Eddings. She's no doubt a bit nervous, so I'll ask you all to put your hands together and extend a warm welcome to...I *hope* I've got the name here right. Darren, your handwriting's very, very small and I haven't got my reading glasses.'

This would be as palatable as unthawed beans, worse than trailing behind Bernadette on those voracious shopping expeditions, worse than attending a church service with her pernickety great-aunt on Christmas Day, probably up there with wondering whether he'd done the right thing by resigning from his job and the year he lost half-a-million in shares.

And he hadn't had time to eat. A hot Italian meal was calling. A plate of Napolitana at Amaretti's. A radish side-salad, a basket of crunchy garlic bread. Better to quit now than to endure a rumbling stomach throughout boring declarations of love and heartbreak. Did he really want to pretend he was another one of these loser poets by reciting verse he wrote some twenty-odd years ago?

An attractive, overly made-up brunette, resplendent in a shawl that sparkled gold and silver, opened the glass door from outside and came hurrying through the foyer. At that moment, Matthew made a sharp turn and bumped his poem-folder against the wall. It sprang open and folded outwards to release each of his writings into the air. Carbon copies of the originals, which he'd tapped out on an electric typewriter as a gawky eighth grader, wafted down to the linoleum floor. He crouched to collect them.

'Clumsy!'

Matthew looked up to see the brunette grinning down at him. She placed one ring-less left hand self-consciously on her hip, gave an eyebrow raise and fake pout, then resumed grinning. Dammit, she was still watching him, and he was no more in control than as the gawky eighth grader he'd once been, a butter-fingers nerd who dropped things whenever he hoped to make a good impression.

'Sorry, folks, all has been sorted out,' chuckled the amplified voice from Room Five. 'The name of our first poet for this evening is Rosetta Melki with "The Piper". A big hand for Rosetta.'

Rosetta! He'd heard that name outside Crystal Consciousness when Conan Dalesford voiced his gratitude to the manager for a sales assistant's help, and again more recently when working late. Jack the cleaner had been calling out to one of his casual recruits, 'Rosetta, could you do the tea room on the other side of the lifts?' and Matthew had thought about that name, thinking how interesting the name had sounded. He'd got home to find Laura watching a cartoon DVD with a little friend of hers. They were laughing at Bugs Bunny planting out a carrot patch in crooked zigzags.

'Now all I need is a Rosetta,' the rabbit said in his nasal drone.

'What does he mean by a Rosetta?' said Matthew, surprised that the name had repeated.

Laura was absorbed in the movie, so neglected to answer.

Laura's little friend shyly answered for her. 'He needs a row-setter because he doesn't know how to set the rows properly.'

He'd been hearing things. Trying to make a coincidence stretch into something more significant.

The brunette smiled coquettishly. 'Need any help with that?'

'Thanks anyway, but I've got it under control.'

Inside Room Five, a low-toned, melodious voice, which instantly gave Matthew a feeling of comfort, began reciting.

The brunette eyed him with aggression. 'I don't bite, moron!' She rushed to Room Seven where a sign on the door read: *Mums without Marriages Assertiveness Training.*

Matthew stopped gathering his papers for a moment and listened to assess whether his own scribblings were better or worse than the poet who now spoke. Her poem had begun with a reference to dreaming:

'When slumber's cosmic travels end each night
 (My flight through stars and cities still unknown)
 I find that I am bathed in silver light
 I feel at peace although I am alone'

Worse, he concluded. My rhymes are an embarrassment.

The woman sounded super-relaxed. Sexy too. He had to get a look at this Rosetta to see if she was as nice as her voice. Matthew sorted through his papers to find the one he was going to read, half listening to the words of Rosetta's second verse:

'Until I hear soft music in the breeze
The piper: I remember him so well
He waits for me beneath the shaded trees
Enchanted, I am woven in his spell'

The piper! I'm with you there, Rosetta, Matthew thought. Peter Piper always greets me beside a tree.

He flicked past the verse he'd jokingly recited to Dalesford. 'I'm not poetic in anyone's language,' he'd told him after that daft suggestion of attending the group. 'Although I've no doubt I could mesmerise them with my eagle poem.'

He returned to the first and second stanzas:

Suddenly starts to circle the sky
Searching the ground with a watchful eye
He's spotted his prey
A field-mouse wee
The merciless eagle has found his tea

'Didn't mesmerise me,' Dalesford had drawled. Matthew had feigned surprise. 'I'm guessing you mean tea as in "meal" and not "beverage".'

'Yep,' Matthew had said. 'And bear in mind "field-mouse wee" is just Yoda speak for "tiny critter". I wasn't referring to rodent urine.'

'Why not add some drama?' Dalesford had said. 'Something like:

'O fragile mouse
Prayers you must pray
Your life is over from today'

Dalesford had then said, 'That's a joke, actually. How about:

'Poor fragile mouse
A sky king's prey
'Tis sad survival works this way

'You'll get the women in with that one. Women love to feel sympathy. But I really think you should try out something light. Get 'em giggling.'

So Matthew had settled on 'Stuntman'. He'd just have to locate it in the jumble he'd gathered back into his folder.

Rosetta's poem went on.

'Some say his name is Pan the woodland faun
And beauty he creates through drowsy tone
The piper at the golden gates of dawn
It's he who frees the eagle turned to stone

'You'll find him in the woods and misty vales
Perhaps beside a babbling brook or stream
Or read of him in myths and fairy tales
I find him at the end of every dream

'So if you hear soft music in the breeze
At dawn or dusk or when the moon's ashine
Look for him beneath the shaded trees
And let him be your friend as he is mine'

Rosetta's conclusion was followed by loud applause. Despite his lack of proximity, Matthew clapped too. He was impressed with the way the poem was related and intrigued by the dream described. An eagle. A piping Pan. Maybe the kid who featured in his—and Rosetta's—dreams was the window-hopping Peter Pan, taking a vacation from the late J M Barrie's imagination.

Matthew sorted through each poem in search of 'Stuntman'. The host of the evening said, 'Thank you, Rosetta, for your whimsical work entitled "The Piper". I understand you wrote this some time ago.'

'Yes,' was Rosetta's reply. 'Back when I was an idealistic ninth grader.'

Matthew breathed out a faint laugh and shook his head.

'I was fifteen when I wrote it, and my inspiration was Chapter Seven of *The Wind in the Willows* by Kenneth Grahame. I thought the part about Pan at the gates of dawn was amazing, really amazing, because it reminded me of a dream I had once. About an elf.'

'An elf?' Matthew whispered.

'An elf?' said the host.

'Yeah, but the reason I probably dreamt this was I was reading Lillibridge's *Our True Ancient History* at the time.'

'Ah, old Lillibridge, eh? You were dreaming about Lillibridge's Pieter. Quite controversial, this author. Some say it wasn't fiction. What do you say, Rosetta?'

Lillibridge's Peter? Who the *frack* was Lillibridge? Where could Matthew get the book? And why had the host pronounced Peter 'P-yetta'?

'To be honest, Claude, I have no real fixed opinion at this stage. Fiction seems to be the most logical conclusion, and yet I feel we should all keep an open mind.'

'Spoken like a true fence-sitter, Rosetta. Have you thought of getting into politics?'

The woman's voice fell into a soft, low laugh. '*Hey*, that's a *great* idea!'

Matthew smiled at the comment.

'We'd be very, *very* proud of you if you did. First Poets' Garret member to govern Australia. Rosetta for PM in 2020 I say. We've never had a rhyming leader. I think it could be quite novel. Hands together again for the delightful Rosetta Melki.'

Now was a good time to go in, during a break in recitals. While the next poet was announced, Matthew darted into Room Five and took a seat at the back on the far left end. The Rosetta woman must have resumed her seat. There was no-one at the lectern except a grizzly looking dude who looked like he wanted to punch someone. He was booming out a ballad about a workmate stealing his wife.

The ballad seemed to be backgrounded by a high pitched treble. Technical difficulties with the mike, no doubt. Matthew scanned the front of the room only to find the poet's amplified voice was all his own doing. The room had no microphone! Tinnitus again. Had to be.

Matthew banged a hand against his ear. No change in sound. He patted his hand against his ear again. Seemed to be coming from without rather than from within. He leaned his head to the side and patted his ear more energetically this time, the impact of each pat resounding thumpishly in his skull.

Aware someone to his right had lurched around to face him, he stopped. Beyond a small stretch of empty seats, an elderly woman with excessively black hair was watching him with wary concern. She edged across to a seat further along. Feeling he owed her an explanation, Matthew pointed to his head and said, 'Tinnitus.'

Mistaking it for an introduction, the woman nodded a frail nod and gestured to herself in much the same way. 'Valerie.'

Low and haunting. The soft, sweet whistle of a pipe made from reed. 'Okay, Peter Piper,' Matthew said under his breath. 'I'm aware you're here. Now push off.' The tune halted immediately.

Matthew looked around the room, at its walls in need of repainting, its low speckled ceiling. He observed the backs of heads in the row of seats in front. Directly before him was a sleek, dark mane of flowing, reddish-brown hair. He stared at the hair for a while, hoping the woman would turn to the side a little so he could catch a glimpse of her face. Maybe he should whistle a tune so that she'd spin round to look at him. Peter Piper's tune would do. He didn't believe anyone in the audience could be enjoying the grumbles of Mr Chip-on-his-Shoulder. Musical entertainment from Matthew might be appreciatively received.

He loved that kind of hair. It reminded him of winter nights as a student of Wimbledon West High, doing homework at his girlfriend's. Flickering light from the hearth would lend her tresses the colour of burnt toffee. She'd looked like some kind of fire sprite: the glow of flames caressing downcast eyes as she'd concentrated on her essays.

Before long, it was Matthew's turn to recite. He retrieved 'Stuntman' from the top of his papers, moved to the front of the room where Claude introduced him, and began to read:

> 'I've jumped from a moving drawbridge
> Surrounded by a moat
> I'm glad that there was water
> Because I missed the boat
>
> 'I've had to do outrageous things
> Like eating camel's eyes
> The actor was a vegan
> It came as no surprise'

A sprinkling of giggles. Not sure whether the other poets were laughing with him or *at* him, Matthew looked up to acknowledge them, and his
gaze fell upon the seat in front of his own. It was empty. The mysterious red-brunette had remained mysterious. He went on.

> 'I've had to use a parachute
> While falling through the air
> But when reaching for the rip-cord
> I found it wasn't there
>
> 'Luckily my neck was saved
> Director Arnold Coppins
> Yelled "Take out your umbrella!
> We're filming *Mary Poppins*." '

A dash of applause. There she was. He could see three-quarters of her through the doorway, standing in the foyer and facing the other way. She was scanning a notice board and murmuring into her mobile.

'And do the gals admire me?
They do *not* by any means
The gals prefer the actors
Yet I do the "hero" scenes

'They couldn't give a hoot about
Us brave and daring lads
Instead they go for poncey blokes
Who star in toothpaste ads

'I'm warning every kid out there
I'm making a confession
If you hope to be a stuntman...Don't!
It's not a good profession'

She'd gone now. Hurried away to the sound of the squeaking door. An emergency? Either that or she'd been scared away by his poetry, fleeing after that phone call, during which she might have said: *This guy's rubbish. I'll see you shortly.*

Matthew became aware of clapping. He gave a nod, then returned to his seat, but the host caught up with him, and he was forced to get up again to answer a couple of inane interview questions before deciding that he too should make an impromptu getaway. An Italian meal at Amaretti's was too good to pass up. He had no desire to sit through the rest of the poetry evening.

Once the poet after him had been given her turn, and while the applause rose up, Matthew quietly left Room Five. He strode through the foyer, then dashed out into the night's chill, into the dull glow of car-park street lamps, half hopeful of encountering a long-haired siren and wondering abstractedly if this was who Rosetta was.

Chapter Ten

XXXI

Eidred drifted through Elysium Glades looking curiously about. Exploring yesteryear's forest was something she anticipated with eagerness upon the arrival of each Sun's Day.

Here in the Pre-Glory Century, a wildly free undergrowth twisted over and around and through every tree, rich and rampant and blooming, variant in shade and colour. The air was heavily fragrant.

Sprites of all shapes and sizes flitted and whirled. Flightier creatures took the form of misty blurs, darting around Eidred with the wispy agility of star-splodged moths. Only the earthed amongst the sprites were distinguishable, calmly absorbed in their care of the fauna.

'Such a shame,' Eidred said to herself. 'Such a shame that sprites are rarely happened upon in the Century of Progress.' And how dreadful it was, that her family—Eidred's very own family—had been responsible for this. The timeframe to which the palace had travelled was far more picturesque than the one it was from, a painful reminder of the fey population's ultimate diminishment.

Entrapping or destroying these gentle forest dwellers would, in a century gone by, cause the demise of much of these surroundings. The strange and lovely flower vines that Eidred had today admired would be gone forever within the next few season-cycles. A plant could not survive without its ethereal counterpart. Sprites were nature's gardeners, and the gardens that formed their homes were soon to be savagely ripped apart.

Eidred sat herself down at the stream. It gleamed like an open treasure box, its reflections of the setting sun and exotic foliage not unlike the gold-encased emeralds that adorned one of the gowns in her dressing-quarter. 'All to go,' Eidred said, brushing away the tear-drop that had trickled over her cheek. She did not recognise any of these waterside trees.

She heard murmurs then, amid the soft gurgling squeaks of playful undines: Gold's Kin conversing in the oak shadow further up the stream.

Scanning to see who this might be, she caught sight of the curved edge of a brown wing beyond the oak's trunk. A guard! Immediately she dashed to a nearby filigree tree and hid behind it. Her wander through Elysium's forests had only just begun. She did not want to be discovered and escorted back to the palace by one of the brusque, winged troopers who guarded all of Gold's Kin. She checked the sun and then slumped against the tree with a triumphant sigh. Only in its twenty-first degree. She had thought it to be later. No, she would not be ushered back home at this stage. The Grudellans had decreed she return by the twenty-second. The guard was not there on account of her. He was speaking with someone.

Intent on remaining unseen, Eidred scampered back to the sandy banks. She sat herself down again and dragged her fingers idly through the stream's rippling surface, discovering soon after with dismay that she was still within earshot of the guard's murmurs.

'I shall fetch you some water, beloved,' the guard was saying. Ah, so this was a gentleman speaking softly to his lady. Which guard would this have been? Eidred knew naught of any current royal courtship. The last known union had been that of her brother, the courting of a widowed Ehyptian queen.

Prior to that, one of Eidred's older sisters had been wooed by an Atlantean solen. Eidred's father was extravagantly pleased with this arrangement. Eidred's sister had received only one previous offer of betrothal, and her future was beginning to look grim.

Eidred frowned at remembering Rahwor, one of the Solen's grasping sorcerers, Rahwor who had dared to imagine himself becoming a prince through marriage. The Solen had regarded the sorcerer's request as an insult borne of stupidity, although he did not berate him too harshly. Instead he punished Eidred's sister for having attracted the interest of a scoundrel.

The young lady had insisted she'd given no encouragement. Her pterodactyl minders had scoffed. Being a marriageable royal woman, they'd said, was encouragement enough. She was then banished to the scullery and expected to scrub even more grime-smeared floors. 'If you do not bewitch a man of grand lineage,' the Grudellans had screeched, 'the Solen will have no choice other than to end your life.' Eidred had learnt of this as a child, through listening to parlourmaid gossip. The event had occurred before her birth.

Twilight had descended in shades of cream and silver-edged pink. The guard's voice rose heartily as he addressed his female companion. 'May the stream water I collect for you be as sweet as morning dew.'

Eidred stifled a giggle and marvelled at the apparent chivalry. Quite the opposite to the gruffness displayed by most men of the royal court. Eidred again peered across at the oak. Could she determine who this was?

Her question was answered when the guard stepped partly out of the shadows, a former gatekeeping guard by the name of Storlem. He'd since been given the title of Messenger. Storlem's other duties, Eidred recalled, involved the collecting together of heart-crystals at all magic-robbing ceremonies and issuing wands to palace bewitchers at crystallings. The woman with whom he spoke remained concealed. The guard had now left the shadows. He was striding to the stream, a goblet in his hand. Eidred gasped and ducked behind the fronds of a pale blue fern.

Once Storlem had returned to the oak, Eidred resumed her place on the bank. 'And so tell me, beloved,' she heard him say, 'were you frightened when you first saw the Solen's residence?'

First saw it? All but those who married into the family had been born in the Grudellan court. What had Storlem meant by this? Eidred listened for the answer.

The reply was warmly melodious, quite unlike the gravelly voices of Grudella. 'We were mystified rather than frightened. A gold sphere appeared in our night sky. Many of us thought it to be a second sun. It descended upon a clearing and then spread across the surrounding land. It unfolded into many, many angles and we looked on in amazement.'

'How strange it must have seemed.'

'Very strange. We sheltered in the Dream Sphere. Our Dream Masters told us that the odd, golden construction we described was the home of earthbound time-travellers. They referred to your glittering residence as a prison. They said we must return to earthly Elysium Glades, and continue on courageously.'

A sprite! Storlem was courting an elf woman or faerie, and yet he certainly wasn't clad in a fey-detection cloak. Could it be true he possessed faerie sight?

'And now your wretched sorcerers have prevented us from visiting the Dream Sphere whenever we wish,' the sprite woman said. 'Now we are limited only to the daytime, through slumber.'

'Do you remember your visits there?'

'Most certainly.'

'Thank goodness for that. I hear they're plotting to remove your memories of that world. You are to remember only fragments. They refer to these fragments as "dreams".' Storlem's tone was sorrowful. 'This is all I ever experienced in the past. Dreams. Not now though. Not anymore. The slumbering memories of our people are created in the Nightmare Realms. And though I am passionately opposed to what they are plotting, I feel I am a contributor in some way.'

'Do not feel guilty, beloved,' the sprite woman said. 'You are nothing like them. You did not cause this.' The woman stepped forward from the tree and into the shadows. All Eidred could see was a silhouette of faerie wings and flowing hair. The two were facing each other with hands linked.

'What a great privilege it is to be silvered,' Storlem said, his tone as gentle as the evening breeze. 'It has blessed me with the presence of your people.'

Silvered! Guards exposed to heart-elixir crystals were ever at risk of surrendering to this condition. Eidred wasn't at all sure what becoming silvered meant, except that it was seen by the Solen to be a dangerous thing, the reason all sprite magic had to be shipped to that faraway land in the south. The last crystal-keeper had been executed for having become silvered. Afraid for the earnest young man who had always appeared less dismissive of her than the other guards,

Eidred closed her eyes and said a silent prayer to her godmother that Storlem's silvering would remain undiscovered.

Perhaps this was what had happened to Eidred. She might also have shared that mysterious phenomenon. Didn't silvering happen only to those in contact with great amounts of heart-elixir crystals? Could it be possible the tiny shard under her pillow had been powerful enough to promote her ability to hear and see sprites?

A stomp of boots and crash of tree branches invaded the dusky calm.

The two spun around and stared into the forest in horror.

Eidred turned. Advancing from the forest were three courtiers, each in fey-detection cloaks. One of them shouted 'I spy a fey woman's wing over yonder!'

Fear descended upon the pair. 'They see me,' the faerie said. 'You must hide.' She pushed urgently at Storlem's chest.

'No!' Storlem stepped forward and grasped her arms. 'I will not leave!'

'Storlem, I beg of you. We cannot allow them to see us together!'

Undines disappeared beneath the darkening water.

Dryad clans fled with their children: frightened bundles of shivering whimpers.

Storlem's voice was thick with emotion. 'I will not let them take you.'

The faerie uttered Storlem's name, over and over, in hushed wails. The two fell into a panic-stricken embrace. 'My love,' the faerie cried. 'Please understand I will be all right.'

'I cannot stand by and...' Storlem's voice was hoarse with tears. 'I cannot...'

The faerie, weeping and shuddering now, stepped briskly away from her eagle-winged guard. 'Would you rather I die of a broken heart? Do not let them seize you.'

The courtiers were now slicing at vines with their swords. Their fey-detection cloaks shimmered eerily through the trees.

'You cannot protect me by staying. You can only protect me by going. Please believe me, my love. It is the only way!'

Eidred waited tensely for Storlem to be persuaded. For his own self-preservation he *had* to comply with the faerie's pleas. Anyone discovered to have befriended a member of the fey was subjected to a slow and painful death, a terrifying notion for Eidred now that she was harbouring an elf in her dressing-quarter. Poor Storlem! She did not want to hear of his demise.

'Then I shall watch over you within the palace,' Storlem said. 'I will always be there to protect you.'

Golden light engulfed Storlem.

The frantic lovers clung to each other once more.

'I will love you for eternity,' he said. 'I will seek you out. Wherever you are.'

'Until we find each other again, goodbye, my beautiful Storlem.' The faerie's tone was a mixture of melancholy and passion. 'I will love you for all lifetimes to come.'

The golden light brightened. Storlem's form faded...and melted magically into the blinding dazzle. Amid a swish of feathers, an eagle appeared in his place. The eagle rose from the faerie's arms and hovered as she darted from the shadows. Eidred saw her clearly then. The faerie was clad in a resplendent array of fiery tones: crimson, russet and amber that extended through her wings in sweeps of silver. She was hurrying towards a clump of ferns by the stream. The glow of fading light upon her gown conjured the effect of autumn leaves in a whirlwind.

Eidred rose swiftly to her feet. She would create a distraction. The men, oblivious to her presence, hurtled past her. One of them dived into the ferns. A cry rang out.

Eidred squealed as the courtier grasped the faerie's wrist. He dragged the terrified sprite from her hiding place.

The eagle was now circling high above, a soaring speck in a purpling sky.

Eidred whirled round and glowered at the courtier, about to command he free the faerie at once.

The faerie's dark, frightened eyes settled for a second on Eidred. As though anticipating Eidred's intended actions, the faerie shook her head in warning. And then Eidred heard a voice from nowhere, outside of the courtiers' shouts. 'Princess, you must go!' The voice was low and hinted of bell chimes. 'Run. Hide.' The faerie's words had been projected into Eidred's mind.

Feeling helpless and hopeless all at once, Eidred slipped across to a nest of brambles within a mossy grove and crouched in the darkness. Sadly, there was nothing she could have done. In defending a sprite, she would have been put to her death. The faerie had understood this.

The faerie's beauty-creation powers would now be snatched from her heart. She would become enslaved. She would be expected to become a bewitcher: vacant-eyed, dark intentioned, robbed of the right to remain in her native home.

The dusk melded into a star-speckled expanse. Sprites crept from where they had sheltered, their grief-filled voices descending into a chorus of moans. The stream unwound into its former peacefulness.

Eidred leaned against a tree trunk for support, about to sink to the forest floor in a torrent of sobs, and was startled by the rustle of feathers. Storlem, in eagle form, was hovering tentatively near the filigree tree. In a single swoop, he circled Eidred and glided a gentle wing across the top of her shoulder.

The words he spoke to the faerie returned to her. *I will watch over you within the palace. I will always be there to protect you.*

Storlem's promise to the faerie meant a nobler sort of love would survive within the cold and gold-hungry palace.

It had arrived: Matthew's day of leaving his banking career. He'd always believed he would leave at the distinguished age of sixty-five after a sterling career climb, hailed at the other end as the best CEO who ever lived.

Sure, he'd climbed to a reasonable level. As boss of thirty-five staff members he was envied by the up-and-coming who vied for his position. They could have it. Imagining Harrow and other competitors tussling over the title he'd once hoped to seize conjured up the image of lions swatting at each other over a buffalo carcass. The job had been lifeless. Now life would be jobless, but only until he got his new venture sorted.

So here Matthew was again, in the bar with the fancy lampshades, realising with a splash of sentimentality that this would be the last time he'd celebrate with colleagues. A recollection of laughs and the smell of cigars and the sense of belonging that came with sharing a win swam by him. End of an era. No more wins. No more deals falling through either, or Doctor Cyanide tributes at charity nights: Harrow's obsession with 'Gimme' had been an amusing enigma to everyone but Matthew.

At last he was residing in neutral territory, master of his own destiny, king of a mysterious new realm that he was yet to conquer.

Scrolling through old messages on his phone, he landed on the one from two Tuesdays ago, when he'd had his phone switched off at the poetry night. *Where the bluddy hell are you?* Where the bloody hell did that woman learn to spell? That and five missed calls, all from Bernadette and thankfully not from the hospital concerning Grandma Carmody's condition.

Matthew took his thumb off the down-arrow, pressed 'forward' and sent the text back to her. She was due there forty-five minutes ago. They'd planned to meet at a café next door to his work before arriving at the bar together. As usual, she'd stood him up.

Davo and Roddie were at the bar ordering Matthew something festive, but apart from these two and the giggling admin girls seated at a corner table and sipping on honeydew daiquiris, the team was yet to arrive for pre-dinner drinks.

Matthew's warm-hearted mid-fifties executive secretary, and 'podner in crime' throughout all his years at the bank, had organised tables for sixty at Opera Underground on Circular Quay. 'Don't go to too much trouble, Celia,' he'd said. 'I'm walking out, after all.'

Celia had corrected him with a conspiratorial smile. 'Retiring,' she'd said. 'And a lot of people will be disappointed if you're not given a farewell to remember.'

Harrow was next to arrive, good-for-nothing Adam Harrow with a dark-haired glamour on his arm who he referred to as 'Rosie'. The girl looked familiar. No older than thirty-two, probably, her skin of pale brown youthfully smooth. She introduced herself just as the deejay started up a *pow-pow* of syncopated drumbeats—her name wasn't Rosie after all—and then Matthew recalled where he'd seen her before. She was the girl with the seductive eyes, the girl Harrow had chatted up en-route to his awaiting fiancée.

Harrow excused himself to go and buy drinks and gave his companion an exaggerated kiss, highly unnecessary, Matthew thought, considering he'd only be gone thirty seconds. Farewelling in advance perhaps. Within a few days the girl would be deserted for someone just as attractive.

Harrow's girl was poised against a backdrop of darkened arched windows, looking like the curvaceous Magdalene of classical paintings. She was smiling good-naturedly.

He had to say something so that she didn't feel uncomfortable standing opposite a bloke, albeit Matthew, who she didn't know...*from Adam!*

'So, Lucetta,' he called over the drumbeats, remembering the snowy fleece of an Alice Springs alpaca that shared the same name, 'What sort of a day did you have?'

'Not so busy,' she called back. 'I had the day off, but it turned into a bit of a disaster.' She told him about a shopping trip that ended dismally when her car broke down on the freeway.

While she related the story, Matthew marvelled at her composure throughout the ordeal of pacifying angry motorists and having to make a spectacle of herself, directing the freeway's cars with another driver who'd stopped to help. This had been endured for ninety minutes because the vehicle service had taken a substantial amount of time to get there. She'd then been told her car had to be towed to a mechanic who wasn't able to work on it for four days.

Matthew nodded every so often, interested to know whether the problem with the car had resolved. Bernadette faced with this would have felt thoroughly victimised. The girl chattered on about it as though it had happened to someone else, someone like that risk-riddled guy on the Comedy Channel, because she laughed regularly at intervals, her wide ironic smile appearing each time she shook her head. Matthew studied her, grudgingly impressed with his colleague's ability to zone in on women who were sophisticated, exuberant and nobody's fool...not counting Harrow of course.

Harrow was moving away from the bar, a daiquiri in one hand and beer in the other. Matthew turned and scanned the doorway for signs of someone he knew. Bernadette walked through it, arriving at his side in a flurry of sickly perfume. She pecked him on the cheek and told him her appointment had run over.

'If I were you I'd give your beauty therapist an ultimatum. When is she ever on time?'

'Wasn't the beauty therapist,' Bernadette said. She stuck her chest forward.

'Implant surgeon?'

'Trust you not to notice.' Bernadette turned away. 'I need a drink.'

'It was an appointment with a designer,' Matthew offered, feeling like he was back in first grade, playing guessing games with peevish Priscilla Smythe. 'To buy that strapless dress you've got on, which you look beautiful in, by the way.'

Bernadette scowled at him while smoothing a hand over her collarbone. 'Doesn't my skin look any different to you?'

'Ah, your skin. You've been to a...one of those...um...day spa things to get an expolocation or whatever it is.'

'No, I got my exfoliation on Saturday, remember? Think colour, Matthew. Colour.'

Matthew stepped out of the game. 'Honeydew daiquiri, Bernadette?'

'Please.'

When Matthew returned, Bernadette was nowhere in sight. Lucetta was alone by the arched windows, gazing at the groovers on the dance floor. She did not have a drink in her hand. Matthew watched the dancers too. A guy in a love-heart patterned shirt was wowing everyone with ceiling-skimming flips and the odd lapse into Cossack dancing. 'Russian acrobat?'

Lucetta nodded enthusiastically. 'Amazing moves!'

'That'll be me after a couple of drinks.' Matthew bent his knees. 'Maybe not. The running injury might hold me back.'

Lucetta roared with laughter.

'What's Adam doing leaving you here like this?' To project a healthy absence of malice, he immediately followed with a closed-mouth smile.

'Not so sure. I think he might have run into someone he knew. That coppery-haired lady you were talking to earlier.'

Matthew was just about to say 'That's Bernadette, my wife,' when the deejay announced in an excitable, ear-splitting blare that they were 'Gettin' the party started.' Informative people, were deejays. What would patrons have done without that vital snippet of information? Hearing the party was *gettin' started* was no doubt a huge relief to all who were worried it wasn't.

'What do you plan to do after you leave the bank, Matthew?'

Matthew glanced sideways at the girl. Her sleek dark hair was piled on top of her head, reminding him of the '60s and Diana Ross, one of his first music-clip crushes. A fringe skimmed brows that arched over densely lashed, amber-coloured eyes.

'I'm going to start my own law firm,' he told her. 'It's sure to beat having decisions made for me by the corporation.'

The bank. Better described as a contrary salary wheel that deleted those who didn't perform to its meteoritic standards. For people like him, who had matched and surpassed these, it became a dispassionate ghoul that took pleasure in breaking apart their souls. Stealthily. With dollar-scented charm. Piece by voluntary piece. The reward? A goal post with legs. He didn't say all that to Lucetta of course. Only world-weary creatures with glass-half-empty mentalities would agree with his take on corporate success.

Lucetta, in response to his law firm admission, toyed with the zodiac bracelet on her wrist and said, 'So you're an eagle also?'

Astrology! Women often tended to relate things back to star signs, yet he wasn't a Scorpio, sign of the eagle.

'I'm actually a Libran,' he said. 'Sign of the scales. But weighing things up is probably good for a lawyer. What's your opinion?'

'Same as yours.'

'But I have the planet Venus in the sign of Scorpio,' Matthew said, 'so there is a bit of eagle lurking around.'

Lucetta nodded. 'I tend to think of Scorpio as a scorpion, but...um...I actually meant eagle in the legal sense.'

'Ah, *legal* eagle.' Matthew clapped a hand on the back of his head. 'How did I not get that you're another lawyer? I'm pretty lame at discerning subtleties.' He checked his watch. 'Particularly after 6pm.'

Lucetta looked down. 'But it's great you know what signs your planets are in. That's pretty impressive. I also have Venus in Scorpio. Makes us fairly passionate people, don't you think?'

Matthew held up his arm in a high-five gesture. She slapped his hand and laughed heartily, shaking her head.

Matthew moved in closer saying, 'I always got the impression Scorpio was a fairly stern sign, but I don't feel much like that at all.' To add a dash of controversy, Matthew switched on a stern expression.

'That's because you've got an air-sign sun,' Lucetta said with an approving nod. 'It lightens you up.'

'And you don't seem stern and serious either. Have you got an air-sign sun?'

'I've got an air-sign moon. But my Sagittarius Sun Sign cancels out any brooding intensity. Although, come to think of it, in private I tend to brood a lot.'

'Sagittarius! I know about that sign. My grandfather was one. They're meant to be quite jovial aren't they?'

'We have our moments.' The girl said it with a light-hearted modesty.

'In fact, my moon's in Sagittarius, according to my sister-in-law, and that makes me very happy.'

'Happy to know your moon's in Sagittarius or happy in temperament?'

'Both. I'm a gratefully elated guy. Over the moon in fact.'

Lucetta's radiant beam froze and fell away. Putting on a Scorpio face the way Matthew had! 'That's an excellent one,' Matthew said grinning. The poor girl still didn't have the drink Harrow was getting for her. He held out the one he was keeping for Bernadette. 'Here Lucetta, have a daiquiri.' She accepted the glass he offered. He'd have another made up once Bernadette emerged.

'Thank you, Matthew.' This was said vaguely. She was still staring ahead, causing Matthew to realise too late that she hadn't been play-acting a Scorpio moment.

He turned to see where her gaze led. Harrow was sitting on one of the couches. Bernadette, seated beside him, was drinking the daiquiri meant for Lucetta. The two were chatting casually.

The insecurity in Lucetta's eyes compelled Matthew to reassure her. The man might be a perpetual drip, but even he had ethics. Harrow wouldn't go around chatting up other men's wives in full view of them. And Bernadette, if nothing else, was a one-man woman.

To show Harrow's date that Bernadette was his other half, Matthew nodded towards the copper-haired beauty on the couch and said, 'Gemini. Sign of the twins.'

Lucetta's forehead relaxed. She nodded at Harrow. 'Also a Gemini.'

'Ha! Two Geminis. Trouble times four.'

'Geminis are the best kinds of talkers.' Lucetta's lashes lowered. 'They've kissed the Blarney Stone. Nearly all air signs have.' She watched Harrow delightedly. 'That includes you, Matthew, since you're a Libran.'

'Aha!'

'So that's pretty cool. Does your wife have the moon in an air sign? Astrologers believe it's a match made in heaven if the husband's sun harmonises with the wife's moon.'

'I actually do know that, believe it or not.' Matthew paused to observe his significant other sitting comfortably against purple cushions. Bernadette certainly had a lot to say to Harrow considering they'd only met twice. 'My brother's wife told us the other week when they were out from England. Her moon...My wife's moon's in the sign of the goat. Is that an air sign?'

'Capricorn? That's an earth sign.'

'Better luck next time,' he said, then thought he'd better add, 'In guessing a sign element I mean. Not in selecting a marriage partner.'

'Of course,' Lucetta reassured. 'Of course!'

Harrow still hadn't returned from his spot on the bar's couch. Matthew continued to keep Harrow's date company while she waited. The conversation had been pleasant enough, despite it having only surrounded astrology. He launched into a new topic. 'What's your specialisation, Lucetta?'

'Er...human rights.'

'Powerful stuff. So how did you find out about astro traits? Do law degrees now incorporate that sort of thing?'

'Wow, I wish they would.'

'Criminology would never be the same again.'

'And anyone like us, with planets in secretive Scorpio, would be considered highly suspect.' Lucetta's voice was deliberately bland. 'Getting back to your question, though, I studied astrology years ago. People's horoscopes have fascinated me ever since. You sound as though you've found out quite a bit yourself. Was that through your sister-in-law?'

'Just the basics. My brother's wife's right into all that.' His sister-in-law had told him that the moon and each of the planets continuously travelled through each sign of the zodiac. A person's horoscope, she'd said, was a snapshot of those planets at the exact time of birth, but most people only knew their zodiac or star sign, which happened to be the sign their sun was in the month they were born, and probably the reason Lucetta had referred to it as a *Sun Sign*. Turning to Lucetta, Matthew said, 'It stands out in my memory as ironic that my wife's moon was in the sign of the goat, because goats eat everything, and my wife is...well...My wife's...particular about food.'

Dette, still chatting to Harrow, was shaking her Diondra-inspired chin-length bob emphatically as she spoke. Her bare shoulders looked the colour of citrus peel, obviously a trick of the light. Blond-headed Harrow looked much the same colour. Two orange-skinned Geminis, conversing as only Geminis could.

Matthew made an attempt to look sly. 'Wait a minute, Lucetta. Adam Harrow's got a Gemini sun you said.'

'Correct.'

Matthew prolonged the artificial squint. 'Do you have a Gemini moon?'

Lucetta collapsed into laughter. It wasn't *that* funny, Matthew wanted to say. Not funny at all, not even if the overly hammy facial expression had been taken into account.

'No, but my moon is in airy Libra, so we'll be fine.'

'Onya, Lucetta. That-a-girl.'

'Then again,' she added, 'the Venus Sign tells a lot about who a man likes.'

'So, what does that have to match? Does he need to have his *lerve* planet in Scorpio like you?'

'Yeah, that'd be perfect actually. Or at least have other planets in Scorpio. Trouble is, he hasn't.'

Matthew was suddenly intrigued. 'What's it in then?'

Lucetta sighed and then brightened, in an effort, Matthew thought, to hide deeper concerns. 'Gemini,' she said. 'The same sign as your other half's sun. I've known the odd two-timer with that combination.'

Matthew took a swig of his beer. 'In that case,' he said, sliding across to the left. 'I think I'll go and retrieve my wife.' To the strains of Lucetta's throaty laughter, he sauntered towards the carrot-complexioned chatterboxes.

He'd wanted instead to stay alongside Lucetta and say 'Screw Harrow', then realised with amusement that this might be taken as friendly advice. It was more than likely on Lucetta's agenda, although in subtler, more elegant language.

Her to-do list might have read:

7pm	Turn up at Adam's workplace's pre-dinner drinks looking drop-dead gorgeous.
7.01pm	Bewitch every bloke in the bar.
7.02pm	Chat charmingly to one of Adam's colleagues.
7.45pm	Attend the colleague's send-off dinner at Opera Underground.
10.30pm	Invite Adam home.

Matthew held out a hand to Bernadette and helped her from the couch. Her skin no longer looked orange in the changing light. It looked yellow: bright yellow, almost metallically gold, as did Harrow's.

'Solarium,' Matthew said in a rush of inspiration. 'You went to the solarium.' He wasn't going to add that she looked as though she'd slapped on brass polish.

'Very close,' she said, smiling indulgently. 'I had spray-tan. At a tanning salon. Solariums are just *errrgh!!*'

'Errrgh?'

'Old-school.' She reached up and stroked the back of his head. The small show of affection made Matthew gulp. It wasn't long now until he'd be leaving Bernadette, and he wasn't looking forward to it. He'd let her enjoy herself first, on the trip away with her cousin. Considering her non-stop dissatisfaction with their relationship, he doubted his divorce demand would turn out to be much of a surprise. Perhaps she'd think over their marriage while in Vanuatu and break up with him on her return. Easier for everyone, but hoping for it was a coward's way out.

Upsetting the stable lives of a woman and her two daughters was a gut-wrenching prospect. He would assure Bernadette that he was not, in any way, expecting them to leave in haste; would insist they take as long as they liked to secure a home they loved.

He and Bernadette wandered back to Lucetta, Harrow trailing oafishly behind them. When Matthew introduced his gold-skinned gadabout, she narrowed her eyes and said to Lucetta in a less-than-friendly tone, 'I've met you once before.'

Lucetta's response was surprisingly warm in comparison, with exclamations of: *Not blonde anymore!* And: *Didn't recognise you in this light. Redheads have more fun! My daughter's a redhead.*

This prompted a half-minute chat. In the first few seconds, Harrow grinned vacantly at the dance floor, and Matthew studied the ceiling. In the remaining seconds, fortunate for Matthew, Charlie arrived with a dozen or so others, booming, 'Where's the retirement boy?'

'Retirement' coupled with 'boy'. A definite contradiction. Thinking of Lucetta as 'Harrow's girl' was probably just as absurd, since it cancelled out all notions of spirited maturity and replaced them with impressions of a giddy nineteen-year-old on a nervous date with the First Year rugby captain.

Charlie's associate director shook Matthew's hand.

Harrow whispered something to Lucetta. Her eyes, darker now in the dimmed light, widened and darted to the side. She placed her empty glass on the nearest counter and seized up her handbag. 'Dette,' she said. 'It was great to see you again. And Matthew, so lovely to meet you. There's been a change of plan. We're apparently not going to your dinner now. All the best for the future.'

Bernadette raised her hand in a feeble wave.

Matthew stepped forward. 'Thanks, Lucetta. Great to have met you.'

'And good luck, Matthew, with your new venture. I'm sure you'll enjoy being an eagle again.'

'Are you right to get going now, Rosie?' Harrow said. He jerked a thumb at the exit beyond the dancefloor.

Why Rosie? Nodding calmly, Lucetta waved goodbye again to Bernadette, then hastened after Harrow, weaving around lamp-stands and bar-stools with energetic finesse. Matthew became aware of Bernadette watching him.

'The flamenco look went out two seasons ago,' she said in a scathing drawl. 'Maybe even three.'

Lucetta's skirt, which swept almost to her ankles, swung from side to side as she followed Harrow to the door. With its layers of black lace, it did have the look of the Spanish dancer about it. The dark-brown bodice fitted snugly over something with white diaphanous sleeves that puffed about her shoulders like clouds, and its front, Matthew recalled, was lace-up.

Matthew glowered at the blond-headed bozo darting towards the door ahead of the girl he called 'Rosie'. Probably had trouble remembering all his women's names. Probably mixed them up occasionally. Harrow certainly hadn't gone out of his way for Lucetta, to make sure she had a drink in her hand.

She was too good for him. Matthew hoped she'd arrive at that conclusion in the not-so-distant future, preferably before the night was over.

On Monday afternoon, when the mall expedition with Lena was no more than a few minutes away, Rosetta hurried into the hallway to collect her handbag and cashmere wrap from the coat-stand.

Seeing again the roses on the foyer table caused a flutter of exasperation that unsettled her stomach. Deep dark red, the colour of desire, coiling into shadows of black, delivered by a Floral Fiesta courier a little over a week ago, courtesy of The Gorgeous GEG.

'Seventeen again and all butterflies,' she recalled herself saying to Eadie and Darren the Friday before. Adam had been due in another couple of hours. Rosetta was off to a retirement dinner for one of Adam's colleagues.

'Is it any wonder?' That had been Eadie. 'He's utterly devastating! And I think he blended in really well at Royston's lunch party.'

Eadie and Darren had been there with a bottle of bubbly to celebrate her getting into the singing semis at Bondi Diggers. Former hairdresser Darren had brought his trimming scissors, and Eadie was only too pleased to practice her new TAFE gained make-up artistry skills with Rosetta's face for a canvas.

Together they'd conspired to give Rosetta the latest 'sixties' look. Darren had worked a darker colour through her hair, gave her fringe a blunter edge, and sprayed it with gloss until it shone like wet liquorice. He'd then wielded it into a teased-at-the-crown French roll that resembled a beehive, a la Diana Ross of her Supremes days, and Eadie had drawn thick lines of kohl across the base of Rosetta's upper lashes that she extended into subtle tilts at the sides before lathering on several coats of mascara.

'We've made you superbly sextees,' New Zealand Eadie had said.

Darren had looked at Eadie uncertainly, and said, 'Did she say "sexy" or "sixties"? For the record, Rosetta, you look both of those things.'

'Ah, thank you, Darren. Sweet of you to say that. I think she actually said "sixties" but with these dear little inarticulate Kiwis, you never can tell.'

Eadie had shaken a fist at Rosetta and Darren, and, as though lining up a dartboard throw, threatened to assail them with a lip pencil. Rosetta had then pacified the mock-angry Maori with a slice of Easter cake, a cup of cocoa and the tarot reading Eadie had hinted at earlier.

...Today, while she listened out for Lena's car, Rosetta unwound the wrap from her coat stand and settled it around her shoulders. Turning again to the roses in their vase, she ran a thumb over the petals of one, wondering vaguely whether the inventor of velvet was inspired by this sort of softness.

To begin with, thinking of Adam had needed no prompting. The man who'd panthered his way across to the glass counter at Crystal Consciousness had surprised and delighted her by asking *that* question when he'd purchased a Conan Dalesford book: whether she was single. A week later he'd gone in at the end of the workday, fixed her with those piercing eyes, and declared in a presumptuously sexy growl that he'd like to have dinner with her once she'd shut shop.

She'd told him with regret that she was busy. Friday Fortnight preparations awaited her at home. Adam had then suggested lunch on Saturday, but she'd had to decline that too because of the potluck luncheon at Royston's. 'But you're welcome to join us,' she'd said. 'Royston won't mind a bit, although I have to warn you we're all vegetarians,' and Adam had happily agreed; had promised to bring along one of his specialties. 'I make a mean Florentine quiche,' he'd said.

They'd gone out to dinner the night after Royston's lunch. Four days after, Adam phoned to invite her to an event two weeks away: the retirement send-off. 'I can't meet up any sooner, I'm afraid,' he'd said. 'I'm taken up for the next ten days. Business trip to Melbourne.'

Saying goodbye and putting down the phone was akin to emptying a packet of Jersey caramels into the rubbish. Rosetta craved him. His kisses had driven her crazy.

Everything from then on had been a reminder of Adam. A surfie on Izzie's favourite soap looked like Adam from behind. In a Target catalogue there'd been a tanned, ever-so-slightly sneering blond man self-consciously attending to a barbecue, one arm draped around an equally self-conscious wife.

'*That* bloke's never cooked a grill in his life,' Craig had commented when he saw the open catalogue on the coffee table. That was the day Craig had brought round his Spanish guitar to rehearse their Bondi Diggers act. Nailing melodic excellence had been put on hold while they settled down to an afternoon tea of Greek Easter cake with lime-rind frosting, a product of the morning's bake-up.

She'd snatched up the catalogue, folded it protectively and jabbed Craig in the ribs. 'Leave him alone,' she'd said. They'd both succumbed to laughter. Trying to sound demure, she'd added, 'He reminds me of Adam. Not as rugged as Adam of course.'

Craig snatched it back and peered at the picture once more. 'Yeah, you're right,' he'd said nodding. 'But rugged isn't exactly a word I'd use to describe that new bloke of yours.'

...Three toots blared. Shaken from the recollections, Rosetta flung on her handbag and hurried out to Lena's little old Ford.

'Such a pretty, *pretty* island,' Dette said with a sigh. 'I'm so glad you decided to come with me.'

No answer.

Dette turned to find him lost in sleep beside a coconut-palm shadow. His incredibly perfect body was taut with stillness, reminding her of a tastefully crafted boy-doll.

'They're *action figures*,' Matthew, years ago, had corrected. 'Boys don't have dolls.'

His green eyes were masked with the upward tilting sunnies that she'd begged him to reconsider. Dette turned away from the sight of them and groaned. They made him look like a cross between Dame Edna Everage and Jaws, nothing like a conservative finance whiz. Ordinarily, he was a superb selector of clothing and accessories, a real winner in the fashion stakes, a man-about-town who was more than familiar with the term 'dress to impress'.

Matthew's random actions had become unreadable. His detached politeness was driving her to distraction. Dette would never have believed when they'd first got married that she could feel so anxious. He'd always got stressed of course. That was a given for a busy man who hauled in a comfortable salary. Nowadays, though, a seeping feeling, which started as dread and ended as fury, would creep into her stomach each time he phoned from work about needing to stay back.

And on the night of his send-off, just when Dette thought she'd won back his interest, with her face having been scrubbed to peaches-and-cream perfection at the day spa, and her body, now at its slenderest, glowing with a quasi suntan—and swathed dramatically in Giovanni's off-the-shoulder creation, which sparkled with teensy-weensy asterisks—he'd eyed the nanny candidate with approval. Who would have thought that someone in a white peasant blouse and lace-up waist cincher could be taken so seriously!

Interviewing candidates had been difficult and stressful, not to mention irritating, and had caused Dette to wonder whether a trip away would be worth all the trouble.

The first had been a veritable Miss Priss whose hair looked as though a Victorian-era nun had styled it. Stern and surly. Demanding to know why Dette was vacationing solo without her daughters during the school holidays.

Then there'd been the New Age hippie flake. Long reddish-tinged hair parted in the middle, loose clothing, Gypsy jewellery, flat sandals. *Flat* sandals! Dette did not want her daughters influenced by this sort of slovenliness.

She'd rung the agency and asked for another candidate. The ex-nurse presented as pleasant enough, but by the time Dette offered her the position she'd got another offer. That was the trouble with good staff. You had to snap them up before anyone else did.

The real bee in Dette's bonnet had been the fourth candidate, the one who had answered her newspaper notice. Too in-your-face attractive for Dette to consider. Someone waiting for Dette's husband to get home before being dismissed for the day needed to be the opposite of a man-magnet. She hadn't been stylish though. Matthew liked women with class. Beginning to run out of choices and reading through this candidate's resume again, which indicated the woman was hard working, had a teenaged daughter of her own and volunteered once a fortnight at a women's and children's shelter, Dette had pondered over whether she could trust her with him. Divorced, however. A big minus. Dette had reasoned then that not everyone was on the lookout, or in an unhappy relationship. She'd been dully dressed in a cleaner's uniform. Dowdy. And certainly not what Dette would call slim.

Overhearing a phone call between Matthew and a workmate had ultimately helped Dette to make up her mind. Matthew's speaker phone had been on in the study. A man named Roddie, who Dette had never met, admitted to falling for a wide-hipped, bosomy Italian. It was Matthew saying 'Voluptuous, do you mean? Woo-hoo!' that had prompted Dette to take up her mobile and coolly inform the final candidate she hadn't been selected.

Bringing her thoughts back to the present, Dette gazed at the aqua of the sea. A smidgen greener and it would be the same colour as the Turnabout Teal she'd asked Dan to use on the bedroom ceiling. A breeze rose up, springing a dusting of sand onto Adam's muscular legs. He stirred. Dette leaned down, planting her elbows on his Berry & Seale 2008 edition beach towel, and kissed his cheek. So beautiful. He was so, *so* divinely beautiful.

Reflecting again on the interview process, Dette closed her lids against the sun's persistent rays and flipped her sunglasses down over her eyes. The whole nanny-candidate thing had been a tedious waste of time. She'd resorted to offering Rhoda double her usual wage, and Rhoda had agreed to give away the idea of hanging around her grandchildren for one week of the holidays at least, confirming that everyone was corruptible with the right offer.

And then one of the interviews she'd conducted had returned to haunt her. Dette had thought she'd seen the last of that final candidate, having barred any possibility of a poverty-wracked and worryingly voluptuous cleaner—devoid of a wedding or engagement ring—attempting to snatch her husband. Embarrassingly, this unsuccessful and perhaps disgruntled nannying hopeful was there at the bar on Friday night. Rosalba? Rosita? Rosalina?

Dette's memory flickered back to the name she'd scribbled down on the phone-pad. Rosetta. That had been it. Rosetta Melki. Matthew had called her 'Lucetta', and although Dette hadn't recalled her actual name at the time, Adam's 'Rosie' reference had sounded closer to it. So very Adam-ish of him, to shortcut something fussy.

Dette had been catching up with Adam in whispers when she'd spotted Rosetta standing alongside Matthew. The woman was laughing uproariously at Matthew's excuse for humour. Dette hadn't at first recognised her, but the hair hadn't been up at the interview, and the fringe hadn't been forward. While Dette had known on arriving at the bar that someone dark-haired had been standing beside Adam, she'd assumed her to be one of the admin girls.

Once settled into the bar's couch, the one with the annoyingly purple cushions, Dette had confided her plight to Adam. She'd omitted, of course, any uncertainty she'd felt concerning employing Rosetta as a temporary nanny, avoiding mentioning too, the way the woman was at that stage gawping at Matthew like a goldfish: a sex-starved one at that!

Instead she'd told him that Rosetta worried her, that she suspected Rosetta was there at the retirement night to seek revenge for having been refused the job. 'She's going to cause trouble, Adam,' Dette had said. 'I know she is.' An exaggeration of course, but she couldn't ignore her first impression when she'd stepped in. The woman's stance alongside Adam had been somewhat territorial. He was, after all, more handsome than her husband, more sought after, and so probably less able to be trusted.

Adam had done the gallant thing; had told Dette he would get Rosetta out of the way. 'She's our office cleaner,' he'd said. 'And she looks to me like she's had way too much to drink. I'll give her a lift home and scoot back to you. Soon as I can.'

'We're all moving on to that Circular Quay restaurant in the next half-hour,' Dette had told him. Afraid he would phone to say he'd failed to find her and gone home, she'd added, 'It's down from the Opera House.'

As the true gentleman he was, Adam had kept his word. Once dinner finished at Opera Underground, the musicians started up. That was when Adam had texted her to say where he was.

Matthew had asked her to dance. Said the band they'd hired for him was his favourite.

'Sweetie, I can't,' she'd said. 'I had to go shopping for quilt covers this afternoon.'

He'd eyed her with affection. 'What does that have to do with not dancing?'

'I walked my feet off trying to find one in a silver-tinted beige. These tootsies are too tired to party.'

And then Matthew's middle-aged secretary, a woman who really needed to do something about that jutting stomach of hers, had urged Matthew onto the dance floor, and while everyone was ensconced in grooving to the rhythms of Matthew's requested song, Dette had seized the opportunity to go to Adam.

She'd raced across to the neighbouring Quay West hotel, announced herself at reception as 'Mrs Harrow' and dashed up the curling flight of stairs to a room conveniently located on the first floor. A room this close to the foyer meant Dette was less than a minute's walk from Opera Underground; no tardy lifts to mar the frantic return she would reluctantly have to make.

High on anticipation, she'd opened the door with her card-key. He'd greeted her from the bed naked, having emerged from a shower that was still running in the ensuite, grinning that bad-boy grin, damp-haired and glistening skinned, his body resembling the statue of a rain-studded Olympian.

So the evening had ended happily. After that climactic hotel visit, she'd returned to the restaurant to find the musicians thankfully packing up, and everyone milling around the small stage in readiness for the 'goodbye and good luck' speech, delivered with back-slapping alacrity by Matthew's boss.

Then there were farewell sentiments for her husband, and teary goodbyes from the tarts in admin who had hugged Matthew a little too tightly to be considered otherwise.

During the cab ride home alongside slurry-worded Matthew, she'd gazed out at the city lights—a jeweller's window of starry reds, greens and blues—while marvelling at how sublime it had felt to be skin-to-skin once more with the incorrigible Adam Harrow.

Two days before the flight, she'd met her cousin in the city and paid her off to keep up the 'Mum and Dad shouted me a trip to Vanuatu and I asked Dette to accompany me', story, then she'd gone to Adam, who had taken ten days off work in May, and presented him with his early birthday present of a return ticket to Vanuatu, all expenses paid.

'Who's funding this?' he'd wanted to know.

'Does it matter where the money's from?' she'd said. And then she'd shocked herself with one of Grandma Carmody's impractical sentiments. 'It's the thought that counts, not the money, and I believe that if there's love, then that's all that matters. Love is more important than money.'

'And I *love* you for doing this,' Adam had shouted. Then he'd picked her up, thrown her on the bed and proceeded to demonstrate his gratitude physically.

On the day of the flight, Diondra had rung to wish Dette 'bon voyage' and to give a friendly warning about being discreet.

'Believe me, I am,' Dette had told her.

Dette, while lily white she wasn't, had still retained her dignity. She was a *lady.* Adam had told her that many a time. Ladies didn't give away all their secrets. Adam had also told her she'd make a great actress, a brilliant one in fact, with all her seamlessly executed cloak-and-dagger darting about, and Adam's opinion was one she valued more than anyone's.

She loved him like crazy, this charming, fiery, ridiculously wealthy finance man with the Wall Street aspirations.

If only...but no. Adam wouldn't ask her to live with him. Six months of hotel room trysts and the plethora of lies she'd told Matthew over the phone while Adam smiled and turned the other way wasn't the smartest method of earning a new lover's loyalty. And solitude was Adam's god.

Being married to Matthew felt so different now. He had plans in place to leave her for someone else, Dette felt sure of it. Having a husband who ignited such nail-biting nervousness was like standing on a precipice, dreading that inevitable push. She could go ahead and break up with him first, of course, but the idea of putting her girls through the disruption of another move, especially if she'd given up on a *second* marriage, was too awful to consider.

She would have to be careful once she got home. She would need to wait around for each mail delivery so as to read and discard Matthew's credit card statement before he did, but that wouldn't stop him from checking his balance online. She would have to arrange a problem. She could hide his laptop...but then she'd probably have to hide the cord of his desktop computer as well, but then...Ah well. She'd think of something. If he discovered she'd purchased ten days' island accommodation at Honeymooner Haven, he'd abandon her within seconds.

Dette stretched out on her beach towel and beamed at her golden Apollo. He did not return the smile. Instead, he regarded her with an enigmatic aloofness that could only be described as smouldering. Mmm!

What if...? Ah yes. What if. A term that was only temporarily cheering, but still...

What if Adam loved her in the same way she loved him and was hesitant to say? What if Adam had quietly decided to put a hundred per cent effort into their relationship? What if she could convince Adam that his life would be better if he lived with her?

She mulled over it all with wistful resignation, then wondered how the same questions would sound if 'what if?' was replaced with 'Needless to say'.

Could it be done?

Did she have the power to change mere longings into possibilities? Dette crossed her fingers and sighed. 'Needless to say,' she whispered. 'I have all the power in the world.'

Chapter Eleven

Matthew eyed the Post-nuptial Agreement forms on his home-office desk, pinned in place by a carved wooden eagle. At Opera Underground Charlie had handed him a box. One of the admin juniors must have taken great care in decorating the box prior to its presentation; there'd been scissor-curled printer paper sprouting from its lid. 'I knew you liked the bloody thing more than I ever did,' Charlie had said when Matthew admired the artefact.

Now, as Matthew glared at the forms, Charlie's retirement gift from Norway stared at him blankly. 'Think it'll work?' he asked the eagle. 'You don't? Matey, neither do I.' He thumped his fist down on the desk and groaned. 'She wouldn't agree to this. Not ever.' He'd realised this way too late.

Pre-nuptials had felt extraneous seven years ago. The ideal for Matthew would have been a twelve-month engagement when he and Bernadette could have lived together to test out compatibility. All going well, he'd hoped they'd plan their family the following year, but Bernadette's surprising announcement had sped things up. His mention of signing a pre-nup had made her sob hysterically. 'This just shows you don't trust me,' she'd said. 'And that you don't care in the slightest about our baby.' There had been no baby; just a four-month disruption to Bernadette's cycle caused by dieters' malnutrition.

He had allowed himself to be shamed into believing a pre-nup was unfair to her. Became concerned that his fiancée would flutter away like a frightened butterfly into the arms of someone who made her feel safer. His lack of foresight proved to him that a man was at his most susceptible when in love. Just as well he didn't have anyone else in his sights. He wouldn't be asking anyone out after the marriage ended. Not until he was strong enough to be vulnerable again.

Mulling over the poetry night, he remembered the book mentioned by the unseen poet named Rosetta, a novel about an elf and an eagle, which sounded like something esoteric outlets would sell.

He looked at the clock, nodded, then reached into his pocket for his car keys. He had to see Marc Garrison at three-thirty, one of his former law colleagues, to discuss the setting up of his new firm. They were meeting at a Wynyard café. If he left now he could duck into that weird little New Age bookshop in Martin Place and snap up the book. Going there after the meeting would mean getting tangled in peak hour. Since leaving his job, homeward-bound traffic had become especially unwelcome, but if he were going to visit the shop, he'd have to leave now.

Maybe not. Matthew dropped his keys onto the desk. He'd go to the bookshop another day and would instead get those phone calls out of the way. A plethora of unread emails was another overdue task. He could start on those now, rather than in the evening. He'd then be free to spend more time with the girls.

The day before, he'd picked them up a game of Monopoly—his favourite game as a child—reflecting on his way home from the toy store that he was pretty much a real-life player now, the thrill of property acquisition having never left his veins. Sara and Laura weren't at all familiar with board games. As far as they were concerned, Park Lane was a London fashion label. After he'd given a lowdown on the rules, they'd all spent the remainder of the afternoon laughing and air-punching with each purchase made and scowling when things went financially down the gurgler. He'd promised them another game once they got home. Better to get his work knocked over before then.

He took up a photograph from his desk, a framed snap he'd always treasured, Bernadette and the girls in California enjoying a lamp lit tea party in the hotel's Executive Suite. When he and the girls returned from Disneyland, Laura and Sara had gabbled animatedly to their mother about Sleeping Beauty's castle and the swivelling teacup ride.

'Teacups?' Bernadette had said. 'Did someone happen to mention teacups?

Both girls had shouted that they had.

'It's funny the two of you should mention tea at a time like this.' She'd led them into the suite's opulent sitting room. A blanket had been set on the floor, picnic style, displaying a four-tier cake stand crowded with tartlets, chocolate ricotta cannelloni and other dainties, and an assortment of gleaming crockery. 'The Mad Hatter dropped by with a tea party for my darling daughters and husband because he knew they'd all be hungry after that enormous trek through the magical kingdom! Have a sandwich, Matthew—I ordered walnut and cream cheese for you. Sara, sweetie, will you be Mother and pour?'

He returned the photograph to its place on the desk, aware it had made him smile. He knew his attitude to Bernadette was often subjective. Frustration with the amount of disharmony in their marriage had caused him to draw on the negatives, but acknowledging Bernadette's nicer qualities didn't have to be done grudgingly.

He reached for the mouse, ready to click onto his inbox, and hesitated. If he left immediately, he'd only be giving up half-an-hour. What, realistically, could be achieved in a measly thirty minutes? He snatched up his car keys and headed towards the stairs. The calls and emails could wait. He was his own boss now. He'd get *Our True Ancient History* today.

Having parked in the nearest underground, Matthew scooted up the escalators, turned left at a news stand, and opened the swing-door of the mystical retailer with its walls of swirling purple and sandalwood scented air.

A man with a grey-tipped moustache was advising an older lady that, while he could certainly order in the book, *Numerology for Pets*, it wouldn't be in the shop for another three weeks.

'That won't do,' the woman said with a shrug. 'I could be dead by then.'

Thinking what a morbid answer this was until he heard a shriek of laughter and the words, 'Noooo, that'll be fine, I'll take the risk. Order it in please...' Matthew made his way down the fiction aisle in search of the L's. Latterby...Lennington...Here was a Lidden. Lillibridge wouldn't be far from that.

242

Vaguely aware of the bell ringing as the shop door opened, Matthew looked up to see the customer with the raucous laugh toddle out onto the street. The murmur of the man at the counter phoning through for the woo-woo literature on animal name-numbers was almost inaudible.

Books on rune stones caused Matthew to get side-tracked, so did the stuff on crystal energy, Out-Of-Body Experiences and theoretical time travel. As the shop drifted into its three o'clock lull, Matthew flicked through various titles, perusing paragraphs here and there, conscious of being due at Wynyard in another thirty minutes, wishing half-heartedly that he owned one of the time machines mentioned in the book he was leafing through to buy an extra hour for browsing.

Total con, he thought, putting the inevitably thin time-travel book back on its shelf. Even a layman like me could write a twenty-pager theorising all that.

The bell dinged again. Matthew scrutinised a graphic in a rune stone book. The text below indicated it to be a representation of Odin, the eagle god of Nordic myth. The idea that eagles had become an obsession made him uncomfortable. So did the explanation of selecting that particular page: '*A warning against trickery...*'

No-one was tricking Matthew. At least, he *thought* no-one was, although the whole point of trickery was to aim it at an ignorant target.

He closed the book with a bang and wedged it back between the other fortune-telling guides, aware of a male voice—faint because he was now in the aisle furthest from the counter—enquiring after a female shop assistant who worked there.

The moustachioed shop man, whose accent might have been German, said, 'She's avay at der moment. On her honeymoon, beliv-id-a-not.'

The shop's phone meep-meeped.

The Lillibridge book was nowhere in sight. He'd overlooked googling it before leaving. At present Matthew had nothing to go on. It would have been helpful to recall whether the novel Dalesford had shown him was minuscule, like that joke of a time-travel book, or voluminous, like *War and Peace.*

The time travel book glared out at him. If it were a *Time Travel for Dummies* title, he might have been interested. That'd be the go.

Travelling back in time, preferably to the beginning of his adulthood and starting all over again with relationships.

No. Earlier than that. Up until the age of seventeen, he knew what it was to be lonely; had been too shy to approach the girls he really admired.

All of that changed in the last two years of secondary school. He grew taller, got contact lenses—the specs in those days frequently resembled frog man goggles—and discovered through relationships that he wasn't as undesirable as he'd always thought. Once he'd met Bernadette in his initial years of work, he'd re-experienced some of that muddled clumsiness.

That the current volatile acquisitionist to whom he was married was the same woman he fancied like crazy when he worked as a junior partner at Garrison Weissler Brumby, was hard to believe.

Bernadette's disarming phone manner and innate sense of style had made a great impression on Matthew and his partners when she'd gone for Garrison Weissler Brumby's 'immaculate Front Desk Clerk' position, and Matthew had taken it upon himself to phone her with their offer of employment.

In his opinion back then, none of the others he dated could match the skinny-legged brunette who giggled at his jokes and moved about the office with a spidery sort of grace. Bernadette's single-mother status had deterred many a potential suitor, but Matthew hadn't seen this to be an issue. Their work connection was the reason he'd discarded his hope of asking her out. Facing each other over the tea-room percolator each day would mean major awkwardness if they broke up, and remaining in control at work was mandatory.

She'd got herself a fiancé named Grant Belfield—a policeman who'd scored a two-storey home in a lottery win—had talked excessively to Matthew about her wedding plans, which killed him inside, turned into a blonde and resigned two months after marrying.

On the day of her send-off, she confided that Grant was the father of Sara, still a toddler back then. He'd been her high-school sweetheart, but she couldn't have married a barman. 'Grant earned an embarrassing amount,' she'd said. 'My great-uncle would never have accepted him into the family. Besides all that, we were way too young.' Her great-aunt had minded baby Sara on weekdays so that

Bernadette could do an admin course at a business college in the city. Not long after graduating, she'd landed the job at Matthew's firm.

Seven years after the send-off, Matthew had come to the realisation, when Bernadette—a divorced mother of two by then—had tracked him down and flitted into the ground-floor foyer of his new workplace one sunny afternoon, that he'd never completely forgotten her.

He went over the shelves and re-scanned them for the name Lillibridge. Nope. Nothing there. He returned to the rune stone book and flicked through it once more, his thoughts settling again on Bernadette. He couldn't ever have imagined she'd become a drain on him in the future. Wasn't marriage meant to be the end of feeling alone? Lonely was the perfect word to describe how he felt in his wife's company.

Perhaps her ability to love only extended as far as her children and the Doultons: the great-aunt and departed great-uncle who had always referred to her as their princess. Matthew indeed had a great deal of respect for Bernadette's motherly devotion. Despite his gripes about self-centredness and a compulsion to overindulge—presents in lieu of presence—he could concede without a doubt that Bernadette cared deeply about her children.

He wandered into the next book-lined aisle, making a note of talking over the postnup process with Marc. He had to get things sorted before she arrived home from Vanuatu. Postnup or none, being allowed to forget Bernadette and all that she'd put him through would soon be reality. He'd tell Marc he didn't believe she deserved fifty-per-cent ownership of his inheritance and everything he'd acquired through sheer slog. While for many years he'd thought a not-so-good marriage preferable to dividing his fortune, the continual put-downs and petulant outbursts had caused him to re-think.

It was a question of living solo or bowing to materialism: his own and hers. While being single again equalled becoming poorer, at least he'd regain his peace, and at thirty-four he wasn't entirely out of the game. He could still take another swing at partnering up, and it wasn't as though he'd be moneyless.

Even with divorce-diminished dough, he'd retain plenty in the way of investments. He wouldn't be giving those up without a fight.

There was a small possibility she'd feel guilty about taking so much and agree to his proposal—retention of the Audi and a paid-in-full four-bedroomer in one of the better suburbs—'small possibility' being an overstatement. This was Bernadette, after all.

He checked his watch once more. Twenty minutes now till his appointment with Marc.

Not so easy was eradicating the guilt that gnawed away at him at breaking up Granddad Weissler's millions inherited ten years earlier. His father and brother had been prudent with their share. More than likely, Matthew would be forced to white-ant the legacy, a fortune built from scratch, the life savings of a man who fled Poland on the eve of the Second World War. If there were such a thing as souls moving up to an otherworld, the gruff elder would be glaring down ferociously at Matthew by now. The results of backbreaking toil, of setting up a modest New York tyre shop in 1942 that expanded into franchises and flourished throughout the four decades that followed, was not left to Matthew so he could waste it within a decade.

'Don't you go marryin' no gold diggers, boy,' the moonfaced man had warned him in a Polish-tinted Southern drawl. That had been when Matthew, as a teenager, had travelled from England for a stay at his granddad's Texan ranch. If the grammatical implications had defined that statement, Matthew could have argued that he'd followed this advice to the letter. He hadn't married *no* gold digger.

Jannali Dalesford's words rang back to him. *Your loving wife...*

Matthew placed the rune-stone book on the counter. He asked about the book he was after. The bookseller punched the title into a catalogue in slow and staccato clacks and viewed his monitor with the classic backwards head tilt of a bifocals wearer. Out of print. 'We could order *Our True Ancient History* in for you,' he advised, 'if the usual wait-time doesn't bother you. I know of an Antiquarian wholesaler.'

'I really need it sooner than three weeks,' Matthew told him. 'Do you know of anywhere around here that might sell second-hand books?'

The bookseller's mouth twisted. His moustache slanted into a diagonal strip. 'Crystal Consciousness has a second-hand section.'

This was said with reluctance. It was an opposition retailer, after all. A guarded pause. 'It's in the station arcade.'

'Thanks for that.' Matthew opened the jangly door, re-checked his watch and headed up George Street towards Wynyard and the café.

Crystal Consciousness. A familiar sounding name. It had immediately evoked the memory of burning myrrh, piped music, and the crimson and orange splendour of an ethereal poster.

He scrolled through last month's schedule on his BlackBerry. Aha! Marked under Friday the 8th was: *Conan Dalesford Book Launch. 5.30pm (Time of finish not provided). Crystal Consciousness Books & Gifts.*

So this was the name of the place next to the first-floor news stand. It was the shop with a mind-body-spirit theme that Harrow had detoured into to buy and then discard Conan Dalesford's *Thoughts on Tomorrow's Tycoon War*. Matthew had intended to revisit because of Laura's 'lotsa dots' gift wrap request but had instead gone to a newsagency closer to work. A few weeks later, he'd shaken hands with Dalesford outside its doors.

No time left today. He'd go next week.

'Sold,' Lena said.

Rosetta gave a nod and drawled 'Eureka!' Combing through the curtain shop's eclectic mix of textures that afternoon had been fun. They'd since agreed the glossy maroon fabric would set Lena's lounge room on fire—metaphorically, of course—and Lena was now darting up to the counter to place her order.

They trolleyed the purchase across the mall's car park, lugged it into the boot of Lena's Ford, and then Rosetta remarked they were due for a caffeine hit at Hansel & Gretel, a tiny coffee shop that exuded the aroma of simmering chocolate.

Once settled at one of the pine tables, Lena made the inevitable comment. 'You haven't told me yet about your last date with The Gorgeous GEG. How was it?'

'Aaaagh!' Rosetta rolled her eyes. 'Disappointing. I'd rather not talk about it.'

But she did. She told Lena how the minutes leading up to the delicious hour of Adam's arrival had hovered in slo-mo. And then he was there on her doorstep, all tall and golden, beaming like the midday sun. He'd said a 'Hello again,' to Eadie (volunteer make-up artist) and Darren (self-appointed semi-beehive stylist) while they scrambled out of the door to make an inconspicuous getaway.

When she locked up, Rosetta couldn't help overhearing Darren muttering to Eadie as he crossed the lawn with her that the look Adam had gone for—navy polo and white trousers—was 'nauseatingly nautical' and that Adam was twenty years too late to be 'an extra on *The Love Boat.*' Although terrified Adam had overheard, Rosetta was heartened to find he'd been taken up with his own thoughts, frowning at the verandah floorboards and relating in a moan his bad fortune of parking further up the street because of a party going on in Ashbury Avenue. And then she'd heard Eadie's words, rich in New Zealander charm, hissed indignantly back to Darren, which sounded to the Australian ear like, 'Eighties *pen*-up boy look' and '*virry en* et the moment.'

'So we went to his colleague's retirement dinner,' Rosetta told Lena, 'And you *won't believe* this. You know the nannying position I went for? The two-week job looking after kids in Cabarita Heights?'

'The one with the interrogative mum? But she phoned you to say you weren't successful!'

'She did. Job's gone. I thought it a shame at the time because when I read the ad I saw some kind of vision, a burst of stars that matched Lillibridge's description of the lights Maleika conjured in the dragon cave. They felt hopeful and positive, so I considered them to be a good omen. But the woman who interviewed me turned up at the pre-dinner drinks. Can you believe it? Dette Weissler is the wife of Adam's colleague! The whole purpose of the drinks and dinner was to celebrate her husband's retirement.'

'And what was the husband like?' said Lena, amused. 'Impossible too, I bet.'

Rosetta paused to consider Dette's husband. Matthew Weissler had got Rosetta's name wrong. She hadn't had the heart to correct him. He'd appeared to be a considerate man and an attentive conversationalist who would probably have been profoundly apologetic if he'd realised. 'He was actually quite the opposite,' she said in answer to Lena's question. 'And a real catch.'

'In a silver-haired sort of way?' Lena was looking puzzled.

'It does sound like that, but no. This guy was young. Thirty years too young to retire.'

'And probably enviously moneyed if he can afford to give up work.'

'Probably.' He'd misheard her name because they'd been introduced when the drums started up. Since she was never going to see Matthew again, his knowing who she was hardly mattered. Rosetta took a sip of her soy latte. 'But I'll tell you something that shocked me about his wife.'

Lena looked up from her coffee, hazel eyes alight with intrigue. 'What was shocking? What did she do?'

'I guess you could say she caused us to leave. One minute I'm at the bar, and the next thing I know, Adam and I are cruising out of the city in Adam's gold Porsche. Everyone was due to move on to a restaurant at Circular Quay.' Rosetta lowered her voice. 'Adam told me that Dette was drunk and flirting with him.'

'No way!'

'It had been really, *really* awkward for poor Adam. He told me he hadn't wanted anyone to be embarrassed and then he mentioned something about not wanting to spoil Matthew Weissler's big night. Apparently he doesn't like Matthew much, but he was sensitive to the fact that Matthew should retire with dignity.'

'Hmm. What's caused Adam to dislike Matthew?'

'Didn't say, but he referred to him as an "arrogant creep" so I'm guessing they're not the best of buddies.'

'What did you do when that was going on?' Lena asked. 'Back in the bar, when Dette went after Adam?'

'It was happening at a distance, and I couldn't be sure it was anything but innocent, although I was definitely feeling uneasy. I shrugged it off when Matthew mentioned Dette was his wife. I mean, there's nothing wrong with chatting with your husband's workmate. But when Adam told me what had really gone on...Well! You know me, Lena. I turn into a she-wolf when I hear about anyone trying to cheat on their partner.'

For a second Rosetta was back on that date with Adam, confiding in him that hearing about cheaters instantly threw up the memory of Angus's icy eyes when he'd marched out of their marriage with barely a grunt. Adam had laughed in agreement and said 'Liars suck.'

'And Matthew's a catch you reckon?' said Lena. 'Wonder what's causing his wife to stray. Maybe he *is* arrogant like Adam said.'

'Whatever the reason, the least anyone can do is allow their partner the courtesy of separation before going on the lookout for someone else.'

'And it's only manners to check whether the guy you go after is with someone else at the time. Ah! There's Crispin again!' Lena turned to acknowledge a senior man all in white, a customer who shopped at the health food store she owned. She turned back to Rosetta, wispy platinum-blonde hair flouncing airily. 'Do you think Matthew knew what Dette was up to?'

'He would have had no idea. I wouldn't have known either if Adam hadn't told me.'

'That's pretty low. She should definitely be candid with Matthew.'

'Absolutely. How many handsome men does that woman want?' Rosetta went on to describe the fluorescent-lit restaurant she'd gone to with Adam after they'd left the bar. Overcooked food and an absence of ambience...the lack of patrons guaranteed quiet conversation, which meant Rosetta's desire to learn more about Adam was amply rewarded. He'd volunteered his opinions: his likes, his dislikes, and an exhilarated description of his favourite gym. Along with a complicated account of the stock market, Adam expressed his confidence in stepping into his boss's shoes. And after that? Well...Wall Street was beckoning. He'd already made two major career jumps, one of them being from journalism to finance. Getting to work for the New York Stock Exchange would be an upwards jump rather than a sideways one, but he had no illusions about the amount of experience this would demand. After the meal, he'd suggested a walk.

'A romantic walk,' Lena ribbed. 'Did that make up for the average dinner?'

Rosetta roared with laughter. 'We walked alongside a stormwater drain.'

'Geez, you go to all the best places.'

A hand-in-hand stumble through the moonless night that ended in gazing into drain water, brown and murky from the afternoon's rain. 'But then he suggested a drive.'

'Wow, where to?' Lena said. 'The local garbage tip?'

XXXII
Many years later in the Devic Century of Ruin Or 'The Century Of Progress' to those of the Empire

Following his Clan Watcher, Croydee hastened back to the glades where the dragon cave began and rushed through its uninspiring depths. 'Look, Aunt Maleika,' he cried. Towards the end of the cavern was an exit that branched off to the right. It was not the exit they had passed through the previous day. 'Why don't we escape the cavern here instead? I'd much rather leave now than walk any further through an atmosphere as heavy as this.'

The two Brumlynds climbed the little incline and pushed their way through a narrow gap in the rock. The craggy doorway opened out to the freshness of the forest.

'The golden residence appears different to yesterday,' Croydee remarked. 'Ha! I see why. A flag is flying. What must the flag symbolise?'

Maleika lifted her gaze to the tower's banner of white, black and maroon. In the centre of the flag was an oval that signified new life. On the outer edges were the spindly lines of pterodactyl claws to give the effect of an egg cradled in talons. 'It means the birth of a royal,' said Maleika slowly. 'This is odd. I did not see the gestation banner yesterday, which is what it always replaces.'

'Perhaps they forgot,' said Croydee with an extravagant shrug. He had said this with irony. He was well aware body kings were the most regimented people in the land.

At that moment they saw, on a balcony overlooking the fountain of gold, a body-king daughter, the bright-haired princess, deep in conversation with a body king. The body king bore the crown of a Grudellan prince.

'The lady has *wed*,' said Croydee, aghast.

'And how does her prince appear?' Maleika said. Before either of them had a chance to observe the male figure, the royal pair had vanished into the palace.

'Quick! Back into the cave,' Maleika ordered.

Croydee scrambled through the jagged opening and somersaulted down the incline to the cavern floor.

When his elfin aunt arrived beside him, Croydee asked whether they should go to the other exit.

'Indeed,' said Maleika. 'We must view the palace from a contrasting aspect.'

The two emerged from the exit, which they had, prior to that day, only ever used in the past, and scanned the castle before them.

'No birth flag,' gasped Maleika. 'Each exit must offer an isolated variation in time! I'm very confused now, Croydee. Three separate versions of the same residence! The one that we see from the river bank and the two that we access through respective cavern doorways. Which one is Pieter in? Which one coincides with the cycles of the sprites?'

'The one we see from the river bank I imagine,' said Croydee. 'It's obvious that the reason for the holograms is this cavern. It must be a portal of sorts that displays past and future images.'

'Lena, how did you guess?' For a moment Rosetta played along with Lena's comment that the drive Adam suggested was a visit to the local garbage tip. 'Actually, you're not far wrong.' Remembering how deflated she'd felt at the next place he'd driven her, she gazed at the

Hansel & Gretel counter where a woman ordering a Vienna and babycino was trying to make herself heard over a face-painted child's impromptu song about the barista's chocolate shaker. 'Adam stayed mysterious about where we were going. He hadn't said much at all, and I felt sorry for him because the night he'd planned had been altered with the escape from Dette. I reasoned that he would have been feeling bad about the awful meal. I wanted to reassure him that dining anywhere decent on a Friday night without a reservation was virtually impossible, but at the same time I didn't want to insult his choice of eatery.' Rosetta shook her head at the craziness of it all. 'So we were heading for the cinemas, and I wondered whether he wanted to surprise me. He'd asked my favourite movie on the phone the day before. I'd told him about my sci-fi fetish, and he'd talked about that re-make they're promoting now. You know the one, Lena. *Invasion of the Star People*. It was about 8 p.m. by then.'

'So you would have caught the late screening.'

'I didn't catch anything. Unless you're counting a lift back home.'

'Aha! You invited him back to your place instead.'

'On the contrary.' Rosetta made a face and relented to laughter. 'At first I thought he was joking. Most people going on dates were still at home deciding what to wear!'

She thought back to her incredulous response to Adam turning into Ashbury Avenue. 'I'm going home already?'

The car pulled to a stop. Adam didn't answer. He leaned back against the headrest, drew in a breath and sighed. Then he turned to Rosetta, raised an eyebrow and slowly slid his arm around her shoulders. He drew closer and her breathing quickened. She caressed his forearms. Adam's muscles radiated warmth beneath his full-length shirt sleeves. The feel of his body invoked such euphoria she forgot her bafflement at him dropping her home.

'You don't have to be by yourself,' Adam said in a growl. 'I can keep you company if you like.'

Adam was under the illusion that Rosetta lived alone. She hadn't yet told him she was a mother. Surely it wouldn't be up to her, though, to suggest they go to his place! This was all so inappropriate. The night was still criminally young.

An avalanche of forceful kissing. Adam untangled his fingers from her spray-stiffened semi-beehive and said: 'So Rosie, I kept this time aside for you. For us. I couldn't have made it a long evening out 'cos I'm in training for a marathon. Have to be up at four tomorrow morning.'

'Uh-huh.' She was still partly lost in that other reality, reeling from the enchantment of getting close to Adam again.

'So. Rosie. As I said. I want to spend that time with you, I've gotta get up early, I don't want to risk a bad start to the marathon, I need to know what you're thinking, need to know pretty much now. Are you gonna invite me in?'

Rosetta's spellbound state fizzled abruptly. 'My apologies,' she droned. 'I didn't realise we were in a traders' meeting. Great pitch, Adam.'

'Whaddya mean?'

She turned to glare at Adam. His green eyes, now two glittery shadows piercing the darkness, were narrowed in confusion. 'I hadn't thought you'd be working towards a deadline.'

Adam's arms, looser in their embrace once he'd begun on his reasons for loving and leaving within the pre-dawn hours, fell raggedly away from her. It was happening a third time. She glanced away from Adam's pouty lower lip. His seduction tactics were consistent: a bout of nagging followed by thundercloud scowls, which cancelled out any notion of shimmying between the sheets with him.

Tapping her fingernails softly on the car door, Rosetta gazed out of the car window, at the purple dahlias in the Dalfreys' front garden.

Why don't I give up now, she thought.

A breeze sprang up. The dahlias rocked forward and back, nodding their heads in affirmation.

Apart from that fleeting blast of passion, it had so far been an unremarkable date. Conversing with Adam was more like conducting an interview with a self-absorbed celebrity. And now, after a few half-hearted attempts to impress her, he assumed she'd obediently agree to his conditions and topple into bed. 'I'm pretty busy this evening,' she said. 'And like you, I have to get up early.'

'Cool! Early night suits me.'

'Goodnight then, Adam.'

'Together, I mean. An early night together.'

Rosetta opened the car door. 'The deal-breaker was that list of restrictions of yours. Thanks for dinner.' She hurried across to the verandah. Deal-breaker? She winced. Not the cleverest retort. She'd failed to find a finance term that sarcastically replaced 'turn-off'.

Adam shouted from his wound-down window, 'I'll call you. Tomorrow.'

'Farewell to you too, Adam.' She marched up the verandah steps as smartly as she could.

...A remark from Lena jolted her back to the conversation in the coffee shop. 'Craig thought Adam was a phoney all along. Sounds like jealousy to me.'

Rosetta contemplated a painted tulip on the corner of the cafe's wooden table. 'I think he was just being big-brother protective. It's six years now since I went out with him. Craig moved on ages ago.' Remembering Craig's latest call, she said, 'And he's notably smitten with this new girl he's seeing.'

'Name's Soozi, apparently.' Lena stirred another sugar through her latte. Amid the rhythmic clatter of stainless steel on glass, she added, 'With a double "o" and a "z". Wonder if she's got anything to do with Craig's "secret project". Has he invited her to the book group?'

'He hasn't as far as I know. And I'm not sure he will. She thinks it sounds bizarre.'

'Do you blame her? A bunch of space cadets getting together every fortnight to meditate and study a book about elves? Andrew reckons I'm cracked. After twelve years of marriage he still doesn't know me!'

'Shame on Andrew.' Rosetta tut-tutted.

'I've got to speak to Craig though,' Lena said. 'He's overselling the idea that *Our True Ancient History* is actually true.'

'Poor old Craig. He's anything but discreet.'

'And as for Adam, don't go missing him too much.'

'I'm not missing Adam at all. I know I've blabbed on about him ad nauseam throughout our coffees but—'

'You really don't miss him?'

'Not at all.' At that moment, Rosetta remembered a side of Adam she loved. On their dinner out the night after Royston's lunch party, he'd confided in her about his upbringing, and it had moved her to tears. His manner that evening had been so much gentler and he'd caressed her hand with such tenderness, she could easily picture him as the dreamy-eyed child he once was, a sensitive novice poet and the tearful object of his father's disgust. Adam's tough-guy stance had made sense to her then. Just like Rosetta, he was vulnerable beneath the surface. Adam had been affected by his dad's vindictiveness; Rosetta by Angus's belief that marriage and fatherhood placed unhealthy limits on a man. Both of them had been rejected by the people they'd loved most. She could understand, too, why Adam felt compelled to sing along to Doctor Cyanide in his car, embarrassing and all as it was for the person beside him. Embodying the nasty mannered '70s rock god would have given him a sense of control. Perhaps he was demanding what was denied him when he snarled the lyrics to 'Gimme': the love of disinterested parents.

'He'll be back,' Lena assured. 'Your men always seem to call after you get angry with them.'

'You're a gem to say that, Lena, but trust me. This one won't. But...ahhh! So amazingly good looking.'

'Yup...he should've been in movies.'

'He did happen to be on the small screen, on Queensland TV.'

'I know. He told me at Royston's lunch party. Former newspaper journo turned finance reporter for Brisbane Eyewitness News. Why did he become an investment banker?'

'He got tired of standing on the sidelines.'

'What'll you do if he does call?'

'I'll rant and rave until he puts down the phone. I'm already feeling sorry for the poor sod.'

'I'm feeling sorry for him myself. Remember the time you told off the guy with the black stubble?'

Rosetta sat upright. 'But that guy stood me up! And...I can't remember his name...Think it began with a 'G'. Hmm. My memory's crazy lately. Maybe Izzie's right. Maybe I am going senile.' She eyed the table's painted tulip and ran a finger across its glossy surface. 'Although, I probably forgot his name deliberately out of spite.

Seriously though, if Adam did happen to phone I'd make it clear I want nothing more to do with him. Ever!' To highlight her resolve, Rosetta slapped her hand down on the table. The latte glasses tinkled, their contents sloshing ominously. 'But that's enough of my gabble, Lena. We haven't talked about you at all!'

'You're forgetting the hour-and-a-half you spent enduring my deliberations in La Draperie. Maybe you *are* losing your marbles.'

'Finding those curtains wasn't an endurance. It was important. Whatever the case, from this point on, I promise to zip up this big mouth of mine.'

Back on her verandah, Rosetta waved to Lena amid the three predictable farewell toots, grimaced at a cobweb that had settled in one of the verandah eaves and took a step towards the door.

The sole of one of her ballet-flats settled onto something softly crackly. Cellophane. She'd stepped on a Floral Fiesta bouquet!

As though attempting to comfort a small, helpless animal, she cooed and caressed the flowers' wounded stems before lifting them from her doorstep. More roses. Pale and pretty, a card attached to them with the same message accompanying Adam's previous delivery: *Am I forgiven?*

'Sweet, very sweet,' she said, cradling the bouquet in one arm. Juggling her eco-friendly shopping bag, she unlocked the door in three staccato moves. 'But it won't change my mind.'

She unwrapped the cellophane from the roses in a series of loud crunches and went on a search for her chunkiest vase. They were a clean, almost iridescent white, these roses—not unlike Adam's bleached teeth—and their variegated edges were a whirl of deep pink.

She placed the vase on a side-table opposite Izzie's room. The phone bleated.

'Eadie for sure,' she announced, rushing to the entrance end of the hallway. Their psychic link was uncanny. Rosetta seized up the phone in a dramatic swoop. 'You won't believe this,' she said into the receiver. 'The Gorgeous GEG's gone all grovelly now with roses.'

'Good for you,' a deep voice purred on the other line. 'Although I've never heard "gorgeous" and "geek" used together like that.'

In a less dramatic tone, Rosetta said, 'Hello Adam.' Thankfully, he'd misheard her Green Eyed-Guy abbreviation.

A yawning gap of silence. At last Adam said in a groan, 'Rosie...'

Abruptly Rosetta said, 'Yes, Adam?'

'I'm going crazy being away from you. When can we meet up?'

'Er...well...' Never. She'd planned to say never, and yet the shock of hearing Adam again after thinking he was gone for good had caused her words to drift away. The effect of Adam's voice, too, was more than slightly dizzying.

'Silence, huh?' Adam was saying, the texture of his voice as luxuriant as his roses. 'This doesn't sound like my Rosetta. Why are you playing games with me, Lush-Lips?'

'I'm not...playing—'

'I'm a desperate man. I'm dying here...I've *got* to see you again. Soon.'

'Really?' Had she actually said that? Said 'really' in a hopeful schoolgirl squeak?

'Listen, Rosie, can't talk long. I'm overseas on a business trip.'

'Where overseas?'

'Vanuatu.'

What was Adam doing in Vanuatu? Trying to sound disinterested she droned, 'Lucky you.'

'On the contrary. I've seen nothing but the four walls of the conference room all week. It's crap knowing the ocean's just a few metres away when you have to discuss the Asian economy with a bunch of trumped up suits.'

'Hmm.' Rosetta couldn't help feeling pleased he wasn't enjoying himself. 'Doesn't sound anything like the romantic commercials.'

'Romantic? Ha! This place is a romance *desert*. There's one romantic thing happening to me though.'

Rosetta's heart dived. He was gloating. Telling her he had someone. In the most patronising tone she could muster, Rosetta said, 'And what's that, Adam?'

'Listening to you. That sensuous jazz-singer's voice: it's sexy beyond belief.'

Her wariness gave way to bashful laughter.

'I want to make it up to you, Rosie, for that stupid rushed date we had. I'm thinking dinner at Chavelle's Saturday night. It's a five-star restaurant near Circular Quay. Overlooks the harbour. Food's as French as it can be.'

'Ooh...um...French sounds tempting.' Going on a *third* date on Saturday with an amazing looking man who had worked as a writer in his early days and so might have been interested in all things literary, including Friday Fortnight—fourth if she counted Royston's lunch party—or stitching her tapestry in time to Danna Nolan's 'Wallflower Blues'? Not a difficult decision. But no. She couldn't allow herself to weaken.

Syrup-coated blarney would not get in the way of her resolve.

She drew in a breath and mouthed her refusal in readiness for the real thing, while Adam continued with, 'So I'll see you Saturday next, okay? I'll pick you up at eight.'

XXXIII

At the emergence of dawn, and while the other Brumlynds were extinguishing the campfire and readying the sleeping wagons, Croydee toddled through the forest dwarfed by tall grasses. He was bound for the Grudellan Palace, a place where Pieter and Fripso might be imprisoned.

At last the structure came into view, emerging beyond the river bank in colours he'd rarely observed. The rays of dawn reflected upon its myriad spiralling turrets.

He had concluded that he must find the true palace, one that wasn't a projection of either the past or future. He must hasten silently through its grounds in an effort to rescue two forest dwellers in peril.

Pools of sunshine, gleaming past the gates upon cobblestone roads, dazzled Croydee's eyes. He was unaccustomed to absorbing so much yellow light—it was normally too harsh for those of devic heritage—yet the need to discover where his cousin and the rabbit might be was far greater than the fear of solar searing.

There ahead of Croydee stood the eagle-winged guards, half gold-skin, leaning upon spears made of the ore they adored so much. Beyond them splashed and sparkled their dragon font, the hideous container of blood the Grudellan Palace's cold-hearted mortals insisted on drinking. While doing so made them a little more magical, the power they inherited through these callous deeds was tainted. It manifested darkness and deterioration and furthered their already voracious need for more of anything they already had.

Seventy season-cycles ago, when Croydee was a young elf, his former Clan Watcher presented him with a gift from the gods, a dragon he'd chosen to name Sluken. A gorgeously jewel-scaled creature was Sluken, as wise as the Oracle and as gentle as the wavelets of a fair-weather sea. The dragon loved nothing more than to bound about the forest with his master. Croydee and his friend were inseparable. Sluken taught Croydee Saurus language and also helped him in his study of magic.

One day, Croydee awoke to a stifled scream. He leapt from his place by the campfire to search for the dragon and was perplexed to find that Sluken was not in his usual spot. When returning to his camp to alert the other Brumlynds, he heard an agonised wail.

The bracken children visited him later, telling him they had seen a hooded one pass by with Croydee's poor, frightened friend in tow. Sluken had been dragged off in the direction of the palace.

Saddened by the loss of his dear friend's presence, he searched for the creature in the Dream Sphere. As with their search in that world for Pieter and Fripso, the dragon was unable to be found.

While this might in a way have been hopeful, meaning Pieter and Fripso had probably not severed their lives in Elysium Glades to pass over permanently to the Dream Sphere, Croydee believed that something in the Grudellan Palace—if this was where they were—was preventing the two from making contact with their clans when they slumbered. Alcor had remained reticent when asked. 'Croydee, let it be,' he had said. 'And take heed of The Oracle's mention of a fruitless quest.' But Croydee refused to be deterred by Alcor's unhelpful chides.

For Sluken, the story would have ended already and done so tragically. Croydee learned that body kings had conducted mass slaughtering of dragons. His idolised animal companion would have been among those trapped in that ghostly void between Earth and the Dream Sphere.

Maleika was the only Brumlynd who had managed to make contact with their imprisoned spirits. Her communication with disembodied dragons had been limited, however, a terrible mix of transparent wings and disjointed words. Croydee was determined to one day restore these lovable creatures to their rightful otherworld. Only then could he lessen his regret at failing to protect Sluken. Would his search through the palace prove that Pieter and Fripso had evaded this awful fate?

Croydee crept to the gates and edged his miniature husk-clothed frame through the gilded bars, only to start at the sound of an urgent voice.

A faerie of the lilac was calling out to him. 'They will see you! They have ways of illuminating your presence with certain objects in the walls.'

'You mustn't do this to yourself, elf,' called another sprite, a poppy faerie wreathed in pink. 'Think first of the peril you invite. Wicked bewitchers cast spells on sprites!'

Acknowledging the flower sprites with his promise to be careful, and advising them to return to their slumber, Croydee continued to wriggle his way through the locked gate. He would be quick. He might well be mortally ended, but he could no longer ignore the disappearance of his cousin and his animal friend knowing they were more than likely trapped by body kings.

He felt certain his life task was to free Sluken's spirit and to rescue Pieter and Fripso. Hopefully this life he was leading wouldn't perish before all was achieved. If it were to end earlier than hoped, then perhaps one of the other Brumlynds would take over the task, and triumph where he had failed.

Croydee kept low and out of sight of the guards. He had not the kindness merits to enable invisibility. Most of his beauty-creation had been used two evenings earlier when he'd hidden from dark magicians.

He wended his way around an open double doorway and found himself within a great hall where fire-luminaries dangled from the ceilings.

No-one was present in this hall. Well aware of the terrible risk he was taking, Croydee tried not to dwell on the idea that the spying

261

lights the faeries had warned him of meant his secret visit might be detected.

He climbed the stairs Maleika told him about, the stairs that branched westward from the great hall, and turned to the doorway at the top. Looking either side of him, he shuffled across to the door, which he presumed was the princess's chamber, for it aligned with the flag-adorned balcony he'd seen from the dragon cave. He was now within eye level of a jagged gap in the timber. Beneath the handle a torn-out piece of the door was stuffed with a knot of tapestried fabric. Part of this fabric had sunk to the base of the gap and allowed Croydee a clear view of the room's interior.

Ah, there she was, the gold-skin lady. The chamber therefore was hers. She was pacing the floor and talking delightedly to someone. To whom was she speaking? Croydee could not hear her gabbled words, but he could see the lady waving her hands about and, at intervals, leaning forward into giggles. She was dressed in a gown the colour of sunshine and moved about blissfully with the grace of a butterfly. She was perhaps of seven-and-ten or eight-and-ten season-cycles and despite the peculiar gold tone of her skin and hair, had a faerie-like prettiness about her.

She was speaking to someone tucked away in a large alcove. The alcove was sealed off with gates similar to the golden ones Croydee had slipped through to enter the palace grounds. The bars on these gates were more decorative than the ones marking the entry of the Grudellan Palace. These were encrusted with a coiling line of diamonds and rubies. From this limited aspect, Croydee could not make out where the alcove, whose far end was crowded out with gowns in the colours that spring blossoms were, began or ended.

And then he saw it. Saw something twitching, alive and familiar that made him smile: an ear that protruded from the barred room, an ear that was elongated, velveteen and white.

The maiden was speaking to Fripso! Pieter might then be nearby.

Chapter Twelve

XXXIV

*C*roydee contemplated wielding his beauty-creation powers to dissolve himself through the solidity of the locked door.

While invisibility took up a great amount of kindness merits, walking through walls did not. Would he have enough kindness merits available? All being well with his magic, he would then creep to the nearest hiding place until he felt safe enough to emerge. It was probable the girl had been taunting the rabbit. Croydee would be of no help if he found himself, against his will, alongside Fripso in the cage-like wardrobe and drained of his magic.

His merits, fortunately, were not diminished. He had just enough to perform his last modest miracle for the moon's phase of Pisces. It enabled him an unnoticed intrusion into the chamber. He hid behind a bronze urn by the door.

'And what is your opinion of it, Pieter of the Brumlynds?' the golden lady was saying.

Pieter was there in the chamber! Where in the chamber *was* Pieter though?

And then Croydee saw a Pieter he barely recognised. It was not a boy that met Croydee's astonished gaze, but a youth, equal in age to the maiden whose wardrobe he was companionably languishing in. He was seated: long lower limbs stretched out comfortably; clearly enraptured by the girl as he watched her from the other side of the expansive alcove's bars. The space this wardrobe occupied, with its collection of a lady's finery at one end, was akin to a sizeable chamber and furnished with a table, three chairs, including a chaise for reclining, and mountains of spun-gold cushions, which looked as though they might be slept upon. Flowers, leaves and grasses were scattered across its floor.

'I think you are to be the jewel of this ball,' was all Pieter said.

'But do you not like its colour and the way the sleeves trail here at the wrists, and what of the skirt?' It was as though asking an elf for advice on the frippery she chose for decadent gatherings was a perfectly normal occurrence. She twirled. The skirt of her trailing gown was bell-like, reminding Croydee of the attire lily-of-the-valley faeries wore. Lily-of-the-valley garments, however, were the colour of snowflakes, pristine and unembellished, free of the sparkles, tassels and flounces that graced this one. 'The Prince of Ehypte will be there. The ladies at court believe he will ask for my hand in marriage should I appear pleasing enough.'

Fripso spoke then. 'Well as I said before, dear Eidred, you look very pleasing indeed.'

Eidred? *Dear* Eidred? A phenomenon! No gold-skin had ever won the trust of animals enough to communicate with them. And none had befriended sprites. Feeling suspicious now, Croydee thought it wise to wait further before introducing himself. This Eidred might be trapping her guests by willing them to believe she was harmless.

'And I must *dance* for him!' the princess said joyfully.

'Will you carry out the dance of the goddess?' asked a playful Fripso.

'Yes, I shall! And it will be as this.'

The rabbit, Croydee noted, was leaping about the wardrobe, carrying out his own impression of a dance. Beside Fripso, Pieter looked especially still. His face had taken on the seriousness of a bewildered child. He had not taken his eyes off the girl—who had begun to tiptoe and glide as daintily as a moon glade sprite would—but those eyes had taken on a mournful quality that Croydee had rarely witnessed.

He's utterly miserable, Croydee thought in alarm, a sobering contrast to the smiles Pieter had thrown Eidred moments earlier.

At that moment Croydee heard a terrible squeal. The squeal propelled all three into frantic motion. Pieter rose and drew himself to his full height, then threw a rug over a quivering Fripso. Eidred ran to one side of her wardrobe to retrieve a cloak, a dark hooded cloak, and flung it over her gown, which had the effect of a thundercloud extinguishing the night sky's stars. Her previously elegant carriage, with head held high, became stooped. The door rasped open. The girl's hair, the only thing bright about her appearance now, fell forward from under the hood as she sank into a subservient bow.

'Come see us at once! You have not yet told the Solen of your answer.'

Four pterodactyls—a species Croydee had seen in his earlier years and was therefore familiar with, yet only slightly less fearful of now that he experienced their horrific proximity—stomped savagely towards their princess and kicked at the statues and urns that decorated her retreat.

'Good minders, what answer is this?' said the girl in a voice that had become soft and lacking in melody.

'That you will join in marriage with the Prince of Ehypte.'

'How very sudden. I have not yet met the prince. And to my knowledge he has not proposed to me.'

Glancing at Pieter, Croydee noted that the elf had taken on a look of relieved surprise.

Ah, thought Croydee. Pieter believes Eidred is already acquainted with the prince. I fancy he might be a silent adorer of this involuntary bride-to-be.

Both elf and princess calmly accepted that remaining unhidden did not compromise the youth's safety. Pieter, although visible to Croydee, had, as expected of non-seeing gold-skins, gone undetected by Eidred's minders. It made sense now, the reason he dwelt inside a wardrobe. He had found refuge there from the spy-lights that would have detected his moving about and, fortunate for him, his captor—or was she an ally?—was blessed with a generous heart and the gift of faerie sight.

'Come at once to the Solen's court,' they said in a scream and, with synchronicity, turned upon their heels.

Eidred trailed meekly behind the monstrous creatures. Before quitting the room, she turned once to gaze upon Pieter, her face concealed by shadow.

Now to present myself to the two, Croydee thought, clasping his hands together in anticipation.

He stepped from behind the urn and said, 'Cousin Pieter and Fripso, it is I, Croydee, here to help release you so that you may return to the forest.'

Pieter and Fripso did not stir. Instead, they remained as they were. Fripso's eyes were closed in meditation, and Pieter was staring at the floor in glum consternation.

They had not heard him! He tried again, this time by repeating his announcement in a louder voice.

Still they did not stir. Fripso, of course, could well have been asleep, but what of Pieter? Pieter must have been terribly unhappy. Too unhappy to notice what was going on around him. Croydee immediately felt sympathy for the lovelorn elf.

He hurried to the wardrobe's decorative gates and waved. Pieter stared impassively at the walls. 'Pieter of the Brumlynds!' There was no reply. 'Fripso!' The rabbit did not move a whisker, even though his eyes were now opened and alert.

It then occurred to Croydee that he was in fact visible to no-one in the Grudellan Palace. Had not the pterodactyls ignored his precarious flit beneath the spy-lights?

Why, after all, had he believed *this* was the present-time palace and not a hologram? He ran to the nearest urn, one that had not been knocked by the pterodactyls, and went to lift it. Alas, his hand slid through the object just as Maleika had predicted concerning the presence of a projection. 'It *has* occurred, somewhere in time,' he told himself, 'this scene I am witnessing, but whether it has already happened or is yet to happen, I have no way of fathoming.'

Never one to give in to challenges, he pondered his dilemma. 'I am perfectly safe,' he reasoned, for his observation of this hologram was simply like an individual from a future timeframe walking into a picture palace and wading through image beams. This was not his cousin's current reality. It was only the capture of a timeframe. As a viewer of this, he was at will to explore the entire residence armed with the knowledge that all he saw was safe to see. No players in this gilded charade were tangible!

He would seek out the princess's meeting with her minders, first of all.

As he retreated from the room, laughing at having used his magic to walk through a solid locked door when none was needed, he heard Pieter say, 'Do you think, Fripso, that she will agree to marry this Prince of Ehypte?'

'Cannot see why not,' answered the rabbit. This was said flippantly. 'It seems she is in love with him already. She has seen his portrait in the Solen's gallery, remember, and she says he is handsome in the way you supposedly are. I have never seen her so happy about attending a dance.'

'Nor have I,' said a crestfallen Pieter. 'And he's sure to love her in return from the moment he sees her.'

The two fell into contemplative silence.

Croydee ventured out to seek the object of Pieter's affection. After much stair climbing and peering into many various rooms, he found her. She was standing at a gilt table, wielding a quill across a document. Before her stood a gold-skin whose strands of gleaming hair fell in ringlets over bony shoulders, and whose ragged golden beard almost reached the floor. The colours of the jewels that adorned his fingers and toes were corrupted and thus made ghastly with encasements of gold that resembled the rising sun's rays. The expression on his face was twisted into what could only be described as cruel.

'You have signed your agreement to marry Prince Adahmos of Ehypte?' he roared.

'Yes, Father,' said the girl. She presented him with a document that one of the servants had rolled and tied with ribbon.

The Solen snatched the scroll from her. 'To think you dared question me on this subject! But I am sure you would rather marry than be dead.'

'Yes, Father.'

'He has amassed many riches from where he hails. Your minders will educate you of his land. You will learn more of our origins, for Ehypte is where your ancestors originated. I should like the majority of my kin to return to this land to assist in repopulating the area. Our blood there has thinned over the past few centuries. We must rise again in the land of triangles.'

'Yes, Father.'

'You must bewitch this man. Understand? If you do not, your life will not be worth living.'

'I understand, Father.'

'Now be away with you.'

Eidred turned mechanically. Her lips quivered and her eyes of blue greyed with tears. Croydee followed her to the door, then into the darkened staircase and looked helplessly on as she wept. He trailed behind her as she moved—with shoulders hunched—down a hallway lit by torch flames. She was sobbing. More than once he heard her utter Pieter's name to herself. Thrice in fact.

The pterodactyls who stood like statues in the stark over-bright room she'd entered, conducted a torturous amount of lectures. When interrogating their student on comprehension, they punished her, and not only for her errors. Her accuracies, also, were treated with contempt. According to these contrary educators, right equalled wrong. The unfortunate princess would forever be taunted for her inability to please them.

At the end of these lessons, which were enough to make even gentle-natured Croydee heated with a kind of anger he'd never before felt, Princess Eidred thanked her perpetrators kindly and exited her school-room.

In the gloominess of a corridor, Eidred knelt low. As she did so, she spoke to a god. Nay, not a god. It was a goddess. A godmother. But who was this godmother? Croydee listened with interest.

'Dear Faerie Godmother,' she said. 'It is true that the only one I could ever...*respect*...is Pieter. This is awful of me, I understand, for I feel sure Pieter would be shocked if I told him as much. I suspect he does not...*respect*...me in return, yet please, Faerie Godmother, should there be any way of escaping this permanent commitment and of being able to win Pieter's loyalty, and to live quite freely with Pieter for the duration of my life, then please show me the way. Show me the way, dear Godmother!'

Croydee regarded the princess with both amazement and compassion. She had fallen in love with one of devic origin. How would Pieter and Eidred escape the consequences of a forbidden entanglement?

She continued onward with her prayer. 'But if I find Pieter is not amenable to me in this way, I promise to be courageous. I shall marry the prince in the hope that he will help me to protect Fripso and Pieter. If he is not good-hearted, I ask that he never learns of their existence and that I may ferry them to safety before I depart this land. And please, Faerie Godmother, if Pieter does not return my respectful devotion, please allow me adequate power to bewitch the Ehyptian prince I am soon to meet.'

Croydee frowned. He had already remained in this hologram longer than intended, although he would feel better about leaving once certain the princess had returned safely to her chamber. He returned there first and waited by the wardrobe. Shortly after, the young lady arrived back and looked in on Fripso, already lost in slumber. Pieter was awake, however, and addressed her almost abrasively Croydee thought. 'Ah it is Eidred,' he said, 'who I suppose is as good as married now?'

'What nonsense,' Eidred snapped. She then turned away from the elf and said, 'I told my father I would only agree to marriage with Prince Adahmos if he makes a favourable impression on me at the ball. But this is five-and-ten suns away yet.' The princess had not told Pieter the truth!

Pieter nodded shakily.

'Contrary to what you may think, Pieter,' she added, 'I do have a say in some matters. And what is important to me is that I marry for love, even if my father cares only for the riches I return to our empire.'

Pieter said nothing.

'Goodnight, my Pieter,' she said.

'Goodnight, friend Eidred,' said Pieter.

Sorry for the two confused admirers, Croydee slipped away from the hologram and galloped through Elysium's forest, eager to reach the glades and tell the Brumlynds of his discovery.

Dette settled back against her beach towel, reached out to Adam beside her and ran a hand over his left arm. The filmy cheesecloth of his unbuttoned shirt chafed coolly against her fingers. 'Why don't you take this off?'

'I'm already brown enough,' he said, clutching at the cuffs. 'Don't want to overdo it.'

'But...oh...um...never mind.' She didn't like to point out that this was only their second stint in the sun, or that Double Bay His 'n' Hers Day Spa had been the reason for his wonderfully even tan, or that he'd already asked to borrow her sunscreen. He'd slapped on heaps of it after his shower. Adam had his reasons for keeping his shirt on over his swim-shorts. One of those reasons might have been Dette's comment that it gave him the look of a guy in an '80s cigarette ad who she'd secretly resolved, at the age of fourteen, to marry someday.

Gazing upon her Apollo now engulfed in sleep, she smiled at the memory of worrying over whether male models were good providers, or 'marriage material' in the words of her cherished great-aunt and great-uncle. The sunny-faced orphan depicted in their shaky home videos, Dette rehearsing a dance routine in her callisthenics leotard, had once been the frightened three-year-old they'd pledged to raise with all the care they could muster. 'You can just as easily fall in love with a rich man, Bernadette, as you can a poor one,' her great-aunt had advised. 'You don't want to go gallivanting around the countryside with motorcycling hoodlums and unshaven hippies. You can do much better than that sister of mine.' And Dette's great-aunt should have known. She'd married above her station: a Brit with a title.

The senior couple had been quietly pleased with Dette's choice of second husband. His financial position and polished English accent won much of their approval, although Colonel Doulton had failed to hide his disappointment in Matthew's lack of pedigree.

And on the subject of marital commitment...Adam had surprised her in bed the other night. He'd said he loved her in a desirous groan.

Things were progressing nicely! It was time to have that little chat. She'd tell him how much she would spoil him if they lived together. And they were yet to play tennis, despite Adam being a keen sports all-rounder. She'd suggest they play a few games tomorrow, on Honeymooner Haven's sycamore-edged courts. Matthew had loved that she was such a skilled player. Many of their first dates had revolved around zealous matches, which Matthew later fondly referred to as 'courtship'.

Adam would have to understand, of course, that she wouldn't move anywhere without her daughters. If he ever dared to suggest she send them to their dad's Punchbowl flat, he would have to contend with the discomfort of her alarmed hostility. Adam's home was a sumptuous, white five-bedroomer. Four of these rooms were unlived-in. What would two more in that palatial house matter to him if she and he were getting along brilliantly? And who wouldn't love having Laura and Sara around? The girls won people over wherever they went.

Matthew had grown to love them as though they were his own. Adam was just as big-hearted as Matthew. He'd undoubtedly make an excellent stepdad. To add to this, he was dazzlingly generous. His gift to Dette from Tiffany & Co was locked away within a drawer inside her walk-in-robe, sparkling with secret beauty, a symbol of their undercover love.

On the day of her flight to Vanuatu, Dette had endured another of Diondra's shopping-spree phone boasts, related, as per usual, in a hushed voice from the Wallaces' poolside. Dominic was indoors, evidently under the illusion that his wife had nipped out to inspect the greenhouse orchids. Once the rave had dwindled into a discontented sigh, Diondra took the phone inside and instantly turned the topic around.

And then Dominic's jarring voice had fired through the earpiece. 'Hullo, Dette! If you're needing a lift to the airport, I'll be happy to oblige.' He didn't know she wasn't going on her own. Diondra was good like that. Knew how to keep things confidential.

Dette was well aware of how Dominic Wallace's mind worked, having resolved months ago he was too twisted for her liking. It had been good at first, sneaking out under the guise of cosmetic surgeon or beauty therapist appointments. He was such a good-looking man, in a clean-cut sort of way. But then he'd suggested she do things she would never want to do, had never heard of anyone doing—despite

271

her own inherent raciness and knowledge of the latest trends—so she'd told him where to get off and scolded him for seducing his wife's best friend.

He'd called her unrepeatable names in the ostentatious art deco mansion he reserved for flings. On its manicured front lawn was a *Sold by Wallace Real Estate* sign, dominated by a close-up of Dominic winking, an aspect of him she'd once considered to be devilish. He'd previously confided that the property hadn't been on the market for a decade, that he'd bought it back in '98 for an exorbitant sum, and every few years ensured it was advertised as 'sold' to garner the interest of prosperous home hunters. Diondra would have been shocked if she'd known he owned a love nest.

The next time she and Dominic had happened upon each other, it was back to normality, free of insult, but also devoid of the flattery...of Dominic saying quietly in her ear exactly how she'd made him feel when she'd swanned around the beach in her yellow bikini.

Dette adjusted the underwire of the bikini she was wearing today, a strapless pink floral that she struggled to keep on in the water. It was lovely to have been appreciated for that yellow bikini for a while. Matthew hadn't been appreciative at all, not once he'd found out it had cost him $2000. She sighed as she remembered his reaction.

'But it's designer,' she'd argued, handing him the bag with the bikini inside.

'For two skimpy pieces of fabric? Come on! You've been conned, Bernadette.' He looked at the tag. 'Is this an Australian designer?'

'Lee-Lee Wagnell? She is now. She's out here from Shanghai. Just started up.'

'Made in a sweat-shop, I bet.' Matthew threw the bikini top down on the dresser in annoyance. 'I don't mind you spending a reasonable amount if it's quality or Australian-made, baby, but this sort of shopping's insanity.'

'But I loved it,' Dette said in her best little girl voice. 'And you're the only person I know who cares about sweat-shops.' Matthew considered himself to be an Ethical Consumer. Dette believed this to be a waste of time, as well as stuffily limiting. 'You're a hypocrite, Matthew. You, just like me, buy things made in sweat-shops.'

'Of course I do. I hate that there isn't total transparency yet.' He ran a hand impatiently through his hair, which tended to fall into waves when due for a trim. 'But if everyone at least takes action and supports fair manufacturing where they can, then we'll ultimately make a difference.'

'How?'

'By stamping out slavery.'

'When are you going to realise that there'll always be rich and poor, Mattie? It's just a way of life. Let the rich be rich and let the poor be poor. That's what I say.'

'Yeah, right, Bernadette, love ya work. Remind yourself of that if ever you wind up in poverty.' That had rattled Dette. Was Matthew still doing okay financially? She certainly hoped so.

Dette adopted a facial expression she'd borrowed from Diondra, which didn't seem to cause unnecessary brow furrows. Pushing her lips forward into a pout and speaking as a mother would to a grizzling toddler, she said in drawn-out syllables, 'Okay, diddums, keep up that ethical consumption of yours. Good luck with getting support on that.' And she stuffed the bikini into her duffle bag, then drove herself down to the beach, only to happen upon Dominic drinking a macchiato at the surf club café.

...'And that,' Dette whispered to herself, basking in the memory of Dominic's unconstrained admiration, 'was when our affair began.' Too kinky. How Diondra put up with him, Dette could not for the life of her fathom. She could never have stayed with Matthew if she'd caught him sneaking her lip pencils. And Geranium Blaze of all colours! So obvious! So...ugh!

At last Adam woke. He brushed the sand from his legs. Adam was kinky too, she supposed. But the difference with Adam was that Dette loved him. With every millimetre of her heart.

Adam raised both the God-awful sunnies and one of his brows. His emerald eyes stared into hers. Why would she bother swimming in the Coral Sea when she could swim in these?

The edge of Adam's lip curled upwards adorably. 'Hey there, Tootles,' he said, and then he addressed her in his naughtiest voice. 'You're looking pretty hot there right now. Wanna go back and make some noise?'

On Sunday morning, Izzie awoke to a knock on her bedroom door and her mother cooing, 'You awake, Sleeping Beauty?' Rosetta's tone turned nostalgic as she tiptoed into the room. 'Sixteen years ago, in late April, a dear little bunny-rabbit leapt into the world.'

'And that rabbit was me,' said Izzie on cue. Lethargically, she opened her eyes. Their annual birthday dialogue from the time she was five. Or had it started when she was six? Six most likely, because the first time her mother had greeted her this way, she'd responded in a toothless lisp. 'A rabbit?' she'd said. 'Yipee! Where *ith* he then?'

Today, Rosetta sat beside the bed nursing an armful of purple-wrapped presents she was yet to hand over, took on a faraway look and said, 'You were *so* much like a rabbit, you in your little fluffy-hooded jumpsuit. In the first week of your life, while I was still getting used to Isobel as a name, I resorted to "Flopsy".'

'I know.'

'And from then on, weirdly enough, you were never satisfied with being a little human. You'd continually ask me to make rabbit ears for you, out of cardboard, and then you'd bound around the garden, happy as anything.'

'I know.'

'Oh, I know you know, birthday girl, but I'm just making sure you don't forget it.' Rosetta waved a finger at her.

'So when will this annual reminder become obsolete?' an amused Izzie demanded.

'When you leave home, I guess.'

Izzie wondered whether today would be the last time she'd hear about her former similarities to long-eared rodents. Before reaching the sophisticated age of seventeen, she might have already secured the full-time job she longed for, since her mum's ability to support her financially through the Higher School Certificate and uni was understandably zilch. A waitressing job in some groovy café would be far more exciting than attending exams and tiptoeing through libraries in search of meaningless facts.

Then she would rent a balcony apartment in the city with a couple of kids from school and hold regular sketching parties and visit pricey hair salons where the stylists excelled at disguising carrot-coloured hair with shades more fashionable. A live-in boyfriend, a Dalmatian puppy, a '60s beetle car and a camper-van with all mod cons to escape the urban scurry on weekends. In her first year of independence, her introduction to the rest of the world would be spent hiking somewhere in Scandinavia during half of her annual leave, to tour castles and swim in glassy lakes. From there, she'd travel to Peru for two weeks where she'd explore the ancients' ruins and converse with locals in the Spanish she'd have already mastered at night school.

She'd hinted this to Rosetta not so long ago, hopeful of getting her used to the idea that her only child had grown up and wouldn't be around the following year. When she'd made reference to the things she'd spend her money on, she'd been disgusted with the patronising tone of her mother's reaction: 'On a junior waitressing wage?'

So she'd kept her dreams to herself. With practice she would become frugal enough to afford these. While Rosetta was a good manager of money, Izzie would be a better one. She felt sure of it.

Her eyes were now fully opened and resting on the chart blue-tacked to the dresser mirror, a horoscope wheel containing squiggly symbols that resembled hieroglyphics. 'Mum, does that horoscope say what my Rising Sign is?'

'I seem to remember Eadie telling us your Rising Sign was Libra.'

Rosetta moved to the dresser and peered at the chart. 'Yep. A Libran Ascendant. And a Cancerian Moon. She's written below the chart that Taureans born around your birth-time of 4.18 p.m. in Sydney have Libran Rising Signs. It says here: *A strong Venusian influence such as this indicates sociability and artistic flair.* Can't argue with that.'

She moved to the corkboard and waved a hand towards Izzie's sketch of a jewel encased in silvery-gold lunar-gilt. 'I really like this pendant, Izzie. Love the shade of pink. When did you draw it?'

'A couple of months ago.'

'It's beautiful! Reminds me of something. Can't think what at the moment. Did you copy it from a picture?'

'Nope. From imagination. It appeared in my mind and I just *had* to get it down on the sketchpad. Did it within about five minutes.'

'Amazing! I thought it would've taken you hours! It has the look of a photograph.'

Izzie leaned back against her bed-head. While Rosetta continued to rave about the 'realness' of an image conceived when her mind was filled with Glorion, she pondered the horoscope over on the mirror. A Rising Sign, of course, revealed more about a person's personality and physical appearance than the Sun Sign did. Izzie had guessed Glorion's might be Libra because of his dimples and diplomacy, but she hadn't known that this was her own Rising Sign. What if she and Glorion had Rising Signs that matched! That would be sooo *sooo* freaky.

Glorion, Izzie had learned, was an early August boy, three months younger than Izzie, and a Leo. Regal, affectionate, sun-ruled Leo. She'd recently asked Eadie the time Dutch Leos needed to be born to have Libra Rising, and Eadie had said around 10 a.m. But what chance did Izzie have of confirming that? They were yet to have their first *real* conversation, and so she could hardly charge up and casually say, 'What time were you born, Glorion? And what date in August is your birthday?'

Now that she'd invited him to the afternoon's picnic, talking to Glorion seemed more impossible than ever. As expected, there hadn't been any feedback on whether he or Tyson planned on turning up. It was starting to look like a boring all-girl get-together.

Perhaps there'd be a group of Year Eleven guys at the beach throwing a party too. At least then Izzie and the birthday boy would have something in common to break the ice: sharing the same Sun Sign. They could discuss their love of comfort and eating, and brag about their generally placid natures.

Rosetta returned to a chair beside Izzie's bed and presented her with the bundle of gifts. Swathes of violet-tinted cellophane fluttered to the floor as Izzie feverishly unwrapped a boxed aventurine-quartz necklace from Crystal Consciousness. Pretty, but something she probably wouldn't wear, not that she admitted to this when she thanked her mother exuberantly...a little carved wooden zebra, which she loved, purchased from the African charity stall at the craft markets...a psychedelic covered journal she didn't believe she'd ever find the need to write in but gushed over its design and voiced how much she valued the energy Rosetta had put into tracking down—and parting-out for—each of the offerings. Added to that was a satin, hideously elaborate, multi-coloured bag that her mother believed would be 'cool' for art.

'Absolutely!' Inwardly, Izzie disagreed, visualising the looks she'd have to endure lugging such a loud and outdated Father Christmas sack into class. 'Wait a minnie, what's in it?' A flat tin fell onto the bed. Pastels. '*Excellent!* I've been wondering how I'd do my next pastel pictures!' The last gift was a hamper full of foodstuffs. 'Awesome!' Izzie seized up two of the eight plastic-wrapped satay veggie pies.

'For your picnic, courtesy of Lena. I'll warm them in the oven just before you leave.'

'Mum this is great,' Izzie enthused, genuinely excited at the thought of presenting her friends with a variety of tastes that she, herself relished. As well as the savoury pastries, Lena had contributed from her shop a mountain of sushi: gleaming dark-green envelopes of seaweed bursting with rice, and a collection of other tempting treats. 'And champagne,' Izzie said in a squeal when Rosetta handed her a bottle with a squiggly ribbon tied about it.

'Not quite. Sparkling grape juice. Take the pink plastic wine-glasses with you if you like.' Rosetta's face grew serious. 'I couldn't get you much in the way of presents this year, honey. I feel awful about that.'

Izzie comforted her mother with a hug. 'But I love everything you've given me. Anyway, I'm practically a grown woman. I'll be buying my own things when I leave school next year. And you know I mentioned the other week that I didn't want presents, so getting these after all is a beautiful surprise. Thank you, thank you, *thank you!*'

Izzie took extra care with her grooming that morning, stretching frizz out of her hair with the aid of Rosetta's chia-seed serum, a paddle brush and the stoic patience deemed obligatory when wielding a low impact heat styler on a slow-drying mane. 'It's a wonder my hair doesn't stay damp for an entire week when I leave it to dry naturally,' she commented at breakfast. 'It's as thick *as*.'

'As thick as what?'

'It's a saying, Mum.'

'I know,' said Rosetta. 'I was only teasing. Eadie uses that term all the time. I reckon it's a stupid term. Stupid *as*.'

When Izzie hurried out to the verandah on her way to the bus stop, Rosetta called from the hallway, 'You look gorgeous in that butter-coloured dress, Izzie. Enviably slim, and radiant as a faerie princess.'

'Great op-shop find. Goes well with these sandals.' Izzie stuck out one foot and pointed her toes to admire the faux-pearl emblems. 'Don't know about the faerie princess bit though. I'm thinking more freckled pixie.'

'But you've hardly got any freckles now.' Rosetta wandered to the front door, tea-towel and dish in hand. 'Like I've said, the lemon juice you've been using works amazingly. And the remaining freckles you have aren't anything to worry about. They make you look sweet.'

'Sweet,' Izzie thought with annoyance, was never used in the same sentence as 'hot'. Not unless it was describing a fried-on-the-spot cinnamon doughnut.

The phone in the hall rang. 'That might be Rella,' Izzie said. 'She said she'd call on the landline if she can't get to the picnic.'

'All right, well, we'll soon find out.' Rosetta lifted the phone and swung her hair away from her ear. 'Caroline!' she said. 'I'm glad you called. I actually wanted to let you know I can work next Sunday.'

Izzie turned to go.

A gasp. 'You're joking,' Rosetta murmured. 'Cazzie, that's awful!'

Curious as to what the bad news was, Izzie paused between the edge of the verandah and the steps.

'Look, I don't mind a bit if you reduce my pay until...Yeah, I know you feel bad about doing that, but just until you're back on your feet.' Rosetta's voice grew soft. 'Please don't cry, hon. Things can still work out. I'm sure the rest of us can band together. We could organise a promotion blitz...we could...Oh I see. Tim too? Oh, no.'

What was going on with the Crystal Consciousness owner?

'I had no idea it was that bad. Caz, I'm so sorry to hear this. No, no, no, I understand. You had no other choice.'

Rosetta's silhouette, a faded grey through the flyscreen door, was folding forward. Her voice had become raspy. 'Hey, I've still got my other job. And Jack Barnaby always has extra hours...No, really. I'll be fine.'

Crystal Consciousness must have been going broke. Izzie crept back across the verandah. Rosetta turned to her. Smiled bravely. 'You don't want to miss your bus, Iz,' she whispered.

The sound of Caroline's sobs on the other end of the line filtered into the hallway. Rosetta slapped the phone back to her ear and spoke in reassuring tones. 'We're funny, you and I,' she said into the receiver. Her attempt at a chuckle didn't quite work. 'Each of us is worried about the other.'

The bus was now creeping towards the middle of Ashbury Avenue. Keeping her fingers crossed that she'd catch it in time, Izzie waited for the call to end. At last Rosetta wished Caroline well and put down the phone. Before Izzie had a chance to say anything, Rosetta snatched the phone up again and dialled the voicemail of Jack Barnaby, her cleaning boss, to request additional shifts.

Izzie opened the door a fraction. 'I was thinking, Mum, it's about time I chip in for rent and food. The bakery wants a junior to work weekends. If I get the job, I could keep the bowling alley earnings for school stuff and clothes, and then I could put the rest towards board.'

Rosetta did not respond immediately. She was standing by the phone table with her head bowed. When she swivelled round to face Izzie, her expression was unnaturally cheerful. 'That's not for you to worry about. Now you go and enjoy your birthday! Go on. Aw, look! Your bus is just about here.'

Izzie hurried down the steps. Remembering something she'd meant to tell Rosetta on Friday, she called, 'By the way, Mum, there's some mail from the letterbox in the wheelbarrow. Two envelopes. I put them there when I answered my phone and ended up forgetting about them.'

'Thanks, hon. If they're bills, they're worth forgetting about.'
Rosetta gave a roll of her eyes. 'Have a fantastic time. And don't
come home without a boyfriend. I mean not *with* one as such, but
with the knowledge of having won the heart of a super-hunk.'

Super-hunk! *Eeek!* Her mother was really showing her age.

While Izzie was at her birthday picnic, Rosetta baked a trayful of
baklava, weeded the fernery by the driveway and swizzled a mop
across the hallway floorboards. Just the laundering left to do.
'Bummer,' she said when she opened the cupboard. 'Out of laundry
detergent.'

The gas-lighter on the stove had seen its last flicker, there were
no matches in the house, and her craving for a hot cup of tea was
increasing by the minute. The corner shop was in walking distance but
a flexi-teller was not. While the fifteen cents in her purse might have
bought a small box of Redheads in 1968, unless there'd been a forty
year inflation standstill, the three silver discs—with their engravings of
the Queen on one side and an echidna on the other—would remain
where they were. In obscurity.

A trip out to an auto bank in the next suburb? Jack Barnaby
probably wouldn't call back until the evening and there was nothing
much left to do at home. Excited at the thought of going somewhere,
she snatched up her handbag and hurtled out to the driveway.

At the front lawn she slapped a hand against her forehead. The
car was still at the garage awaiting a generator replacement. Despite
being wheel-less for the past three days, she still hadn't beaten the
automatic reaction of reaching for her keys. Eadie wanted help that
afternoon with browsing over colours and prices for a patio she hoped
to afford the following year.

With a shrug, she thought: I'll top up on supplies at the mall.

The freeway freeze—resulting in her car being towed away after
sputtering to a stop in peak-hour traffic—had occurred the day after
she'd taken Izzie to the dentist. A bill for two fillings was never
especially welcome, even less so now that Rosetta's sole mode of
transport had performed that spectacularly costly dummy-spit.

And now Crystal Consciousness, a workplace she'd cherished, had folded under the pressure of February's slumping sales figures. She would need to work full-time in her cleaning job now, a demanding job physically, but a good hourly rate all the same.

She flipped on a CD, 'Serene Lunacy', a hit made famous in 1967 by New Zealand vocalist Danna Nolan, and strolled out to the back garden to open the two letters received Friday that were lying, crumpled at the corners, in the wheelbarrow where Izzie had left them. They were sprinkled with petals from the nearby daisy bush and soggy from Saturday's rain. From the sitting room, the chorus rose up in a whirl of soprano splendour. Humming along, Rosetta peeled open the damp windowed envelope. The words *Eviction Notice* in bold, angry lettering sprang out.

Shock prickled over her spine.

The home that she and Izzie loved was no longer theirs! According to the letter that shook in her hands, the developers had brought the demolition date forward. A month to pack up and be out of there.

She checked and re-checked the real estate agent's letter while the reality of it seeped into her heart. One month! Sinking down onto the lawn, she stared at the shadows.

Finding a modestly priced home in an area close to Izzie's school would take nothing short of a miracle. Double income families were almost always given precedence as tenants. Understandable, Rosetta supposed. A single mother, a Jill of all Trades with no career, no work that could be considered permanent and a continually changing address, was often viewed as a potential rent-dodger.

Evicted!

And then there was the pregnancy. To top it all off, she had a pregnancy to deal with.

Lena, an expert on cats, confirmed a week ago that Sidelta's kittens could arrive any day.

'I love kittens,' Rosetta had said mournfully. 'From a distance though, when they're owned by other people...' and Lena had warned that finding homes for six or more kittens was not an easy task.

The clouds had begun to gather when Rosetta returned inside. She scanned the accommodation section of the local paper, mouth agape at the ludicrously high rental prices, and groaned at the idea of having to put Izzie through yet another locational change.

She had to consider the positives. It wasn't as though Punchbowl—or its surrounds—was so terrible. She and Izzie might be luckier this time, with a neighbourhood free of intruders.

She filled her glass at the kitchen tap, checking the clouds from the window. The temperature had dropped a few degrees in the past hour. Had she reminded Izzie to take a jacket? Had Izzie remembered to grab an umbrella?

She surveyed the back lawn. 'I'll miss that jacaranda tree,' she said. 'And the two citruses.'

Her gaze moved to the clothesline. She froze.

The scene before her snatched the air from her lungs.

'Can't be,' she whispered. 'No.'

Someone was out there, crouching on the path. A figure made shadowy by the darkening sky. A man in a trailing black coat.

She slipped to one side of the window. She would phone the police, but first she would need to watch him to make sure he didn't approach the door. She would need to lock it. Now. And she would need to lock the front door too.

She fled to the indoor laundry. The images crashed through her thoughts...crazed eyes, curling talons. Her only barrier against the stranger was a flimsy flyscreen, a small flight of concrete steps and a distance of five or six metres. She reached for the heavier door to close it, all the while watching him, anxiety rising in her chest like a wave.

He had not moved from where he was crouching. His head, veiled in the jacaranda's shade, was bowed. He was inspecting something on the ground.

'God, no,' Rosetta breathed.

He was watching Sidelta. Grasping at her. Sidelta raised a paw in defence. The stranger collected her up in his arms and stood.

Without pausing to consider the consequences, Rosetta flung open the screen door and stepped out. In a shout, she said, 'Put that cat down!'

The man dropped his arms in fright and stepped sideways into the sun. Sidelta sprang out and sought shelter under the wheelbarrow.

'Oh.' Rosetta stared at him, at the face now visible in the sunshine, a face conveying shock and embarrassment. Eyes of light blue observed her warily.

'Dominic!' Rosetta's fear turned to anger. 'What were you doing with Sidelta?'

'We were having a cuddle,' Dominic said. 'But I think you might have startled her.'

It was feasible of course. Dominic had no reason to kidnap her cat. On the rare occasions he'd dropped Izzie off, he'd only been kind to Sidelta.

'You scared the bejeezus out of me! Why didn't you knock?'

'I did. You weren't hearing me out the front, so I thought I'd try your other door.' Dominic's thick lips curled into an apologetic grin.

Aware of the tautness in her shoulders, Rosetta breathed out. 'I see.'

Sidelta, recovered now from her initial alarm, crept up to Dominic and leaned dreamily against him, grey fur tipped with silver in the afternoon glare. Dominic stooped and glided a hand over her back. Definitely not a cat thief. Definitely not the lizard eater. 'I was wanting to have a chat with you about this gem of a place of yours.' Dominic flourished his hand outward and smiled benignly at the yard.

'You want to talk about this property?'

Dominic flickered his eyelids, dark lashes trembling delicately. 'And a great little property it is too. Cal Bungs are going like hotcakes lately. Reminds nostalgic forty-somethings of the homes their grandparents once had. Feels comforting. Secure. You probably already know that their high demand has pushed the prices up?'

'Ye-es.'

Dominic strode towards her and produced a business card from his coat pocket. 'If ever you're looking at selling, Rosetta, I'd be delighted to oblige. In fact, I insist.' He raised an eyebrow and imitated his TV-commercial self. '*Call us at Wallace*...as the ugly guy on the idiot-box says.' He chuckled at his last comment, at what he considered to be an irony.

'Thank you, Dominic.' Should she tell him the grim truth? That in one month's time her cosy California Bungalow would be reduced to a rubble heap? No point in admitting to being a renter. Diondra already had enough ammunition.

'I recommend you meet me for a drink, Rosetta, to discuss values.'

'That won't be happening.' She placed her hands behind her back, the card crushing in her fist. 'I won't be selling anything, but if I were, I'd talk to one of your staff members.'

Despite her non-committal response, Dominic appeared to be encouraged. 'Good girl,' he said. 'Good, nice, girl!'

The patronising choice of words made her seethe. Until she realised Dominic had been addressing Sidelta. The indiscriminate feline was lying shamelessly at his feet, pregnant abdomen poised upwards in readiness for a belly-rub.

Dominic murmured a few more terms of endearment to the expectant mother, examined his watch, mentioned needing to pack his suitcase for an 11 p.m. flight to Port Vila in the South Pacific, and said goodbye to Rosetta with a smile that wasn't sincere.

Once he'd exited through the side gate, Rosetta escaped inside and flopped on the couch. She was safe. Sidelta was safe. But something still bothered her. What was it? Dominic's manner? His appearance?

The eyes. They were different. A shadow at the rims that hadn't been there before.

Rosetta sat upright.

The corners of Dominic's eyes had looked bruised, as though charcoal had been smudged into the corners and then haphazardly wiped away.

She tried to recall the man in the unlit laundry at Punchbowl. His mouth would have been painted. Its redness had been too bright. And his eyes? They'd been pale, almost glassy, yet darkly sinister. Lined with kohl? She couldn't remember. If only she could remember!

Sidelta, now settled on the edge of the rug, watched her with sedate amusement.

'I'm getting paranoid,' Rosetta said.

Sidelta launched into a food-demanding, 'Yeee-ow!'

'And you're getting hungry. Now, how would you and your un-born catkins feel about another can of tuna and a big saucer of milk?'

XXXV
Back in the past timeframe, the Devic Pre-Destruction Century Or 'The Pre-Glory Century' to those of the Empire
THE TIMEFRAME IN WHICH THEIR PALACE RESIDES

'Tell us!' The command was screamed at Eidred.

'I do not know.'

'Tell us!'

'I cannot tell you. I do not know!'

'Then you will have to suffer the sorrowful consequences. Who do you harbour in your room? Who is living in your dressing-quarter? Who are we to imprison at the sun's twenty-fourth degree?'

Eidred glared at the spindly creatures whose eyes—piercing, un-feeling, eager for the sight of blood—burned holes of terror in her heart.

'You are mistaken, good minders. There is no elf and no rabbit stowed away in my room.' At that, she sank her teeth into her lip and knew she could never forgive herself for this utterance, a disastrous error made in the name of fear.

'An elf?' they screamed. 'A rabbit? This is news we are yet to hear.'

'But you must understand. They are not here of their own accord, they—'

'Oh but they are, they are.'

'They are not!'

'We shall kill them! We shall offer them to our gods! We shall rob the elf of its magic!'

'I have imprisoned them for myself. Therefore *I* shall kill them.'

'You?'

'I, as Princess of Grudella, possess the powers to do so. 'Tis written in our laws. Have you not seen Law Seven-Six-Eight in the *Book of Rightitude*, good minders? Are you willing to go against the Solen's decrees?'

A nod was given to one of the servants, and Eidred, despising the stillness that followed, waited wordlessly for the *Book of Rightitude's* retrieval.

Silence enveloped the room, a silence that allowed Eidred to remember she hadn't dared to breathe until now. Her hands, clenched into fists, were beginning to shake forcefully to match the state of her shivering shoulders.

The delay caused by the troopers' errand allowed her greater time, although not enough. Very soon they would find her claim to be a fallacy. Very soon, Pieter and Fripso, and possibly Eidred as well, would be flung into dungeons.

May the gods have pity on me, Eidred inwardly pleaded, and allow me to go with them. May they allow me to die with my beloved friends. May they remove me from my life as a princess!

Life might as well be death, with the demise of her only companions. Waking to each sun in a state of mourning, with the memory of her failure to protect them, would be far worse than a torturous end.

And yet, events had wound to such an extent that she could not reverse them. The pterodactyls scanned the Book and sniggered at Eidred.

Her arms were clamped into chains.

Two troopers exited the hexagonal room in search of an elf and a rabbit, both of whom would be cowering in the princess's chamber.

'You cannot do this,' Eidred shrieked. 'I demand to see the Solen! I demand to see the man who is my father...I demand...'

A sack was thrown over her head. An ugly scent of toadstools and other hallucinogens enveloped her.

Eidred slumped to the floor.

Chapter Thirteen

XXXVI

'Eidred?'

The princess awoke to the memory of troopers hauling her down flights of stairs and into a prison beneath the palace.

'Are you conscious, Eidred?'

'Fripso? Is that you speaking?'

'Yes, Eidred, only me.'

'So dark! It is so dark I can't see anything! Where are you, Fripso?'

'Eidred! Tell us you are all right. Tell us you are not unwell. You have been screaming in your unconsciousness, and Pieter and I are concerned.'

'My dears,' squealed Eidred, still trying to make out shapes before her in the darkness. 'It is I who should be concerned, I who have given you such misery. Oh my poor, poor darlings. Forgive me, forgive me, forgive me.'

'Eidred,' a familiar voice said, and it might as well have been music because it belonged to Pieter. 'Do not berate yourself, friend. We are not so badly off in here.'

'But what will happen next?'

'A question we might well ask of you,' Fripso said. 'It is you, Eidred, who knows the ways of the palace.'

Eidred noted she was lying on something soft... something as soft as the mattress of her chamber. Her tear-wet eyes adjusted to the darkness. She could see a window over yonder, one just like her own, and a little pool of starlight on the floor. ''Tis my room,' she exclaimed.

'Of course it is,' Pieter's voice rang out, and Eidred heard a soft chuckle. 'Did you travel in the Nightmare Realms? Did you travel somewhere especially awful?'

'The shouts, indeed, were almighty,' added Fripso.

'Oh! Only a nightmare!' Eidred hurried to light a candle. Her heart, only moments ago aching with petrifaction, was now bubbling over with joy.

After ensuring a flame had materialised upon the wick, Eidred leapt from her bed and across to her captive guests. She unlocked and opened the dressing-quarter door, scooped up Fripso, kissed his ears wildly, then with motherly tenderness set him back down.

Eidred turned to gaze at Pieter, her beautiful friend Pieter, and stepped towards him. She reached up to touch the side of his neck, felt the keen stretch of jawline above it, and the slope of his face—a face that was even more handsome by moonlight—and searched his dark eyes, which at first had become wide in surprise yet were now dreamily heavy-lidded.

'Our skins are different,' she said bitterly, wanting not to turn away from the one she had grown to respect with fervour.

She hoped she had not alienated him with this defeated remark. Thankfully, he did not retreat. He watched her with quiet interest, his expression aglow with an intriguing brand of kindness. Could it just have been kindness, though, or was it something more?

'But our hearts are not,' he said, and with that his arms went about her, and Eidred felt as though she were soaring through the very stars that danced outside the chamber window. Pieter's lips were brushing lightly across her cheek. The dizzying sensation of embracing a youth she hadn't meant to grow fond of, invoked a happiness that was almost too much to bear, but then he released her and stepped back.

Now achingly aware of the fullness of her feelings for him, her happiness presented itself as something of a burden, weighed down by a dread that had grown greater in strength since the terrible dream. 'Oh Pieter, I fear so dreadfully for your safety and the safety of Fripso. I have had the most frightening premonition. 'Tis a warning, I feel, of what might happen. I don't want them to find you. I can't let them find you. You cannot live like this, you cannot live like this, you cannot...' Her breathing had become panicked. Her entire being cried out to be held once more by that lad of fey origin who had, only seconds ago in his closeness, wreathed her in a momentary state of ecstasy.

'We will find a way,' said Pieter, although he shrugged as though devoid of ideas. 'I must tell you, Eidred, your hope of marrying your prince is breaking my heart, but I understand I have no power to persuade you otherwise.'

Liberated for a moment from her morbid concerns, Eidred giggled. 'And why does it break your heart, my Pieter?'

'Is it not obvious enough?'

Delighting in Pieter's admission to being heartbroken should she wed, Eidred encouraged him to re-word his concerns. 'I am not sure I understand what you mean to say,' she said, wanting to laugh and dance and sing. Pieter's jealousy of a suitor was maddeningly delicious.

'Well, I embraced you a moment ago, Eidred, not just as one who is a friend, or even...' Pieter was quite lost for words. 'Or even as a sprite might comfort a body king daughter...I mean, a gold-skin.'

'How then?' Eidred's pulse had become as rampant as a river current.

'It was an embrace of adoration,' Pieter said with a sigh.

'He means,' a small voice from the other side of the clothing-quarter said, 'that he has fallen in love with you.'

Eidred squealed and threw her arms around her elf. Pieter held her tightly. Tears from Pieter's eyes fell onto Eidred's hair and face. Eidred wept too—so great was her joy—and was no longer sure whether the tears dampening her cheeks were Pieter's or her own.

'What's more,' continued Fripso. 'He wishes you wouldn't marry that prince. He wishes it was he and not the prince who you'd decided to marry.'

'I am afraid,' Eidred said slowly, 'that I cannot abide by Pieter's wishes.'

'You cannot?' Fripso's voice dulled. 'I suppose you are barred from it. After all, a sprite and a gold-skin together in matrimony would never do.'

'Oh, yes it would,' said Eidred wistfully. 'But I cannot agree to Pieter's wishes, Fripso, for they are unfounded. There is no prince with whom I plan to share my life, and there is no offer of marriage.'

'No prince?' Pieter was visibly overjoyed.

'Not yet.' Eidred lowered her voice to a tone that was soft and questioning. 'Unless of course Pieter of the Brumlynds would like to become one.'

Pieter's expression sobered. 'A sprite and a gold-skin wedded! How could this possibly be?'

'I have thought much of this, Pieter. There could well be a way of fooling my family into allowing us to wed and to at the same time keep Fripso safe.'

The elf, reaching out to Edired, clasped her in his arms once more, then lifted her up and spun her into circle after circle. Eidred, immersed in bliss, clung to his shoulders laughingly. With gentleness, Pieter returned her to where she'd been standing and murmured, 'Marrying you would be my greatest wish fulfilled.'

Pieter's enthusiasm for the plan was divinely reassuring. His sunburst smile was broader than ever, and his eyes were no less filled with affection than when Fripso had uttered those beauteous words. *In love with you.* In love with *her*! Eidred had won the heart of someone she would eternally idolise. That he might have felt some of the ocean-deep reverence she harboured for him was the most magnificent news she had ever in her life received.

The faerie godmother, Eidred believed, had been responsible for granting nearly all of her requests. One last wish remained.

She related her hopes to the young man before her while he held both her hands in his. Tentatively, she asked if he agreed to her scheme. 'Becoming a prince would indeed be dangerous. Are you truly willing to take a risk in marrying me, elf?'

'Princess,' said a solemn Pieter, 'how could I not be willing to take that risk?' He laughed a little and shook his head, evidently marvelling at the surprising turn of events. 'If both of us were competitors for a title of Most Powerful Spell Wielder, the medal-bearer would no doubt be you.'

'Me? But I am unmagical! Whyever so?'

Pieter's eyes shone with elation. 'In requesting I marry you, enchanting Eidred,' he said, 'you have miraculously transformed me into the happiest sprite alive.'

Sara was the first to greet Izzie when she arrived at the beachside meeting point. 'No word from Tyson I guess?' Izzie asked.

'He rang this morning,' Sara shrilled.

'No *way.*'

'And he'll be here a bit late.'

'Just Tyson?'

Sara looked unsure. Realising Sara didn't know of the Tyson/Glorion alliance, Izzie hurried towards the other guests lolling on a picnic rug beneath the pines.

Sara caught up with Izzie. 'Tyson isn't seeing anyone, is he?'

'I doubt it. We would have heard by now if he was.'

'I made up some fairy bread,' Sara said lolloping along beside Izzie. 'So we'll have to pretend we're primary schoolers.'

'You're a star,' Izzie said absently. Could Tyson attending mean Glorion would be along too? 'Hundreds-and-thousands or sprinkles?'

'Hundreds-and-thousands.' Sara nodded, eager for approval. 'All sweet and sugary like the ones on chocolate-freckle lollies.'

'Cool,' murmured Izzie, recalling Rosetta saying the freckles on her nose were 'sweet.'

At least, Izzie thought, mine aren't multi-coloured.

The sea, seething and grey, gleamed in the smooth curl of its frothy waves. Whether the girls could remain outdoors without having their lunch diluted by the anticipated rain had become an issue of debate.

'Let's just start anyway and try and beat the showers,' suggested Izzie. ''Cos I can't *wait* to unpack this picnic basket! Wait till you see the delicacies!'

The girls huddled forward, and clapped and whooped as Izzie announced each item from Lena's health food store. Rella's butterscotch popcorn and Charlotte's box of designer chocolates were already laid out on the tartan rug, as were the Singapore noodles that Marla brought, a recipe her Chinese mum cooked for special occasions. The African coconut slice of Jandy's got the loudest cheer.

'This is an absolute banquet,' food-lover Izzie roared. She examined the unremarkable photo of Tyson on Sara's camera. 'You guys are sooo kind. So what are we going to do about the lack of talent so far?' She inclined her head to indicate two middle-aged men tiptoeing into the shallows. 'Where are the hotties?'

'They're probably scared of storms,' said Andrine. 'And of mega-intelligent women such as ourselves.'

'Then let's go seek 'em out and scare 'em,' said Izzie. 'Because this party's gonna be a *party.*'

'Woo-hoo!'

'Gimme a "b"!' yelled cheerleader Dalia.

'B!'

'Gimme an "o"!'

'O!'

'Gimme a y"!'

'Y!'

'Gimme an "s"!'

'S!'

'And whaddaz it spell?'

A dilapidated car decorated with painted flames screeched to a halt.

'Spells yobbos,' said Izzie. 'If you add B.O. and turn it into an anagram.'

Three teenaged boys leaned out of the car's windows to eye Izzie and her party guests, their heads moving in unison with pulsing drumbeats.

'Ha! Travelling ostriches,' said Dalia with a snicker.

'Ay, girlies,' yelled one. 'Wanna come for a ride?'

'Ignore them, ignore them, *ignore them,*' whispered an anxious Andrine, staring at the ground.

The girls bowed their heads too, in deference to Andrine who was shielding her eyes as though afraid another glimpse of the rhythm-happy speedsters would turn her to stone.

Refusing to hide away, Izzie held Sara's camera at arm's length, angled the lens at the car, then leapt to her feet to take a closer shot.

'Izzie!' her friends hissed.

'You'll come for a spin then, will ya?' yelled the driver. His mates rolled around in their suede car seats, helpless with laughter.

'Just taking your picture!'

The greasy-haired head-bopper in the driver's seat revved the motor and snarled.

In one dramatic move, Izzie pointed to Sara. The girl ducked, curling inward like a daisy at sundown. 'Her dad's a cop,' Izzie called. The camera snapped and whirred. 'Do you think he'll recognise you?'

The driver took off in a squeal of burning rubber.

'That's one camera-shy dude,' Izzie said, returning to her guests.

They embarked on their lunch and chirruped animatedly, commenting every so often on the eeriness of the gathering clouds. One of the girls happened to mention Glorion, a subject that had the effect on Izzie of an invisible hand reaching beyond her ribcage and grasping at her heart. The topic wafted briefly through a conversation which, just as it began to flourish—thanks to a certain amount of persistence on Izzie's part—changed direction and bypassed Glorion altogether. Not that the news was all that interesting. Izzie had heard the same about him before. A few kids at school thought he faked his Dutch accent. Probably just a rumour. The undeniable appeal of Glorion's stilted English would have become the target of jealousy among other guys at school.

As the day grew older and darker, Izzie and Sara resigned themselves to Tyson having changed his mind about the party. Izzie was already acutely aware that no Tyson would mean no Glorion. Teens travelled in packs, after all, particularly boys, who seemed only capable of boarding public transport in threes. In fifth grade a party passport was as simple as arriving solo with a present tucked under one arm, after having been driven door-to-door. A comb through the hair, a soap-shiny face. Now it was peers on either side, like bodyguards, clothes no better than a slightly varying uniform that went under the guise of fashion, and hair that had to be gunked with product and reverse-vacuumed into an imaginative shape. Faces were daubed with tinted zit-cream, lips smeared with chap-sticks, ears decorated with gold and silver, or glass that imitated gems.

'Maybe Tyson thought it was called off because of the rain,' Sara said in a small, sad voice.

'Could've phoned though,' Izzie said, 'before jumping to conclusions.'

The girls went for a walk along the cliffs in search of hotties, but the only form of life they found was a scattering of seagulls. They discussed the latest movies and Charlotte's new shoes, collected a few pearlescent shells for the summer corner of Izzie's four-seasons collage and returned to the beach again to gossip some more and bemoan the boylessness of the landscape.

Then it came time to depart. Darkness had fallen, rain had begun to pelt, and the headlights and taillights of cars on the esplanade turned the road's glossy blackness into a ribbon of blurry reflections.

Swinging the now empty hamper, which had, a few hours earlier, harboured a surprise butter cake her mother had baked—with the words 'Sweet Sixteen' mapped out in liqueur boysenberries on liquorice frosting—one bloated, bedraggled wet-haired party-thrower made her way down the street, feeling a pinch of grief and a spark of anger at a certain person not bothering to RSVP.

The street was now a festival of faerie-lantern luminosity. A guitarist in the nearby pub started up a yodelling ballad that sounded as lonesome as Izzie had begun to feel. Wishing she'd accepted a lift with Rella's family, she glared at the empty bus depot across the road. Buses on Sunday evenings were generally few and far between. She would flick through the teen magazine Marla had lent her to pass the time.

She went to cross the road and spun round at the sound of a familiar voice. 'Can I help you with that basket?' The word 'that' had been pronounced 'dat'.

'It's not heavy,' breathed Izzie, unable to temper the pounding of her pulse.

'What are you doing here on a Sunday night all by yourself?' Dark-eyed, be-dimpled Glorion! Glorion of the caressable biceps and sun-kissed brown hair!

'Having a birthday,' Izzie said. Glorion would have to think up an excuse for not going. This would be very, *very* interesting.

'A birthday!' Glorion beamed. Without hesitation he said, 'Well if I'd known today was that, and if I'd known I'd run into you on my way to the supermarket, I would have brought a present with me.'

'But...didn't you get...' The invitations via his locker and Tyson: he hadn't received either! Would she admit to having asked him to her picnic? Better to stay coolly detached. 'Yeah, it was pretty good,' she said. 'Everyone was there.'

'So is this party started yet?' Instead of 'this' he'd said 'dis.'

'Finished,' said Izzie, smiling bravely up at him.

Raindrops were dampening Glorion's fringe, lending him the cuteness of a just-washed puppy. 'Drat!' he said, in his inappropriate and adorably uncool way. 'If it was still on I would have *crash-gated*.'

'Gate-crashed?'

'That's it. Gate-crashed.' Glorion smiled and shook his head, having a silent laugh at himself. 'My English isn't as good as my Dutch.'

'My Dutch isn't as good as my English, so we're square.'

'That's funny, Izzie!'

Wow, thought Izzie. If Glorion thinks that's funny, he's easily amused. I can be sooo much funnier than that.

'Where are you off to, Izzie?'

'To the bus depot to catch um a...' He was standing very close and was looking directly into her eyes. 'Um...a bus home, so I'm going home. By bus.' She'd really stuffed that one up. Why couldn't she think of something more upbeat to say? Something witty or smart? She was still spinning from hearing he'd be prepared to turn up uninvited. If only she'd kept the party going longer!

But where was Glorion off to, anyway? 'Where are *you* off to, Glorion?' she asked, with a numb-tongued shyness she felt sure would have looked ridiculous on someone like her.

'Supermarket. To buy some dinner.'

'Oh! Ha! Of course.' Stupid question. He'd already mentioned this! 'Um...well...better not stand in the way of that.' Her own fringe was plastering to her forehead, and her scalp felt soggy, an indication that this must be a significant downpour. Rain was rarely able to seep that far through Izzie's thick tresses. Suspecting she probably looked like a shipwrecked sheepdog, and now, as a result of this realisation, a red-faced one, Izzie turned to say a hurried goodbye.

But Glorion's fingers pressed lightly on her elbow, causing a giddiness that rendered her motionless.

'Wait,' he said. 'Does it have to be so soon? Australian supermarket trolleys are scary. I have no idea how to operate them. Could you show me some ropes Miss Birthday?'

Izzie's stomach gave a small skip of excitement. 'So you've got a trolley phobia?'

'And a rejection phobia,' grinned Glorion. 'Come on, Miss Birthday, let's go.'

XXXVII

Eidred's eyes reminded Pieter of the serene pools wherein his friends the undines dwelt: blue and vibrant with emotion, and now they overflowed with love for a Brumlynd who considered himself to be undeserving.

Pieter's days were bittersweet. His own impulsive actions had re-moved him from the trees, rivers and crystalline air that he'd treas-ured without thought during his boyhood. Life was now immeasurably altered. Becoming a youth had brought him a treasure of a different sort, in the form of the golden girl who had captured his heart. While he missed Elysium Glades, he knew he could not do without Eidred.

With fondness he remembered back to when he had begun to find her intriguing. She would return from her lessons each evening to converse animatedly. Had he not felt responsible for her slumber, Pieter would have been happy to continue talking and laughing with Eidred until sun-up. There would be a delaying at first, when she'd tell him she was all right to stay awake, but Pieter would continue to coax until she reluctantly admitted to weariness and agreed to bid them 'goodnight'.

The word goodnight was just as much a blessing to Pieter as it was a bane. When considering Eidred, the sound of it made him glad. She would be renewed by the star-spun in the Dream Sphere. When considering himself, it caused the opposite of gladness, reminding him that he would immediately be robbed of something precious, something that would trigger within him an ache for its return. When first this happened, he told himself it was the variation in company he missed, for chatting to a member of the rabbit species he was forced to live alongside tended, after a time, to descend into mundanity. Only so much could be said about Wakkel-Weed and parsnip.

Even when away from her chamber, Eidred had still been there with Pieter, emanating an unassuming loveliness, for she and her influence had become part of his mind, the memory of all words and mannerisms almost as exquisite as her presence.

Falling in love with a gold-skin had in its initial stages been a burden. Pieter had felt powerless to speak of this, certain she would shun him laughingly. And then there had been an angry emotion, which Fripso told him was 'jealousy of a rival,' when Eidred had talked incessantly about Prince Adahmos in a tone that conveyed she was eager to meet and impress him.

Eidred, now seated beside him in the dressing-quarter, looked up from her sewing, a costume of disguise, and said, 'Our ceremony will be so lovely, Pieter.'

'The only thing lovely about our ceremony will be your attendance,' Pieter said. He did not fancy the idea of marriage by gold-skin standards. It sounded as though it were to be a sombre affair, where many useless rituals took place, including a dawn chant and then a heckling of sorts that Eidred described apologetically as a 'lunar spoiling' when both bride and groom were expected to express their contempt for the moon.

'You must become an actor,' she cautioned him. 'And for all that you do that is not you, Pieter, you must feel no guilt. Never forget it is all a game. A silly non-reality that will vanish when we leave.'

As the sun streamed in on Pieter, he felt a tiredness he'd never before felt. Prior to this he had been livelier than ever, elevated to extremes of happiness, which he accredited to the powers of love.

He imagined, as he often did, himself and Eidred returning to their proper timeframe, The Century of Ruin, after their hundred-year sleep. Perhaps they would wake earlier than the guards and flee to Elysium Glades. He could then introduce his bride to the Brumlynds. If they did manage to escape, their time in the forest would be short. He and the princess must remain in hiding thereafter.

Sensing Pieter's concern over his lack of usual zeal, Eidred said, 'I believe staying conscious in the daytime is having its effect on you.'

'My beauty, I believe you are right.'

'You are not your laughing self this day. You have become listless, yet if you fail to practice living by the sun, you will never cope when introduced to palace life.'

'This is true.'

'And so, although I feel wretched encouraging you to take leave of your nocturnal nature, I fear it must be done for your higher good. It hurts me to watch you suffer this, beloved.'

Pieter missed his clan greatly. When Eidred, many seasons ago, had righted a misunderstanding, telling Pieter she had *not* imprisoned them, he'd asked her to convey a message to his own mother and Fripso's to advise they were in the Grudellan Palace of their own free will. The Backwards-Winding occurred soon after, and so Eidred missed her chance to locate Maleika and Karee. They were all now distanced by a century. To hide his disappoinment, Pieter made the remark that Eidred's eight-and-tenth birthday was closer than ever now. 'I therefore have something to look forward to, besides being wedded to you,' he said. 'And the Brumlynds aren't entirely isolated from me. I am sure I would be visiting them in the Dream Sphere.'

'And yet, you rarely sleep in the day, now, Pieter. They must search then wonder what's happened to you each time their spirit selves go there. Even if you returned to that routine, it would do little good. Remembering Dream Sphere visits is impossible without—'

'I do miss the remarkable benefits of Remembrance Essence.'

'I have been unsuccessful in finding any.' Eidred's voice had dulled.

'But I would never expect this of you, Beauty!' The task had not been an easy one for Eidred. Grudellan women were permitted only small amounts of time to themselves. During the afternoon of each Sun's Day, she would wander the forest in search of a devic clan who might allow her a flagon of Remembrance Essence.

Although Eidred was possessing of faerie sight, she'd happened across few of devic heritage. Pieter concluded that many of the sprites would have seen the princess first and warned the others to hide. Even if they hadn't managed in time to conceal themselves, an unconsciously created shield of invisibility would have meant Eidred overlooked them.

Upon the rare occasion of encountering a sprite—once a bluebell faerie, another time, a pixie of the bracken—both had told her the same thing: that they were not permitted to help someone of power-mongering heritage.

'I roamed Elysium Glades this morning, in fact,' Eidred said. She re-threaded her sewing needle with twine that flashed lustrous gold in the streaming sunlight. She'd discovered a group of gnomes who, to her dismay, shrugged and shuffled away when approached with questions. 'I suspect they knew what I meant and were being deliberately non-committal out of fear,' she said. 'And who could blame them? With the terrible reputation my family holds, a sprite could be quite excused for distrusting me. Guarding their magical elixir is a heroic thing to do. It quite impressed me.'

Pieter felt differently. 'Sprites always strive to be truthful,' he said. 'Their evasiveness would not have been deliberate. Perhaps in this part of time, Remembrance Essence hasn't yet been discovered.'

'It is possible, I suppose, but I am resigned to sprites' suspicion. I pay the price for being associated with the wicked. Oh, Pieter, I wish I'd been born one of the fey...I mean, one of the devas, with the same skin colour as you.'

The tone of Eidred's complexion, once grotesque to Pieter, had become something he considered to be beauty personified. It added uniqueness, he believed, to her myriad qualities. He comforted her with, 'They're radiant, those colours of yours,' and smiled secretly at Eidred's care in using language that didn't offend. 'Fey' had always been a derogatory term, just as 'body king' had. The two had agreed that morning to eliminate both words from their vocabulary, and Pieter was surprised to learn that the term 'gold-skin' was not as he'd assumed it to represent. 'It pleases me that you're a gold-skin,' he added finally.

Eidred reminded him that he'd again pronounced the term wrongly.

'It's because you have gold skin,' Pieter said, after apologising for his forgetfulness. 'That's why we all thought you called yourselves that.'

'Indeed that is not it, but I commend you for seeing something else in the name. Our skin, without consuming the dragon gold, is blue, Pieter. Blue-grey, the colour of our blood.'

'This is common knowledge amongst sprites. To think I am marrying a blue blood!'

'To think my future husband is non-possessing of golden tokens,' Eidred threw back with a smile.

'A blue blood! So tragic sounding, and yet my mood surrounding this is the opposite.'

'And it's Gold's *Kin*,' Eidred said laughing. 'Remember that. Not gold *skin*, as you so unceremoniously put it. We are the family, or kin, of currency. Our currency of gold makes us powerful, and to gain greater supremacy we coerce those with lesser resources to either work for us or give something up for us so that we may accumulate more.'

'Unlike the currency used by sprites,' Pieter said gloomily.

'The currency of kindness was a much better system of exchange,' Eidred agreed. 'But because you receive your kindness merits for assisting someone only in the Dream Sphere, it is difficult for you and most unfair. You know not whether you've even received them.'

'My dreams have become little more than a puzzled haze,' Pieter admitted.

'Think of all the magic that might well be available to you, Pieter, if only you knew!'

Pieter shrugged. 'I am not at all concerned. Magic from accrued merits is nothing more than beauty-creation. What help would beauty-creation be to me? Being in love with *you* holds more than enough beauty.' He took Eidred's small hand in his. 'Escape is deceptive. My magic doesn't work on deception. Invisibility as a protective device might be allowed...'

'But you no longer require invisibility. The palace's frequencies have given your atoms solidity, and now you are more like us.'

'It's odd having to hide now like Fripso does when the Grudellans storm into this room.'

'Indeed. But at least you can wander around the chamber unde-tected. The spy-lights no longer recognise your devic energies.'

They'd discovered Pieter's visibility to those of the court when a Grudellan had spotted the top of the elf's capped head behind Eidred's gowns. Pieter had been ushering Fripso to the edge of the wardrobe. All three of the chamber dwellers were stunned to learn pterodactyls could now discern him. 'My milliner,' Eidred had said with studied nonchalance. 'He's donned one of his creations for me to see.' The Grudellans had responded to this with disinterest.

'There are many laws, however,' continued Pieter, 'as to when magic can be used. It is sacred and therefore mostly elusive. I am merely a novice in this art.'

'But if I'm able to get you a flagon, Pieter, you could recall exactly how much magic you have at your disposal. I wonder where the devic clans source this.'

'In the Century of Ruin we collected it from rocky springs known as the Wondalobs, but I could never ask you to make that arduous journey. Please, beloved, forget about Remembrance Essence. I am perfectly happy with the way things are.'

'Wondalobs?' Eidred's eyes brightened. 'There is talk within the empire of this newly discovered resource! I had no idea Wondalobs water was also Remembrance Essence.'

'Remembrance Essence is Wondalobs water infused with a silver-pink crystal.'

'But I possess a silver-pink crystal! Remember the shard from a bewitcher's wand that I told you about? The one that was hidden under my pillow at my naming ceremony? Already sorcerers are collecting Wondalobs water to examine its power-giving properties. I understand they keep it locked away in their workshop, but surely I can find a way to secure some. I can now concoct your very own Remembrance Essence!'

'No, Eidred,' Pieter said gravely. 'Please promise me you won't ever attempt this. You must never put yourself in danger, Beauty. With or without Dream Sphere memories, you and I shall live a life that's happy.'

Despite Eidred's promise to forget the idea, Pieter feared he saw a glimmer of mischief cross her features, as though she were already constructing a plan.

Eidred gazed down at their hands entwined and marvelled at the contrasting shades. 'Fey and Gold's Kin united,' she said teasingly, and it provoked Pieter to answer in mock indignation.

'Do you not mean deva and body king?'

'Sun and moon then,' she said.

'*Moon* and sun,' Pieter chided, feigning pedantic ire at not being mentioned first.

Defying this, Eidred added, '*Gold* and silver. *Day* and night.'

'Dull and bright,' Pieter growled.

'Mortal and Sprite!'

And then Pieter, chivalrous now in their juvenile game, gave in and mentioned Eidred ahead of himself. 'Princess and willing servant.' He placed a kiss on Eidred's hand.

'Self-proclaimed elf-adorer,' a giggling Eidred announced, 'and the Prince of her Heart.'

'Or,' said Pieter, 'as the colours of our flesh might suggest...'

'Black and white.' Eidred caressed Pieter's hand, a deep, dark brown against her own sallow paleness. 'You are of dark skin,' she said, 'and I am of light. What an unusual pair we make!'

⋯⟨♪⟩⋯✳⋯⟨♪⟩⋯

The rain had vanished, a birthday wish made true for Izzie. A wind had sprung up soon after she'd begun trudging along the beach with Glorion.

Glorion was carrying two supermarket bags, each full of tinned asparagus and tinned asparagus only, a reason he had remained on a lower level of admiration than he'd originally been placed.

'So where is this house by the sea you've been telling me about?' Izzie asked, shivering.

'It's not so much a house. It's...more of a shed.'

'A shed?'

'But less bigger.'

He rummaged through his supermarket bags, muttering about something he'd neglected to buy.

'Toothpaste?' Izzie suggested. 'Bread? Coffee? My birthday present?'

'I wanted to get another tin.'

'Of what?'

'Of asparagus,' he said with a sigh.

Maybe it was an addiction. Izzie's mum was probably addicted to the corner shop's Jersey caramels; Andrine at school was clearly addicted to choc teddy bear biscuits; Eadie from the Friday Fortnight group was addicted—by her own admission—to condescending men.

It had to be an addiction. Or maybe his preferred vegetable contained a nutrient most boys his age didn't know about, something that gave him his awesome muscles. Maybe asparagus was soon to be hailed as a new superfood, one that would rival the spinach gulped down by that ancient cartoon dude, Popeye.

Izzie had taken on a brisk walk to match long-legged Glorion's amble, following from half-a-step behind as he wound around the cliffs abundant in yellow-tinged scrub. This was the same part of the beach she'd meandered through earlier with her friends. Recalling her despondency at finding the beach devoid of boys, she laughed inwardly. Such a waste of energy, but how could she have guessed she would stumble across her favourite two hours later?

The sea was dark, snarling like a lion and crested with foam that glinted silver beneath the waxing moon.

'Izzie, you're cold,' Glorion observed, and he said it in a tone of gentle concern.

'Sure am.' She nodded wholeheartedly, hoping in some small way that this might be a cue for him to put his arm around her, or fling his jacket about her shoulders at least. His words sounded so gorgeously intimate, like something a boyfriend would say. And she wanted *so* much for him to be just that.

The notion of visiting Glorion's home was exciting enough as it was. And she'd been invited to dinner! Even if it turned out to be just a quick bite to eat in a school buddy's kitchen—with nothing for future retelling that could be remotely described as flirting—none of this mattered. Just being able to say she'd *walked* alongside Glorion Osterhoudt and *talked* with him was a jewel in the crown of all privileges.

No offer of a jacket. Glorion's arms stayed glued to his sides. 'I don't often go to the shops.' He stared directly ahead. 'That's why I'm angry with myself for not getting everything I needed.'

'Why asparagus?'

Glorion didn't answer.

Perhaps she should have feigned being an asparagus fan, to avoid him clamming up.

At last Glorion said, 'It contains glutathione.'

'And what does that do?' ventured Izzie.

Glorion took on a faraway look, as though canned fodder and the nutrients it contained had vanished from his thoughts. 'It helps...Actually, it doesn't matter. Okay Izzie, I'm going to ask you to stop here.'

'Stop here? But why?' Surely Glorion wasn't getting tired of her company. Not already! Was Glorion going to reply or was he planning to leave her, and on top of this, leave her in suspense?

Glorion did *not* linger any longer, nor did he answer. Instead, he launched into a slow sprint. Izzie watched the rise and fall of Glorion's sturdy shoulders. Unbelievingly, she focused on the back of his pale jacket. It bumped upwards with each stride. He wound around the sandy path, then disappeared from sight.

But why? Could he be dodging any further stumble-bum attempts of hers at getting to know him better?

Her abandonment might only have been temporary. Glorion's dash might have been nothing more than a short run to oxygenate his lungs—or to burn off glutathione-induced energy—but he'd given no indication of coming back.

I'll give him five minutes, she decided.

Five minutes passed. No sign of Glorion.

Okay, another five, she told herself, but her wait in the discomfort of the cold stretched closer to fifteen.

This had to be the shortest friendship in existence! Of all the things she'd experienced with Glorion in her imagination, none came near to winding up wondering whether he was a self-sufficient loner who lured in those he bedazzled before abruptly deserting them.

Thoroughly miffed at this, Izzie crept through the scratchy wilderness skirting the beach. What had happened to him? Was he sheltering in theobscurity of his 'shed'? Maybe he'd just gone home. Not once had he mentioned his family. At most, he'd given impressions of living alone. A fifteen-year-old boy was hardly capable of supporting himself through school. Perhaps he was an orphan with an inheritance. But if that were the case, school gossip would have had it covered by now.

A harsh breeze tickled Izzie's rain-damp forehead, and the waves made dramatic sounds, a continuous stretch of gasps and sighs that seemed to echo the anguished cries of a monstrous, soul-weary water god surfacing from the ocean's coral silence to bemoan the loss of love. She'd never known anyone to run off because she'd asked a couple of questions. She couldn't help it if she had an enquiring mind, one of the reasons her English teacher said she'd make a good journalist. No-one could be expected to twist their personality into impossibly tiny knots in the hope of pleasing someone else.

Disappearing guys! If the propensity for this was hereditary she'd hate her mother forever.

Her eyes smarted from the wind's chill. She had the good fortune to cry then. The tears were strangely soothing. She whispered, 'But why?' and continued to wonder this with growing ferocity on her march back to town.

The higher part of the beach was horribly quiet and the night was exceptionally dark, thanks to thunder clouds crowding out the moon.

Reaching the esplanade again would be comforting. She was anxious to leave behind the isolation of an unpeopled shore. An uneasy feeling had seeped into her veins. The empty surroundings held a bleakness that encroached on any illusion of safeness.

A thump rang out on the path behind her.

Izzie's heart dived. She didn't have time to turn.

A pair of large hands clamped over her shoulders. Izzie winced at the pressure of the hands, her voice stalling in her throat.

Nervousness gave way to panic. And then terror.

She tried to turn but couldn't.

Had they followed her? Or had they waited and watched from some hiding place in the tea tree grove?

Flooding her mind in split-second flashes were grimy images of news headlines...her mother at home weeping...the yobbo occupants of the flame-painted vehicle seeking revenge for her impulsive comments...

The grip on her shoulders tightened.

Izzie began to scream.

'Help!' Izzie shouted.

The breath of her pursuer was rasping. His hands continued to grasp. If she squirmed enough she might be able to wriggle free.

She cried out again.

The hold on her loosened.

Propelled now from a frozen state to one of frenzied fighting, Izzie thrashed her head and shoulders from side-to-side and shrieked: 'Get away from me!'

The hands fell away.

Like a bird released from its cage, Izzie fluttered forward.

She ran and ran, not seeing, not hearing, a slave to the rhythm of her steps with no other thought than to reach the safety of the esplanade where subdued lights dotted the distance. Her hands and feet were numb, but her heart was pow-powing with machine-gun velocity.

'Is-o-bel!' A voice from behind was calling to her. The voice, croaky and old, had broken up each syllable with a gasp.

Was someone here to help her? But who? Who? She couldn't look back. It might be a trap. She had to push on and escape.

'It's only me,' rasped the voice.

She continued to run.

'And I'm sorry! Really sorry!'

It was as though her legs couldn't stop. Haltingly urging herself towards the streetlights, Izzie ran on. In an impulse of curiosity, she suppressed her fright and looked over her shoulder. She glimpsed two arms—encased in light-coloured sleeves—waving above a hooded head, which the esplanade's dazzle of traffic blocked out.

The faceless hooded one shouted, 'Help me, Izzie. I need–' *Gasp!* 'Your–' *Gasp!* 'Help!'

With the realisation that she might now be at a safe enough distance to observe the person who knew her name, Izzie turned again. The traffic glare cleared, the face fell into clarity, and Izzie felt incredibly foolish.

'Are you okay?' she called.

He was leaning over. Another car wound around the cliffs, and the light it shed revealed the faint sparkle of silver and red snow boots, confirming to Izzie that this was Glorion with the hood of his jacket pulled over. No-one else wore footwear like that.

How could she have been so stupid? It was more than likely he would return to her. But those hands! They'd been grasping and threatening and had compelled her to take off. Still charged with the distress his touch had infused, Izzie contemplated whether she was safe to go to Glorion. After all, he'd acted strangely from the time they'd left the supermarket, and she didn't know this guy from a bar of Pears. What reason had he given her to trust him?

Glorion straightened from his lunge forward and wheezed. 'Can't breathe, Izzie. Can't...'

Asthma! Izzie dashed towards him. She cupped her hands and pummelled Glorion's doubled-over back, the way she'd seen a First-Aider at school treat someone who didn't have Ventolin.

'Tiny breaths, Glorion,' she ordered. 'Try to relax and don't breathe too deeply.' Glorion's back was taut with tension. His chest was heaving. Choking sighs escaped from his throat. 'No, no, no! Glorion, you *must* relax!'

'Izzie,' he groaned. 'I'm—'

'Shush, shush, shush! Just concentrate on breathing gently.'

'Izzie, I'm sorry.' His voice exploded into a series of coughs. 'Sorry to scare.'

'Not a problem! Just let me help you sit down here, and we'll breathe together.'

Glorion sank down beside her onto the damp sand. He reached into a pocket of his jacket.

'You've got a puffer,' Izzie said, relieved.

But it wasn't the grey and navy chunk of plastic she'd hoped to see. He handed her something smooth and jagged that felt like a chiselled icicle. It was a stone. A clear stone. A crystal. No ordinary crystal though. Mostly colourless, with sparks enlivening its core: sparks like gas flames, blue and bright.

'Hold...hold above me,' Glorion told her, and she did so immediately.

'Wave from temple to temple,' Glorion said, his voice less clouded with restriction.

Clasping the stone in a trembling fist, Izzie took it slowly to the left of Glorion's forehead, then to the right. Intently, she watched the twisted angles of his eyebrows settle back into shape, a sign he'd begun to recover from his oxygen-starved torment.

Crystal healing. Plenty of people were into that. A bucketload of them had their business cards pinned to the Crystal Consciousness Books & Gifts notice board. And yet, did any of these healers experience such a dramatic change in temperature? The stone, icy to the touch just moments before, was pulsating, now as warm as her hot-water bottle at home, something she'd had to prepare with increasing regularity now that autumn insisted on nightly rehearsals for winter.

Thankfully, Glorion's gasps subsided. All Izzie could hear now was the wail of the sea. Not convinced she should at this stage finalise the healing, she continued to wield the stone. The rapid thawing of her fingers was an incentive to continue curing her poor buddy's breathing, relished to such an extent that when Glorion grinned and gestured for her to pass the stone back, she was reluctant to part with it.

'Izzie, you're my saviour,' he said.

Feeling coy, Izzie turned away and said, 'It was nothing I did. That stone of yours is amazing.'

'It *is* what you did.' Glorion willed her to face him. 'If I'd had the ability with the stone I would have used it at the onset of my attack. You were the one who accessed its power.'

'I was?' Izzie's imagination soared.

To herself she said: Maybe I have some kind of Otherworld magical power. Cool! I'll have waitressing as a day job and do miracle-healing appointments on every second Saturday. Then I'll be able to afford everything I want so much faster.

Where had he got the stone? She was fairly sure it had done the main part of the work. She envisioned going shopping with Glorion Osterhoudt after school. He'd help her select one of these crystals for her newly launched clinic.

'The stone won't work on your own stuff. It only works if someone else treats you,' Glorion explained.

'Oh,' said Izzie, adding hopefully, 'Can it be just anyone? Or does it have to be someone special?'

'Everyone's special, Izzie,' Glorion said quietly, and it made Izzie redden and feel distinctly unimportant. The megastar medicine-woman image of herself dissolved and was replaced with a greater respect for the stone. 'Where did you get it?' she asked.

'Not from anywhere here. Izzie...about my running off...'

'Don't worry about it.' The sight and sound of Glorion's suffering had thrown things back into perspective. Whether they were friends or not, whether he'd burnt her off—out of boredom—or ditched her out of disgust, he'd needed her help. She'd given that help freely, as anyone would. She'd *Stood Aside From Ego*, as her mother was prone to say.

'So you're sure you'll be okay now?' she asked.

'Absolutely. Thanks again, Izzie.'

''Kay. Bye.'

Her rising to leave was punctuated by tones of surprise. 'Where are you going?' Glorion called. 'Hey, Izzie! Why are you walking away?'

Izzie shrugged and walked onward, knees still wobbly from those two major scares. What did *he* care? It wasn't as though *he'd* had any trouble upping and leaving without warning.

'Tell me where, and why, you're going!'

Izzie turned, glared into Glorion's darkly bright eyes and said, 'Like...explanations are now suddenly compulsory.' She trudged on, realising she'd never texted home to say she was eating at Glorion's. Just as well. She was looking forward to dinner, even though the over-consumption of party food had made her wonder how she could ever feel hungry again.

Glorion's footsteps drummed behind her. Izzie marched on-wards. Glorion had almost caught up. Was he about to give an explanation for abandoning her earlier?

In typical Glorion style, he said very little. Once Izzie turned, he mumbled, 'Just here to say goodbye back to you.'

'Uh-huh.' Did this dude ever communicate beyond the one sentence? Did it not occur to him that someone, right now, was mirroring his act of running off?

Glorion watched her with outstretched hands, then dropped his arms to his sides. Shoving his hands in his pockets, he said, 'I didn't mean to grab your shoulders. The asthma had me doubled over. Please accept my apology for frightening you, Izzie.'

Izzie couldn't help smiling. He looked so adorable when he was apologetic, kind of like a sad little boy, with his hair sticking up in fluffy spikes. The hood, before falling off, had tousled it out of shape. 'Don't worry about it, I'm fine,' she said. Feeling well within her rights to also receive an apology for his deserting her on a dark beach, she said. 'Glorion, why did you run off on me before? I think it was really mean.'

Glorion reached out and patted her shoulder in a distracted way.

Silence.

'Well?'

'Well, I had to go to the little room in a hurry. There were people in it. I got rid of them, did what I had to do, then ran back to you as fast as I could.'

Little room? Little room! Did he mean *the little boys' room*? Disenchanted with this confession, Izzie snorted. And this was the same boy who'd argued for a better world in the upstairs debating section of the school library?

Her time spent with Glorion that evening had felt more like a chat with a three-year-old. Rushing off to the loos in the middle of a conversation was far from cool. As for 'getting rid of people' who also had a right to the beach's amenities...Huh! Could Glorion *be* any weirder?

Could it really have been Glorion who'd described, so effort-lessly, his altruistic dream for a world where each and every person experienced a rewarding work life that was both 'purposeful and pleasurable'? Probably not his own words. Probably got bookish Alexander Whitford to write the speech.

At least she'd got to see the real Glorion Osterhoudt. For a while there her rose-coloured glasses had misted her discernment, but she'd since concluded that the boy standing opposite her was *not* a normal fifteen-year-old. Thank goodness she hadn't blabbed to friends about her fascination with him. How stupid would she look if Glorion's space-cadet strangeness became common knowledge? The snow boots had been the giveaway. Nearly every other sensible girl was put off by those, but Izzie had been blindly determined to like him.

'So could you forgive me for that too? I'm sorry about it. Really. Then we can go and have something to eat.'

The thought of dinner was tempting. The idea of stewed, fried, boiled or roasted asparagus, however, did not appeal.

'Thanks anyway Glorion, but I think I'd better get home instead. It's been a big evening.' Big because of all the trying emotions he'd put her through.

Once more, Glorion reached out to her. This time his hand rested on her elbow and slid over her forearm with a certain amount of tenderness that she couldn't deny felt lovely. Glorion's fingers glided over the top of hers. The action of his arm falling back to his side was like an invisible rope willing her to move closer. Without thinking, she let her body fall towards him, the dreamy need for his nearness radiating from every pore. The feelings were so powerful they cancelled out any concern over Glorion's mentality. Being in physical proximity of him was exhilarating beyond belief, something she could very easily get used to if given the chance.

She regained her balance, turned, and stood beside him. Glorion watched her, awaiting the decision. So he was a little bit backward. So what? It reminded her of a book by Colleen McCullough—wherein the smart American heroine crushed on a guy with the mind of a primary-schooler—and of the subsequent film that starred a magnetic Aussie actor. Inspired by the recollection, Izzie decided that going out with Glorion, despite what other kids might say about her, could still be done. Sophistication wasn't everything. Good looks and a calm temperament and a knowledge of healing were important factors too. 'Okay,' she heard herself say. 'Let's go and eat.'

Allowing him to steer her to face the cliffs, she trudged alongside him and breathed in the refreshing salt air. She regarded Glorion with a long sideways glance and smiled at him. He returned her gaze and looked down, dimples forming in his cheeks.

She was completely at ease now. Glorion wanted her to stay! Perhaps a small spark of superiority had replaced her need to convey maturity or a sparkling wit, unnecessary to someone who neither had nor valued these qualities. Discovering Glorion's deficiencies had definitely been a good thing.

The path along the cliffs wove through rows of boatsheds painted in shades that individualised each. The older ones could have even been built in the late nineteenth century.

While they walked, Glorion told Izzie his parents didn't live with him. 'I'm an exchange student,' he said.

'So what's your host family like?'

'Terrible.' Glorion shook his head. 'I'm not with them anymore. I had to leave.'

'Then who do you live with now?'

'Um...no-one. It's lame, I know.'

Wondering how Glorion could get away with leaving his allocated guardians and continuing his education in Australia without being called back to The Netherlands, Izzie asked if he rented a place on the beach.

'Kind of. Here it is now.'

Izzie spun round to look for Glorion's house. There was nothing before them but a jumble of glossy vines trailing over the cliffs.

'Come on Izzie, it's this one over here.'

'Over where?'

Glorion fumbled in his pocket for a bunch of keys. To see which was which, he held them up to catch the moonlight. Unless he was some kind of magician with an invisible cottage, the sight of him about to unlock a non-existent door did not add up.

It's either him or me, but I'm guessing one of us is crazy, she decided.

Glorion turned and, astounding her, unlocked one of the boatsheds, flicked on a light to reveal a sofa of yellow and aqua, gestured to the indoors and said, 'Welcome to my little room.'

The 'little room'. Not a public restroom at all! Little room was a perfectly logical description for where Glorion lived! Izzie continued to stand at the door, wondering whose boatshed Glorion had emptied out and taken over and whether the police might arrest them during their asparagus entrée/main course/dessert.

Glorion leapt firstly up one step and then into his boatshed, the type of home that only a teddy bear crammed into a dolls' house could envy. He emerged with a plastic bottle filled with pink liquid. 'Here's something to drink, Izzie. Catch!'

The bottle hurtled towards her. She grasped it and checked the label. 'Fresh watermelon juice from the fruit shop! My favourite!' The coldness of the bottle had her puzzling over where Glorion might have refrigerated it. Apart from sorely lacking in space, the boatshed appeared to have no connection for electricity. That light he'd switched on was a campers' lamp for sure.

He disappeared back into the boatshed calling, 'So are you gonna let me cook you dinner? Or are you still recovering from taking in the immensity of my castle?'

Irony! A sprinkling of reasonable vocabulary! She liked that. Maybe she'd judged him too harshly. English, after all, was not Glorion's first language.

'So what's with you serving me drinks? Is it the butler's day off?' She hopped up to the single step and skipped in. It could have been a one-person dormitory belonging to an army cadet. The three-seater—which would have also doubled for Glorion's bed—was nestled beside a mahogany, gilt-edged coffee table. A jungle of potted palms lined the end wall.

Glorion was standing at a small waist-height table to the left of the shed. He was slicing onions and singing a Boyd Levanzi favourite. Noticing Izzie's confusion at spotting the indoor palms, he nodded towards them. 'We don't have tropical trees where I come from.'

Izzie's gaze moved from the palms to a picture on one of the timber walls. The picture seemed to emanate ripples of silver and gold as though it had an aura. Strangely, as she neared it, the mysterious overlay disappeared. In its place was a depiction of a black boy and white girl around the same age as Izzie. The boy's eyes were deep. They emanated a liveliness that Izzie found to be mesmerising.

The girl beside him had long blonde hair, a light tan and huge blue eyes.

Izzie moved from one corner of the room to the other, trying to comprehend the artwork's holographic effect. 'Amazing! Who painted this?'

Glorion gave a modest shrug.

'Did *you* paint this Glorion?'

'Yup. In art class the other week.'

Glorion was an artist! Not just an artist but an art genius!

'This is too cool for words.' Izzie ran across to the painting again. 'Really beautiful! Who are they?'

'They're very, very ancient. The girl married someone who...Have you ever heard of Adahmos and Eid?'

'Is that Dutch for Adam and Eve?'

'No. Just a variation.' He gestured to the sofa. 'Sit down, Izzie, and I'll tell you a story.'

'About how someone of your age manages to run away from their guardians and live in a furnished boatshed? Legally?'

Glorion continued chopping. Still concentrating on the onions, he shook his head. Even though he was turned three-quarters away from her, Izzie could tell from the dimples denting his cheeks that Glorion was smiling, possibly even laughing. 'Not right now. The story about the silver boy and the golden girl.'

Right now Izzie didn't care what he talked to her about, as long as he talked to her. She was falling for him again, and everything about him—his voice included—had lulled her into a giddy sense of awe. 'Silver boy and golden girl,' Izzie echoed. 'Any relation to Obamos and Weed?'

'Adahmos and Eid, you mean. Yes! You and I, Izzie, have an important connection with them.'

'You're right. We're probably something like Adam and Eve's great-great-grandchildren thirty million times over. So we *are* related, or at least connected I guess, although I wouldn't say strongly.' Again she surveyed the makeshift bedsitter. 'Why here, Glorion? You sure weren't joking about living in a shed. Why are you *here?*

Glorion rested his knife on the chopping board. He leaned forward with his palms on either side of the table. Gazing above Izzie's head with the same distant light in his eyes she'd noticed earlier, he said, 'I'm here because of *them*. That's why I have to tell you their story.'

Chapter Fourteen

XXXVIII

*S*he watched the Solen warily. 'Father, as you know, I am a keen observer of the *Book of Rightitude*.'

'Sacrilege it would be if you were not.'

'And it so happens that I have a question that I believe only you, Father, can answer.'

'You are arrogant to squander my time. Do you have no awareness, Eidred, of my importance? I have had you educated on the hierarchy of Grudella, you claim to be an adherent to the *Book of Rightitude*, and yet you assault my ears with the impudent demand for advice on one of your twisted presumptions!'

'It is a delicate matter, Father, one that I believe must not be conveyed to our minders.'

'Oh?'

'You see, Father, I should like to know when I am to have my future told. As you are already aware, the *Book of Rightitude* states that a princess's agreement to marrying, regardless of whether it is written or spoken, must be followed by an audience with one of the palace soothsayers.'

'Why do you plague me with things I already know?'

'Please listen to what I mean to say. This meeting with the soothsayer must take place exactly ten days before the union. As I understand it, Father, once I bewitch Prince Adahmos, and once he requests of you my hand in marriage, you will wish to establish a ceremony on the first day of the new moonth, since this is the sacred day for weddings.' Eidred glanced at the Solen whose hand rested on his bearded chin while he scowled at the floor. 'Because our next moonth arrives in eleven days, three days after I meet the prince, I expect you would command us to marry then. Or would it perhaps be the following moonth?'

'And wait thirty-one more suns to witness an Ehyptian noble gain insight into your guilelessness and thereafter renege on the union? Do not patronise me. You know already that I would expect you to marry immediately. Hierarchical relations are critical to our expansion in power. Be mindful that if you fail me, daughter, I shall have no hesitation in inflicting upon you all punishments my counsel deals traitors.'

'This is understood, Father.'

The ordering of afore-union rites would be arranged by the Solen only once an official marriage proposal was made. It was clear to Eidred that he had misjudged the honour of the document he'd commanded her to sign five suns earlier, a document that officially earned her the privileges of a bride. If he'd continued to ignore this, he would no doubt have received a harried visit from one of his advisors to cancel a decided-upon marriage date because of its contradiction with the soothsayer visit ten days prior.

'I am most certain, Father, that you are knowledgeable of the fact that I have signed, under your guidance, my agreement to marrying Prince Adahmos and that, providing he proposes to me, the marriage will take place eleven days from now. Therefore, I wish to ask my question. At what sun's-degree on the morrow am I to visit the soothsayer?'

Evidently resentful of being shown his neglect of Rightitude law, the Solen glared at Eidred, icy eyes dull with hatred.

Pleased with herself, Eidred bowed her head lower in the hope of concealing a smile. Not even a monarch could dispute the *Book of Rightitude*. To go against its content was a severe breach of palace code, expected to invite the gods to send a luck so black that starvation, ruin, disease and diminishment of gold would in hindsight be deemed the milder of misfortunes to be cast upon the Grudellan Palace.

'I have,' he said, turning away, 'already planned to inform your minders at today's twenty-second degree of the time you are to attend tomorrow's future-telling. Impatience is an ugly trait of yours, Eidred.

You have succeeded in making a most unnecessary interruption to the valuable work I do.'

'I apologise, Father. I am wrong in questioning your excellent foresight.' With that, Eidred bowed low and left the Solen's gilt-smothered chamber. Once reaching the floor beneath, she pranced through the hallways as a deer would, consumed with fits of laughter. Contrary to his assurance of having done so, the Solen had not thought to arrange a soothsayer. If he had, Eidred's minders would have consulted her by now.

Eidred's assumed ceremony would now take place on the up-coming moonth. Any date further along would not have worked. Unthinkable to the Solen was the delaying of a lucrative union, and this was exactly to Eidred's advantage. An earlier wedding was critical to her plan.

On returning to her chamber, she spoke nothing of this to the elf. Pieter must not yet know of all she'd agreed to do. She continued to stitch together the robe she was secretly constructing, plying the needle with tense precision while contemplating the urgency of her quest.

The following day, at the sun's seventh degree, Eidred was summoned to the western division of the palace grounds. Before her loomed the dwellings of the Solen's bewitchers, three-and-ten black pyramids glimmering grimly in the morning mist.

Filled with wonder at the events the soothsayer might forecast, Eidred made her way down the winding cobblestone lane. Beyond these stark three-dimensional triangles was a dome of crystal, a temple devoted to Flurena, Goddess of Fortunes. Within that indigo-hued receptacle was a hooded figure seated at a tree-stump table.

'Greetings, Highness,' said the soothsayer bowing. The bridal fortune teller's utterance echoed gratingly and was not unlike ptero-dactyl screeches in the effect it had on Eidred.

With a twisted hand, the soothsayer gestured to a seat laden with glittering cushions.

'Sounds too much like a fairy story,' Izzie said. She scooped her fork through the last slivers of capsicum in the stir-fry Glorion had prepared for her, a scrumptiously aromatic dish which, thankfully, had been free of asparagus.

'I guess it is a fairy story,' said Glorion. 'But everything I told you is true.'

'I don't know, Glorion. It sounds great, it really does, and I wish I could believe it happened, but I just don't. It's another version of *Sleeping Beauty.*'

Glorion's relating of the folktale had prompted a display of that debating team captain eloquence—marred only slightly by his Dutch accent—and had held Izzie spellbound right up until he'd uttered the words 'The End'. At the unravelling of a tale that began with '*The modern world in which you and I now live...*' Izzie was enthralled by the hero, an elf from ancient Norway who had pushed the boundaries of the times by befriending one of Gold's Kin.

Glorion was unafraid to believe in sprites and dragons and greed-twisted rulers of long ago. He'd been right there inside the story while he conveyed it, nostalgia spilling from his eyes. She felt as though they'd gone on a voyage together in a hot air balloon, one emblazoned with colours from beyond the spectrum. Izzie had since landed with a thump back into reality where logic was encroaching on all she'd dared to believe.

'You should write it down,' she told him softly. 'It'd make interesting reading.'

Glorion's dimples appeared and he said, 'Have you heard of an author by the name of Edward Lillibridge?'

Izzie tried to recall where she'd seen the name. The recollection of an unillustrated cover with a silver title floated into her consciousness, along with the inkling that it had been written well over a century ago by a minister perhaps, or a priest. Of course! It was the book belonging to Royston. 'My mum and her friends formed a reading group they call Friday Fortnight,' she told him. Excitedly she added, 'That's the exact book they're studying! Royston described it as a lost history.'

'Have you seen inside the book, Izzie?'

'Not yet. So that's where you got this story! I'm amazed you can remember it all. Mum's still got Royston's book somewhere. She's borrowing it until the antiquarian bookshop delivers her order for the group. I'll check it out when I get home.'

'Do that,' said Glorion.

'It's really old, the story. Apparently that reverend guy was alive in the eighteenth century.'

'He was. So when did Rosetta Melki start this group?'

'She started it...Wait a minute!' Izzie blinked, confused. 'I never told you my mother's name.'

'You're kidding! Are you telling me *Rosetta Melki* is your mother?'

'But she is. How did you know of her?'

'Back in my home country I googled Edward Lillibridge and accessed the Friday Fortnight website. But your name's not Melki, it's Redding!'

'Mum went back to her maiden name.'

'I see! Has she told you anything much about *Our True Ancient History?*'

'As far as I know she tried reading it years ago when she was my age. Said she couldn't make much sense of it back then. Probably more interested in romances written for teenagers and those glamour glossies they had in the '80s.'

'Uh-huh.' Glorion's eyes registered surprise.

'Although she loves the story now that she's studying it.' Pondering its moral, Izzie said, 'So it was written by one of these men of God, but it really didn't have a churchy message, did it? Well, not the version you've just told me.'

'Lillibridge was primarily a prophet,' said a serious Glorion. 'And it was a philosophy, not a religion that he wanted his readers to embrace.'

'And what would you say that philosophy was?'

Glorion threw the question back to Izzie. 'What would *you* say it was?'

The thought that rocketed its way across to her was that love was the answer to everything, but she wasn't going to embarrass herself by saying something as schmaltzy as that. If she did, she'd probably only redden, an unbecoming give-away to Glorion concerning the effect he had on her.

The law of love, which sprites had always lived by, did not acknowledge selfishness. This didn't exist within them, and the presence of kindness acted as a robust shield against fear.

As Glorion had explained in his story, love's absence sparked two major afflictions within the body king race: conflict—known to dissolve into the cruelty of war—and currency territorialism, which resulted in nourishment-depletion for much of the devic and fauna population.

A mortal and a nature-spirit had united, and their unity represented the harmonious blending of black and white, moon and sun, silver and gold. Their love, sadly enough, was forbidden.

Eidred, or 'Eid' as Glorion referred to her, had not been any ordinary Gold's Kin princess. She was quite happy to move away from her Scandinavian home of Norwegia, with her firstborn and the guy she married, to the Land of Mu, where eleven of her twelve children were born.

In the Land of Mu a new society emerged, which embraced harmony through beauty-creation, a form of natural magic sprites used, to pretty-up the world with greenery and gorgeously fragrant blossoms. This was overseen wisely by Princess Eid and her prince. They were protectors of the devic clans, faithful servants of sprites, discreetly shunning Gold's Kin enforcements while resurrecting the Currency of Kindness.

Mu's society was built upon a deep respect for the family, the community and the planet, and this nurturing energy beamed outwards to honour all living things so that a sense of belonging and connectedness prevailed.

Romantic love—sharing life with a soulmate—never had to be anxiously sought. Those seeking partners were granted their wish at certain times of the year when the power of lunar grace weaved a subtle form of synchronicity that drew seekers together.

Aeons after the prince and princess moved to the Land of Mu, a place known in other legends as Lemuria, Gold's Kin of Ehypte—now present day Egypt—turned their 'land of triangles' into a political minefield. Ehypte and Atlantis, a neighbouring continent, began plotting against Lemuria.

Lemuria was a nation far more technologically advanced than the society of 2008 that Izzie knew. Lemurian crystals were responsible for creating flight, light, healing and temperature control. Ageing didn't exist because the crystals prolonged life and preserved youth for thousands of years. Glorion told Izzie that these incredible technologies were too numerous to name. 'I really couldn't describe them fully, Izzie,' he'd said. 'The concepts are too complex. People from the twenty-first century cannot hope to understand how these remarkable innovations worked.'

Paradise was then blasted apart. An apocalyptic war destroyed the sublimely progressive lands of ancient times when Gold's Kin of Atlantis attacked the devic nation of Lemuria with laser missiles. This obliterated all other nations and everything on Earth's surface.

Millenniums later, when enough laser-radiation had risen from the earth into the stratosphere, vegetation returned. The increase in oxygen that resulted from these new patches of jungle allowed life to emerge once more. Evolution was now free to begin again. 'Those ruined civilisations were *pre*-prehistoric,' Glorion had said. 'But the radiation devastated nearly all that was left of the old world. Archaeologists have never accessed proof of our true history. They believe that the second evolution of humanity was our first and only.'

'But the thorn thicket, the kiss, the hundred-year sleep! That Lillibridge dude might have gone short on ideas and borrowed from fairy tales.'

'How do you know this *Sleeping Beauty* story wasn't a fragment of *Our True Ancient History?*'

'So you still think it's the original?'

'I know it's the original.'

'Okay, I'll mull over that. But at home, when I'm alone with my thoughts. You still haven't told me why you live in a boatshed.'

'And you haven't told me why you didn't invite me to your birthday.'

Izzie turned to avoid his gaze. She'd been too nervous at the bus stop to tell him he'd been welcome all along, doubly invited in fact. Changing the subject right now seemed the most sensible option.

'That veggie-fryer of yours is crazy. I've never seen one like it. Where do you get these things?' She waved her hand towards the hive-shaped appliance on his coffee table. 'How does it work without electricity?'

'Well unless you want me to be evasive, like you were being just then, the question still stands.'

Izzie coloured. Maybe she hadn't got the locker number wrong. Glorion might have received the envelope after all. Instinctively she glanced up to where a fridge should have been, but wasn't, to check for a magnet-affixed invitation.

Glorion drew closer to her on the sofa, leaned towards the coffee table, opened the fryer's rounded door, drew the crystal from his pocket and directed it at a circuit within the interior. The small light at the side of the fryer blinked on.

Izzie gasped.

'Crystal power does work,' Glorion said. 'You just have to know the secret to it.' He tapped the left side of the crystal and directed it at a heater in the corner. 'Sorry, Izzie. It's a cold evening...for Australians that is. I should have done this earlier.' The heater hummed obediently. A soothing warmth wafted around Izzie's ankles.

Glorion tapped its right side and waved the crystal about like a wand. Boyd Levanzi's 'Ain't Been Nothing No More' thundered from speakers assembled on the coffee table.

'Wow,' said Izzie. 'You Europeans are so ahead of your time. There's no way any of us could find a gadget-activator like that in Australia. Not even at Dick Smith.'

'But it's pure crystal. It's not some technological device.'

'Glorion, I'm kind of finding that hard to believe. My mum works at a crystal shop.' Remembering Caz's bad-news phone call, she added, 'Worked, I should say. She lost her job there this morning. It kind of proves that crystals aren't popular like they once were. Crystals aren't really...well, this one you've got here is made to look decorative like a jewel. It's a gimmick.'

'It is *not* a gimmick.'

'It *is*. Wanna settle this for good? Are you cruisin' for a bruisin' Glorion Osterhoudt?' She waved her fist about like Popeye and stuck out her lower lip.

Glorion laughed, snorting a little as he leaned forward, consumed in a fit of chuckles. Izzie took the opportunity then to take in his profile, to admire the light-brown eyelashes brushing shut, the angular line of cheekbone, those Best in the Solar System lips locked in a smile.

It was then that Glorion reached out a hand to Izzie's shoulder and gripped it with a gentleness far more intense than the affable contact of friendship. Electrified by his touch, Izzie took in a sharp breath. She edged closer on the sofa so that she was next to him, almost, but not quite, touching.

Then everything became a blur of bliss as she melted into his arms, aware that he had enclosed her in his embrace, that he was smoothing her hair back while continuing to hold her tightly. He was brushing his lips against the top of her head, murmuring her name in a husky sigh.

All Izzie could think was: It's happening...*it's really happening.*

Izzie nestled her forehead against Glorion's chest. Driven by her need to nudge further against him, she found herself moving her head slowly across to his shoulder before raising herself up to slide the side of her face against the roughness of his jaw.

She leaned back to look at Glorion. The eyes before her were bright as fire, exploding with affection.

He was going to kiss her!

And then, his arms left her. His arms left her! And so did he.

Glorion had shot to the other end of the sofa. Any further along and he would have crashed into the arm-rest.

He rose, turned away from her and said, 'I shouldn't have done that.'

Jolted from drowsy-eyed elation to stunned panic, Izzie tried to speak but couldn't. What could she say? Had she hurt him? Unnerved him? Repulsed him?

She'd always suspected aluminium-free deodorants weren't effective. Angry with her mother and with Lena's health food shop and with her own ignorance to the fact that Nature-Woman Minus Metal Roll-On—manufactured by Organic Manic—might turn boys off in droves, Izzie covered her eyes with her hand and groaned.

Submerged in a sea of despair, Izzie clung to the arm of Glorion's sofa, contemplating the lacklustre days ahead. On Monday she would ask Sara to email a complaint to Organic Manic. Sara's mum, Dette, someone Izzie had never met, was apparently good at making formal complaints, the reason for Sara's refund savvy.

What help was a refund, though, when the painful truth about a dud purchase had chosen to show itself now, through Glorion's startling response?

'I'm sorry,' was all Glorion had to say. He turned to her with sad eyes, or at least, with what *someone's* interpretation of sad might be. Izzie couldn't be sure of anything about Glorion now that her trust in him had shattered. Snuggling up to someone who attracted you was one of those unstoppable things that normally led to slow caressing and fervent kisses. If Nature-Woman Minus Metal Roll-On hadn't been the reason, then Glorion must only have *thought* he was interested in her and then decided he'd been mistaken.

How humiliating! How would she ever live it down? Her very first attempt at giving in to the desires she'd felt had made a boy dash away from her. Her way of loving was wrong. Unacceptable. Punishable by the sight of a tense-shouldered Glorion staring un-smilingly at the walls.

'I'll go now,' said Izzie, and a sob escaped from her in a sput-tering gasp. How she would manage this, she didn't know. Her legs felt as though they'd been turned into over-boiled fettuccini and her heart was beating so hard it stung. Now she'd have to trudge to the bus stop, alone, through the darkness.

Glorion repeated his apology. 'I'm sorry, Izzie.'

'...Don't...need your pity, Glorion.' Her throat rasped. Where was her voice?

Glorion contemplated. 'I really wanted to get closer, I really did.'

Glorion was still fifteen. Maybe he thought most sixteen-year-olds were scarily experienced and that Izzie would insist they go for it on the sofa there and then. 'If you thought I wanted to have sex, you were wrong,' Izzie hissed. Like she'd do something as risky—and unfamiliar to her—as that! She'd just wanted to be beside him. They'd kiss and talk, and then he'd walk her back to the esplanade. But this was not to be. Ever.

'I didn't think that at all, Izzie. Neither of us was planning on having shagging.'

Izzie didn't even bother to correct his English.

Glorion continued. 'I love being with you Izzie, and I loved *that*.'

Izzie sighed. Her hands, crunched into fists in her lap, slackened a little. The distasteful image of a girl outside a windmill appeared in Izzie's mind. 'There's someone else you like,' she said glumly. 'You never liked me. You like *her*.'

'Who?'

'I don't know. Someone in Holland. Or someone at school with shiny hair.' It didn't matter to her that she'd said something stupid. Nothing mattered now.

Glorion grinned at Izzie, then shoved his hands in his pockets and said, 'Not true. It's only you, Izzie. I only like you.'

Izzie gulped. 'Did I scare you then, Glorion?'

'No. It took me plenty of willpowers to detach from you.'

Izzie's spirits rose. Not daring to say anything, she waited for further explanation.

'But we can't get together yet. Things are complicated.'

'Yet?'

'Later, in the future, if you're still liking someone such as me, then...' His voice trailed off.

'What do you mean? Glorion, what's complicated for you? Forget the whole getting together stuff, I don't care anymore about that.' This wasn't strictly true. 'Just tell me what's wrong. Is it being an exchange student? Do you have to go soon, is that it?'

Glorion shrugged. 'I don't know.'

'Are the authorities after you now that you've ditched your host family?'

'I don't know.'

'Do your mum and dad know where you are?'

'I don't know.'

Izzie groaned. Finding out Glorion's reasons for putting romance on hold had become a game of Charades. Should she wiggle one ear and demand a 'sounds like' to prompt a more informative clue?

The tea trees rustled. Glorion leapt forward.

'Possums,' said Izzie vaguely. She went to peer out one of the windows, only to remember that the building was devoid of these.

A bang shook the walls.

Izzie shrieked. 'What's that?'

Glorion was poised like a lion about to pounce, the muscles of his jaw taut with apprehension. He stared across at Izzie with widened eyes, then held a finger to his lips to quieten her.

A thump. Another bang. It rattled the far wall, causing the indoor tropical plants to shudder eerily.

Glorion stepped forward. He raised his hand in the air, palm facing upwards, and said something in another language, just one word. At the instant he said it the boatshed's light went out and they were left in darkness.

Assuming he was swearing in Dutch, Izzie whispered, 'Someone's out there tinkering with your electricity.'

'What electricity?' Glorion whispered back. He had a point. 'That was me, Izzie. I switched off the lights so my inhabiting of this place wouldn't be detected through the gap under the door.'

Izzie was tempted to say, *Isn't it a bit late for that now?* It was obvious whoever was out there—more than likely the foreshore authorities who she'd feared would land on them during dinner—had been focused on the building well before Glorion zilched his lights. Perhaps it was someone more sinister. She remained silent, anxious to hear Glorion's next words.

She could hear Glorion taking in a breath. 'Izzie, I have to ask you now to co-operate with me. We're gonna have to run for it, okay? We're gonna have to get away from the people who came here before.'

The people before. Could they have been the people in Glorion's 'little room' story that he'd mentioned getting rid of earlier in the night? She hadn't entirely believed it at the time, but now it made sense.

Nodding shakily, then realising Glorion couldn't see her, Izzie squeaked, 'Okay,' and allowed him to take hold of her trembling hand, his touch a reminder of rejection that engulfed her like a wave. She wanted to pull away, but the need to follow Glorion's guidance took precedence over injured feelings.

Glorion squeezed her hand before letting go of it, then crept to the back of the boatshed.

Izzie froze at the sound of scrabbling on wood. 'They're *getting in*,' she wailed.

'That's just me,' Glorion said. 'Again.'

'What are you doing?'

'You'll find out in a moment.'

Glorion took hold of her hand once more and guided her to where he'd been scuffling about. A light flicked on. Glorion was holding a torch. But it wasn't a torch. It was the asthma-healing crystal! From the crystal beamed a powerful golden glow. 'You have to go through the tunnel,' Glorion said, looking ominous when he pulled the crystal close to his chest. The glow illuminated his chin, and shadows blanked out the sockets of his eyes. 'Follow the light.' During the next shivery moments, Glorion crouched to aim the healing crystal /torch at a trapdoor between his foot and a rug. Izzie was surprised to hear him laugh. He said, 'And that doesn't mean I'm telling you you've gotta die.'

Thinking of it now, it did sound like the accounts people gave of near-death experiences. The tunnel. The light. Not a pleasant thought at that moment. Being pursued by someone who might be of murderous intent had her frightened enough without Glorion joking about the passing over process.

Glorion lifted the door in the floor to reveal a spiralling staircase. 'I don't believe it,' Izzie breathed.

'It's okay if you don't believe it.' Glorion lowered the floor-door outward onto the rolled-up mat. 'Izzie, I have to ask you to go in there first. Don't be scared. I gotta lock up this place.'

Izzie stepped into the beam of Glorion's crystal that guided her down to a platform beneath the floor. With caution, she edged onto one of the steps, which, bizarrely, appeared to be sculpted from marble: glimmering and purple. She gripped the iron railing, narrow and chillingly cold beneath her grasp, and wound her way down each echoing step. The light from the crystal flicked off. She was at the bottom of the stairs now, again in darkness.

Glorion was still up in the boatshed. From what Izzie could hear, he was dashing from corner to corner, presumably snatching up his most valued belongings. She shuddered at the idea of Glorion's pursuers forcing their way in, robbing him of his chance to exit. Was this some kind of dungeon beneath the boatshed? How long would she and Glorion be trapped within its walls? She gripped the end of the bannister to steady her shakes.

And then the bannister rattled beneath her fingers.

At the shuffle of steps on the platform, Izzie darted away.

Resounding through the subterranean hideaway was a shuddering, thumping clang as someone—who Izzie feverishly hoped was Glorion—clambered down the staircase.

Rosetta hastened to the sitting room as the clock struck seven, and stared out of the window. No sign of Izzie still. Her state of concern turned into panic when an array of greyed-out golds flooded the empty streets. That was well over an hour ago. Darkness dimmed Ashbury Avenue now...and the images, those gruesome images of the intruder, were on continuous play, triggered earlier by Dominic's appearance in the backyard.

She dialled Diondra who expressed concern at the hoarseness in her voice. 'Um...er...That's a worry. Charlotte's been home for ages. We picked her up along with her friend Sara. But I'll get her to speak to you because Izzie might have told one of them where she was going next. And...maybe Dominic could go and look for her. He's out at the moment, then he's due at the airport, but...anyway, I'll put Charlotte on.'

Once her mother handed her the phone, Charlotte said in a worried little voice, 'We all said goodbye at around four-thirty. Izzie was going to catch a bus.'

Rosetta then made the perturbing discovery that Izzie's phone was still at home, dead as a doornail under the desk in her room. Rosetta plugged it in, but the battery was still far from charged. She checked the bus timetables, went outside to pace the verandah where curtains of darkness had closed out the twilight's charcoal muted purples, then gave Royston another call.

He greeted her with a nervous, 'Still not home?'

Rosetta did her best to ward off tears. 'If my car hadn't packed it in on the freeway the other day—'

'Now don't you worry yourself, lovey. I'll be there ASAP.'

As soon as Royston arrived, he drove her to Brighton le Sands. They checked the bus depot, then got out to scan the shore in search of a wandering sixteen-year-old. Rosetta surveyed the ocean, trying desperately to calm the fear tensing her shoulder blades, telling herself this was silly. Why would she expect to see Izzie struggling against the stormy waves? But then, why would Izzie be roaming the beach at this hour?

'The police station's across the road,' Royston said gently. 'We'd better report her missing.'

'Not yet.'

'Rosetta love, the sooner you can report this, the greater the chance there is of locating her.'

Rosetta gulped. Royston was right. And yet going to the police felt like conceding defeat. 'I...I have to get home.' She hurried back to Royston's car. 'Izzie's phone will be charged by now.' She would grab some of the numbers in it and start ringing around. She opened the door and wilted into the passenger seat, saying as Royston climbed in to sit behind the wheel, 'I can't believe she left her phone at home. I guess she probably thought it was no use to her with the battery at zero.'

Royston started up the motor. 'We'll go back,' he soothed, 'we'll access those numbers of friends she keeps in her phone, and we'll give them a call.' His methodical slowness eased the race of her mind. 'Who knows? She could have bumped into a group from school she's friendly with. They might have decided to throw her a party of their own.'

Uncertain now, Rosetta shook her head. 'If that were the case, I'm sure she would have borrowed a phone to let me know where she was.'

Royston's car lurched out onto the esplanade. Blurs of light emanating from street lamps were half smudged out by layers of misty gloom. The faint echo of a lone singer rose up from somewhere, yodelling a teary ballad.

'I have a feeling a boy might be involved here, Rosetta,' Royston said. 'Someone Izzie fancies who has her losing all sense of time.'

Rosetta eyed Royston's profile. At that moment his hairless scalp shone, illuminated by the lights of a passing car. It was like the Dalai Lama had spoken. Her heart flickered with hope. 'Do you think so?'

Normally a statement like that would concern her. Considering the circumstances, the idea of Izzie being with a boy she felt safe with was far preferable to the idea of Izzie being in danger. A teenaged daughter letting passion override sense was every mother's fear, but it wasn't the worst fear a mother could have.

Royston attempted a cheery voice. 'I'm sure that's all it is. A party or a romance. Teenagers are chronic at forgetting to arrive home on time when there's fun to be had. You have to remember how you would have been at that age.'

'Let's not go there.'

'But Izzie's no wild child like you apparently were. She might even be home by now.' Glancing away from the road, he flashed a comforting smile. 'Scampering up the verandah steps as we speak.'

'I hope you're right, Roystie. I certainly hope you're right.'

Beyond the Norfolk Island pines lining the road, the foamy blackened sea curled upwards and crashed as though angry with the moon that played on its edges, a wind-billowed cloak enveloping a collar of silver-flecked lace.

It had been a difficult day. The house, the car, the cat, the job, and now Izzie, had all given her grief. Nothing else mattered, though, if Izzie came home. She would cease to obsess about their plummeting circumstances if Izzie returned safely that evening.

Rosetta noticed then, on the other side of the road, the outline of a figure. He was wrapped in a cloak, the same kind of cloak she'd moments ago thought the roiling waves resembled. They neared him. Not a cloak at all. He stepped onto the roadside, fixed his gaze on Rosetta and regarded her with a sneer. The hatred in that disconcerting glare threatened to bore holes through the windscreen. Rosetta twisted round in her seat to observe him. Another car passed. Its headlights threw up a glimpse of pale goatish eyes and pinprick pupils.

Black trailing coat over stonewash denim jeans. Boots. Long black hair that skimmed his waist. Rosetta's skin turned to ice. 'Stop the car!'

'What's the matter? Did you see her?' Royston checked the rear-vision mirror. Swerved the car to the kerb.

'It's not Izzie, it's *him*,' Rosetta said in a gasp. 'The laundry man...the man with the long fingernails. Him.'

'Who's the laundry man?' Royston was shaking his head in confusion. 'Oh! That creepy guy at your old place?'

Rosetta clasped the handle of the car door. She levered the handle and scrambled out of the car. There he was. Further back alongside the footpath, wending his way around the pines. She marched forward.

'Rosetta! What in Christ's name are you going to do?'

'Demand to know what he's doing out here.'

Royston jumped out of the car. 'You *can't* do that!'

She flung herself around to face him. 'Royston, my daughter's gone missing. That man...' She tried to keep her voice from screeching. 'That man is a stalker. I've got to confront him.'

What was he doing in Brighton le Sands of all places? He'd been in Punchbowl the last time she'd seen him. Punchbowl was miles away. Why here? Why was this twisted individual lurking around the site of Izzie's birthday picnic?

'Then I'm coming with you.'

Rosetta rushed towards the stranger, her eyes on his outline: menacing jagged angles against the night sky.

'It might just be that he's developmentally delayed, Rosetta. Not harmful. Like you said, he was crouched over the dryer watching the clothes go round.'

They were now within a few steps of him. He hadn't moved much, having now stooped over the base of a pine tree to stab at the ground with a twig. To conserve her breath, Rosetta slowed to a brisk walk. 'He was caught looking in bedroom windows,' she said. 'He *eats reptiles*.'

'It's possible of course that he might be dangerous.' Royston's words had quickened. 'Why don't you stay here? I'll go and have the chat with him. It's better doing it like that because he doesn't know me, whereas he knows you from the flats.'

'Like that matters to me.'

'But he might get nasty. I don't think we should take that risk.'

Before she could protest, Royston told her he'd be better able to get information out of the stranger because of his less agitated state. 'Mind these,' he commanded, passing her his wallet and keys. He gave her hand a reassuring squeeze. She noticed his fingers were trembling. He turned and ventured towards the pine trees.

In the little amount of light available, Royston contracted into a faint and ghostly figure as he made his approach. The man was now crouching, just as he'd crouched in front of the laundry dryer. Rosetta shuddered. Slowed her breathing. How could anyone sane lower a lizard onto their tongue?

The man held up a small rounded container with a handle.

Royston looked at the sky, nodded, then looked at the sky again.

Royston returned. He shook his head. 'Harmless,' he said. 'Just as I expected. Has the mind of a child. Said he was collecting seaweed with his bucket and spade. Asked if I wanted to join him and whether it was "gonna rain?" '

Royston's verdict was heartening. His youth counselling experience allowed him insight into developmental conditions. It was doubtful some kind of abductor with something to hide—even if faking a juvenile persona—would invite a potential witness to remain alongside him.

They returned to Burwood in nerve-wracking silence. Once they passed Izzie's floodlit netball court, Rosetta grasped the door handle.

Almost home again, almost back at Ashbury Avenue. But if Izzie wasn't there when they unlocked the front door...

Rosetta closed her eyes and sent a silent, passionate plea to her daughter's guardian angel: Please look after my Izzie. And please, *please* bring her back to me safely.

Thinking aloud, she said, 'The guy at the beach could have been bluffing. He might have just been pretending he was juvenile and harmless. I didn't take in his face, only the eyes, and it was only for a split second. Light and bright. Blue I think, but perhaps I'm—'

'Trust me,' Royston said. 'That guy under the pines wasn't faking his persona. There was no embellishment about him, Rosetta, unless we're counting the makeup.'

Rosetta whipped around. 'Makeup?'

'Kohl.'

Her thoughts zoomed back to slimy Dominic. The black smudges around his eyes...His getaway later that night to Port Vila in Vanuatu...Diondra's mention of his absence from home. 'Are you serious, Royston?' Her voice rose harshly. 'You didn't tell me he was wearing kohl!'

'Of course I didn't. It didn't seem important.' Royston watched her in concern. 'Is there some relevance in that, Rosetta?' Confused now, he added, 'Perhaps I've missed something.'

Chapter Fifteen

Izzie had at first been afraid of the footsteps descending the staircase.

She'd looked up to see red reflective fabric underlining the base of two space-age boots, then flashes of white and navy enveloped in light, the combination of Glorion's jacket and backpack.

'Okay, Izzie.' Glorion had jumped from the stairs and reached towards her. 'Grab my hand!'

Glorion had broken into a run. He'd hauled Izzie into some kind of passage. She'd sprinted alongside him as speedily as she could.

And now they were rushing through a subterranean corridor. They'd been running for ages. This sudden escape was mad. Where would it lead? Eating dinner in a boatshed that evening had been weird enough. Discovering an underground tunnel beneath it was even weirder.

The interior here was not unlike the ferny, stone-walled underpasses wending through The Rocks: a conglomerate of crooked old buildings that graced the turquoise brilliance of Sydney Harbour.

Glorion's voice was a panicked shout. 'Nearly at the exit!'

Izzie knew, having sketched The Rocks tunnels from photos, that this underground escape route she and Glorion were hurrying through could well have been built in the late 1700s. Apart from an absence of growth between the bricks, it was identical to the harbourside ones built by early convicts.

Afraid her fingernails would tear holes in Glorion's hand, Izzie willed her eyes to focus forward, following the light. Her legs were beginning to tire, but she forced herself onward, thankful for her marathon training in phys-ed class, praying that the running wouldn't aggravate Glorion's asthma.

They ran on, past glimpses of damp sandstone, their footsteps an eerie echo. Hastening through this thru-way was rather like being lost in the ancient world of Lillibridge's depictions, the dragon cave of Elysium Glades that Glorion had described.

'We stop up here,' Glorion shouted.

The crystal lit the end of the tunnel, but *was* it the end? It seemed an exit couldn't have been farther away. The end was visible but entirely closed off! A dead end. Not a single way out. Looming before them was an uncompromising wall of steel.

Again Glorion yelled what sounded like a Dutch swear-word. Astoundingly, the wall slid up to reveal a flight of mossy steps. A ceiling made of criss-crossed metal blocked off the top.

'Oh no,' squealed Izzie. 'We're sealed in!'

Unperturbed by this, Glorion climbed the stairs. He reached up, his fingertips making contact with the square of metal, and flipped the ceiling upwards and off. It fell onto a surface above them with an almighty clatter. 'It's just a grate,' he said.

Then he turned to Izzie, and the sight of him there, majestic against the darkness, made her catch her breath. Imprinted now on Izzie's memory was a snapshot that would remain with her forever, Glorion on the steps, backgrounded by a rooftop vista that opened out to the fabric of the night. Light from beyond, perhaps from the moon or a streetlamp, had etched his outline in gold-tinged silver. Outside of this glow was a scattering of stars. A halo. He looked like a celestial super-being with a halo.

Can't help it, she affirmed. I love him.

Despite its ethereal charm, the scene was misted over by a thought that unsettled her, a kind of premonition that echoed Glorion's earlier words, a vague indication that she wouldn't see him again for a long time. Perhaps never.

His dark eyes radiated gentleness and concern. 'Are you all right, Izzie?' he whispered.

'Yup.' Climbing the stairs, Izzie shook off the negative notion and concentrated on being alert to their next move.

'Okay, once you get out of here we're heading for the nearest Mylanta bush.'

Izzie couldn't help laughing now that much of the panic had eased. Considering the nauseating fear they'd endured, a bush growing heartburn medicine could well prove useful.

She stepped towards the surface, accepting Glorion's hand as he helped her up to a scrubby wilderness. 'Mylanta bush?' she said between chuckles. 'You mean lantana I reckon.'

'Yes! This is what I mean.' Glorion patted her shoulder with an affectionate smile.

They were surely a quarter of a kilometre ahead of their pursuers, whoever they might be! Glorion had assured her, as they ran, that their escape had been neatly concealed. Some months before, he'd created a decoy to promote confusion. With the help of magnets, he'd worked out a way of replacing the mat after locking off the trapdoor. How he'd done this, Izzie could only wonder. As far as she knew, magnet controlled trapdoors and voice activated steel barriers were not in common use.

Relieved to be back above the ground, Izzie took in her surroundings. The soil here was soft and powdery. Contrary to nervous visions of emerging onto a railway track and dodging an oncoming North Shore Express, she was still at the beach in a tangle of undergrowth, the lights of Brighton's esplanade winking not so far away through a veil of she-oaks that had taken on the appearance of feathers in shadow.

Knees almost buckling from her frantic run, Izzie stumbled across to the lantana bush where clusters of pink and yellow florets livened the air with their spicy scent. Glorion knelt. He reached in beneath the base of the lantana and hauled out a structure of sorts that looked like a cane basket. It was the size of a small fishing boat and had flat, wooden bench-seats in it.

'You're not going to get us to sail in that,' said Izzie, unable to resist giggling. 'It's got holes!'

'Nope. But we can still travel in it.'

For a second, Izzie marvelled at Glorion's sombre-faced humour. The home he'd made for himself would have already been discovered by the foreshore authorities. The police, who would have been alerted by now, were probably rummaging through the boathouse's treasures to check for drugs or stolen goods. 'Okay,' said Izzie, playing along. 'Let's travel. Where to?'

'That's something I should be asking you.' Glorion seated himself inside the oval boat-basket and gestured for her to take the seat opposite. 'Where do you live?'

'Um, Glorion, I don't think it's relevant to joke too much right now. We've got to keep moving. We *don't know* where the Feds are.'

'Feds? Aussie cops?' Glorion drew the crystal from his pocket then waved one of his hands across a tapered end, intent on activating it. The boy was obviously from a well-off family. His casual acceptance of luxury inventions consistently bordered on boredom. Sounding suddenly like a slangy Australian, he said 'Nah, I'm not running from a couple of local coppers.'

'The foreshore authorities then? For squatting in a boatshed?'

Glorion shook his head. 'More serious than that.'

Chilled by this, Izzie stepped back. 'Then who?' Was someone homicidal stalking her friend? '*Who* is *after* you?'

'It's SAPO,' he said, his mouth stretching into a grim smile. 'The Swedish secret police are after me, Izzie. See, I'm not all I appear to be. And I hate having to lie about my heritage. Especially to you.' He patted the seat opposite him. 'All right, Izzie, jump in.'

Izzie's temper ignited. Her nerves had been jangled by one too many scares that evening, and Glorion's random reactions had ratcheted her tolerance level down to zero. 'Cut the crap,' she yelled. 'How dare you lie to me! If you were for real and the Swedish police were after you, I doubt you'd be sitting in that excuse for a boat pretending it was some kind of...I don't know...magic flying machine. For all I know those rattling sounds might have been nothing more than a few clumsy fruit bats.' She stopped to draw in a breath. 'It's either paranoia or a really bad joke.'

Perhaps she should have listened to the rumours at school, that he faked his Dutch accent. His version of an Aussie drawl moments before had been spookily accurate. If he was right about SAPO shadowing him, then he might have been Swedish, but why would Scandinavian detectives be concerned about a boy of fifteen? Glorion didn't look or behave like a crook. Odd and all as he was in the way he swung erratically between naivety and brilliance, Izzie doubted he was some kind of Mad Dog Morgan. Burwood High was too public a place for an immigrant escaping the law.

Would he give her a rundown on his past, or would the cryptic remarks continue? Another game of charades that Izzie was destined to lose.

'I'm not paranoid,' Glorion yelled back. 'Get in. Quick! They're gonna get us if we don't go now!' He leapt out of his toy, clutched Izzie's wrist with a firm hold and gestured for her to hop into the cane construction that he believed—thanks to some sad breakdown between his imagination and logic—was something he could travel in. Curious to see how long this delusion would last, Izzie got in.

'Stay there,' Glorion commanded. 'Please.'

He waved his hand across the crystal again. A light, this time a violet one, flickered from it. And then something uncanny happened. The structure rattled. Izzie squealed. Its shakes intensified, then shuddered to a stop.

'Now hold on tight,' instructed Glorion. Izzie grasped either side of the vessel.

'What's happening?' she screeched. The vessel seemed to be growing legs! Izzie wasn't imagining this. The vessel was rising higher; was jolting them upwards in alarming bursts. They were level with the lower branch of a tea tree now. And now they were hovering shakily beside the tree's crowning foliage!

'Must be attached to a tree lopper,' Izzie muttered. 'What *is* this? I'm scared, Glorion.' She attempted to peer beneath the container, which continued to lift them higher and higher, to try and establish what was propelling it.

Glorion was too busy concentrating on the crystal to notice the daze Izzie was in. He tapped one end, frowned at it, then turned it over and tapped it again.

They were now suspended over the tree-tops. Nothing beneath them! So much for the cherry-picker theory.

Stunned, Izzie looked down, taking in shop rooftops and car surfaces that gleamed softly in a haze of neon far below.

They were flying! Floating in mid-air!

Izzie screamed. And screamed and screamed, louder than she ever had, even louder than she'd screamed on the Easter Show Pirate

Ship, which was really saying something, considering the stomach-swivelling scariness of that ride.

This had to be a dream. No-one wandering below was aware of her shouts. Oblivious to Izzie, and to Glorion and to the vehicle that had pushed them into the sky, the wanderers on the street continued to wander, looking at their watches or speaking to each other or drawing out their phones from pockets and handbags. Even Glorion didn't seem to be alerted to her terror.

Izzie's voice was hoarse from pressure. She silenced herself, clung to one side of the contraption and peeked over the edge.

The pub singer she'd passed earlier had, after a break, taken up his guitar to embark on a yodelling sort of song, his words rich in tuneful lonesomeness.

Glorion uttered nonsensical words.

Shivering from shock, Izzie said, 'Is that a command to bring us back down?'

'No,' said Glorion, and he threw down the crystal in anger. 'I was swearing. In my language.'

'Please Glorion,' Izzie rasped. 'Take us back down.' The basket-boat then pivoted to the side and, as though having heard Izzie's plea, zipped back towards the lantana.

With stomach-churning velocity it plummeted, then bumped back onto the ground. Puffs of sand from impact flew up around Izzie and sank away floatily.

Glorion was sitting with his head in his hands. 'Yeah it brought us back down,' he said with a groan, 'but that wasn't my intention.' He rose, collected the crystal from the basket-boat's floor, stepped onto the sand and held out an arm to Izzie.

Accepting his hand, warm and invitingly enclosing, Izzie stepped out.

'The crystal's Sonic and Visibility shield was starting to fail. Being seen or heard would have been too much of a risk.' Glorion kicked one of the boat-basket's sides. 'There's too much radar around. Someone must be speed testing nearby.' He paused for a second, brows knitted thoughtfully. 'Then again, it could just be that I'm low on glutathione.'

'The stuff in asparagus?'

'Mm. It acts as a conductor for crystal energy, in tandem with the zilconic fabric of my boots. Come on, Izzie, we'll have to walk now to deliver you back home, and we'll have to be quick.'

Hurrying beside Glorion as he suggested they hail a cab instead, Izzie tried to gather her thoughts. Not even European technology was as advanced as that. And those boots. They'd always struck her as futuristic.

The future boy. The boy who had glimmered in her destiny. The boy who had told her many a time in recurring dreams that they'd have a few years to wait and then the world was theirs to share. Had it really been a vision of Glorion?

Since meeting him, Izzie assumed her mind was playing tricks on her. She'd told herself she'd unconsciously recalled the guy in the dream to be Glorion because it suited her to think their paths were fated to cross. The dream boy had probably been nothing like Glorion in reality, but he wasn't *from* reality that boy, he was inside her head. And yet, hadn't she felt as though she'd recognised Glorion when they'd met in the canteen queue? Didn't her introduction to him somehow feel like seeing a movie for the second time?

'Awesome crystal,' she said when Glorion halted at the kerb of the esplanade to wave down a cab. Not an electronic device as previously thought. Glorion had already denied that. 'Where did you get it?'

Glorion, clearly mindful of being followed, looked beside and behind him. He shrugged. 'From one of those crystal shops.'

Some store catering to New Agers like Crystal Consciousness Books & Gifts. Probably tagged with a brief set of instructions listing its uses: Ridding the lungs of congestion...Illuminating escape routes...Becoming airborne with or without an invisibility shield. A strong warning to keep its abilities secret would have also been printed on the tag. Bought at a crystal shop? Yeah, right! As far as telling fairy tales went, Glorion was an ace.

'I have a special way of recalibrating crystals to give them their power. But they're a poor imitation of...Look Izzie, here's a taxi now.'

His casual statement baffled her. 'A poor imitation?'

A poor imitation of what?

A technique of empowering crystals sounded logical enough, but how did it explain Glorion's capacity to control lights vocally, or doors at the end of tunnels? How did he even *know* there was a hidden underground escape beneath that particular boatshed? 'So you get a crystal, any old crystal and then you make it magic.'

Glorion shook his head. 'Magic is just an illusion.' He signalled the cab. The cab stopped, but only to pick up a group of pub-goers. 'It's an alternate form of creation. You call it that because you've never seen it happen before. The Victorians would have called anything you see around here magic.' Glorion nodded towards the beach where a group of younger teenagers were scurrying across a shore that wetly mirrored the cloud-crowded moon. 'Including that frisbee those kids are throwing to each other.'

The singer-guitarist outside the pub had since donned a sheepskin coat and bright blue beanie to shut out the cold and was beginning on a cowboy song with lilting chords, something about loving someone longer than the lifespan of asteroids.

"'Cos my galax-eee
Is you
And the starlit charms you throw at me
Are worth a year or two'

Izzie gazed up at Glorion, at those mysterious eyes, wishing she could decipher just by looking at him who he really was and where he was from.

But hadn't she already pieced it together? 'I've always believed in time travel,' she said quietly. 'At first I wondered whether you were from the future. But now I'm starting to suspect something else.'

The musician strummed another verse of his galaxy song.

'But the person
Y'really are
Means my years of love
Will far exceed
The lifespan of a star'

Glorion waved his arms above his head at the approach of another lit-up taxi. In one smooth move, it veered across and stopped beside them.

'And now...' Izzie continued, halting for a moment when Glorion opened the door for her while mumbling something about escaping SAPO, '...now that you've told me about the crystal tech of that civilisation, I'm wondering if you've travelled here from the past.'

'The past?'

Undeterred by his reaction, Izzie pushed on, the strength of her convictions fuelling her courage. 'That ancient time you told me about. You know so much! I reckon you're from the place Eid went to once she and her prince had finished with Norway. You're not from the future. The future is what you're in right now.'

Inside the cab, within the cosy interior of a moving capsule that reeked of vinyl seat covers and tobacco, Glorion placed an arm around Izzie's shoulders and gave her a little shake. 'Izzie,' he whispered. 'We'll talk about this when we get out of the taxi. Let's talk about other stuff.'

The combination of feelings that accompanied Glorion's touch, and the realisation of his true origins, submerged Izzie in a sadness that overwhelmed her in its intensity.

'Where to, friends?' said the cab driver.

Izzie took in a breath to answer.

'Eighty-nine Ashbury Avenue, Burwood,' Glorion said, as though it had been his own, as though he were used to telling cab drivers Izzie's address.

'I've never told you where I live, Glorion. And we're not listed in the White Pages yet.' Teasingly Izzie added, 'Have you programmed your crystal to tell you? Does it also connect you to a telepathic address book?'

Glorion looked down. Izzie felt his arm tighten around her. 'It was an automatic reaction. I'm intuitive, that's all.'

'That's exactly right! You're intuitive and powerful, and you're not from here.' Izzie gazed upon his angular profile, then settled back against him, basking in the safeness of his arm encircling her. Less than an hour ago he had shunned contact. Here he was getting close again. He'd apologised since then, and he'd told Izzie he liked her and no-one else. It was only now, after their crazy race from danger, that Izzie could pause long enough to savour the dizzying impact of those words.

Royston's prediction from Friday Fortnight returned to her. *I don't even feel he's from...anywhere. It's like there's this emptiness, this void...*

Glorion's home was much further away than The Netherlands or Sweden. Once Glorion went back, Izzie would never be able to visit him. He might as well have died. He would have, in fact.

That was what it was in truth. Once he returned to his world, he'd be dead in hers.

'You're a Lemurian,' she said. 'And you're much, much older than me.' She stared out of the cab window and up at the gems of light in the heavens, flecks of distant shimmers against the sky's velveteen mystique. 'Ancient. You're totally ancient. Just like all of those stars.'

XXXIX

'Greetings, Soothsayer Zemelda,' said Eidred, awed at the sight before her. Upon the wooden seat, which was carved into curls of contrived oak leaves, were peculiar cushions. The patterns they displayed weren't static; they moved of their own accord. Stars danced across each cushion, radiant bursts of celestial swirls. Fascinated by their magical qualities, Eidred allowed herself to be distracted awhile from her purpose. She sat herself down to inspect each cushion, delighting in the wealth of imagery.

Zemelda rapped on the table. Eidred set down the cushion whose changing images she was at that stage admiring and leaned forward to listen. The soothsayer peered into a sphere of solid quartz. Eidred eagerly awaited the wisdom of her words.

'You are to travel the seas soon after marriage,' she announced.

'With whom?' demanded the princess. It must *not* be with Adahmos! Eidred would evade marrying the Ehyptian prince, surely. How could she bring herself to wed anyone who wasn't Pieter?

Zemelda looked up from her quartz and glared at Eidred. 'Do not ask questions until invited,' she said. Her gaze drifted back to the globe. 'You are to travel the seas soon after marriage. You are to travel to the Land of Triangles.'

Ehypte! Zemelda could not be right. Or could she? Perhaps marrying the prince was imminent! Perhaps her carefully laid out plans would flounder.

'You have an animal by your side.'

'He will travel with me? On my husband's ship to the Land of Triangles? Or do you see him in the present, somewhere within the palace?'

'Hush!' ordered the soothsayer.

The princess bit her lip, although not at the chiding of insolent Zemelda. Any reference to Fripso might spark suspicion amongst her minders.

Thankfully, they seemed not to have heard her. They were leaning upon their spears with an uncharacteristic listlessness. Half-closed eyes, devoid of their usual watchfulness, gazed blankly ahead. Eidred had never before seen her minders in this state, swaying subtly to an imagined tune as though immersed in a drunken daze.

Eidred looked about the sloping-walled chamber. Small paintings lined the left corner: one of the Solen, another of the Grudellans, a third of three eagle-winged troopers and a fourth of a galloping unicorn. 'My art,' said Zemelda.

'You paint very well,' Eidred said. 'Soothsayers, I'd thought, were versed in spinning and weaving only. I did not know art was also encouraged.'

'Generally it is not.'

'That one over there is very much my father,' Eidred said, marvelling at Zemelda's accuracy in perspective and colour. 'And the eagle-men. All three are beautifully portrayed, Storlem especially.'

'Who?'

'Storlem.'

Zemelda tilted her head.

'The tallest one. That is Storlem.'

'Oh, is that who it is?' Zemelda ran gnarled fingers across the quartz on the table. 'Their names are of no importance to me. Let us proceed now, shall we?' She closed her eyes. 'There is an animal in your midst.' Her gaze fell upon the drowsy minders. 'Ha! The goblet of bitter fern I served these Grudellans hasn't agreed with them. Ah well, I am sure they will wake in time.' At that, one of them opened an eye. Hurriedly Zemelda said, 'There is *no* animal in the present. There is *no* animal in the palace.'

Fortune teller indeed! The woman could not decide which story to tell. It was just as well, Eidred supposed, that Zemelda had failed to intuit Fripso. Mention of him in the presence of pterodactyls might undo her scheme. Disappointed she wouldn't receive anything of value, Eidred leaned back in her chair and scowled at the table.

'Your marriage partner's name must begin with the letter "A".'

Oh but it won't, thought Eidred, smug at having perceived the soothsayer's limitations so quickly.

She now disbelieved all this charlatan had to say. Zemelda's magic would have disintegrated, perhaps many years earlier. The quartz sphere was proof of this. Eidred had only to glance at it to confirm that her falsehood-telling soothsayer was incapable of summoning up future scenarios. It sat in the centre of the temple's table as clear and as empty as a raindrop on a rose petal. Far livelier was the moving mosaic of scenes on the cushions.

'*Must* begin with *A*,' repeated the soothsayer. 'His skin is...his skin. His skin is to be of dragon.'

Yes, thought Eidred, stifling a yawn. The Prince of Ehypte has golden skin like the rest of us, but that doesn't mean I shall marry him.

Unless a proposal was made, no-one of the Solen's court was permitted to know the name of Eidred's intended husband. The Solen had been betrayed. The soothsayer's ramblings were a product of court gossip, pieced together neatly and conveyed in dramatic fashion to appear convincing.

'You and your prince are to be the co-creators of a new breed.'

'A new breed?' What a lot of nonsense the soothsayer was gar-bling! Still, Eidred nodded to her to continue, idly interested in the story about to be spun.

'A new species will come about. One that is both god-like and material.'

'Gold's Kin are already god-like and material, Zemelda,' said an irritated Eidred. 'I hardly think a new species has to be created to exhibit these qualities. You tell me nothing new.'

'You?' said Zemelda. '*You?* A body-king daughter? Do you honestly believe your people are an example of unchallenged divinity?'

Body king. The same unflattering term that Pieter had used to describe royalty. For a moment Eidred gave thought to the soothsayers and their somewhat stark history. She could hardly blame Zemelda for viperish comments considering the splendour of her former self. The woman who sat before Eidred was, as were all soothsayers, a bewitcher whose time was over, a once beautiful rose now wilted and old.

How unjust it was, faeries from the glades imprisoned by the palace. Luring fey with illusory glamour should never have been allowed. It then occurred to Eidred that she, herself, had been guilty of the same misdemeanour. Hadn't *she* bewitched a member of the fey? For Pieter, his separation from all that he knew would have been suffocating. His association with a princess had cost him his nightly life in the forest. She might free him a little by making him known to the Solen by means of marriage and a clever disguise, but for the duration of their union, Pieter would never be free to roam beneath the stars.

Without thinking, Eidred said, 'Oh, I have been so selfish.' Being married to someone royal was wearyingly onerous, a duty requiring stoic adherence to the *Book of Rightitude*. The elf's deep respect for lunar grace would be cast aside and replaced with a reverence for harsh golden heat, a sorry disruption to his Dream Sphere journeys. 'So selfish,' Eidred repeated, her heart weighed down with disgrace.

'*Nonsense,*' Zemelda said in a hiss. 'You have never been selfish!'

The words were of little comfort. This faded faerie knew naught of Eidred's dilemmas. With pity, Eidred looked upon the creature who, many season-cycles ago, would have been a beacon of silvery joy. Grudellan rituals had turned any magic she had, dark. Now that her radiance was denied her, along with fey powers and eternal youth,

Zemelda was destined to crumble with the advance of each season-cycle, forced to humbly advise a princess from a bloodline she despised. The mortifying role of court soothsayer was all that endured, a task made up of grappling at truthful-sounding tomorrows, despite the frailness of her second-sight.

'Princess!' Zemelda's voice had taken on an urgent tone. 'You have done everything right. The presence of your prince is a blessing. He has gone to you, remember, of his own freewill. There is a blissful balance in this arrangement. The two of you are significant in the legacy you will gift this world.'

Surprised at the passion in Zemelda's voice, Eidred wondered whether there might yet be a little magic left. It would still have been combined with the pre-meditated statements borne of fear, of course, for word of a soothsayer's failure reaching the Solen almost certainly resulted in death. Despite all that, a gentleness in the soothsayer's tone made Eidred dare to trust her. Feeling she could confide in the mystical woman, Eidred wailed, 'But, Zemelda, how do I marry a man I cannot love, and find blissfulness? Princes are almost always cruel to their wives. I want someone nobler, someone—'

'Of devic origin?' Zemelda's voice had become a whisper.

Eidred turned to observe her pterodactyl minders. Astonishingly, the eyes of all four were tightly shut. The minders were dozing! Could this be invisible help from her faerie godmother? The godmother had been wonderfully generous of late, granting Eidred a myriad of longed-for eventualities.

Eidred scolded herself for trusting the soothsayer. Zemelda had quite likely peered into her mind; might well have been collecting thoughts and memories to use against her. She must steer her thoughts away from Pieter.

'The silver and the gold unite,' Zemelda said.

'Of course they do,' said Eidred. 'And it should never have taken place.' Adopting the same superiority of other royal ladies, she added, 'Look at what has happened to *you*, Zemelda! Your powers have been corrupted from dallying with the men of our court.' Remembering how Storlem's faerie woman had been callously forced away from the forest and realising then that she had no reason to disparage elderly bewitchers, she added, 'I am sorry for you, Zemelda; sorry you have had to bear the indecency of this empire.'

'We talk not of the bewitchers and courtiers, my child.' Zemelda's hood fell to her shoulders, revealing trailing snow-white tresses and a heart-shaped face. Wise eyes, the colour of mud, were encased in folds that radiated out towards ruckled temples. 'We talk of the one who has stolen your heart.'

'But I do not yet know the Ehyptian solen's son, and he is of gold, not of silver, so there is no-one and...'

Eidred closed her eyes to make a silent wish. Dear Godmother, she prayed. Please keep concealed anything Zemelda might discover about Pieter.

'It is *all* kept *secret*, child.'

The soothsayer was reassuring her! Eidred shot a furtive glance at the minders. They slept on, opaque grey lids aflutter with every breath. Zemelda's face relaxed into a smile, and Eidred glimpsed a shadow of the fragile prettiness she would have once been renowned for, the very thing that had made her vulnerable to courtiers well-versed in charm. Trust had been the fey women's downfall. From their pure-intentioned standpoints they'd found it difficult to believe that those they had come to love were not as they appeared.

An insatiable desire to possess all that appealed to their senses was the hallmark of royal kinsmen. Fey-detection cloaks, designed to echo goodness and saturated in auras of allurement, were one such example. The privilege of their occasional wear was bestowed on the Solen's most reliable men. These veils of virtue, crafted by dark magicians, were encrusted with gemstones containing moonlight. The jewelled cloth, once sewn, was infused with an alchemical elixir Gold's Kin termed 'Fey Toxin,' a delicate form of magic stolen from the hearts of captured sprites, the true name of which, according to Pieter, was *beauty creation*. The beauty-creation allowed cloak wearers the gift of faerie sight, along with a talent for communicating pleasingly with sprites of the feminine persuasion.

The garments were only complete once marked with the sign of the pterodactyl, a code to indicate their idol Grudas endorsed the ensuing chaos, and were worn as infrequently as possible to avoid their silvering effects. Last season a young guard had been duly slain after having become silvered. All in the court spoke in savage whispers of the guard's deplorable 'kindness affliction', all save for Eidred. Only Pieter and Fripso voiced their disgust at the cruelty. Knowing the poor lad's capture would also have repelled the silvered guard Storlem, Eidred ventured to acknowledge the faerie's lover with the odd reassuring smile during her weekly wanders around the sunflower beds, and beseeched her godmother, wherever she might be, to send him protective angels.

Hands clasped into fists, she thought back to that awful day, when Storlem's beloved faerie was whisked away to the palace. From what Eidred could gather, the faerie had been immune to the cloaks' mesmerisation. Her abductors had removed her from Elysium by force when she'd resisted their manufactured enticements. As Eidred mulled over the sly ways of Gold's Kin, she studied one of the cushions in her lap, only to find it reflecting her thoughts. The cushion was synchronised with Eidred's memories! At first it revealed the temple of sorcerers and then the spinners, weavers and cloak seamstresses within. It then showed Storlem turning into an eagle...courtiers seizing his quivering-winged companion...undines wailing in the twilit shallows.

A coincidence, Eidred told herself, although the notion was wreathed in doubt.

'Nothing is a coincidence,' Zemelda said. Voice hushed, she continued. 'The two friends of yours from the forest will be safe. Your beloved Brumlynd will become your betrothed, providing you are wise.'

Eidred gave a cry of amazement.

Alas, it was to her detriment. The eyelids of the beaked monsters flickered open. The pterodactyls snapped into a formal stance and allowed their steely stares to settle on both the princess and her fortune teller.

Shakily, Rosetta put down the phone. 'All of them,' she said. 'All of Izzie's friends said the same as Charlotte. They've been home since six. Saw her off at the bus stop.' Trying to steady her panicked voice, she said, 'Royston, tell me honestly. Are you *sure* the lizard man was harmless?'

'Positive.'

They'd driven straight back to the beach after Royston's eyeliner revelation; had searched the entire esplanade of Brighton Le Sands, but the object of Rosetta's terror was nowhere to be seen.

'Not harmful in the slightest,' Royston said, sinking into the sofa. 'And I *don't* believe he's that Dominic guy you mentioned, in disguise. Not that it's beyond the realms of possibility. There are definitely people out there with a hidden side, but...I feel positive someone from school is looking after Izzie.' He stared down at the coffee table. Waved his hands about. 'I feel there's a familiarity.'

With the boy you mentioned in the car?'

'Yes. A boy she likes. Look, lovey, get out the cards and we'll see what they tell us.'

Rosetta turned, hesitated, then pivoted back to the phone. 'I can't do that right now.' She would have to call the police. Why was Royston talking about tarot readings at a crucial time like this?

Somewhere in the next street, a dog howled.

Royston scooped her tarots from the coffee table. 'A quick shuffle,' he said, 'and pick out three. That's all I'm suggesting.'

Numbed with indecision, Rosetta took up the tarots Royston offered, shuffled them clumsily and gave the top three cards back to him.

The photo album in the bookcase. She'd have to take out this year's school pictures of Izzie to show the police. Now.

She fled to the other side of the sitting room where the bookcase lined the wall.

'Rosetta...' Royston's voice filtered through to her softly. 'Sit down for a second. These cards look very promising.'

Rosetta gulped. 'Promising?' She halted and put down the photo album, then turned and made her way back to the couch.

'The Lovers card,' said Royston with a knowing nod. 'Just as I thought.'

Rosetta took in the golds and reds of the 1910-designed tarot. The card depicted a nude couple standing apart. An angel, whose hair looked more '70s punk than early twentieth-century up-do, hovered between them. Rosetta frowned at the angel. 'Hope that's a chaperone. Who knows what they were about to get up to?' Despite the card prompting concerns about teenage sex, the Johnny Rotten celestial messenger was comforting in an odd sort of way.

Royston was thoughtful. 'I never noticed this before, but the man and woman on this tarot must be Adam and Eve. See the apple tree in the background? Shame about the absence of fig-leaves.'

He then turned over the second card, the Two of Cups, a picture of a fully-clothed couple about to clink wineglasses. Its representation of innocent love—a friendship blossoming gradually into romance—heartened Rosetta a little. 'Exactly,' said Royston. 'The beginning of a romance.'

Rosetta covered her face with her hands and groaned. 'What am I doing asking the tarots? I'm stupidly putting off the inevitable, that's what I'm doing.' It was time she acted; went ahead with that last resort. The police. Fighting back tears, she rose from her seat. She moved to the other side of the room again, murmuring, 'I'm getting those photos now.'

'I've turned over the last one,' Royston said. 'And wow! Do you know what I got?'

Past caring, Rosetta turned to face Royston. He held up the Three of Cups, a card that conveyed a trio of dancing curly-haired women in flowing robes, each raising a goblet of ridiculously large proportions.

'I feel it's saying you'll be celebrating Izzie's return tonight. The taller one is you, and the smaller one is Izzie—both of you with '80s perms—and *this* one on the left-hand-side...'—Royston affected a small, meek smile—'...is me.' He glided a hand over his shiny scalp. 'Back when I had hair.'

Drearily, Rosetta said, 'Fantastic choice of frock.'

Perversely, the image of Royston, herself and the prodigal daughter skipping together daintily in Grecian garb, and toasting a triumph with goblets capable of holding a good litre of Moet, seemed all of a sudden hilarious.

The build-up of hand-wringing emotions caught up with her then. Her laughter flew out of control. She slapped her knee and folded forward, gasping and giggling all at once in a laugh that had a beginning and middle, but no end. Royston's stunned stare made her laugh all the more. The chortles she was unable to kerb would have been far more at home in the throat of an unhinged kookaburra. But the whoops of hilarity changed direction. They melted into sobs, into huge wracking waves of fear that insisted on washing away hope.

After what seemed like a terrible waste of searching time, Rosetta dried her tears and headed for the phone.

A key jangled in the lock. The front door squeaked open...and a dishevelled Izzie ran into the sitting room.

Rosetta and Royston screeched in unison. Royston knocked the coffee table as he jumped to his feet. The cards tumbled off, scattering the floor in a sweep of colour. Rosetta trampled over them in her rush to Izzie.

Hugs, tears, smiles.

Rosetta, like a magpie mother in springtime, swooped on her daughter with reprimands. Izzie gabbled an explanation, something to do with a boy from school who lived near the beach and made great vegetable stir-fries. Rosetta wiped away tears and laughed again, although this time quietly. Her treasured daughter was safe and sound and back where she belonged.

'So you've got a new boyfriend,' Royston said, after hugging the pretty redhead fiercely and wagging a finger at her. 'Your old "Mumsie" here, wouldn't believe me, but I felt sure this was the case.'

'Kind of,' said Izzie. 'It's kind of hard to explain. Glorion's...Well he's...he mightn't be here for very long.' She contemplated the floor. 'Mum, I'm really sorry I left my phone behind. Firstly I forgot to call. And when I remembered, Glorion talked me into letting him cook dinner, so I forgot again and then...we had to run...had to run to get a cab because I realised I didn't have my phone and you'd be worried. The taxi driver thought we said somewhere in Wollongong and took us in the wrong direction.'

'Just don't *ever* do it again. Ever!'

'Promise I never, ever will.'

'And he's called *Glory-Lon*,' Rosetta said. 'So unusual.'

Izzie's blue-grey irises slid sideways. 'It's actually *Glorion*.'

'Hmmm,' said Royston. 'Glorion. Sounds foreign.'

'Dutch,' Izzie said.

Royston then leapt into a quirky little tap dance and launched into song.

'He's not an Aussie, is he Izzie?
He's not an Aussie, is he, eh?
Is it because he's not an Aussie
That he makes you dizzy, Izzie?'

'Where'd you get *that* one Roystie?' said the wide-eyed teen.

'From a 1920s Flotsam and Jetsam record I have at home. My interpretation. Embellishments added to match the current situation.'

Rosetta pressed the side of her head against Izzie's, and they both giggled.

'Well,' said Izzie. 'In answer to your tongue-twister, Royston, he's *not* an Aussie. He's a foreign exchange student.'

'So *that's* why you asked me last Friday Fortnight whether your future boy would be from overseas!'

'Hey! That was confidential. Between you and me only.'

Rosetta patted her daughter's back and hugged her once more. 'Thank God you're home.'

'I had a beautiful birthday,' Izzie said, and her eyes were like stars.

'Ah, look at you,' Rosetta cooed. 'Bitten by the love bug. I left some tofu laksa in the saucepan for you to heat up.'

'Thanks, Mum, I'm *starved.*'

'Between you with your Taurus Sun Sign, honey, and me with my Taurus Rising Sign, I don't think we'd ever allow ourselves to go hungry.' She turned to exchange a grin with Royston, but he was busy readjusting a shoe that the impromptu choreography loosened. 'We two girls never seem to lose our appetites, Royston. Not even when we're sick.' She shot Izzie a sly glance. 'Or *love*-sick'

'I am *not* lovesick.' Izzie, hands-on-hips, was clearly impatient with the cheesy references to her budding romance.

Clasping Royston's arm, Rosetta chuckled conspiratorially at Izzie's reaction, then told him, 'I've made plenty of laksa. I'll go and get you some."

'No thanks, darl. Already had dinner and I'll be pushing off soon.'

'Easter cake then?'

'Lovey, I'm fine.'

'Baklava? I've got some lovely baklava there.'

'Rosetta!' Royston rolled his eyes in exasperation. 'This must be the fourth time since I arrived that you've offered me food and drink. Much as I appreciate your concern, I'm not hungry, my love. And it's too late for coffee. Even for decaf.'

'Blame it on my Greek upbringing. As I've told you millions of times before, we're programmed from an early age to push food onto people. They're the reason I'm plump. A childhood of indulgence European style. That's *my* excuse.'

Royston gave a nod in Izzie's direction and bulged his eyes. 'And European Glorion cooked Izzie-Whizzy dinner,' he said. 'I think you've got a point there, Rosetta, about Euro food-pushing. Clearly, he held her there against her will until she ate every morsel. That's why you're late home, isn't it now, birthday girl?'

Izzie nodded enthusiastically. 'Leg-roped me to a chair and in-sisted I tuck into a gourmet meal. Scariest dinner of my life.' Izzie gave Royston a peck on the cheek and excused herself. 'Thanks for worrying, both of you. Sorry for being such a pain.'

Once Izzie had bounded off to the kitchen, Royston inclined his head to the verandah. 'Can I speak to you about something?'

Surprised at the urgent tone in Royston's voice, Rosetta opened the door and led him out. The darkened neighbourhood felt cosy once more, a contrast to the forbidding stretch of emptiness it became when Izzie was gone. Maybe Royston intuited something not quite right with Izzie. Surely not! Izzie was okay. More than okay. Happy as anything in fact.

Royston, standing within the glare of the hanging light globe, ran a hand over his whiskers, a pained expression wrapped across his forehead. More bad news? She'd had enough letdowns today, with the loss of her living situation, Crystal Consciousness going broke, the impending birth of a litter of felines, and five of Izzie's friends saying they had no idea where she was.

He began with: 'The potluck lunch at my place. Bit of a laugh, wasn't it?'

What was going on with Royston? Was his relationship with Darren still okay? 'Heaps of fun, Royston,' Rosetta said. 'You were the perfect host as always. You never told me what you thought of Adam.'

Adam Harrow back in her good books! His persuasiveness on the phone that afternoon was nothing short of impressive. No harm in meeting up one last time, she supposed. And if he happened to be moody again...she'd be there on the spot, able to tell him straight that she wouldn't put up with any spoilt-boy insolence.

Royston looked at the floorboards and stuck his head to the side. 'Hmmm,' he said.

'What's wrong? What didn't you like? If it's about us having to leave early, I take full responsibility for that. Adam's a busy man. He had to prepare for a ten-day business trip.'

'Hm.'

'Gee, Royston. I'm really sorry. Maybe I shouldn't have left when Adam did.'

'Don't be silly, Rosetta. If you've started seeing someone you'll naturally want to be with them more than with us. It was lovely you made the effort in fact. That's not what I want to talk to you about.'

'What is it then?'

Royston rolled his eyes upwards, searchingly, as though the exact words he wanted were pinned in the eaves. 'Er...About Adam. How well do you know this fella?'

Feeling as though she were being interrogated by her overly protective foster father, Rosetta replied, 'Enough to make my own decisions. We're going out again on Saturday. He rang from Vanuatu.'

'I hate to have to do this Rosetta, *hate* it, but I couldn't live with myself if I didn't admit what's troubling me.' Royston drew in a deep breath and sighed. 'It concerns this new man of yours.'

Chapter Sixteen

Rosetta's heart lurched. 'This is about Adam? Why? What happened?'

Silence.

The feeling of being squeezed through a mangle.

When Rosetta spoke again, her voice felt separate, as though at a distance. 'Tell me, Royston.'

'How do I put this?' Royston turned away and then turned back. 'When I was in the kitchen making up our coffee at the pot-luck lunch, I pulled out the cannister of sugar, and then Soozi, Craig's new girlfriend, found the cannister of coffee etcetera, and then she went up the hall to the linen-press to find a fresh tea-towel and, well you see, Darren had put the tea higher up, on top of my raspberry preserves.' Royston gave a nod and raised his eyebrows.

'If you don't mind me asking, Royston, what's that got to do with Adam?'

'I'm getting to that. It's not easy telling you this. What happened, was...well, it was to do with the tea cannister. Your Adam came up and he...offered to help, and...well, Adam whispered—'

'Whispered? To you? In what way?'

'Not to me, to Soozi, when she was reaching for the tea. He must have thought I'd gone, but I'd only ducked into the laundry to grab an oven mitt. Anyway, when I returned he was all over Soozi, pretending to be of help. He deliberately brushed against her when he retrieved the tea cannister. Then he said something rather pathetic.'

'In a whisper to Soozi.'

'In a whisper to Soozi, yes.'

Trying to detach herself from what had been revealed, Rosetta stared at Royston. 'What was said?'

'Something about hooking up sometime. I won't repeat the exact phrase Adam used. It was utterly distasteful.'

Rosetta felt nauseated. Weak. In a small, weary voice she asked how Soozi had dealt with the situation.

'She dealt with it quite confidently. Said to Adam, "Aren't you here with Rosetta?" I couldn't believe what Adam said next. He said, "No, I'm actually not," and then he tried to convince her that you and he were only friends. Soozi had the last say. She said, "Well I'm here with Craig, and I think you're a dishonest slime," and she marched out, so that left Adam and me in the kitchen, standing opposite each other.'

'I see,' Rosetta said numbly. Poor Soozi, faced with behaviour like that! Dishonest slime was an understatement.

Royston crossed his arms. 'So I ploughed forward and made myself heard. I told him where to go, basically. Said, "How dare you treat my friends like this." He's not your type at all, Rosetta. He's a phoney.'

'We were going to eat out at Chavelles,' she said, surprised to find her voice cracking.

Don't cry, she told herself. Don't be a sook.

And yet the tears over Izzie going missing seemed not to have left. Royston enfolded her in a hug. Relenting once more to the feelings Angus had sparked fifteen years earlier when he'd deserted her for someone comparatively slimmer, she wept into Royston's thin shoulder.

'Just think, darlin',' Royston said. 'Painful and all as it is, the veil has lifted now.'

'Ah, well.' Ashamed at her blubbering outburst, Rosetta swiftly dried her eyes. 'It wasn't like I was madly in love with him or anything. I was falling though.'

'You were falling for an idealised image, Rosetta, not for him. Besides, even when you didn't know he was a two-timing low-life, do you think he treated you well?'

Rosetta fixed her teary gaze on the chink of light beneath the front door opposite, a blurred and washed-out rectangle. 'No.' She gulped. 'Not really. I kept...kept waiting. Kept hoping that he'd...I don't know. He wasn't how I'd imagined he'd be.'

While resisting Adam hadn't been easy the last time she'd been out with him, the moment she became separate from all that nearness, the moment those churlish demands turned into dis-comforting echoes, she'd ceased to regret her haughty departure.

He'd been poor company. He'd let her down. A pattern had emerged; Adam only being attentive once he'd dropped her home, a transparent attempt at being invited in.

Rosetta told Royston how Adam hadn't known much about her and hadn't bothered to ask. Prior to getting acquainted with him, she had frequently visited his workplace. Adam's office was on Level Twenty-three of the Metro building, the same office Rosetta cleaned in tandem with Jack Barnaby, not that she'd ever mentioned *that* to Adam. His knowing her as a lowly retail assistant was humiliating enough. Apart from working in the same location and the fact that they'd both toured the Greek Isles in the early '90s, she and Adam had very little in common. They were poles apart; spiritually, economically, and, as she'd discovered this evening, ethically as well.

Encouraged by Royston's *tsk*ing, Rosetta went on. 'All those months of wanting to date him, and then there was this giant so-what factor when it happened. He had an emptiness about him.' She dabbed again at her lashes with the back of her wrist. 'And he was a difficult person to get to know. In the three times we went out he never wanted to spend much time with me. He'd neglect to buy me a drink, then he'd go and talk to someone else. And then he'd want us to leave really *really* early.'

'Why did you tolerate that?' Royston had his professional counsellor's voice on now.

'I'm getting less fussy in my old age, Royston.'

'That's ridiculous, Rosetta. You must think better of yourself.'

'But since I hit thirty-eight it's been a joke in the dating department. Nowadays it's slim pickings.'

'Rubbish. You've had plenty more opportunities than a lot of women your age. Slim pickings, my arse.'

'It's true. Men "pick" "slim" women to ask out. They don't want weighty old me. It's slim pickings! And when Adam came along I guess I was amazed that anyone as attractive as he is could take an interest.'

'And you'd up until then liked Adam from a distance,' said Royston understandingly. 'So you would have been extremely flattered by the time he asked you out.'

'Too flattered. And too willing to overlook inconsistencies.'
What had happened to her vow in the coffee shop earlier in the day?
That steely resolve to give up on Adam Harrow had sneakily grown
legs and scurried away!

'From now on,' Royston said, 'I don't want to see a minute more
of this passive damsel stuff. I don't want to see a friend of mine
enduring a date's bad attitude just because she thinks she's
undesirable and he happens to have made overtures.'

'And as you, and Soozi, and I have discovered, he's very good at
making these overtures.' Rosetta shook her head again, annoyed with
herself for not having spotted Adam's fickleness.

'Don't ever think you can't do better,' Royston commanded.
'Claim back your inner goddess and get back to being the gutsy girl I
used to know. And...Newsflash: your extra weight doesn't detract
from your beauty. It just adds to your va-va-voom.'

'Such a sweet compliment, Royston! I think you're right about
me letting my standards slip.'

'It's the same for all women. If they don't expect enough for
themselves, they end up fodder for sharks like Having-a-Bob-Each-
Way Harrow. Nothing wrong with being fussy.'

'Fussy! That was one of Mama's favourite descriptions of me.
She was furious when I told Thaddeus Georgioupolis that I'd never
go fishing with him.' Her foster mother's outraged squawks could only
be regarded as funny now. Back then, though, Rosetta had been hot-
headedly indignant.

'I'll use the word discerning then,' said Royston. 'Discernment is
a good thing.'

She thought of Adam's colleague, the married English guy, who
had diplomatically kept her company while Adam zigzagged about the
bar hobnobbing with workmates.

It had been a lovely place, that bar, art deco design with huge
arched French windows and exquisite lampshades glowing in autumn
tones. A smoky jazz song had been cut short when the deejay ordered
everyone to get excited about some party *gettin' started.*

The married guy, Matthew, had chatted with her in his easy way.
She'd adored conversing with him, although she couldn't determine

why. Nothing remarkable had been said, although a man with a genuine interest in astrology was always refreshing to talk to.

Guilty about the tear stain on Royston's shirt, Rosetta said, 'Matthew got me a drink. Adam didn't.'

'Who's Matthew?' Royston pulled Rosetta briefly away to look at her, his eyes aglow with question-marks.

'Just a guy from Adam's work. It was Matthew's retirement send-off, and Adam went and talked to Dette Weissler, among others, the woman who interviewed me for a two-week nannying stint, which I didn't end up getting. Matthew kept me company, and he was really kind and nice. Really nice. And he got me a honeydew daiquiri, the most expensive drink at the bar.'

'That was good of him darlin'. Guys in their sixties are generally pleasant like that. They mellow.'

'Definitely wasn't in his sixties. Wouldn't have been more than thirty-two.'

'Ahem. Rich, then, if retiring at that age.'

'Could have even been younger.' She didn't like to add *still had hair*. Royston was sensitive about losing his. 'And he was *heaps* more fun than Adam was that night.'

'Hmm? What did he look like?'

'Well, he was...' Rosetta recalled the man who was Matthew. '...He was much taller than Adam, and he wasn't all bulging biceps. More like a swimmer. Narrower in the hips.'

'A good body? Now that's a start.'

'Ooh, there isn't any start...um...'

'I didn't say it at the time, but that Adam fella was rather steroidal looking. And something special happened between you and this Matthew?'

'No!' Royston had misunderstood completely! The guy was *taken* with a capital 't' and she hadn't viewed him as a prospect before she'd found that out—she'd only had eyes for her date. 'No, it was nothing like that. He was just the sort of man who was...well, amazing really. One of these people who have all these appealing things about them. Someone who felt like a friend.'

'Always good to make new friends.'

'Adam's strikingly attractive, but he's a pretty boy.' Overly groomed shallowness. It felt good to voice those reservations at last. 'But Matthew...' She recalled Matthew's reluctant smile and the radiating lines that had formed around his eyes. Adam Harrow, rarely straight-faced, had a smile which, although dazzling, appeared to be fixed on with superglue.

His more refined workmate tended towards seriousness, even when being funny, although when Rosetta attempted the odd quip with Matthew, he'd broken into a slow grin and had instantly gone from quite good looking to downright gorgeous.

'Yes?' said Royston. 'Do tell. I'm waiting.'

'Tell what?'

'Well, you just went like this.' Mimicking Rosetta, Royston stared at the front door and said in a high-pitched semi-whisper, 'But Matthew...'

'Sorry, Royston. I'm still in shock. I don't even know what I was about to say. I'll let you get home to bed.'

'I'm not going anywhere till I know you're feeling happier.'

'I'm absolutely fine, Roystie. You get going.'

Matthew...

Adam had said in the car on the way back, after having made a ludicrous statement about the poor having 'dug their own graves,' that Matthew was retiring from a call centre supervisor's role. Because she'd observed at the bar earlier that Matthew had an authority about him when he talked, as though used to addressing large numbers of people, she'd asked how many staff members he'd directed. Adam's answer had been eight. Eight, Adam had said, and they all hated him.

Rosetta hadn't believed for a second that the man could be as disliked as Adam had implied. Twice during her conversation with him, men in suits had darted up, shaken his hand effusively and said things like, 'Sorry to see you go, boss.' Contrary to what Adam had said, Matthew's staff members looked and acted more like accomplished executives than chirpy customer service operators. Now that the extent of Adam's deceit was so apparent, the conclusion that hit Rosetta was that most of his jabber would have been questionable.

'Royston, I haven't mentioned this to anyone, but on the odd occasion, I felt a teensy bit scared around Adam.'

'Scared? In what way?'

Remembering their last date, she drew in a slow breath. 'It's weird. I never gave this much thought. I guess because I was so rapt in him I kind of edited out a lot of his unusual behaviour and instead focused more on the sweet, charming stuff. But the last time we went out, he took me for a walk along a stormwater drain and—'

'A stormwater drain? That's more than scary. That's horrifying. Not to mention severely unromantic.'

Fighting off giggles, Rosetta said, 'That actually wasn't what scared me.' She shivered. 'Although the area did happen to be fairly remote. It was what he said when we went there. We were standing looking at the water. Adam had let go of my hand and he'd become distant and kind of fidgety.' Rosetta gulped. 'I was kind of trying to make conversation, attempting polite comments about the stormwater, which was difficult to do because it wasn't unlike a bubbling sewer, then Adam spun round to me, so quickly it made me jump, and said, "What would you do if someone attacked you just now?" '

Royston's eyes widened. He stepped back. 'Don't like the sound of that. What did you do?'

'I kind of shrugged it off and said to him, "If I were attacked right now I'd warn the attacker of my brown-belt karate skills." And it occurred to me when we were walking back that Adam hadn't got the joke. I mean, it was a stupid joke. I wasn't expecting him to laugh. What I didn't expect was for him to stare at me seriously for a second then march back to the car.'

'Why brown belt? Why not black?'

'That was the question I'd expected Adam to ask. And I planned to tell him what I'm about to tell you. Everyone *pretends* they're a black belt when they're horsing around. Brown belt is one down from black belt, so it's still very threatening and sounds like less of a lie.'

'And Adam fell for it.' Royston was watching her with concern. 'You are definitely well rid of this guy, Rosetta. Now you're sure you'll be all right?'

'A thousand times yes. And a thousand times thank you!' Rosetta drew in another deep breath. 'Stunned at my gullibility though. Still processing what you told me.'

Royston took his keys from his pocket and rattled them. 'Well, why don't you process something nicer? Process the idea of Matthew. Sounds like you really fancy him.'

'I don't fancy him at all,' Rosetta said. 'I've given you the wrong idea by mistake, but you already know I don't go for married men.'

'He's married?' Royston did his drama-queen thing of hands flying to his face.

'Didn't I tell you that?' Rosetta suddenly felt embarrassed.

'Nope. I got the impression he was single from the way you were talking.'

'I was sure I told you. Must have slipped my mind.' Biting her lip, Rosetta followed Royston out to his battered car, which tended to resemble an unhappy bumble bee.

Royston told her then that with all the turmoil that had gone on, with Izzie going missing and his anguish at having to retell the 'Adam incident,' he'd been looking for an appropriate time to tell her about something inspiring that had happened to him. 'It's probably not the ideal time to tell you,' Royston said, 'but then, this news of mine might serve to cheer you up.'

'I'm cheered up already, Roystie! I'd love to hear something good that's happened to you.'

'It's to do with the guy Craig's known for however many years. Conan Dalesford, the man you invited to Crystal Consciousness. You did his Sydney book launch.'

'Ah, the author of *Thoughts on Tomorrow's Tycoon War.* Lovely guy.' The white-haired man with astonishingly jewel-like eyes had discussed his ideas on the greed-lack cycle with her before she'd rushed home to make rosemary and lentil soup. Izzie had been preparing for Charlotte's birthday bash that night, the standard junk-food gobble, and Rosetta had insisted she fill up on broth first. 'What news do you have on him?'

'To begin with, I was inspired by Craig going to Conan for advice on his "secret project" although I couldn't imagine journeying all the way up to the Northern Territory. Mortgage and renovations and rego have taken precedence these last few months and I don't have family to stay with up there like Craig has.'

'Craig didn't stay with his family. He stayed in a luxury hotel.'

'Did he now? Ah, well. Not all of us are pampered professional liars.'

'Don't you mean lawyers?'

'That's what I said. Liars.'

'A professional as opposed to a fledgeling "liar" like me, I suppose.'

'Exactly. You're a *student* liar.'

'He's spending a fair amount of time in the NT lately. Perhaps that's where that "secret project" of his is based.'

'Hey, anything's possible. Anyway, Conan Dalesford agreed to a phone consultation with me. He's quite renowned for his predictions, you know. He's been amazingly accurate about world events.'

'Extremely intuitive, yeah. I would love to have talked with him after the launch, but I *did* get to talk to him before it.'

Conan had quoted passages over the phone from *Our True Ancient History* and Royston, delighted at this, had referred him to Rosetta's Friday Fortnight website. 'He said he has good reason to believe Lillibridge's book is based on truth rather than some fairy story. Conan backs the unpopular theory that it's an authentic glimpse of pre-history, the world prior to rebirth. Our little Sydney book group believes the same. We all knew it was never fiction.'

'Knew it months ago.'

'*Felt* it in fact. Can you imagine the average Joe believing that? They'd reckon we were crazy.'

'Maybe we are. But we sensed the story was real. And four of us now have dreamt about that forest.'

'Four and counting! What about the time you and I had the *same* dream about being in that forest? Just as I was about to tell you the trees were rich fuchsia and an exquisite shade of aquamarine, you said to me, "The trees in my dream were a greenish-blue and there were dark pink ones as well." So anyway, what do you reckon my first question to Conan Dalesford was?'

'Probably who Conan was in past incarnations.'

'Close.'

'Was it who *you* were in past incarnations?'

'Getting closer.'

'Ah! Got it. You asked him whether you'd been *Reverend Edward Lillibridge*.'

'How did you guess?'

'Hm. Something to do with your much-verbalised affinity with him I think.'

'Affinity is an understatement. The book felt familiar from the moment I picked it up, and I'm crazy about anything to do with eighteenth-century Europe. Anyway, I asked Conan straight out whether I was Reverend Edward Lillibridge in one of my former lives, but he said I wasn't.'

Nudging him playfully, Rosetta said, 'Ouch, Royston, that's a shame. I would have felt privileged to know the reincarnated author of *Our True Ancient History*. Were you disappointed?'

'Very.' Royston unlocked his car, pulled a cardigan from the front seat and shrugged into it. 'But I trust Conan. The good news is I could well have a connection to the book. Conan said he received a visitation on the morning of my appointment. A Dream Master appeared before him.'

'Dream Master?'

'It's kind of like a guardian angel, just like Alcor in the book.'

'He gets visited by his angelic guides? Unreal!'

'And guess what the angel said? You won't be able to believe this. He told Conan that many of the individuals documented in Lillibridge's work are not only real, they're real now.'

'In what way?'

'They've reincarnated. They're here *now* in *flesh-and-blood*, existing somewhere in the present. And they're going to usher in The Silvering in 2022!'

XL

Zemelda shifted in her seat cagily. In an effort to avoid attention from the glowering pterodactyls, she nodded subtly towards the cushion as a way of indicating to Eidred that its pictures were altering.

Eidred leaned forward and moved the cushion away from her minders' sight.

'I repeat. Your husband is to be Ehyptian.'

To Eidred's amazement, the scene that appeared on the cushion was an image from the future. Eidred held an urn of sacred water from the dragon font. Pieter, repulsed by the idea of ingesting animal blood, was refusing to consume it. Eidred took from her sewing chest a square of linen. She saturated the cloth with the liquid from the urn and proceeded to wield it like paint, pressing it in gentle daubs across her beloved's face.

The Eidred of the present shook her head in concern. Surely this would not change the colour of his skin!

But then the cushion showed Eidred clapping her hands and dancing about the dressing-quarter. Pieter rose from where he'd been seated on the floor. He no longer looked like an elf! The tones of his face, neck and limbs were now lightened. Upon seeing how happy this had made Eidred, he clasped her in his arms and whirled her into a devic jig.

The future was just as Eidred had hoped. She hadn't thought, however, that Pieter would refuse to drink dragon blood. It had not occurred to her that painting his skin with the liquid would give the same effect. Silently, Eidred thanked her godmother for sending such an ingenious idea. Zemelda was proving to be an ally, but Eidred still had to be mindful of trickery.

'I repeat,' said Zemelda. 'His name must begin with an "A".'

Upon the cushion appeared a moving image of Eidred outfitting Pieter in the costume she was, in the present, still hurrying to complete. 'You look so very similar to Prince Adahmos,' the future Eidred said. 'I thought this when I first ever saw his likeness in my father's gallery. You will have no difficulty passing yourself off as him. I have modelled your clothes on the ones in the portraits. Ehyptians dress so differently to us!'

'Zemelda,' Eidred whispered. 'I have already begun sewing this.'

With a detached nod, Zemelda continued. 'His "return" to Ehypte need not be any earlier than necessary.'

What had Zemelda meant by that? Upon the cushion appeared a scene in which Eidred was pointing to the sculpted calendar that graced one of her chamber walls. The date indicated it was two suns before the arrival of the true Adahmos. 'On the morrow we must flee the palace,' she told Pieter and Fripso. Pieter nodded gravely, plainly aware of the burden that was soon to be theirs.

The scene dissolved then, into shards of jagged light. An image of the Solen replaced it. He was pacing his quarters, screaming to several advisors who stood anxiously in the doorway. 'The traitor has not arrived! There is no word of his delay. Either he is killed or shunning my authority. If it be the latter, I'll declare war on the Dorweldian realm.'

Eidred's cushion took on the colour of night. Concerned the pictures had ceased to play out, she set it aside in frustration.

'Look!' Zemelda pointed at the quartz on the table. Eidred saw nothing within the crystal sphere and discerned Zemelda's order to mean 'Look once more at the cushion.' Taking form upon the cushion were the words:

The promised one will not arrive
The promised one is not alive
The promised one exists no more
Exist did he, though, e'en before?

He was no longer living! Ehypte's prince must have met his death during his journey to Norwegia. A deep sense of guilt overcame Eidred. Stricken by the idea of Adahmos having been shipwrecked, made victim of a deadly disease or hunted and devoured by wild beasts, Eidred wept. As well as having a similar handsomeness to Pieter, the prince also shared Pieter's look of compassion. Tearily she whispered, 'Zemelda, it is all my fault. My hope of replacing—'

'*Say no more!*' Zemelda's stern voice was now inside her head. Just like Storlem's faerie, the soothsayer was speaking to her without a voice. '*Highness, be careful of your words,*' she warned. '*The Grudellans are awake now, remember. Tell me with your thoughts.*'

Without uttering anything at all, Eidred confided in Zemelda that she feared she had brought black luck upon Adahmos in wishing to replace him with an imposter.

Aloud Zemelda said, 'It is fate.'

She turned to Eidred's minders and addressed them with a command. 'When Prince Adahmos of Ehypte arrives in seven suns,' she said, 'he must visit me at once!' To Eidred she projected a silent thought. *Here I refer to Pieter.* She turned back to the pterodactyls. 'Tell the Solen there is huge wealth to be amassed, and that the path to this fortune can only be perceived by a sorceress of my calibre.'

'We shall deliver this message to the Solen. We do not promise an agreement to your answer,' shrieked the four nastily.

To Eidred she said with a wry smile, 'Blessings for your impending marriage, my child.'

'May I ask my questions now, Zemelda?'

'Indeed.'

'I would like to know about the precious gems my family has hidden in a faraway land. Where is this treasure buried?'

⋯⋯⋯

'Wow...' Rosetta tried not to remain underwhelmed. Royston's comment that the characters in *Our True Ancient History* were now reincarnated, and alive and well in 2008, felt decidedly far-fetched. Royston was right, but only in his tongue-in-cheek reference to her not being able to believe all that.

'It feels like a truth to me,' Royston said. 'Lillibridge hinted at this on the book's fourth page.'

'He did?'

'Check back to before the prologue. The verse Lillibridge wrote is highly insightful.' In his signature drone, Royston added, 'It's all coming together, it really is. What if we actually already *know* these characters? What if they're not only reincarnated, but somehow connected with our little Sydney book group?'

Rosetta gave Royston a sideways hug, luxuriating in the mohair fluffiness of his cardigan. 'I'll never dispute Elysium Glades once existed in Norway, and I love the idea of The Silvering. Not so sure about sprites and Gold's Kin returning to new lives here in human bodies. And as for reincarnation...' She hesitated. 'Well, I mean...'

After Royston laughed off her scepticism and related a couple of Conan Dalesford's more modest prophecies, he climbed into his car, started the motor, gave an affectionate wave, then zipped off into the darkness.

Royston's parting words about Matthew remained with her. *Sounds like you really fancy him.* She didn't of course. And even if she did, there was no harm in silently and anonymously admiring someone married. Quite different to working on attracting them, as the woman who ensnared her ex-husband had. As for Angus, he'd been equally selfish, too wishy-washy to walk away. How convenient, to suffer from Cheater's Amnesia, an impaired ability to remember he had a wife and baby who loved and needed him.

The other words of Royston's lingering in her mind was his speculation that their tiny book group was 'connected somehow' to the ancient history Lillibridge conveyed. For Rosetta, it didn't ring true.

Trying to imagine what Pieter and Eidred and Maleika would be like if reincarnation were real and if they were in this world today, Rosetta floated inside. She dashed to her bedside table and with great care picked up the book that she'd read and loved as a teenager. Back then she'd seen it as an interruption to her important task of reading every '80s teen romance ever written, but it had brought something precious to her, some awareness that she was more than just her personality.

Conan Dalesford had said Royston was 'a being with unlimited potential', but wasn't everyone a being with unlimited potential? Perhaps every person in this current point in time was shackled by shrunken memory-banks that cancelled out recollections of worlds beyond.

She ran her hand over the hardcover of the 1920s edition of *Our True Ancient History*—the copy she'd been borrowing from Royston until her order from the Antiquarian arrived. She skimmed her fingertips over its matt roughness and tarnished sunken title, and went over Royston's conversation with Conan Dalesford.

According to Royston, Conan had found a way of breaking down 'the memory divisions' initially put in place by body kings. Royston had said, with an enraptured smile, that Conan had the ability to remember each of his 'incarnations' on Earth and was referred to by many as a 'fully realised being'. He'd been visited by his past 'selves' who'd prompted him to welcome them into his consciousness. He'd then apparently melded with these selves, and absorbed the valuable skills, talents and wisdoms gleaned from each particular life.

Rosetta opened the book and breathed in its familiar woodsy fragrance. She couldn't help wondering whether all Conan Dalesford's ramblings were just philosophy-speak for the multi-faceted expressions of the self. Interactions that life demanded meant different selves were accessed and swapped over frequently. Everyone relied on varying shades of their personalities to make it through each day, as workers, as parents, as lovers, or thinkers or dreamers. Conan Dalesford's nod towards rebirth might have been nothing more than a metaphor, a fancy way of espousing postmodernism.

She turned over the cover-page. There it was. The tiny verse in the front of the book Royston had told her to read. How could she have missed it previously? The verse was preceded by an introduction.

Perhaps the people whose lives you are soon to learn of, dear reader, will return to the Earth in future times.

Let us be fanciful for one small moment, and allow ourselves to suppose that an important silver-coded link will be embedded within their Christian, middle and last names:

The silv'ring link
'Tween he and she
Is little more than 'i' and 'e'

If not as such
Then 'o' and 'r'
Within each name these rascals are

The page had evidently been Conan Dalesford's inspiration for concluding sprites and body kings were living in the here-and-now. According to a linguistics professor Royston had emailed last week, the reference to 'rascals,' had probably been a wry substitute for the term 'letters of the alphabet.'

Rosetta turned to Chapter IV where Maleika explained its meaning to her clan:

'The Silvering is a time of repair in the extreme future. It is expected to occur when the gold-tainted illusion of greed equalling lack and lack equalling greed has multiplied to an unbearable point.'

What, in the sprites' ancient world would have been considered the extreme future? Centuries? Millenniums? The 1700s when Lillibridge was alive? Perhaps The Silvering had already happened. Perhaps not. Kindness was certainly not the present currency. If it were, children would not be dying of starvation.

Could it be possible the extreme future was soon to come about?

Closing the book, she contemplated the names of each of the ancient people documented in it. Pieter, Eidred and Maleika each had 'e' and 'i' side-by-side in their names, while Orahney, Croydee and Kloory each had 'o' and 'r'.

The phone rang. Rosetta rose, then sat back down at the thud of Izzie's eager footsteps and her voice echoing in the hall. 'Oh, hi! Yes, I'm fine. Sorry about the mix-up.' Her voice loudened. 'Hey, Mum! Charlotte Wallace's mother is on the line.'

'So glad she's okay,' Diondra said, once Rosetta gave a quick account of Izzie's return. 'Dominic ran out of time. His Port Vila flight left at ten, so I was going to call Matthew.'

'Matthew?'

'Matthew Weissler. Dette's husband. I thought he and Sara might be able to go and look for her. I've been caught up, unfortunately.'

'Dette Weissler is Sara Belfield's *mum*?'

Diondra's tone became accusatory. 'Didn't you know that?'

'Well, no. See, Izzie and I know Sara through her dad, Grant Belfield.'

'You don't know Dette?'

'I don't know her well. I've met Dette twice now, but neither of her girls was with her. I guess I didn't make the connection because Grant always refers to his girls' mother as Bernie.'

'Bernadette is her full name.'

'Yeah, I see that now. Ha! How funny!' Rosetta couldn't resist laughing. To think that one of the unnamed daughters Dette mentioned at the nannying interview had been Izzie's school buddy! 'Dette would be in Vanuatu by now, would she?'

'She's there for another week.'

'Sara and Laura's mum! Such a surprise! I happened across Dette a couple of weeks ago at her husband's retire—'

'Glad Izzie's safe and sound. Have a lovely evening.' The call ended in an irritable click.

Not long after, the phone rang again.

A familiar husky voice said, 'How are you? Got time to talk to a telemarketer? I sell socks.'

'Craig,' Rosetta roared. 'Great to hear from you! What was your trip to Alice Springs like? And how's that "secret project" of yours going?'

Craig summed up his trip in a few words and neatly dodged the second question by launching into another topic.

Falling into a flippant mood while chatting to her old buddy, Rosetta scribbled down her full name on the telephone pad: *Rosetta Sophia Melki* and circled the i's e's o's and r's it contained.

Craig's girlfriend had already told him about the Adam incident. He asked how she was bearing up.

Halfway through saying she was taking it very well, Rosetta interrupted herself with: 'How could I have been so naive?'

Craig, in a stream of swear words, constructed a colourful description of Adam. Finally he said, 'Despite shenanigans from that joker, though, how are things?'

'Izzie stayed out longer than she should have and I was scared to pieces, but she's home now, so as you can imagine I'm happier than ever, although the cat's pregnant, the house is being sold on us. Crystal Consciousness has gone bust. Car's still with the mechanic.'

'You've been evicted, Rosetta? That's terrible.'

'Craig, I can't even bear to talk about it.' She lowered her voice. 'And Izzie doesn't know yet. I'll tell her tomorrow.'

'Okay, but remember I'm here if you need help with anything. I'll help move you; that's no problem at all. Just give me plenty of warning.'

'I can always rely on you, Craig. You're a gem.'

'And as for the cat getting knocked up...well, that was preventable, Rosetta.'

'Oh, really? I'm sorry, but I don't remember asking for a lesson in veterinary science. Knowing it's preventable and not being able to do anything about it are two different things you know.'

'I know, I know. No need to get narky. Why didn't you tell me you couldn't afford to get Sidelta desexed?'

'I couldn't have worried you with that. It was my responsibility to come up with the cash and I stuffed up, but no matter how hard I try saving, random expenses always crop up.'

'And wipe out your non-surplus income? When are you gonna realise I'm here for you? I know you wouldn't have accepted it as a gift, but what's wrong with asking for a loan? Think of me as a benevolent bank manager. I love lending money to the people I love! Anyway, what I was phoning about might at least remedy one of your worries. How'd you like a smooth-running vehicle for the next month? I have to go back to the Northern Territory.'

'Your BM? For the time you're in Alice Springs?' Rosetta took the phone from her ear, squealed and ran on the spot, then said into the receiver, 'I'll delay any further enthusiasm until after you assure me you're covered for Comprehensive.'

'Covered for Comprehensive, but not for deafness caused by an excitable woman's squawks. Eadie told me your car broke down on the freeway.'

'It's a junk heap. Insists on making a spectacle of me by breaking down wherever the traffic's heaviest.'

'Mine can tide you over till you win that singing competition. Then you can cash in your prize and get yourself a good one.'

'Aw Craig! In our dreams.'

'I mean it, Rosetta. Being in the semis at Bondi Diggers means you're a serious contender.'

It had been a brilliant night the week before, when, high on the knowledge she'd become involved with Adam Harrow, she'd sung for the judges a jazzy rendition of 'My Moonlight Prince', released in New Zealand in the mid-sixties by Danna Nolan. Craig's skilful playing of the Spanish guitar had done justice to her song.

It hadn't been all bad news. Some truly lovely highlights had enlivened the past few weeks. Life had taken on a vibrant quality, and Rosetta was determined to keep it that way. And now Craig, bless his heart, was offering to lend her his plush, super comfortable, midnight-blue sports, and she'd have it for an entire month.

'Craig,' she said sighing, 'this is the best news I've had in ages.' She told him about Royston's consultation and Conan Dalesford's thoughts on The Silvering.

'Lena and Eadie reckon it's gonna happen in 2012,' Craig said. 'Something to do with the completion of astrological cycles and an end to the Mayan calendar, but we're not even sure what The Silvering is.'

'Except for that one mention in Chapter IV about it being an end to the greed-lack cycle. Conan believes we'll experience The Silvering in 2022.'

'Mm. We're hardly seeing any evidence of that. It'd make a good blog topic though, Rosetta.'

Their conversation wound up. The phone rang once more. Jack Barnaby returning Rosetta's call.

'Yaaaay,' she hollered. 'Jack! Thanks for calling back.'

The commercial-cleaning proprietor sounded off-guard. 'I...er...didn't expect you to be still up at this hour, Rosetta. I was about to leave a message.'

'No, still up. We tend to be owls, Izzie and I. Listen, I'm in a bit of a pickle at the moment. My poor boss at Crystal Consciousness phoned me in tears this morning. Profits are down, and she's had to let us all go. So I made up my mind to tell you as soon as I could that I'm free to do those extra shifts.'

Her words were met with a prickly gap of silence.

'Jack?' Rosetta waited. 'You still there?'

'Hmmph!'

'So...er...are those shifts still available or—'

'I'm not happy, Rosetta.'

'Not happy? What's caused you to be unhappy, Jack?'

'You letting me down on Thursday, that's what's made me unhappy.'

'When my car broke down? But I phoned you as soon as I could. Like I said before, I'm honestly sorry for the trouble caused, but a car packing it in isn't something we plan.'

'Yeah, well, you should have kept your car in better order. Turns out the junior I hired needed a couple more shifts, so I'm afraid I'll have to ask you to quit.'

Rosetta hastened to answer and failed. Could this really be happening? Could her commercial-cleaning boss really be firing her over one lone absence? 'Surely you wouldn't do that,' she said, her voice dissolving into panic. 'Four whole years, Jack! Not a single missed shift until now. No sick days, no lateness—'

'I'm sorry, Rosetta. Times are tough. The market's looking uncertain. At this stage, I have to demand total reliability.'

Bitter at this, Rosetta said, 'How alike we are. I value reliability too. Especially when it comes to employers.'

Jack Barnaby made a hurried goodbye, his voice conveying more than a hint of guilt.

Long after she'd placed the phone back into its cradle, Rosetta stared glumly at the walls. No job. No home. No more than $2.65 in the bank. Unemployed. Homeless.

The Women's and Children's Refuge, with its noise-ridden fluorescent-lit dorms and barely nutritious dinnertime mush, loomed gloomily in her list of solutions. So this was how it was meant to turn out. A switch from volunteer to victim. Had fate collapsed the world around her to point out the irony of greed equalling lack? Was expecting full employment a sign she'd been too greedy?

The dread of failing her daughter had always been there, cloying and pungent like old cigarette smoke. Now it took the form of a stifling vapour. Her throat was constricted and tense. Oxygen seemed to elude her.

Starting up EGS to combat global suffering would be impossible now. The hope of helping others escape poverty had been reduced to little more than a pie-in-the-sky delusion, cancelled out cruelly by her own need for survival. 'Can't afford to think like this,' she told herself. Dwelling in pessimism would only sink her deeper into that inevitable mire of despair. 'Have to be positive. Have to keep alert to opportunities.'

Eager to scour the internet for jobs, she darted across to the study. Izzie was in there, compiling a group email. 'I'll be out of your way in a sec,' Izzie murmured. 'You look like you need the internet pretty urgently.'

Rosetta opened her mouth to relate Jack's phone call and stopped. Did she really want to ruin the final minutes of Izzie's birthday? Izzie was already concerned about the demise of Crystal Consciousness.

Once Izzie left the study, Rosetta emailed her CV to a variety of retail and cleaning advertisers. She then acted on Craig's suggestion of blogging about the 'Silv'ring' verse. Communication with Friday Fortnighters would serve to distract her awhile from the dire prospects ahead. She threw out a question to Friday Fortnighters:

I'd love to hear your thoughts on The Silvering. Do you believe the people Lillibridge consulted during the writing of his book (referred to as 'The People of the Sea') were making an intuitive prediction? If so, when do you believe The Silvering might happen and how do you imagine it would come about? We'd love to hear your thoughts and feelings on how the world's greed-lack cycle might start to diminish. What's *your* interpretation of the sprites' 'Currency of Kindness?'

Despite a resolution to remain light and bright, she found herself concluding the blog with mention of her job and home situation to illustrate the lose-lose aspects of shrinking accommodation affordability and growing unemployment. Realising she'd descended into maudlin self-pity, she promptly deleted them. The goal of these blogs was to inspire, not to depress. Besides, she was sure to receive a thought-provoking post from someone in far greater turmoil. Not every sole parent had just the one dependent. She altered her approach.

The response she received astounded her. The Currency of Kindness had somehow struck a chord. Posts flew in lamenting the unfairness of the current economy.

'We're each expected to have a job,' *Deborah, a Friday Fortnighter from Cardiff in the United Kingdom wrote*, 'and yet there aren't enough jobs to go around. For this, we are punished. We live in constant fear of losing our rights to survival. Go back to how we were meant to live, I say. In line with nature. Oh, what I'd give to live in Elysium Glades! (Minus the body kings of course!)'

The numerous accounts of job losses and home losses happening to neighbours, to sons and daughters, to friends and relatives of Friday Fortnighters, and to Friday Fortnighters themselves, were, in their own sad way, a comfort to Rosetta, a sobering reminder that she wasn't alone. The plight of those unfortunate enough to live in developing nations, or in areas sullied by conflict and persecution, was also a prominent theme.

'And yesterday a psychic told me that here in the States we're going to plunge into a financial crisis,' *Betty from the USA wrote.* 'She predicts it'll happen sometime in September, and all I can say is I sure hope she's wrong. Things are bad enough. Can't bear the idea of my friends and family having to cope with another thrashing.'

One of the Fortnighters had posted a question about the book's prologue. What did Rosetta and other Fortnighters think the author meant here when he talked about sounds that could actually be tasted and textures that were able to be heard? Rosetta flipped back to the page that followed the 'Silv'ring' poem and examined Lillibridge's cryptic introduction:

PROLOGUE

Beyond ancient history, before the bubble-transience of Greece of yore and of Belladeneire's people (a cell of creation wherein majestic diminutives fevered away at their mission) wove a solid world where senses governed life for those who embodied them. Here, where depth of bodily sensitivity divided this realm from many others, the devas dipped and glided through myriad darknesses. Only momentary was light's feathery touch. Only once certain receptors dared to accept was music beheld in all of its hues. The place in time where expansive sensing might be summoned at will was no longer a part of devic life. It had faded into the far distant future.

Command of the fuller senses had found discomfort in the realm of belief. Non-acceptance was an enforced ethic of body kings. Bodies were obliged to *feel* music in one allocated area, to *hear* texture with certain receptors, but to never wholly succumb to them. Such magic would release bodies from their sabotages. Body kings were not equipped to withstand such disorder.

Other worlds, vaster worlds such as the Carousel Star, where Carousellians' voices, high and haunting, sung welcome, had not the force of persuasion to teach earthly incarnates fuller senses. Senses to them were *lilac-lemon-silver. Bell chimes hushed to dawn, then sunset entwined in a rosebud so delicate it might burst into tears.* Madness was all the bodily rulers could call it, from their limited points of perception. Oftentimes the devic sprites would stumble across Carousel but would, just as fleetingly, pirouette out again to the rhythm of the stars. The merfolk wept, but their tears were shed unhappily. They had lost their inspiration to cry for gladness, so it was then and there that they disintegrated into the tide of obscurity, aeons later remembered only in the dreams of wise men and in children's utterances, which younger souls housed in older bodies dismissed as something known as *non*-sense: another term body kings used when denying reality's presence.

Body kings: dark and menacing, and responsible for a kingdom built by their own paper-fragile words and deeds, delighted in existing singly and scorned the support of clans. Their thinking was not to be invaded by the melding of monadic whispers. Gold, the division of the senses and the introduction of separateness had become dependable weapons to hold above heads. These barred bothersome thoughtforms built of bliss, which sprites created unconsciously.

Unsaid mysteries surfaced in future millennia through writings, teachings and experiments borne of the Enlightenment. Nonetheless, naught was solved as to why certain ancients were imprisoned in solidity. The answer to who guarded the Dream Sphere Key: this too appeared unreachable for it lay just beyond Elysium's waking consciousness, as taunting and as frolicsome as the autumn breeze.

Not long after she'd read this, a lengthier post arrived, from Conan Dalesford of all people, the inspirational author she'd been discussing earlier in the evening with Royston. The post read:

Greetings from Alice Springs!

Thank you, Rosetta, for challenging us with your blog questions.

A warm hello to my fellow Friday Fortnighters. Allow me to introduce myself. I am an alpaca farmer with a penchant for books. I take great pleasure in both reading (and writing) them! I have been fortunate enough to meet Rosetta Melki personally through the Crystal Consciousness store on my most recent book-signing tour and was afterward treated to a lovely meal by a reader who missed the event, at a pub that specialised in surprisingly good vegetarian fare. Sydneysiders are expert at making their interstate visitors feel welcome!

May I say, Rosetta, that your website is a credit to you. As a dyed-in-the-wool Lillibridge fanatic I am delighted to have found an area in which I can compare notes with other readers. Viewing insights from those within the various *Our True Ancient History* reading groups is also a treat.

I have noted that a number of readers are confused by the abstract nature of the prologue. Some argue that Lillibridge deliberately made his prologue evasive to conjure the fantastical dreaminess of Elysium. I will take this a step further by saying that I believe Lillibridge wrote it as such in order to convey the ethereal aspects of sprites' powers.

My interest in The Silvering lies in references Lillibridge makes to the 'fuller senses'. Prior to body kings' enforcements, sprites did not need to visit the Dream Sphere in spirit form. Their soul-selves were melded into their physical bodies and moved together in harmony.

Please note that I write this from the viewpoint that the book's described events actually occurred here on Earth.

Once the body kings arrived, a kind of magical warfare would have ensued, where sorcerers would have worked on violating the laws of nature. By clipping the 'celestial wings' of those native to this planet, body kings were able to extricate sprites' soul-selves from their physical bodies. The sorcerers among these gold-obsessed invaders callously removed sprites' access to the higher realms. In doing so, they ensured that sprites, in their solid bodies, were unable to exercise the *synaesthetic* qualities of colour-hearing, music-seeing and fragrance-feeling (expressions of the fuller senses). Body kings did not manage to keep sprites earthbound entirely. Those of devic origin were still able to return to the Dream Sphere when asleep. At night, once sprites woke, their soul-selves returned to limited bodies that no longer held the power of sensory expansion. Decreased intuition made them vulnerable to capture.

When enslaving sprites, body kings would confiscate all heart-centred magic. They stored this magic, or beauty-creation as it was known, in hollowed-out vessels fashioned from crystalline mineral.

Once drained of their beauty-creation, elves and gnomes were forced to mine gold. Faeries were imprisoned within the palace grounds, sent to live in marble pyramids and kept in check by pterodactyl minders.

As a less evolved species, body kings could not fathom what it was to co-operate within communities. They lived by a tenet of separateness. Retaining this cold isolation resulted in that fear-motivated and destructive element named greed.

I feel strongly that in these current times neglect of the heart is the basis of all earthly problems. From the time in our prehistory that Lillibridge chose to convey, a pattern has emerged. Our collective memory tells us that Earth's people have been robbed of their former bliss.

When we are born, we are full of expectation and innocent love. As we evolve further into this world of imbalance, we learn that we cannot trust. We learn that fear is our protection against hopes getting crushed. We live much of our lives guarding our own survival, frightened that our rights to food, shelter, health, wellbeing, and to life itself, will be snatched away from us, or from those we love. And so, fear closes down our ability to empathise. Distrust has led to giving ourselves permission to dislike others within our planetary family. Discriminating against universal siblings, though, means the brunt of sufferance is shared equally. No-one escapes it.

I believe that The Silvering will mark a time of healing. The healing might well be directed at our kindness barometers: our tender, broken hearts. Our ability to acknowledge the connection we have with everyone else who shares our world has been compromised by body-king instilled beliefs that we are separate, imperfect, damaged, and unworthy of love.

Gold-tainted prejudices will fall away when we find a way to live through our hearts. And through doing this, we will bring about a return to limitless compassion and contentment. When all conflict-sparking behaviours dissolve into higher forms of expression, we will create quite effortlessly an environment in which the Currency of Kindness is able, once more, to flourish.

I feel sure that when all hearts are unashamedly open we will discover new abilities that have, for aeons, remained hidden within our

DNA. We will discover our fuller senses.

And magic will return to the earth.

—Conan

Hi to all from Mumbai!

Conan, I couldn't agree with you more. At present, however, trying to get the world's population to exercise total trust would not work. Being a hundred per cent trusting in a world that knows untrustworthiness would surely result in disillusionment. Surrendering to total faith in humanity could only occur if we all, in unison, achieve an enormous level of respect for each other. I can virtually hear other Friday Fortnighters saying, 'But that's what I already do! I respect *everyone* who crosses my path.' Everyone? Are you an enlightened being then? I'm sorry, but only someone who's attained disciplined mastery over their mind and emotions can claim that. The rest of us are wired to judge.

Ravi

Wendy from Scotland here!

While we're locked into body king belief systems, we'll continue to obsess over lack.

Sadly, it is the majority of the world's population that lives in poverty. A teensy-tiny, wee percentage of the population have scrooged their excessive fortunes thus damaging severely the flow of exchange. They've created a kink in the hose of plenty!

At this point in our evolution I think we're still, as Buzzie Bavasi once said: '...living by the Golden Rule. Those who have the gold make the rules.'

Wendy

Wow! What wonderfully thought-provoking posts!

Thanks, Conan, Ravi and Wendy for your heartfelt insights. Conan, I'm delighted at your knowledge. Your mentions of *Our True Ancient History* in a 2007 article was our inspiration for studying it. Since you've examined OTAH for a number of years, I guess we could say you were a Friday Fortnighter even before Friday Fortnight existed!

Any chance of you becoming a guest blogger? Owing to your extensive research, I can say with all honesty that your contributions would be greatly valued.

And if you do accept our invitation to write the odd blog for us (no pressure—really!) then a topic I'd love to learn your thoughts on is the 'Silv'ring' verse at the beginning of the book.

Could it be possible Lillibridge alluded to reincarnation? He was a reverend after all, so it does seem odd. And, at the risk of sounding a bit loopy, I'll pose this question: Supposing reincarnation is real. Supposing the people Lillibridge wrote about do happen to be incarnated in our current timeframe. Is there any way we would recognise them other than looking for certain letters in their names?

The mention of these letters seems rather vague, considering a good number of us in existence right now happen to have this 'i/e' or 'o/r' combination. That being said, I think it's a fascinating idea, a parson exploring the idea of rebirth. I'd love to hear your insights into what Lillibridge might have been hinting at.

RM

Dear Rosetta,

I would be honoured to be a guest blogger in the future—it would be my privilege.

You raise valid points in your mention of Lillibridge's 'The Silv'ring'. I have emailed you a copy of a purchase I made at an auction in the early '70s during my antique collecting days, a page from a lost journal that apparently belonged to Lillibridge's teenaged son, written on 8 July, 1768.

You have my permission to upload this to your website. In the third of his four paragraphs, which mostly record the mundane task of selling firewood at markets, the boy states:

Father and I are puzzling over the last message from The People of the Sea. They say that when the sprites and 'the three silvered' Gold's Kin return to the Earth to usher in The Silvering, they will retain their ancient names, although these names will be hidden somewhat; mixed about and therefore disguised. Father was most interested to hear that these names will also contain the letters 'e' and 'i' or 'o' and 'r'.

Here is what I make of this. Since each of the people Lillibridge documented already had these letters in their names, then the mention of these letters recurring might have been a clue to the recurrence of all letters. Perhaps their entire names are present as *lexigrams* inside their new ones. A lexigram is a word, name or phrase hidden in other words, names or phrases. A lexigram is similar to an anagram in that it involves word jumbling, but the difference is, an anagram requires the rearrangement of *all* letters, whereas a lexigram might only rearrange *some*. For example:

Assuming Eidred is incarnated in this world today, her first, middle and second names, this time round, might read something like:

'Lindy Maree F*i*elds'

L̶I̶N̶D̶Y̶ M̶A̶R̶E̶E̶ F̶I̶E̶L̶D̶S̶ = EIDRED